THE GIRL FROM DARK DAKOTA

BRYAN DEVORE

MONDAY

*Midway in our life's journey, I went astray
from the straight road and woke to find myself
alone in a dark wood.*
    —Dante Alighieri, *Inferno*

1

Professor Donovan Graves walked across the University of Chicago campus at one in the morning after another long day trying to unravel the arcane mysteries of the cosmos. He had worked all afternoon and evening reviewing an exciting new paper from London. He felt as if he had been lost in a time slip for hours—how else could it have gotten so late?

His cane clicked on the concrete, precisely with every other step he took. Walking the same path he had taken for twenty years, he still exulted in how the sidewalk lamps on this part of campus reminded him of paintings of Victorian London. But not even the gothic beauty of his favorite walking path in the city could relax his mind after the disturbing revival of hope he had encountered tonight.

He often stayed late at his office in the Psychology Department to review the latest case studies posted online by the various parapsychology and psychic-research organizations scattered across the globe. Many teams traveled to haunted locations on Friday and Saturday nights and posted online stories of their experiences, on the Sunday after. Much of the research concerned recorded events of telekinesis, spirit sightings, premonitions, electromagnetic disturbances, clairvoyance, and ESP, all of which fell into the realm of abnormal psychology and paranormal research. Most came from the Society for Psychical Research, or SPR, based in London, or New York's American SPR. Some sightings were endorsed by the Vatican. Other research emerged from private institutions like the Rhine Research Center in Durham, North Carolina, which had historical ties to Duke University. And others came from amateur groups. These Dr. Graves despised because they lacked scientific credentialing, were often conducted in a slapdash manner without fraud controls, and seemed more focused on sensationalism than on hard science.

But the case that now disturbed him was a news event coming out of London. It was tied to the upcoming trip that a large number of paranormal researchers were going to make for an annual gathering at a cemetery in India. A father claimed to be receiving messages from his dead son telling him he had to go on the trip. A child communicating from the afterlife wasn't an unusual conceit, but what had grabbed his attention was that the son had died the same year as his David, and at the same tender age.

He strode over the bridge and worked his way carefully down the wide concrete stairway to the faculty parking lot. The black Lexus waited half hidden in the shadows beneath the last crimson leaves of a maple tree. Winter would be here soon. The car chirped and flashed loyally, unlocking itself for him. He laid his cane on the back floor mats, started the engine, and crawled along the narrow, deserted university streets toward the fast and frenetic interstate highway cutting across Chicago.

For the next fifteen minutes, he sped along the freeway, with his thoughts for company. Then, leaving the highway, he drove through tree-lined neighborhoods until the streetlamps and houses grew sparse in the hilly urban section of the city, which had been on the outskirts of Chicago a hundred years ago and held its ground, refusing to change as the city grew around it.

He pulled up to the black iron gates that rose a dozen feet high at the opening in a high stone wall. Leaving his cane, he tottered the few feet to the front crest and inserted his key. On the third try, it turned, recessing the stubborn tumblers, and he levered the latch and pushed open the gates as they groaned in protest. Only a few people besides the groundskeepers had access through the gates after dark, but as the head of Chicago's largest paranormal research institute, he had long ago convinced someone in authority that there might be an even higher authority calling out from the great beyond.

He stepped back to the car, drove it into the cemetery, and locked the gate behind him.

*   *   *

Professor Graves moved among the tombstones with the familiarity of one who frequently wandered through this place at night. He never used a flashlight until he was close to David's grave. The last thing he wanted was for anyone with a vantage point outside the walls to see a small light flitting about the cemetery. They might think it was a ghost orb, a will-o'-the-wisp, or a grave robber or vandals. Whatever the viewer believed it to be, it would bring the same result: police.

Moving past a line of trees, he sidled his way down a hill, careful not to slip on the many fallen hazelnuts that may as well be ball bearings, left there to throw the clumsy or distracted. After descending the slope, veiled by the night, he stood in front of David. He decided to leave the flashlight at his side turned off. He stood silently for several seconds, listening for any faint crunching of leaves or snapping of twigs or voices in the dark. Once assured of his solitude, he relaxed.

"The SPR reported another incident today," he whispered. "The witness accounts are as serious as the last three reports from Scotland. They believe the increased activity is from the recent advances in technology, which are awakening the possibilities for stronger communications. This hasn't happened since the last upward trend, nearly a hundred and twenty-five years ago." He paused. "Not since the Victorian era have they seen this degree of activity. Not even during the spike in reports from Great Britain around World War One has there been so much going on."

He paused, staring at the cold, dead grass on his son's grave.

"Something has changed," he said. "Something is happening. The scientific community doesn't understand it yet. *I* don't understand it, and that scares me."

He shuddered as if an icy breeze had just washed over him, as if something very cold were near him in the darkness. Sometimes, he wished an angel would appear, just for a moment, to reconfirm his dwindling faith. He would even settle for a demon or the devil himself, just to stop the endless torture of not knowing whether awareness of any kind survived on the other side of death. He knew that energy survived, but did any trace of a person's consciousness or soul live on? Was any part of David still in existence anywhere, in any form?

His gaze became heavy and unfocused. His eyes watered.

But no angel appeared. No Devil. And no David.

He was just an old man, alone in a cemetery, surrounded by lifeless tombstones. And an eternity of darkness surrounded him.

He thought of how far off the path he had wandered in his life. Years of his youth spent believing in magic and ghosts and the power of the mind through telekinesis, clairvoyance, and telepathic abilities. Years spent as a young man studying parapsychology at Harvard and conducting paranormal investigations of mediums as a member of the Society for Psychical Research. But his uncovering of one fraud after another had drained him of all youthful belief in magic and spirit contacts, until the world became so full of charlatans that even the idea of angels and demons faded into myth, and his entire faith in the afterlife shriveled and died.

Deflated, he turned and walked back up the hill. He had been a fool to come here, a fool for hoping to find some relief from the pain that still lingered all these years after his son's death. He was now more convinced than ever that death was nothing but a tragic, empty void.

A cool gust splashed across his face and whipped around his hair and overcoat. He had to lean into the gust just to keep moving forward. The strong wind was now swaying the hazel trees so much that from here, the gnarled branches along the short ridgeline became giant, twisted hands and fingers, clawing their way out of the graveyard's soil.

He continued his climb, telling himself that he was still alone in the cemetery. But when he gained the top of the hill, he froze at the sound of three soft thuds on the ground right in front of him. A chilling, creeping tingle crawled up the back of his neck. Something was here with him in the darkness. He slowly drew the flashlight from his coat pocket. As if holding a gun he was afraid to fire, he kept it off as he held it out in front of him with a trembling hand. Other than the strange blustery wind, he hadn't heard any other new sounds. He hated to risk revealing himself with the flashlight, but not being able to see whatever was here with him was worse. So he widened his stance in preparation for a fight and turned on the flashlight.

The beam illuminated only a narrow swath of ground, so he played it to the left and right. And as the amber beam reached out across the ground, it at first found nothing but pale, sturdy tombstones staring back at him like the solidified remnants of a hundred souls. But then his flashlight drifted down, and he saw three hazelnuts, aligned on the ground just a few feet in front of him. He half-covered the end of the flashlight with spaced fingers and pointed it straight up. Above him he saw tree branches stretching every direction, in what looked like a giant spiderweb in the half-moon's light. The branches swayed back and forth and bobbed up and down, moaning and scraping against each other. He watched the moving limbs in the dim orange light escaping between his fingers, mesmerized by their unsettling movement, as if the tree were coming alive and might reach down and snatch him.

He lowered the flashlight and took another step forward. But the moment he moved, he heard four more thumps. Stiffening, he raised the light and saw a new line of four hazelnuts, just past the first three. His insides clenched in alarm. He turned right and took a step just as five nuts fell through his light beam and smacked on the ground in a straight, equidistant line, as if to block him from going that direction.

He pointed the flashlight up and saw that the branches were swaying even more violently now. He watched them as he took another step. A small, round object fell fast through the light and struck his raised wrist. Instinctively lowering the flashlight and pulling his hand close to his body for protection, he barely had time to register the slight pain before another hazelnut hit hard on the bridge of his nose. Then another wacked his ear.

He grabbed the lower flap of his overcoat and pulled it up and over his head for protection. He was about to dart out from under the overhanging branches when he paused abruptly. Realizing that no more nuts had fallen since he stopped trying to move forward, he waited at least ten seconds, unsure what to do. Motionless, he hunkered down in the darkness, the flashlight now turned off, his coat draped over his head as if he were a kid hiding under a blanket. The wind continued to build, whispering and moaning in the branches above. He was too old to stay hunched over out here for much longer, but some instinct told him to wait just a bit more, to remain silent and motionless for just enough time to let his racing heart slow back down to a calm, safe level.

Then, with his head still covered, he heard a flurry of taps and thuds behind him. Straightening up, he pulled the overcoat from over his head and watched in the pale moonlight as a batch of hazelnuts fell from the tree and bounced and rolled down the hill, toward David's tombstone. Even the nuts that had fallen from the far branches had somehow curved unnaturally in their descent, joining the others.

His chest quivered as he took a slow, deep breath of cold air. The building wind from behind him was pushing his overcoat tight against his back, almost propelling him forward, as the bottom wrapped around his calves and flapped wildly in front of his knees. The cemetery felt colder. The next hard gust threw a hundred dead leaves past his face like a swarm of crazed bats. And the tree shook again, and more hazelnuts fell and rolled down the hill, looking like dark little beetles scampering toward David's tombstone.

Dr. Graves grabbed his coat's lapels with his left hand and squeezed them together to keep out the shifting wind. Then he took slow, wooden steps back down the hill, returning with some trepidation to David's grave. He heard new sounds now, little clicks, as if things were moving all around him. In his peripheral vision, the pale shapes of other gravestones seemed to shift and lean and rock. He felt that he might just have a heart attack or stroke and drop dead right here. They would find his body in the morning and have no idea what he had seen and experienced in the last moments of his life.

He heard things behind him, but he wouldn't look—couldn't look, because his eyes were fixed on some strange object moving in the cloudy darkness before David's tombstone. The wind in the trees on the ridge behind him moaned louder than ever, and more hazelnuts rushed past him toward his son's grave. A distant, dangling chain beat hard against the cemetery's gate far to his right, disturbing the night with loud, eerie clangs and clanks. Still he moved forward, trying to ignore the wild tumult around him, his eyes still locked on the dark object spread over the ground at his son's grave.

He stopped at the foot of the grave and stood looking down at it in the darkness. He couldn't make it out exactly, but whatever was there had stopped moving. Breathing fast and deep, he pressed the rubber nipple on the flashlight and pointed the beam down at David's tombstone. And gasped. There, in front of his son's grave, the fallen hazelnuts had rolled together to form two words: *FIND HER*.

2

Williston, North Dakota

Rachel sat up in bed with a sudden fright. Her heart was racing, her breath fast and shallow. Her wide eyes searched the dark surrounding her until they found the red glow of the digital alarm clock: *2:17*. The screams in her head had woken her. Her adoptive parents called them nightmares, but she knew that the screams were real.

Sliding to the edge of her bed, she rubbed her eyes.

Tonight, the screams had been unusually loud and horrifying. And this time, they had interrupted a wonderful dream she was having. She had been lying on a blanket in the grass with Scott, looking up at the stars while the tips of their fingers coyly rubbed each other's palms. Brushing fingers was exciting, for she hadn't even realized he might like her. Growing up in Williston, they had known each other forever, but now they were in their senior year of high school, and maybe their casual friendship was turning into something more. She had felt him looking at her, so she had turned her gaze away from the stars to lie sideways and look at him. She had felt the coming of their first kiss. But then, before it could happen, the screams had woken her.

They were coming more often now. She usually heard them at night, but one time they had occurred while she was playing basketball in gym class, and another time while she was taking the test for AP calculus. She couldn't figure out any pattern, although she was tracking their frequency. She had first heard them nearly a year ago, and once they started, they had recurred nearly every night for weeks. Then they got weaker and less frequent. By spring, they were happening only once every seven to nine days—she kept a log in her journal. Then every four to six days in the summer. Then every three days. And now they were happening every night. And they were growing stronger.

She wasn't surprised they were getting worse. She knew what they were—who they were. Everyone in town knew what had happened last year. The anniversary of the murders was less than a week away. This Saturday night. She wondered whether the screams would go away afterward. She hoped they would, but didn't really know what to expect. This was the first anniversary, and the screams were already louder than they had been even right after the murders. It was obvious to her that Annabel was much angrier now. And she seemed to be getting even more enraged each night.

Last Halloween, on the night of the murders, Rachel had dreamed of Annabel's death while the unconscious woman lay in the hospital and doctors fought valiantly to save her life. Annabel had somehow been still alive after her husband shot her in the head. In that real-time dream vision, Rachel had felt the woman's soul struggling to stay with the body, frantic to avoid the beckoning light. But Annabel was dying, and there was nothing the trauma team could do to stop it. Her soul felt pain, then fear. And as she was finally pulled from her body, Annabel's spirit screamed and screamed in its wild refusal to leave this world. Then the doctors and nurses dissolved and vanished, along with the bed and now-lifeless body. Then a conference table with surrounding chairs slowly materialized.

But despite these changes to the room over time, Annabel's spirit continued to scream and scream—and Rachel was the only one who could hear her.

Rachel got out of bed and opened her window. It had stormed hard earlier, but now the skies were clear. She put on warm clothes and climbed out onto the roof to look at the stars and the half-moon. Lightning sparked too far away for her to hear thunder. In the faint light, she could see the muddied dirt drive leading away from the farmhouse toward the nearest country road, a mile away.

She often came out here after the screams woke her. Looking at the stars, she would pretend her mother could hear her, but she had to whisper so she wouldn't wake her adoptive parents.

"They came again, Mom. They're getting worse." She paused, her eyes stung by the cool wind. "I don't think they're going away, and I don't know if I'm supposed to keep listening, or if there's something else I'm supposed to do."

The roof was cold and damp, and she pulled her knees to her chest.

"You'd tell me, right, Mom? If there was something I'm supposed to do? You'd give me a sign?"

And she listened to the night, giving her questions time to find their way, time to be understood.

She waited ten minutes for some sort of answer, for any indication she had been heard. Her special abilities made her feel like an outcast, a freak. She hid them from her friends because she didn't want to be treated differently. She downplayed it with her adoptive parents because she didn't want them to worry. Only her real mother could understand what she was going through. But her mother was gone.

It was cold and dark, but she found something peaceful about being out here alone. She sensed a faint connection with the infinite cosmic awareness surrounding everything while so many slept. She kept waiting for any answer, any sign.

But tonight, as on so many other nights, she received no answer.

3

They were spiraling toward death. Jason Hardy gripped the narrow armrest and squeezed until his knuckles were white. Glancing around the small cabin, he was annoyed that the other forty passengers didn't seem appropriately nervous. Maybe there was nothing to worry about. Maybe he was just paranoid. He hated flying on these small jets, especially in the cool autumn months this far north. Icing and all sorts of mechanical problems could occur. And both pilots looked fresh out of high school. During a crisis, experience went a long way, and at twenty-seven, he couldn't help feeling uneasy about temporarily giving control over his personal safety to someone even younger than he.

Jason prayed he was just phobic. They had to be getting close to their destination airport in North Dakota. The pilots wouldn't hold back information from the passengers if they were in trouble, right? They would have to announce that everyone needed to straighten their seats and duck their heads. Wouldn't they? He was fairly sure they had to tell the cabin if anything was wrong. They wouldn't dare keep it a secret.

He closed his eyes and took a deep breath. It was going to be okay. He wouldn't die today. Not here, in a place he didn't even want to be. Not after what had happened between Nicole and him last night. Not with everything he still had to figure out.

The plane dropped hard, and he felt himself rise in his seat until the seat belt snugged, holding him down.

He heard a few gasps around the cabin. They weren't from him, so he felt a little braver, although his heart had iced over during the drop—just as he feared was happening to the wings. Things were getting really rough now.

He had given up looking out his window thirty seconds ago, when they entered a deep, thick cloud bank. That was when things had started getting bad. With his view limited to a blank white void, he stared at the back of the empty seat in front of him. It vibrated harder with each passing second, rattling the folded tray table against it. He looked back at the window as they fell out of the clouds. The ground was right there, less than a thousand feet below. He saw horses in a green field. The plane was so low, it terrified him that they were still bouncing around so much. Those young fools flying this small jet were actually trying to land in these high winds. Now he *knew,* this was the end.

Had he lived a good life? He didn't know. Had he had fun? Yes—for a while, anyway, though not recently.

Had he made a difference?

He hadn't. Not that it mattered anymore, for he was suddenly out of time.

The plane jerked, jostled, and shook as the earth rose toward it. All the other passengers were now silent, as if they had already lost themselves in solemn prayer until their maker took them. He couldn't believe this was how his story ended: crashing into the cold, barren landscape of North Dakota. He was an accountant, not a police officer or a firefighter. He wasn't ever supposed to be at risk in his work. If an accountant ever died on the job, it was from a heart attack, not impact.

He could see their shadow now, gliding through the grass beside the runway. The jet tilted. Why weren't they pulling up? How could they just crash into the asphalt without giving everyone on board a fighting chance to survive?

The jet rose, then fell. Then rose again. Then fell farther. They were almost touching their shadow, which had now slid onto the runway.

A hard jolt hit the aircraft from underneath, and Jason was certain it would break apart and scatter in sliding fragments around a ball of fire racing along the runway. But by some miracle, the jet held together, and the engines soon screamed in reverse. He slid forward in his seat, and again the seat belt restrained him as he tensed to keep from slouching over. The small overhead compartments groaned. The entire cabin was a chaotic environment of terror and shaking and unexplained noises until the jet slowed to a reasonable rolling speed that suggested they all would survive this.

He took a deep breath and exhaled. This was far too stressful a way to start his workweek. Most of the other passengers wore jeans and sweatshirts. He was the only one he saw in business slacks and a nice blue button-down collar shirt.

The two men across the aisle, to his right, stood up as the jet stopped. They looked like shale oil workers or project engineers, both bearded with ruffled hair and a commanding appearance of toughness. The one closer to Jason looked at the other and said, "Once again, we've survived the Flight of Death."

"Amen to that," the other man replied.

Flight of Death? Seriously? These men had actually given it a name. Would it be like this every time he must fly here from Chicago? What had he gotten himself into this time? A job in Williston, North Dakota—the middle of nowhere and about as far away as it was possible to be from the now-fading Wall

Street dream that had carried him through business school. A place of drifting roughnecks and dirty riches beneath windy, barren plains. A week before Halloween. A place where he already felt lucky just to have arrived alive and well after enduring the Flight of Death.

The cabin door opened, and passengers began to move down the stair platform to the runway surface at Sloulin Field International Airport. It was one p.m. He had to keep moving. Pick up his bags. Get the rental car. Type the address into his phone's GPS app and follow the directions to the only hospital in the region. And from there, he would begin his investigation of the strange financial data coming out of the hospital, while praying that he wouldn't have to confront any more close brushes with death.

4

Jason parked the rental car in a dirt patch under a sycamore tree and killed the engine. All his luggage was buried in the trunk, except for his computer bag, on the front passenger seat. He stepped out into the bitter chill of late October. Moving around the car, he grabbed his computer bag, slung it over his shoulder, and locked the car while walking away.

Most of the cars in the small parking lot were old, and none were expensive. As he drew closer, he studied the old three-story stone hospital through the half-bare branches of skeletal trees. It looked at least a hundred years old, and he wondered what on earth had motivated someone to build a thing like this out here so long ago. At one point, this hospital must have felt like the Taj Mahal to the local dwellers of depression-era America. Now, as the town grappled with the changing fortunes of boom and bust and second boom in shale oil prospecting and extraction, no one seemed to know how to bring this hospital into modern times.

And then, as he bore right on the main path, he saw his answer.

Like a mirage, a larger hospital of glass revealed itself behind the older stone building. The modern facility stretched away from its predecessor with the sort of impressive might that an aircraft carrier would have beside Ahab's whaling vessel. It was as if there were two hospitals, one growing out of the other, like a butterfly spreading its lovely wings after completing its transformation and crawling out of the worn-out husk of its past.

He continued toward the door of the older building, where his emailed instructions directed him. Following the short concrete walkway from the parking lot through the landscaped grounds, he reached the door embedded incongruously into the side of the old stone hospital. He pulled it, but it was locked. He had nothing to show to the black plastic badge scanner on the door frame, but he had the next best thing: a phone number.

Scrolling to the contact email on his phone, he selected the number and waited as the call went through, sending a signal on a radio wave that bounced off a nearby cell tower and kicked back to the specific cell phone of his contact person in an act of modern-day sorcery that few truly understood.

"Hello?" a woman's voice answered.

"Mrs. Franzen? It's Jason Hardy from Chicago. I'm here in Williston—I think by the back entrance you described in your email."

He waited a beat for her to reply.

"Mrs. Franzen? Hello? Are you there?"

The silence continued. He pulled the phone down and saw the time lapse of the call still counting forward, so they were still connected.

"Mrs. Franzen?"

A strange whisper came through the speaker—distant, mumbled, rushed, and inaudible.

"Mrs. Franzen?"

"No, no, no …" it whispered. "Run off con … off con … Run!" Then a high-pitched screech burst from the speaker.

"Holy hell!" He yanked the phone away from his ear. Holding it away from him, he looked again at the display. The call time was still ticking away, now at three minutes and fourteen seconds … fifteen … sixteen. And then it stopped, pausing for an instance before switching back to the original email screen. "Damn," he muttered, realizing the call had finally ended.

Just then a red face emerged behind the door's small window before it flew open. He jumped back, alarmed.

"Mr. Hardy?" the plump woman said with a friendly smile.

"Yeah." He was still rattled.

"I'm Molly Franzen. Sorry, it died."

"What died?"

"My phone. Lost the signal. Happens a lot in this building."

"It *just now* died?"

"A few minutes ago. Right after you said you were here. Figured I'd just come down instead of waiting for the signal to come back. Did you have a nice flight in?"

He was trying to process what she was saying, and was still confused, but he shook it off when he saw her waiting for a response. "Oh, actually, it was probably the worst flight of my life."

"Oh my!"

"Yeah, it was pretty rough. I was terrified the whole time, and at the end I was pretty sure we all were going to die."

"Goodness! It is like that out here sometimes. Little planes don't do well in high winds. I'm glad you made it through in one piece."

"Me, too."

"Let's get you set up, and then I'll give you the tour."

He followed her inside. They walked down the bland concrete hallway until they reached the wide elevator doors. She pushed a button and waited in silence. He glanced down the rest of the long corridor. Small windows lined the left side of the hallway at eye level, like portholes in an old-school ocean liner. They admitted bright patches of sunlight onto the opposite wall.

The old elevator arrived with a strange electronic knell unlike anything he'd ever heard from a machine. It was a sound he hadn't heard since his grandmother's funeral, and it sent his mind back to that crowded sanctuary in Belleville, Kansas. He saw his parents, still together. He saw the bell ringer by the pulpit. And he saw the shiny walnut casket. Then, in an altogether different place and time, he saw the metal doors of the elevator slowly creep open.

He just stood there woodenly as Mrs. Franzen stepped into the car. When she turned around and saw him, she said, "Oh, I know it looks and sounds awful, but it's completely safe. Just old, that's all. Inspector checks it once a year. State law."

His strange, sudden flashback had gone away as abruptly as it came. It had given him an eerie, unsettled feeling, stealing him from the present to enchant him with a jarring memory of the first time he faced the reality of death. He hadn't thought of it in years. Why here? Why now?

He forced a half smile and stepped in beside her.

She pressed number three, and they rose two levels so slowly, he could barely sense any motion. The car was large with stainless-steel handrails lining the three sides. It was probably the oldest elevator Jason had ever been on, and he trusted it only slightly more than the jet that had brought him here. When they finally reached the top floor, she led him down the hall to an open doorway near the end.

The room wasn't fancy. There were no pictures on the wall, but it made up for the Spartan decor with a number of small windows and a huge mirror. An oblong conference table, with nine ratty office chairs and space for a half-dozen more, filled most of the space. In the center of the table were three stacks of papers with many yellow sticky notes protruding from both sides.

"So this will be your home," she said.

"Looks great," he said. "Network connection?"

"Somewhere under the table. I can call our IT person if you can't figure it out."

"Excellent."

"Most of the documents you requested are in those piles." She pointed proudly at the paper stacks. "Still a few things we're pulling. Should have everything in a day or two."

"Thanks."

"We've numbered everything as you asked."

"Perfect." He set his computer bag down on a chair.

"Ready to continue the tour?"

"Sure."

Mrs. Franzen led him back out and down the hallway, pointing out that this room was for the human resources team, that one for payroll, this one the copy room, that one for her accounting staff, and this one for herself. As she walked him past the rooms, he noted they weren't as nice as offices typically found in the corporate world. They had worn furniture, battered file cabinets from a time before he was born, and really nothing aesthetically pleasing other than a few personal touches added by individual occupants. Even windows were scarce, limiting the natural light. And she pointed out only a small number of offices in the hallway, making the floor seem half abandoned.

"Well, that's it," she said. "Everyone from my team is in the main building, helping put up Halloween decorations. We'll do another round after people get back, so you can meet them."

"Yeah, I didn't realize so much had moved to the new building. And it looks a lot bigger than I had imagined."

"Oh, yes, all hospital operations have moved next door except for my team and HR. No more patients in this poor old building. No more procedures take place here, either. All medical equipment has been moved. This entire building is vacant now except for this one area up here on the third floor. Eventually, we'll probably move over there, too. The new hospital construction was finished this summer, and the official opening was in August. As you probably know, the costs ended up running way over budget, and payor mix has also been really bad the past few quarters. So, in their infinite wisdom, the national office imposed a 'turnaround initiative,' which forced me to lay off half the people on my team. So all that is why you see so much empty space in this building."

"I'm sorry to hear that," he said solemnly. "The national office had a lot of cuts, too. It's been a tough year."

She nodded somberly. "Well, it's a skeleton crew now, Mr. Hardy. But we've worked very hard with the resources we have. Hopefully, you find all our accounts and supporting documentation in order. Please let me know if you don't."

"I will," he said.

"Well, I've already eaten, but I could walk you over to the cafeteria if you're hungry."

"I ate something on the drive from the airport. Thanks, though. I might have you point me in the right direction later. How late are they open?"

"Until six. Will you be working late?"

"Most nights. Flying out Friday afternoon. The audit shouldn't take longer than that."

"I'll get you a spare key. No one else will be working late."

Back in the room, he pulled out his laptop and powered it on. While waiting for it to cycle through its startup routine, he unpacked his power cable and mouse. To make the power cable reach from the nearest wall outlet to his laptop, he needed to stretch it awkwardly across the table and dangle it through the air like a low hanging clothesline. He popped open the plastic container of pens, pencils, sticky notes, flags, and everything else he had swiped from the main supply room at the national office last Friday.

Then he pulled one of the stacks of papers close to him and studied the reference numbers written on the protruding yellow sticky notes. He opened the client request file in the planning folder on his computer's desktop screen and began reconciling the stacks of paper with the reports, records, and supporting documentation he had included in his advance audit request, emailed to Mrs. Franzen two weeks ago.

He had a lot of work to do. A lot of information to sift through. It was going to be a long afternoon. Perhaps a long night, too.

5

Chicago

Helen Bovell felt as if the life had been drained out of her. She sat in silence with her eyes closed as her assistant showed the next sitter into the small, musty-smelling room. The low, heavy breathing told her it was a large man. It was a sound anyone would have recognized. Beyond this, her mind searched to detect anything else about this man. She couldn't open her eyes yet—not until she had exhausted all efforts to reach beyond the barriers blocking her mind. Barriers that, for the past thirty years, had kept her excluded from the fully realized world she once knew in her youth.

Now, at the age of fifty-five, she tried not to ruminate on all she had lost, for right now she had to focus on yet another disgraceful reading.

"Madam Bovell," the man said.

She remained silent. Her thoughts clear now, she searched for his mind's energy. And she searched for any transmissions from spirits close to him.

"Madam Bovell?" the man whispered.

"Shh," she replied. "Sit. Silence."

She heard him take a seat at her small, round table, felt the slight pull on the black cloth that draped across it to the floor.

A tingle of excitement sprang up inside her when she thought she felt the energy of his mind. A fuzzy picture appeared in her sight. Rain on water. A swamp at night. An old boathouse in the dark. A child crying with a chorus of locusts. Poverty. Neglect.

Then the vision left. She sensed nothing else. And she couldn't even be sure she had sensed anything more than her own imagination grasping at elusive strings of truth.

This wasn't going to happen—not the way she wanted. Not the way it used to happen. She knew that now. But the man was waiting for answers, expecting her to give him guidance or some crumb of hope or comfort. So she would try to give the answers he sought, even if they were just conjured from her imagination.

"You're from Florida?" she asked, eyes still closed for theatrics.

"No," the man replied.

"From Louisiana?"

"No."

"I see a swamp."

"I'm from Iowa City."

"But you've spent time in a swamp. As a child."

"Not that I remember. My parents always lived in Iowa."

Helen concealed her concern. She had been here before. She knew how to shoot blind.

"Your father is here," she said calmly, opening her eyes to look at him. It was a gamble, but the man looked about sixty. There was a good chance his father had passed away.

"Here? In this room?"

His expression had softened, as had his tone. She could now read faces nearly as well as she once read minds. She had regained some trust and was back on track.

"He died violently," she said.

"It was a heart attack," the man said, his brow lowering.

"A violent heart attack. It was very painful."

"I wasn't there," the man said, his voice weakening from the burden of sorrow and perhaps regret.

"He's very proud of you. Of what you've done with your life."

"He was never proud of me when he was alive. Failed business. Failed marriage. Why would he be proud of me?"

"You're his son. He's always loved you, now more than ever."

"Because he's not a drunk anymore?"

"Yes." She sensed something from the man. Something she'd seen before. Time for another gamble. "And because you've stopped drinking."

The man's jaw dropped. "He can see that I've stopped?"

"Yes."

"I've been sober almost a year. I haven't missed a meeting. He sees this?"

"Yes," she said. "He's been with you the entire journey. He loves you. And he's proud of you."

The man choked up, then sobbed.

She felt for him, for his pain. And she truly wished she still had the ability to help him as she had once helped so many. Every night, she prayed that her gift would return. Someday, it would come back to her. It couldn't be lost forever—it had been too much a part of her life. She had felt a faint tingle in the middle of the reading—a subtle sense of energy emitted from the man's mind. Perhaps even another force in the room. Maybe his father's spirit really was here with them. But she hadn't been able to hold it, let alone get any understandable reception from any transmissions. Her powers were gone. It was just another night of her weakened faculties being unable to produce connection. Her gift would not be coming back to her tonight, just as it hadn't come back in the past thirty years. But she still had to take care of this man. He believed her—for the moment, anyway. They had reached a high point in the reading, and if she tried to take it any further, she would likely be exposed as the fraud she was. That had already happened twice this month. This would be a victory for her reputation only if she stopped now.

"He has left us," she said. "I have lost contact."

"Can you reach him again? Please."

She closed her eyes for a few seconds, then shook her head. "I'm sorry. I sensed his emotional state fluctuating before I lost contact. He was very happy. But it's difficult to hold contact when emotions become overwhelming. It breaks the concentration they need to maintain connection. I don't think he'll be able to make contact again tonight."

"His spirit feels emotions."

"All spirits do. Not the same way that we do. Their emotions aren't magnified by chemistry. But they do feel things like love or anger. Before I lost the connection, I felt enormous love."

"Is he still here … with us?"

"I can't know for sure. But I believe he is."

"Can he hear me?"

"If he is here, he can hear you."

"Thank you," the man said, beaming gratitude through his tears. "God bless you. I can't believe it! All these years I felt he was watching me. I knew he was there. Can you do this again? Make contact?"

"Not tonight. He was too emotional."

"But another time? Another night?"

"Yes. Nothing is guaranteed. It's up to him. But yes, I'm here to help. And I believe he wants to communicate more with you."

"Oh, thank you. God bless you, Madam Bovell. God bless you."

She nodded while gesturing toward the door he had arrived through. "The spirits watch us and frequently try to communicate with us. Together, with strong faith, we can receive their messages. I hope you do return."

The man stood and, after some hesitation, left the reading room. Bovell heaved a sigh. The man seemed to have needed to hear the words she said. She hoped she hadn't gone too far. She hoped her lies would do more good than harm.

But most of all, she hoped that the spirit of the man's father hadn't really been in the room. The last thing she needed was to have another soul angered by her fraud and fakery.

She got up and left the room through the narrow exit door in back. She had no more readings for the night, and she desperately needed a drink. Or two. Or however many it took to drown the memory of all the voices she used to hear before her connection with the spirit world was severed, leaving only the endless, haunting silence.

6

It was late at night, and Jason was horrified at what he had seen. The accounting records were atrocious.

He was alone in the old wing of the hospital. The skeleton crew had left many hours ago as the autumn sun was setting. And as the sun retreated, a storm had swept in after it, battering the little windows in the conference room with bursts of high wind followed by intervals of heavy rain that sounded more like hail. Occasionally, he would stand up and peek out the window, staying long enough to watch the clouds bloom with the next lightning strike.

He had snacked on a granola bar an hour ago, and his stomach was already grumbling for something more substantial. And he still needed to check into his hotel. Thirty more minutes, he told himself, and he would pack up, find his lodgings, and track down a place to grab a late bite.

Something thunked against the window behind him. Startled right out of his seat, he stared back at the black glass. Lines of water slid down the outside, sporadically shifting left as gusts slapped the building. He suddenly worried that this weather might spawn a tornado, even though it felt too late in the year and he hadn't heard the wail of a tornado siren. Growing up in Kansas, he had been through a dozen tornado scares. Most had only involved sitting quietly in the basement with his parents, flashlight in his pocket in case the power went out, listening to weather updates on the battery-powered radio as the funnel drew within ten miles of town, then five miles, then to the edge of town, while he waited anxiously, praying that the monster not find their house and eat them alive. And it never found them. His parents were together back then, still in love, and during those dark minutes Jason had fantasized that it was their family's bond that protected them from nature's dark forces.

He thought of checking his cell phone for any weather alerts, but he had powered it down and buried it in his bag an hour ago because he could never get a signal in this room and didn't want to waste the battery. Another thunderclap rattled the window. He instinctively stepped back from the wall until he found himself in the doorway to the long, dark corridor. Sensing something, he slowly turned his head to look down the black void of the hallway. Why were the lights off? The darkened corridor looked cold and uninviting except for a strange, soft blue reflection beneath the distant blood-orange exit sign.

He moved toward it as if enchanted by a Siren's song. As he approached it, the object's shape distorted, morphing into a series of Rorschach images that originated in a circular center, with arms or lines reaching out from it, then contracting, then stretching away again. It continued to change as he moved toward it, as if it was also watching him. It seemed to coil into itself like a snake sensing the approach of either prey or danger. Seeing the sliding, curling movement triggered an animal alertness in him. His skin tingled, and he could hear his own heavy breathing as his instincts warned him not to go another step. But curiosity drew him forward.

As he moved past the small copy room, lightning flashed through its window and blasted his shadow onto the wall beside him, making him jump twice: first at the lightning, then at his hulking shadow. A third jump followed two seconds later, when the chasing thunderclap arrived. The force rattled the windows and walls and unseen objects in the darkness around him. It was like the booming voice of some imagined giant from his childhood nightmares. He slid down the wall to the linoleum floor and knelt there for a moment.

When he looked ahead once again, the blue thing still floated at the end of the hallway, still reacting to him by shifting its shape with each movement of his head. He now wished he had taken the time to fish his cell phone out of his bag so he could have some light. But he was halfway down the corridor already, so he stood up and shuffled in the dark toward the blueness. It shone like metal, and he could see movement within it. He was twenty feet away now, and he worried that even an inadvertent blink might shatter this illusion—like waking from a dream that never returns.

He was fifteen feet from the spectral thing that shifted and glowed and spun and twisted into itself. It couldn't possibly be natural ... but how could it be anything else? It must be in his mind ... but he didn't believe that, either.

He was now ten feet from it.

Two little eyes appeared inside the blurred, swirling light. They grew and swirled and blurred into the rest of this strange psychedelic phantasmagoria.

At five feet away, he froze, pausing to give his eyes one last chance to make sense of this object before he reached out to touch it. It no longer moved like a snake. Now the blurred tubes of light twisted and curled over each other like dozens of serpents in a tight den. But as he tried to explain the inexplicable, he also perceived a strange beauty from the thing, as if he were watching an incandescent jellyfish moving through dark waters.

The open break-room door was on his left. Another lightning strike flashed through its windows, and from the corner of his eye he saw the silhouettes of two or three figures standing by the sink. But by the time he jerked his head to look left, the lightning was gone, and he winced at the thunderclap in the darkness.

He flinched again and waited for some sign that other people were here with him. He counted to ten in his head, getting braver with each count, and finally told himself that he hadn't seen anything more than the Halloween decorations taped to the window.

He turned. The blue swirling glow was still in front of him. He held his breath as he reached out to touch it, as the full outline formed from the darkness.

His fingers touched metal, and a slight groan responded as it flexed inward a half inch. As this happened, the image warped. When he withdrew his finger, the metal straightened and the image returned to its original state, with one salient difference ... Now he saw a face within it. The face was stretched like an expanding bubble reflection he had once seen in a hall-of-mirrors funhouse as a child. His own reflection—and that of the blue object. The metal he had pushed was the door of a tall locker for supplies. It had been left ajar just enough to alter the angle of reflection.

He turned to look behind him. And there, inside the open doorway to the payroll staff's office, was the blue object: the glow from a computer monitor with a screen saver depicting ocean waves. He exhaled a sigh of relief.

Closing and latching the supply-locker door, he walked back down the hallway to the conference room. But just as he turned to step back inside it, again something caught his eye. Turning slowly, he saw the blue reflection—it had returned at the end of the hallway. The door had cracked open again, even though he was quite sure he had latched it. There was no way it could be open again unless someone opened it. Lightning flashed and thunder rumbled like a busy bowling alley. Not understanding how it had opened, and not wanting to tempt the darkness a second time, he turned and stepped back inside the conference room. But just as he walked through the open doorway, he jumped back in alarm and wacked his funny bone on the metal doorjamb. Wincing and holding his left elbow, he tried to ignore the vibrating numbness in his elbow and stared at the room. Every chair around the conference table had been pushed back all the way to the walls. One was against the tall mirror, which now had a long crack near its base. And the chair he'd been sitting in lay on its side near the far wall.

This wasn't possible. This was no illusory reflection like the image of the screen saver on the locker door. During his short hallway excursion, something had been in this room and moved everything, including chairs that were now broken and looked as though they had been pushed or thrown with real force. He had been gone only a minute and only just down the hallway—never more than a hundred feet away and always within sight of the doorway. But he had never looked back when moving down the hall. He had never imagined there might be something behind him.

The thought made his head whip around to look behind him, searching the dark hallway for movement. He winced again and kept rubbing his elbow, frustrated that his arm had gone half numb just when he might need to defend himself.

He saw nothing but a hallway cloaked in darkness, with periodic gray squares from the outside lamps casting faint light through the rain-streaked windows. Hundreds of little black lines ran down the gray square spaces along the far wall of the hallway. Nothing else moved in the corridor, although he felt certain that someone else was here with him.

Stepping back into the lit conference room, he squeezed and relaxed his fist, feeling the strength return to his arm. He had to think … No, he had to get the hell out of this place as fast as possible. Even the light in the room seemed to make him more vulnerable, more exposed.

He rushed back to the table, slapped his laptop shut, and
threw things into his bag as fast as he could. He should have left
hours ago, and now his haste made him even more frantic, as if
the noise he made packing up would attract danger of some sort.
He wanted out of this place now. It was as if the building were
on fire, with only a minute or two before escape became
impossible.

The zipper on his computer bag gave a faint screech as he
pulled the slider across the top to interlock the little plastic teeth.
Slinging the bag's strap over his shoulder, he rushed to leave the
room. Pausing at the doorway, he stuck his head out and glanced
both ways down the dark corridor. Now that he was truly
terrified, he did something he wished he had done five minutes
ago. Opening the side pouch on his bag, he dug past the clutter
of pens and chargers and headphones to find his cell phone.
After fishing it out, he pressed the side button and waited fifteen
excruciating seconds for it to power on.

When he finally had the phone light on, the hallway loomed
dimly out of the dark void. He shined the light down the hallway,
then turned it the other direction. It was too weak to show him
much beyond thirty feet, but that gave him courage enough to
turn his back on the shadows long enough to kill the lights in the
room and close the door. He held the light on the gleaming brass
handle as he locked it with the key Molly had given him.

Then he turned and jogged down the hallway, with his
computer bag slapping his side, and the phone light jarring up
and down with every step. He cringed at the thought of
something jumping out at him from one of the many doors he
passed. At the end of the hallway, he rushed down the stairs as
fast as he could without rolling an ankle. He was relieved when
he turned the corner on the final landing and saw the straight
shot to the exit. Barreling down the last flight, he slammed into
the door's horizontal bar handle, throwing it open, and raced out
into the storming night.

Jason hurried across the rainy parking lot as lightning flashed above him. The rental car looked cold, having sat wet and abandoned for hours while the storm raged above it. Splashing through an unseen puddle, he unlocked the door while still a few feet away, yanked it open, and fell inside the car while pulling it closed. Water dripped from his hair and ran down his face. The windshield began to fog up. As his breathing slowed, he was already doubting his memory. It had occurred only a few minutes ago, yet it suddenly felt distant and dreamlike.

Tomorrow, his job would take him back into that building, back down that hallway, back into that room with those creepy chairs and God knew what else. For all he knew, a serial killer had escaped from a local asylum and now wandered the halls at night—especially on stormy nights, especially when out-of-towners visited and worked late and alone.

He had to go back. But not tonight. Tonight, he had to get the hell out of here.

He started the engine. The headlights lit up a ghostly sycamore on a temporary pond the storm had created in the grassy low area beside the lot. The taillights gave him no real visibility through the storm, so he reversed blindly from the tree, cranking the wheel and pointing the rental's fat nose toward the lot's unlit exit. The windshield was defogging fast. He shifted into drive, but before fleeing, he took one last look at the old hospital. And through the streaks of water racing down his window, through the raindrops cutting through the black night, he saw an elongated blue object take up half the space in the window of his conference room. The moment his eyes locked on to it, the blue object faded away from the window, and the room returned to pitch darkness.

And then, as if in answer to any lingering suspicions that he was imagining things, he saw the room's light flash on and off like a strobe light with a faulty interrupter. *Flash—flash ...*

flash ... flash—flash. Then it paused, and again: *Flash—flash ...
flash ... flash—flash.*

He gasped as he floored the accelerator, roaring out of the
parking lot and away from the hospital, as lightning and thunder
exploded above him.

TUESDAY

Deep into that darkness peering,
long I stood there, wondering, fearing,
doubting,
dreaming dreams no mortal ever dared to dream before.
    —Edgar Allan Poe, *The Raven*

7

Madam Bovell felt the icy air chilling her skin as she floated within a reef of clouds below the stars. The dark countryside a mile beneath her looked peaceful in the moonlight. She was flying. Then floating. Then suddenly, she was falling.

Falling toward the shadows of an Earth colder than the icy celestial heavens.

She looked over her shoulder, pleading for the clouds to elevate her again. Asking to be returned to the standing of her proud past, with all her youthful powers in play. But yet again it was not to be. Abandoned, she fell toward the rising landscape, away from the ethereal beauty of the firmament and down toward the realm of dirt and grit and pain and struggle and death, known as Earth.

A town slumbered below. She felt the wind whipping past, and the soft mattress of air that seemed to hold her aloft. The town rose toward her, lazily at first, then gradually faster. A huge, sprawling building stood directly beneath her. It seemed to be her target. She would soon crash onto one of its many wings. She sensed pain and suffering within it, people near death. Somehow, she knew that it was a hospital. Now she could see an

ambulance outside. She could make out more details as she got
closer. She was falling directly toward a red X on the building's
roof. It looked like a helicopter pad. And in another half minute,
she would splatter all over it.

"Rachel Black," a voice boomed from somewhere.

Her eyes widened, then quickly narrowed against the biting
wind of free fall. She was confused. How had she gotten here?
What had happened? Was this real?

"Rachel Black," the voice yelled, this time from right beside
her.

She turned her head and saw a gray woman falling with her.
Falling? Or flying?

"Rachel Black ... " the woman yelled again.

"Help me!" Madam Bovell shrieked. She had only seconds to
live. The hospital's roof was coming at her faster and faster.

"Find Rachel Black," the woman said, more calmly now, as
if oncoming death made for easier communication.

"Help me! Please!"

"Find Rachel Black ... "

"How? Where?"

The woman's lips didn't move, but her words spoke
themselves. *"Dakota. Dakota."*

Madam Bovell looked away from the gray woman, back
toward the roof. It roared up at her as she streaked toward the red
X on the helipad.

She let out a scream, as the terror of certain death
overwhelmed her.

She woke up, her nightclothes clammy with sweat. The L
train rumbled past on the tracks outside her window. Buried
under layers of rumpled blankets, she drew in a deep breath.
Then her thoughts crystallized. It had been decades since she felt
such a potent dream. Excitement rushed through her. This wasn't
a nightmare or some tormenting spell from a demon. It was a
vision. Perhaps a crisis apparition. And unlike the last one she

had received thirty years ago—which she had ignored, ultimately to her great horror—this one she must chase down.

She got out of bed and scurried across the room, her white nightgown flowing as she moved. Entering her spare bedroom, she sat at her old rolltop desk and powered up her laptop. Within minutes, she was scrolling through pages of results for Rachel Black on the Internet. She narrowed her search to North and South Dakota but found no reference. Then she changed her search words to include the Dakota territories and found the wife of a blacksmith, who died of tuberculosis in 1867. She considered this for a moment before moving on. She changed her search to just "Rachel Black" and "Dakota" but found nothing except the same reference to the blacksmith's wife.

She started her search over again, focusing only on "Rachel Black." The web search engine showed eleven thousand hits. She began scanning the brief captions for each one.

She didn't know quite what she was looking for, but she had to find the answer to the message. It took a lot of energy for an uninvited spirit to communicate with a medium through a dream vision. Crisis apparitions were always important and urgent.

For so long, her life had been stuck in a dull, sleepwalking routine of a charlatan—a worthless, parasitic existence. Everything she had become was an insult to the memory of her brilliance, which continued to fade. It was as if her old life had been nothing more than a distant dream. But this vision had changed everything. For the first time in decades, she had truly been in touch with the spirit world. And now, after so many years of drifting and waiting and hoping, she was once again awake.

8

Madam Bovell's eyes were tired, and her hope was flagging. She had found nothing. Thousands of Rachel Blacks haunted the Internet like souls lost in the ethers, but nothing she had read connected to the Dakotas in any significant way. And perhaps that was the problem: she had been given so little information that she was forced to rely on some indescribable power within her to *feel* the path to take and the right Rachel to pursue. A power that had left her thirty years ago.

This was ridiculous. She had wanted so badly to have experienced her first powerful vision in decades. But maybe it was just a vivid dream of the sort that ordinary people had all the time. There was nothing unique or powerful about her anymore. And the knowledge from her lost abilities was handicapping her efforts to live a normal life. Worse, that esoteric knowledge was perhaps leading her into madness, which she feared more than death itself.

She closed her laptop and stared absently at the little white light that changed to a slow blinking, like a pulsating star in a distant galaxy. As she stared at it, thinking of a distant dying star, she realized she must be missing something from the dream.

Something that the unknown spirit was trying to communicate must have gotten lost in translation—something else she was meant to hear before waking.

But how could she retrieve any missing piece of the vision? She could try to fall back asleep, to wait for the spirit to find her again in an unconscious state. This, however, was one of the most unpredictable means of spirit communication. She could sleep ten thousand nights and never make contact with the gray woman again. She could try to organize a séance, enlist others to help her into a trance state so she could attempt spirit slate writings, as she had so famously done in the past. But it would take days to organize such a gathering, and also, she wanted to keep things private.

Then she realized, with a sudden chill, that there was another way, another method—something she hadn't used in a very long time.

She went into her hallway, to the small closet past her kitchen. Pulling out a step stool, she climbed up and stretched till she felt the long, narrow wooden box pushed to the back of the top shelf. Excitement surged through her like a direct electric current. This box, and the memories it contained, had been stored away for so long. But just hefting its weight again and preparing to bring it back to life made her heart quicken.

Setting the box on her living room coffee table, she paused to look at the coats of dust layering its plain, drab lid. Was she truly ready to open up her past, to unleash this misunderstood power after so many years? A power that popular culture believed was controlled by dark forces? A power that she was no longer sure she could even conjure?

She opened the lid.

And there, like an old acquaintance staring at her from a haunted past, was the worn brown face of the Ouija board. It stared up at her with the same silent impudence as on the day she last closed the box, shuddering in horror. Its intimations of dark secrets scared her as much as anything she had ever encountered in her heyday as a reputable medium. As much as anything, it was this little wooden plaque, configured with letters and symbols, that had ended her career. She should have burned it long ago, but she had lacked the will. It had some mysterious bond with her, some link to another world that she was terrified of abandoning.

She lifted it from the box. After clearing the box and everything else from the table, she lit a few candles and dimmed the light. She needed to create an aura of strong positive energy, which wouldn't be easy without a group of séance sitters. But what she was about to do, she must do alone.

She moved the Ouija board closer, then took the last object out of the box. The planchette was the real device driving the power of the board. It was a heart-shaped, wooden object the size of her hand, with a large hole in the center containing a crystal disk. When the planchette was moved on the board, one could see through the crystal to whatever letter or number it was over. The board contained three main rows of symbols: the first was "A" through "M," the second was "N" through "Z," and the third was "1" through "9," followed by "0." The rows of letters arced over the straight row of numbers. A human-faced sun and the word "YES," and a moon and "NO" occupied the upper left and right corners respectively. At the top center of the board was the trademark name "OUIJA." And at the bottom center were the words "GOOD BYE."

The board brought back a kaleidoscope of memories from her youth, when the psychic power had been so strong, she took it for granted. What she wouldn't give now for just one more chance to feel that power again!

It took her a solid minute to pry her gaze away from the Ouija board. Her eyes felt dry. Blinking a few times to clear them, she got up and went to the cabinet against the far wall. From the bottom drawer, she took out a dozen white taper candles and an old box of matches. She set out the candles in silver holders throughout the room, lighting each with a separate match. Turning off the lights, she shuffled back to the Ouija board. It was still hours before sunrise.

Pulling the coffee table away from the couch, into the center of the room, she sat cross-legged on the floor and rested her elbows on the short table. She stared at the two rows of black capital letters arcing over the numbers. They seemed twice as large in the glow of candles as they had in artificial light. After all these years, the board was waking up.

She placed a hand on each side of the planchette. The wood was warmer than it should be. The crystal eye seemed to witness her staring through it at the number six on the board. She consciously slid the planchette forward so it was between the "6" and "U," with only blank wood visible through the crystal viewer. This was the place to start.

She closed her eyes and relaxed her muscles. She breathed deeply. Steadying her mind with positive energy and an openness to any transmission or contact seeking her.

And then she waited.

For a long time, she sensed nothing. Maybe twenty minutes passed as she waited with welcoming thoughts, trying to exude only positive energy. Then, eventually, she felt a tingling and quickening within her. Her mind became more alert, stronger, more focused, as if a drug had kicked in and was heightening her senses. Something had happened. Something *not her* had touched her mind. She could see in her mind's eye every detail of the room she was in. With eyes still closed, she made a quick pass over every photo and art print on the walls, every book on the shelf, every tchotchke and drip of dried wax on the mantel. She remembered everything. It was a state of heightened alertness she hadn't known in decades.

She felt a slight smile form and quickly willed her lips to relax again. She didn't want to lose this contact. It was stronger than she had ever felt before. Something astounding had happened. It was time for her to begin.

"Who are you?" she asked out loud, eyes still closed, hands still resting patiently on the planchette.

She waited thirty seconds without feeling any movement from her arms.

"What is your name?"

Again she waited, but still nothing happened. It was terribly difficult for just one person to conjure a spirit enough to move the planchette. It usually required a group of three or more to channel a spirit's communication into the subconscious act of moving the planchette. Only those with a rare gift, highly tuned into the spirit world, could successfully communicate alone with a planchette on the Ouija board. In the past, many mediums had preferred automatic writing for communications. They would fall into a trance state and scrawl on paper, then come out of the trance and see what the spirit had written when in control of their hands. But Madam Bovell had never been great at automatic writing. Her gift, other than performing séances and having visions, had been communication through a Ouija board.

She couldn't get the spirit's name, so she tried another question.

"Are you the one from my dream?"

She felt a twitch from her left hand, then a tingle in her right arm. Then nothing.

"Are you the one from my dream?" she asked again.

Her hands got warmer, and a rush went to her head. She felt the planchette move a little. Then it moved some more, sliding in small jerky increments, away from her and a little to the left. As it moved, her hands remained on it, holding or pushing it, she wasn't sure which. It was difficult to tell, for her arms felt numb, and feeling had left her hands. She no longer felt in control of her muscles.

She waited with her eyes closed until the faint sound of the planchette's felt-tipped "feet" moving across the board's surface stopped. Opening her eyes, she saw her arms outstretched, and the crystal lens of the planchette centered over the word "YES."

"Welcome," she said, relaxing a little, a bit of her faith returning, a sliver of her power restored. She felt back in her old element for the first time in ages. "You want me to find someone?"

She closed her eyes again and felt the planchette move briefly in a circular motion. When it stopped, she opened her eyes and saw that it was again centered over "YES."

She had to be careful. Spirit contact through a Ouija board was usually a short-lived experience. Unlike automatic writing or séances, which could go on for hours, only a very limited number of answers could come from a Ouija session. This was partly due to the slow process of spelling out answers and partly, she believed, because the contact was being made while conscious, rather than in a trance state as with automatic writing. So she had to ask the most important questions in the simplest way before losing contact, with no guarantee that she could ever get it back again.

"You want me to find Rachel Black in Dakota?"

She closed her eyes. This time, however, the planchette moved right, away from "YES" and to the right, toward "NO." But when it stopped and she opened her eyes, she was confused. The crystal viewer was at the top center of the board, over the word "OUIJA."

"I don't understand," she said. But that wasn't a question, and she had to move forward with questions before contact was lost.

"Where is Rachel Black?" She closed her eyes, but there was no movement.

Time was running out. She could already feel the connection weakening. She was too far in the dark to ask simple questions.

She could guess that the spirit—the gray woman—was becoming frustrated. She must gamble on one last large question that gave the gray woman flexibility to answer openly. This could require all the energy that both she and the spirit contact had left. She had to ask the one right question.

With eyes still closed, she calmed herself with deep breaths and asked, "How can I find this person?"

The moment her lips closed, the planchette began to move. It was coming back almost straight toward her. When it stopped, she opened her eyes and saw the crystal over the letter "S." But before she closed her eyes, it moved again. Startled, she watched as it slid right one letter—"T"—and stopped. Then it slid again to the next letter, "U" and stopped. "S," "T," and "U" were contiguous on the lower of the two letter rows, nearly in the center of the board.

It seemed strange and insignificant that the three most centered letters were the first chosen after the word "OUIJA," but she willed herself to keep a positive and open mind as the planchette moved again. It moved up and to the right, stopping at "L." Then it moved in a small circle, again stopping over "L." Then it moved right and down to "W." Then back left to "O." Then in a small circle back around to "O" again. Then up to "D."

Her eyes had watched each motion, mesmerized with excitement, wet with tears of joy that she had once again made real contact with the hereafter. She had merely been going through the motions of life for the past three decades, trying to search again and again for her lost gift, not really living, only surviving. But now she felt at home with herself again after decades wandering in the wilderness. At peace. She was once again doing what she had been born to do.

But she also felt weak. This sitting was taking its toll.

And the connection also felt much weaker now.

"Is that everything?" she asked after the planchette hadn't moved in thirty seconds. It sat over "D."

Nothing.

She hadn't yet put together the letters in a meaningful way. Her thoughts were becoming foggy. She was losing contact. She sensed that it was ending, and that awakened a sense of desperation.

"Please tell me more. How can I find her? Why do you want me to find her? What has happened? What is wrong? Why me? Please, tell me something … something more … anything."

The planchette began to move again, pulling toward her, centering as it slid to the bottom of the Ouija board. It stopped over the words "GOOD BYE."

"No, wait. Please don't leave."

But it was over and she knew it. The connection was lost. And her mind was suddenly tired, weaker than she had felt in a long time. Her eyelids became heavy, and the strong urge to lie down on the carpet came over her. But she couldn't let herself fall asleep. Not yet, lest she forget the exact letters from the message.

Removing her hands from the now lifeless planchette, she grabbed the small notepad and pencil she had placed on the carpet by the coffee table. She could still remember the letters, but she had to hurry—she could sense an exhausting, forgetful sleep rushing toward her like a blue norther on the horizon.

Slapping the notepad onto the coffee table, she tightened her grip around the pencil and pressed it to the paper. Her vision blurring, her mind succumbing to the desperate hunger for sleep. All her remaining strength went into summoning enough willpower to stay conscious for ten more seconds. The message, whatever it meant, was too important to lose. She moved the pencil carefully, precisely, writing out the word "stullwood" before she let go of the pencil and sank down onto the carpet, swallowed up by darkness.

9

Jason awoke to the nightmare reality that he must now return to the hospital. He took a long shower, as if the cocoon of falling wet heat might forever shield him from whatever had spooked him last night. Afterward, he stared at himself in the mirror with a look of dread as he scraped his face with the razor. He moved in slow motion as he dressed, prolonging the process of putting on each new article of clothing, as if he were a man contemplating the expected but unwelcome results of a medical test.

Leaving his room, he forced himself to act normal as he reentered the greater world of other guests and hotel staff. He went down to the hotel's small dining area for the complimentary breakfast of eggs, bacon, toast, and orange juice while browsing the top stories in the *Williston Herald*. A man's body had been found in Devil's Lake, and the coroner said that multiple drugs had been found in his system. Another story described decreasing fracking activity as more drilling investment left the region. A short article said that some weekly direct flights between Houston and Williston were being cut next month. Then he found an article about people in the area bemoaning the rise in housing costs because of the shale oil boom from last year. It was hurting local family budgets with higher taxes even during the pains of the region's recent economic contraction. The article also talked about other problems brought by the rapid oil boom and bust, such as the influx of people from out of state who had come to Williston looking for jobs, many of whom ended up living on the streets when the economy soured. He couldn't imagine the struggles of these people just trying to find work and survive, and for a brief moment, it took his mind off his own fears after his experience at the hospital.

But the sense of dread soon returned.

As he made the brief commute from the hotel to the hospital, his mind kept replaying the events of last night. Before he knew it, he was driving his rental car past the final row of houses and trees and turning into the hospital's back lot. A sense of gloom weighed on him as he walked under the gray skies toward the old stone wing of the hospital. His badge got him through the door, and he trudged up the same stairwell that only last night he had raced down in fright.

As he walked down the third-floor hallway, he looked with fascination at the aluminum supply locker at the end wall, now clearly visible in daylight. He shook his head in annoyance. The locker door was shut, but he would never again see that as its normal position.

Then he reached the doorway to the conference room.

Looking inside, he did a double take. The chairs were all spaced perfectly around the table. It wasn't the way he had left it, but any member of staff or cleaning crew could have set them straight. He might have even questioned his memory of last night's events if not for the large crack along the base of the wall mirror.

Not knowing what else to do, he unpacked and powered up his laptop to continue his work that had been so abruptly interrupted.

He worked for an hour before a knock at the door pulled his mind from his construction-in-progress audit workpaper. Looking up from his computer, he saw Mrs. Franzen smiling at him from just outside the room.

"Morning, Molly," he said.

"Morning," she replied. "How's everything going."

"Good," he lied. "Maybe we could set up time this afternoon or tomorrow to go over some initial questions from my testing."

"Sure," she said. "I have a conference call with Fargo from two to three, and I'm leaving at four to run an errand for my daughter. Free to meet anytime in between, and I'm open all morning tomorrow."

"Perfect. Maybe we should do first thing tomorrow." He glanced at the calendar on his computer, then looked up again. "Oh, I do have a quick question. You guys keep the building pretty secure at night, right?"

"You mean, like, for leaving your work binders here overnight?"

"I mean, have you ever had any security issues? Break-ins? Thefts?"

She cocked her head. "We haven't had any thefts that I know of. Why? Is something missing?"

He hesitated. "I worked late last night, and I just got a little nervous because of the storm. Just wanted to see if there had been any security issues in the past—make sure I'm safe, I guess. Sounds silly when I say it out loud, but the storm rattled me a little."

"Did you see something move?"

The question made his throat go dry. It would normally have been a strange question, but it wasn't. Not to him. Not right now.

"How did you know to ask that?"

She grinned. "Wow! You really did see something."

"How did you know?" he repeated.

"Hold on," she said, hand raised. Then she turned her head and shouted, "Peggy! Peggy!" She left the doorframe, sliding back into the hallway, vanishing out of sight. "Pe-e-e-geee!"

He stared uncomfortably at the vacated doorway. Why had he mentioned anything? He had a job to do: fly in, audit, fly out. When he was done here, he would move on to another project in another town, then another, just as he had done for the past five years. After this engagement, he might never again see Williston or anyone he met here. It seemed like a nice place, but he had grown weary of meeting people he would never see again once he left. He wanted to stop moving, to settle down and grow roots somewhere, to feel that sense of home that had evaded him ever since his parents divorced years ago. And until he could stop moving and find a spot to settle down, he wanted to avoid new friendships with people who would soon be out of his life forever.

He heard rustling near the doorway and glanced up, half expecting to see a crazed escapee from a psych ward waving an axe or a ridiculously big kitchen knife, just like in the scary B movies he had seen growing up. Hollywood loved firearms unless it was a horror film, in which case only a sharp metal object would suffice. But instead of discovering the imaginary serial killer he had barely escaped last night, he saw only Mrs. Molly Franzen, with a wide-eyed woman in tow. This must be Peggy.

"Okay! What did you see?" Molly asked him excitedly without even introducing the woman.

"Hold on," Jason said. "What's going on here?" Auditors were naturally suspicious people by profession, but right now the alarm bells going off in his head would drown out the carillon in the National Cathedral. He wasn't going to tell them *anything* until they told him *something*.

"Just tell us what you saw," Molly said gleefully, like a little girl with a delicious secret she just couldn't contain.

He shook his head and looked at Peggy. She was staring at him stone-faced, pale and still.

"You know something, don't you?" he said to her. "What aren't you telling me?"

"Where did you see it?" Peggy asked in the scratchy voice of a lifelong smoker.

"I don't know what I saw," he said, surprised by his own defensive edge.

"Where did you see it?" she whispered, her expression now a little sad.

Her somber gait touched him, and his suspicions eased. "In here," he answered.

"In this room?"

"Yes. Why? What is it?"

"This room is where she died," Peggy said.

"Where *who* died?"

"Annabel."

He looked at Mrs. Franzen. "Someone died in this room?" He had trouble voicing the question around the lump in his throat.

"A number of people have died in this room," she said matter-of-factly. "This was one of the old hospital's operating rooms."

"Here?"

"It was one of the few rooms big enough for a conference room. Most were only big enough for offices."

"And people died right here over the years? How many?"

"I have no idea. It's not like they kept a spreadsheet back then listing the deaths. This hospital is over a hundred years old, so probably a good number. A lot of the rooms have a history of deaths."

"They died on the operating table?"

"I assume so."

"Where was the table located in here?"

"I'm sure it changed position over the years, but since I've been here it was always right there." She pointed a stubby finger at the conference table.

"Right here?" he whispered, rolling his chair back from the table. He stared at the dark waves of grain in the wood.

"What did you see?" Peggy asked again.

"Nothing," he said quickly. "I didn't see anything."

Molly and Peggy exchanged a glance. Their tight lips and knitted brows matched so precisely, they could be twins.

"What do you think I saw?" he asked.

"You might have seen Annabel," Peggy said.

"Like, a *ghost*?" he asked. Just mentioning the word made him feel ridiculous, and he would have dismissed it entirely if not for the serious response it got from the two women. Both nodded, as if unwilling to answer out loud.

"Come on! You're telling me you've got a *ghost* in this hospital?"

"Yeah," Molly said. "Cool, isn't it ... in a way?"

"A haunted hospital?"

"Probably a lot of them are haunted, really," she said. "When you think about it, all those deaths over the years ..."

"So what's so special about this Annabel?" he asked, intrigued enough with their shared fantasy to play along.

"She died here under horrible circumstances," Peggy whispered.

"Horrible how?" he asked, his tone more respectful now that he could see how serious Peggy, at least, took this subject.

"She was murdered by her husband."

He grimaced. *"Here?"*

"She was having an affair with her neighbor," Peggy continued. "Her husband worked the shale oil fields. He came home one night and found Annabel in bed with their neighbor.

Shot them while they were still in bed. When the police arrived on the scene, the husband wouldn't put the gun down and was shot and killed. The neighbor had died at the scene, but the paramedics got a faint pulse from Annabel. They rushed her here, but she died within minutes of arriving in this room. Some things on the first floor were moved to the new hospital building as construction was wrapping up. The changes created a bit of upheaval, so we temporarily had to use this OR as the ER surgery, too."

"Okay, that's bad," Jason said. To Molly, he said, "You should have told me about this."

"It doesn't have anything to do with your work," she replied.

"You put me in this room."

"It's just a room."

"Doesn't sound like it," he said. "Peggy thinks it's haunted."

"What do *you* think?" Molly asked, any trace of amusement gone from her face.

"I don't know."

"What did you see?" Peggy said.

"Some chairs moved when I was out of the room. One cracked that mirror. Okay?"

"Whoa!" Molly said.

Peggy nodded. "How many chairs moved? One or two?"

"All of them."

"All of …?" Peggy's eyes were wide.

"Whoooaaa!"

"Come on. You guys are messing with me, right. Something you always do to the new guy? I get it. Very funny—hah, hah. Now, please stop."

"We didn't do anything," Molly said. "But it's happened before."

"Um-hm." He didn't know how much more he could take of this. "I'm afraid to ask."

"Did anything else happen?" Peggy said.

"Well, I thought I saw something at the end of the hallway, but it was just a reflection of your computer monitor in the locker's door."

"Whose monitor?"

"Yours."

"What room?"

"Your room, Peggy. Last door on the right."

"My monitor has been broken for weeks. I've been working off my laptop until IT gets my replacement. And I take my laptop home."

"Well, it was turned on last night."

"You don't understand—it can't turn on."

"I *saw* it on." He paused. "Anything else you guys want to tell me about this Annabel?"

"There's a lot to tell if you have time to hear it," Peggy said.

"I'll make time."

Both Peggy and Molly moved toward the table to grab seats.

"Oh, hey, wait," he said. "Is there somewhere else we can talk about it? I don't want to be in this room."

"Let's get a coffee in the cafeteria," Molly said.

"In the new wing?" he said. "Great idea."

He stood up, locked his computer, and followed them out the door. But even as he left, he thought he heard, from no discernible direction, a low whisper saying, "*No, no, no ... Run!*"

10

Rachel took the side entrance into the massive high school building. The sounds of ambient chatter ricocheted off the hard walls and filled the corridor. She smiled when she saw Tommy at his locker. They had been friends since third grade, but she had never admired him more than when he chose not to play football this year, even though he was a senior and one of the top players on the team. He had decided that it was more important to help on his family's farm than to devote countless hours honing his skills as a star tight end and defensive end. He had also confided in Rachel that his disgust with the head coach's verbally abusive treatment of less-skilled players had made his decision to walk away from the sport that much easier.

"Hey, Tommy," she said. "How are the chickens?"

He pulled his head out of his locker. "Hey, Rachel. Chickens are good, growing big now. Couple are sick, but that's not bad out of fifty thousand."

"Has anyone decided about Halloween yet?"

"I haven't heard anything," he said. "But we should figure it out soon. You still thinking Annabel?"

She nodded.

They heard a bang from behind them. Looking back, they saw three boys pushing some other kid against a locker. The three wore blue letter jackets with white leather sleeves, and Rachel recognized them from the football team. They pushed the kid again, knocking him back against the line of lockers with another bang. Other students just stared at the scene while walking past.

"Bastards," Rachel said.

"Yeah," Tommy agreed. "I'll stop it."

"Against three guys?"

"I used to own them on the practice field," he said. "They won't have forgotten. Hey, let me know what the other girls decide about Halloween."

"I will—I'm heading there now," she said. "*Good luck* with those trolls."

"I won't need it," he said, grinning.

As he left her and advanced on the three bullies, she realized that some part of him really missed the challenge of aggressive contact sports. But his aging parents had really needed him to take on more of their farming responsibilities. She stood there only long enough to watch Tommy step between the three guys and the kid, and to then slowly back the three up with words and a few light shoves until the guys turned and walked away, muttering. When Tommy turned back to talk with the kid, Rachel decided to keep moving. She needed to get to the central commons before first period, to respond to the strange text message she had received.

She had made it only halfway to the commons when she saw Aaron walking toward her. Being taller than almost everyone in their class, he was always easy to spot. He was also one of the smartest people she had ever met, at least when it came to math and science.

He smiled when he saw her. "Where you heading?"

"The commons," she answered. "You seen Shelley or Jessica?"

"Yeah, they're both there. I had to leave early."

"What for?" she asked.

"I'm trying to hack into Mrs. Dodson's laptop."

"What? *How?*"

"I embedded some malware into the file I emailed her for my last assignment. I need to check and see if it's been executed yet."

"Are you crazy! Trying to hack our computer teacher's laptop? Aaron, you're going to get yourself expelled!"

"I won't get caught. And if I do, she might just give me extra credit. So many kids are just goofing around in her class, she'll probably be thrilled to have someone so passionate about computers."

"If you were really smart, you'd find a way to hack into the school's grading system," she joked.

"Working on it," he said with a wink.

She looked hard at him, then laughed. "Well, I better get to Shelley and Jessica before the warning bell."

They parted, and she continued toward the commons.

Rachel walked through the chaos of the high school's central commons before first period. As she swam through the crowd, she saw Shelley and Jessica talking.

Sneaking up behind Shelley, she was careful to barely touch the back of her friend's ear with one finger. She held the faint contact for nearly a second before Shelley twitched and swatted at her ear while jumping forward. Jessica laughed as Shelley spun around and gasped.

"Okay," Rachel said. "What's this important text you got?"

"It's from my mom," Shelley said with a grin. "There's been another sighting at the hospital."

"Of Annabel?" Rachel asked.

"An accountant from Chicago was working late last night and saw all the chairs move in the conference room."

Rachel stared in silence. She had sensed something powerful occurring last night and had assumed it was directed toward her. But she had never considered that she might pick up things that were happening to others.

"We have to check it out," Jessica said.

"When?" Shelley asked.

"Tonight," Rachel said. "While the trail's still fresh. Can you get the key?"

Shelley nodded.

The five-minute warning bell rang throughout the commons. The swarm of students drifted away from the central space and shuffled into herds that flowed into the hallways. But then the speaker system crackled, spewing garbled white noise for a few loud seconds before a distant, raspy voice screeched, "No, no, no … run off con … off con … Run!" Then came a long scream before the speakers hissed, gave a brief high-pitched ring, and fell silent.

Rachel had covered her ears at the end, as had most of the kids around her. She looked behind her, trying to find Shelley and Jessica in the crowd of faces. Some students looked shaken. Others laughed uncertainly. All were surprised.

When Rachel finally located and locked eyes with Jessica, then Shelley, she could tell that both her friends were thinking the same thing as she: the disturbing noise was not some random radio-wave intercept or a joke from some kid who had grabbed the microphone in the principal's office. Not this close to the anniversary of Annabel's death. Not when there had been a sighting at the hospital just last night. No, this felt like some sort of message, a warning from someone urging them all to *run*.

But from what? And to where? The message had seemed fragmented, its warning useless. They could do nothing except continue as planned, all of them, while holding in the back of their minds the thought that maybe they should be running from some unknown peril while they still had the chance.

11

The hospital's cafeteria was a large open area with long stairs leading down from the main floor of the new wing, giving it the feel of a wide pit. It was just before nine a.m., and the breakfast rush appeared over. A few tables away, four women in lilac scrubs ate yogurt and bagels. At the end of the tray bars winding past the food windows, a big, round-faced kid in his twenties, wearing an apron and a plastic hair cap, stood behind the checkout stand.

Jason set his green tea down and sat across from Molly and Peggy. "What was her full name?"

"Annabel Heller," Peggy said softly.

Molly, who had been typing something on her phone, finally set it down on the wooden table. "Her family had been in these parts forever—probably longer than the original hospital."

"Had been?"

"They're all dead now. Annabel was the last one."

He looked at Peggy, as if to get a second opinion.

"Annabel's family are all here," Peggy said, with her Earl Grey steaming in front of her. "They're all buried near Annabel in their family plot at Highgate Cemetery. Her grandparents died decades ago. Her mother fought breast cancer for years before she died ten or so years ago. A year after that, her father died of a heart attack. Her older brother, Joe, took over the family business and died in a farming accident a few years later. He was her only sibling, so after he was gone, she was alone … except for Rubin. They were high school and college sweethearts before they got married."

"And a year ago he murdered her," Jason said sadly.

"The family was cursed," Peggy said. "Any family with that much tragedy must be cursed."

"And now she's haunting our hospital," Molly said. "Making things go bump in the night. Causing lights to flicker, slamming doors, moving chairs, phantom footsteps, and now, apparently, turning on broken computer monitors. She'd be dragging chains along the attic floor if we had one. Boo!"

"Don't joke about it, Molly," Peggy said.

"Oh, she can't hear us in here."

"What do you mean?" Jason asked.

"She only stays in the old wing."

"She doesn't come over here?"

"No one's ever seen or heard her in the new wing. She doesn't like it, so we're safe here."

"We don't know that," Peggy said.

"Then how come she's never come over here?" Molly asked. "There hasn't been one reported incident."

"She can't! She's trapped!"

"I bet she could if she really wanted to," Molly said.

Jason didn't know what to think of all this. He liked a good ghost story as much as the next person, but these two didn't seem to be telling tales—at any rate, *they* believed them. He studied them as he sipped his tea.

"Well, don't you think she would have left if she could?" Peggy said to Molly. "Why would she *choose* to stay in the old wing?"

"Maybe she likes it there," Molly replied. "I do."

"No. You. Do. Not," Peggy said as if disgusted by such a claim.

"I do!"

"In that dark, drab place? No!"

"I like the quiet. And I bet Annabel does, too."

Peggy swatted the air and looked at Jason. "Don't you listen to a word she says. Ghosts don't want to stay *anywhere*. They want to move on. It's unnatural for them to be stuck between this world and the next. Poor Annabel is trapped."

"What makes *you* the expert?" Molly asked.

"I've researched it."

"Researched," Molly said, laughing.

"How?" Jason was serious. He wanted to know.

"Would you like to see the book?" Peggy asked.

"Don't show him that. He'll think we're crazy."

"Yes, I'd very much like to see it," he answered, overruling Molly's objection.

"It's in my office," Peggy said. "I'll give it to you when we head back over. You can borrow it this week. Just don't forget to return it."

"You keep it in your office?" he asked.

"See?" Molly said. "Now not only does he think we're crazy, he also thinks we don't do anything but read ghost stories at work."

"Only during my lunch," Peggy proclaimed.

Molly chuckled, then looked at Jason. "We do actually get a lot of work done around here, Mr. Auditor. Just ask us any questions you want."

Jason set his teacup down. "Well, actually, I did want to ask you about the reserves for the private-payer receivables."

"What about them?" she asked.

"Why have they increased so much? They're twice as high as last year's numbers."

"We had to increase the reserves. Bad-debt write-offs have been going up."

Jason thought about this for a second. "People aren't paying their hospital bills?" he asked.

Molly shook her head with disgust. "We can't *find* the people."

"What do you mean?"

"People are going missing," she said.

"Missing?" he asked, a little startled.

"They're just vanishing."

"Wait. People around here are *vanishing*? What are you talking about?"

"A lot of people around here are migrant workers from other states, who come up here on buses and get jobs working in the oil fields. They live in temporary housing pods set up by the oil companies. When they need health care, they usually come in through the ER. Many don't have insurance, because the oil firms contract them on a short-term basis. And they don't have permanent mailing addresses, since they're living in temporary housing. No place for us to really send the bill. We can't turn them away from the ER, so we treat their emergencies and sometimes a little beyond that; then we discharge them. When we try to send the final bill out a month later, we have a hard time getting paid. So we end up writing them off, sell the account to a collection agency for pennies on the dollar, and just take our licks and keep on ticking."

"Until you go bankrupt," he said.

"Until we go bankrupt," she agreed. "Welcome to the world of rural nonprofit hospitals."

"But at least you're saving lives," he said.

"As you said, until we go bankrupt." She gave a sad smile.

They had finished their coffee and tea, and it was time to get back to work. They walked back to the long staircase that connected the cafeteria to the upper mezzanine.

"Any other major problems with collections?" he asked as they climbed the stairs. "The numbers just seem so high."

"There's also a bad homeless problem here right now," Molly said. "Usually, towns our size would have just a few homeless people if any, but we have hundreds. The shale oil operators aren't doing as well these days, because prices are down, which means job cuts. Lot of places across the US apparently got word last year there were jobs up here, but no one sent out the memo informing everyone that those jobs are gone. A lot more migrant workers are getting off the bus every day than can find jobs, and many of those end up too broke to leave. So they get stuck here, hoping a recovery happens so that jobs come back."

They reached the top of the stairs. The wide hospital floor stretched the length of a football field, with them on the fifty-yard line. The new building was four stories tall and had an open center, with staircases and walking bridges connecting atriums and passageways on all the upper levels. People in white lab coats and soft-hued scrubs moved purposefully about. Family members, looking half lost, went in small packs, trying to navigate the maze.

"So yeah," Molly said. "For one reason or another, people around here are vanishing. Even crime is up."

"Crime?" he asked.

"There's not too much crime in the area," Molly replied. "Even with our problems. But sometimes, people do seem to just disappear without any trace of what happened to them. Probably they just left town, but there are legends that some ancient evil has found its way to our town and is taking people at night. Scary stories fueled by the fact that it's hard to have a missing-persons alert for a migrant worker who might have simply left town, or for a homeless person that nobody ever really knew in the first place. So yeah, when people go missing around here, no one looks too hard for them. Not unless they were a local resident, but the last really horrible thing that happened to any locals was the Annabel thing."

As they walked past a registry station with a few dozen people sitting in rows of chairs, he found himself scanning each face as if he might decode their struggles. He was still young and healthy, which he too often took for granted. It took a long walk through the main floor of a large hospital to remind him what happens to the body when one's time or luck begins to run out. Some were grossly overweight, some rail thin, some on oxygen. Most were old but not *that* old. Some read magazines; others read their phones. Some looked exhausted; others seemed to be happy enough and taking everything in stride. They all had *someone* with them.

"It must have been tricky moving people over from the old hospital," he said.

"A logistical nightmare," Peggy said.

He chuckled. "How many patients had to be moved?"

"Forty," Molly answered.

"Think any of them are still here?"

"Sure, some. But probably not many. Why?"

"I was just wondering something …" he said, idly watching the foot traffic through a large concourse intersection. "Just wondering how many patients here might have had an experience with Annabel's ghost in the old hospital. Maybe some of them saw something that they're keeping a secret."

"Something bad?" Molly asked.

"I don't know. Just a thought."

"Well, for the record—in case any of this makes it into your audit report—I don't believe in any of this ghost stuff. But off the record, I can tell you that you're going to *love* that book of Peggy's."

He smiled.

But as they kept walking, he noticed an old woman in a wheelchair coming toward him, pushed by a big orderly with bushy sideburns. The woman was hunched down in her chair. Thick blankets covered her lap, and a bony hand gripped one arm of the wheelchair. She had a mop of wild gray hair that was hard to miss because her head was bowed with her chin touching her chest. She looked as though she had been here a long time. For some reason, he couldn't take his eyes off her as she drew closer. Then, when she was within thirty feet, her head rose slightly as if she sensed something, and her shining eyes caught his. She stared at him through the gray hair that curled and dangled over half her face. And she seemed to see something in him that she recognized, for just before she was pushed past him, a mad grin spread across her face as if she knew some dark secret about the hospital that she would never tell—not to him or anyone else—but would take to the grave.

12

A nauseating chill passed through Rachel after she finished the last few lines of "The Black Cat." She jolted in her seat when the classroom bell rang out as loud as the terrified screams that she had imagined from the story's condemned narrator. She slammed the book shut, only to be further startled by Poe's thoroughly creepy face staring back at her, his deathly countenance captured perfectly in the icy black-and-white photograph. Stuffing the book into her backpack, she hustled out the door with the other students as Mr. Coleman bellowed out warnings of tomorrow's quiz on Poe, Lovecraft, and Le Fanu.

Rachel followed the current of students down the wide stairway and passed a large glass case filled with trophies and plaques listing school records and championships in track, wrestling, and volleyball. At her locker, she spun the cheap combination dial and pulled up on the thumb lever. When it didn't budge, she hit it with her fist on the sweet spot a foot above the latch and pulled the door open.

She unzipped her backpack and started swapping out books for the ones she needed to take home.

"Hey, Rachel."

She looked up to see a classmate a few lockers down. "Oh, hey, Tiffany. How'd you like that story?"

"It was scary. I can't believe that guy gouged out one of the cat's eyes. That's messed up! And then he *hung* the cat!"

"Poor kitty."

"Yeah. Hey, what were you writing when he was reading the story? No one else was taking notes."

"I didn't take notes," Rachel said.

"Sure you did—didn't you? You were writing furiously for a while there."

"During the story?"

"Yeah."

"I never wrote down anything," Rachel said.

"Look, it's okay. I was just asking. I didn't realize it was so personal. Don't worry about it. Look, I'll see you later, okay?" And with that, Tiffany closed her locker and walked away.

"What the hell?" Rachel whispered to herself. Then, turning back to close her locker, she saw the spine of Poe's selected stories still sitting inside her backpack. She frowned, staring at it as if it might do something. She took it out and turned to the first page of "The Black Cat." Then she flipped each page until she came across one that made her stop. Jumping off the page in bold black ink scrawled across Poe's tale of terror was the number *623*, written manically dozens of times—*623, 623, 623.*

Her eyes jumped randomly about the mad scattering of the same three numerals in the same order—*623,* scribbled in different sizes at various angles. Some were giant and crossed the entire page, some were upside down, and some were even written inside the curves and loops of others. Her knees buckled, and she had to lean against her locker to keep her balance. When she realized that the numbers weren't even in her own handwriting, she had to close her eyes to keep from panicking as heat flashed through her head and down her throat, and an uncomfortable tingling spread throughout her body. She turned and pressed her forehead to the cold locker and silently counted while taking slow, deep breaths. This hadn't been her. Something or someone had invaded her mind during class and taken control of her. Why was this happening? She was just a girl who had been sitting in a classroom, surrounded by her peers. What had she done to deserve this curse?

Rachel opened her eyes and saw the book shaking almost uncontrollably as she held it by one hand, dangling open with the page now sideways and still facing her. She snatched at it with her other hand and tore it from the book, wadding it up in a tight ball.

Lurching into the tide of bodies in the hallway, she felt the strangely hard edges of the crumpled paper trying to pierce her palm and fingers, as if the page were gnawing at her skin with tiny, pointed teeth. It hurt, but she dare not relax her grip until she made it to the nearest trashcan and threw the wad of paper in with rather more force than necessary.

She had been so upset by the violation of her mind that she hadn't even considered what the number might mean. *623.* It meant nothing to her, but now it stood glowing in her mind's eye, haunting her, and she couldn't tear *that* out and throw it away.

As she left the main hallway and headed for the side exit door, she decided to keep quiet about this—no need to mention it to her friends. There was no pattern to any of it. Nothing made sense. She tried to pretend it was only worthless spirit clamor. She was just a radio that was starting to pick up strange overlapping static from nearby broadcasts by the departed. Just random cosmic noise, nothing more.

She joined the migration from the building out into cold afternoon sun.

The high school was at the foot of a long hill clad with old-growth elms, oaks, and chokecherries. The area had some of the richest mineral composites in the soil, making it one of the more verdant and scenic parts of the county. West of the campus was a middle-class neighborhood. East was Highgate Cemetery, with its low stone wall stretching the length of the high school and beyond, past the practice fields and into the deepest patch of woods.

The overcrowded high school had scattered islands of parking built around various expansion wings from the core building. But all these lots had room for just half the students' cars. Like many, Rachel would rather park on neighborhood streets than joust and jockey for a space in the lots. She liked the long stretch of road on the far side of the cemetery. Maybe a hundred students parked in that area, resulting in a twice-daily migration of students across the cemetery. Every morning, they came like zombies staggering out of their graves to descend on the high school. And again in the afternoon, they would make the trudge back across the hallowed grounds, past leaning tombstones and somber trees, without a thought to all the vibrant beings like themselves who had left their mortal remains here.

Rachel stepped through the narrow entrance in the stone wall and began her afternoon walk past the dead. She admired the cemetery's gothic beauty. Family mausoleums projected the myth of strength, and mastery of their surroundings. Grand tombstones competed with each other into eternity, boasting of material wealth that their owners could no longer wield or enjoy. The unknown lives of the souls she passed were condensed down to the dash between the first and last year of their earthly existence. Anything over seventy-five years was excellent, anything over forty-five was okay, anything under thirty was tragic, and anything under eighteen was devastating. Her mother had been twenty-seven when she died. Rachel was now seventeen, and she mused that she still had ten years left before she would meet her mother's fate.

Her pace quickened as the ground sloped down. An errant breeze whispered through the trees above, shaking loose dozens of crimson and gold leaves that fluttered down to cover the slowly disappearing green. As her black shoes rustled through the fall leaves, she heard wicked laughter from a big granite headstone fifty feet ahead.

"Hello?" she said. "Who's there?"

"Hark! Art thou friend or foe?" A faint wave of smoke rose from the tombstone, followed by a wave of wheezing laughter.

"Friend," she announced.

"Just what a cunning foe would say to entrap the unwary," replied the smoking tombstone.

"A friend, I assure you. One of only a few, I'm sure, for a fool like you can't have collected many over the years."

"Cruel words," the tombstone groaned. "Most cruel."

She picked up a stick, looked briefly at its gnarls and knots, and tossed it just over the stone.

"Hey!" Leaves rustled, and a boy's blond head popped up and looked at her. He grinned and said, "I yield, fair lady! I YIELD!"

"Wise decision, Scott. You bonehead, what are you doing smoking that stuff out here? You could have been caught. What if it had been someone other than me who came along? A teacher, groundskeeper, even a cop—your ass would've been grass."

"Speaking of which, you want some?" Stifling a giggle, he held the joint out in front of his eyes and jiggled it as if ringing a little bell.

"I'm being serious."

"I could tell it was you."

"Oh, really."

"Sure. You're the only one that goes out of their way to walk through the leaves. You make so much noise out here, it's as if you're *trying* to wake the dead."

"Maybe I am."

He laughed. "Speaking of which, you're going tonight, right?"

"Yeah. Why—you thought I wouldn't?"

"Honestly, I wasn't sure. After what happened last time …"

She stared at him, surprised at his intuitive grasp of all the concerns she had from the group's last outing. She hadn't talked about it with anyone and had almost convinced herself that no one even noticed how hard it had been for her. But clearly, she had underestimated how closely Scott was watching her and how in tune he seemed to be with what she had been feeling.

"No, I'll be there," she said softly. "Jessica's house?"

"Yeah, that's right," he said. "You want to talk about it? The little panic attack or whatever it was you had? I mean, I don't really know what you experienced, but it's probably best to talk about it with someone."

"Maybe at some point. I think I would like that. But not yet, okay?"

"Sure. But you think you'll be okay tonight?"

"I think so." Then, with what she hoped was a reassuring grin, she added, "And if I'm not, you'll be there to help me out. But I'll be fine, really. I just need to stay focused on …" She paused as a slight, sudden swishing interrupted her thoughts.

"What?" he asked.

"Hear that?"

He froze and listened and then shook his head.

"Something's walking through the leaves," she said.

"Something?"

"Someone's coming."

They both scanned the area around them.

"I don't see anything," Scott whispered. "I mean, there are cottonwoods scattered everywhere, so line of sight is terrible, but I don't even hear anything."

"Something's out there, and it's getting closer."

"Are you sure it's not just in your head? It could just be ..."
Now he, too, paused. "Oh, crap, you're right. There."

Rachel turned but saw nothing except big, crooked trees and
tombstones.

"What is it?" she asked.

Scott lowered the joint as he studied whatever had caught his
eye. Then he groaned. "It's that big security guard. The one
that's always patrolling the parking lots with his walkie-talkie.
Thinks he's Dudley Do-Right."

She ducked behind the grave and followed Scott's eyes. Sure
enough, here came the husky security guard, lumbering down the
hill straight at them, like a bear that had picked up the scent of
food. He held the radio to his mouth as he moved, as if in
constant communication with some secret military command
center that lived in his imagination. Then his searching eyes
must have caught them, because he jerked up and yelled
something at them.

"We're dead meat if he catches us with your pot," Rachel
said.

"I've got a plan."

"What?"

He grabbed her hand. "RUN!"

A slight tug was all it took. They dashed off through the fifty
yards of tombstones that stood between them and the street
beyond. The security guard was yelling at them. Rachel glanced
back once and saw the man's flushed face as he labored in
pursuit. She giggled as they ran, and this set Scott off into giddy,
continuous laughter. He kept hold of her hand as if the only
mistake they could make in their flight was to split up. For to his
credit, the huffing, sweating security guard was refusing to give
up the chase.

They pounded up the slope and exploded through the
shrubbery along the edge of the cemetery. On the street, they

darted between two pickup trucks, cut right toward the next street corner, and stopped on the side street.

"I'm this way," she said, motioning right.

"I'm down there." He pointed the other direction.

They heard a shout from inside the cemetery—distant but getting closer.

"See you tonight?" he said, letting go of her hand and grinning.

"Wouldn't miss it," she replied.

They heard more shouting from the cemetery. They looked at each other one last time and started giggling again as they ran in opposite directions toward their getaway cars, keen to avoid the torture of in-school suspension.

And as she jumped into her Volkswagen Beetle and sped away, Rachel basked in the afterglow. This little adventure with Scott was even more fun than her dream from Monday morning. And in a few short hours, she would be seeing him again. The thought made her heart quicken, and she temporarily pushed aside all her concerns about death and murder and Annabel's growing anger.

13

Shelley Franzen marched through the front entryway of her house after closing the front door. "Mom?" She waited a tick, then called out louder, "MOM?"

She opened the side door to the garage. Half the garage was filled with storage boxes from their old life in Oregon, before her mom got the job at the hospital. Had it really been two years now? It seemed crazy that so much of their old stuff was just going to sit boxed away for so long. Most of it probably dated back to when her parents were still together, which was likely the real reason it stayed buried away.

It was a big house for one high-school girl to spend so much time in alone. Some girls her age would no doubt have taken advantage of the situation by inviting boys over after school. But Shelley was too shy, and she didn't want to get into trouble—at least, not *that* kind of trouble. She had her dreams of med school to think about. Then she could become a doctor like her dad, and maybe even move back to Portland someday and work in the same hospital.

She went to the kitchen and opened the drawer next to the fridge. Amid the jar openers, penlights, pencils, and soda straws, she saw the round-headed silver key, its sharp teeth grinning at her in the bright overhead light. It was always risky to steal the spare hospital annex key for a night, but her mom hadn't noticed the past few times. Picking it up, she stared at it and wondered how she would explain such a strange crime if her mom caught her. Her eyes rose and met her dad's stare from the family photo on the wall. The three of them, standing near a footbridge on a verdant trail along Oregon's Tryon Creek. It was the only picture with her dad in it that her mom allowed on display.

Shelley raised a finger to her lips. "Shh, okay, Dad? Our secret?"

Her dad stared back without a word, frozen in a bygone moment of a happy family that no longer was.

She closed the drawer, threaded the key onto her ring, and rushed upstairs to her bedroom. She dropped her backpack on her bed and emptied her pockets, placing her keys and cell phone and pocket purse next to her pack. She had a few hours before she needed to be at Jessica's house for their Ghost Hunting Club meeting—enough time to go to the pond before dinner.

She threw on a wool fleece, clomped back down the stairs, and rushed out the back door. The sun was near the horizon. It would be dark in half an hour. The sky was already turning a bright orange. Her mom didn't like her going to the pond by herself, especially so close to dark. She would have to hurry so she could be back before her mom got home.

She ran through the mostly bare trees with spindly branches. Leaves rustled as a sharp breeze swept through the surrounding thicket. The tall, narrow poplars and birches swayed, their long branches dipped and bobbed. She couldn't remember ever seeing so much movement along the path to the pond. She had no idea how old this batch of trees was, but she was certain that this isolated pocket of woods was older than the town.

Shelley strolled down a last slope to the edge of the pond. A little aluminum dinghy was turned upside down on the grass. She flipped it over and dragged it the few feet to the water's edge. Tossing in the wooden oars, she stepped in with one foot, grabbed the metal sides, and pushed off from the shore.

The boat rocked as she lowered herself to the seat. Then she fitted each oarlock to its mounting hole and rowed toward the center of the pond. The murky body of water was not much bigger than a football field, but over the past two years it had become her private refuge from the world. She would often come here and just sit floating in the middle of this placid little ecosystem. In summer, she would watch the dragonflies cut arabesques over the cattails, and the water striders sculling in the shallows. And in the fall, she would come out on evenings like this to enjoy the peaceful solitude before winter turned the surface to thick, dark glass.

She pulled the oars in and listened to the soft lapping of ripples against the dinghy. As the silence deepened around her, she watched the apricot sunset through a wild tangle of black branches. What had seemed beautiful at first now began to twist into something darker. Her eyes looked into the moving branches. It seemed almost as if they were tightening together to block out the fading light, enclosing the pond in a dark shroud.

Her breathing quickened.

The breeze picked up, chilling her as it passed over the black water. It even stung her eyes and nose, as if there were something toxic in the air. Strange hollers and whistles and groans came from the trees as the wind cut through the remaining tight spaces.

Shelley was panting now as her heart raced. Something wasn't right. This was not the peaceful pond where she had found refuge and solace so many times in the past. Something was different. Every inch of her instincts told her that something was very wrong.

The last of the orange light vanished, turning everything to shades of dark blue and gray and black.

Strangely, she felt cold water soaking through her sneakers and socks. Fumbling the small Maglite out of her pocket, she clicked it on and found an inch of water in the bottom of the boat. Alarmed to see the water level rising, she played the beam along the seams, hunting for the leak. But after working all the way around the boat's bottom, she found nothing. The boat hadn't been taking on water during her first ten minutes on the pond. It didn't make any sense.

The reality of the situation hit her. She had no way to plug the leak even if she found it. She must get this boat back to shore before it sank. She reached her hand into the standing water to search one last time but jerked it back when she felt something brush against her wrist. Swinging the beam back down, she saw that the water in the boat had turned dark red, and in it writhed a dozen black snakes, curling and twisting over one another.

She screamed and dropped the flashlight. It splashed inside the boat and cast a blood-red glow below her, with shadows of serpents flitting between her legs.

Arching backward, she tried to throw herself out of the boat to escape, but her left foot was caught on something under the middle bench. She screamed as the serpents slithered about her ankles. The water was still rising and reached her lower calves. She jerked her leg, but her foot was wedged. She screamed again, louder this time. Imagining and praying that there was someone out there in the dark, she let loose with a bloodcurdling scream for help. She yelled until her throat burned and her breath gave out.

The water spilled over the three benches and continued to rise. The flashlight was still on, revealing the frenzied motion of the snakes in their red-tinted medium. Shelley had only seconds before the water would sluice over the edges and pull her and the boat down into the dark depths.

She grabbed both gunwales and pulled her leg as hard as she could. Pain fired in her heel, intensifying with her efforts to free her foot. But no matter how much she fought and struggled, she couldn't get herself unstuck.

The freezing water rose right up to the gunwales and paused. She stopped struggling, afraid that the slightest movement might slosh the water over the rim and swamp the dinghy. Panting and shivering, she stared at the rising water.

The boat turned slowly, as if something below were pushing it. The boat was now completely swamped, so that the flashlight's glow reached beyond the tiny vessel to the water directly around her. At this point, it looked almost as if there were no boat and she were sitting motionless in the middle of the pond.

A few seconds later, the rest of the boat began to sink.

Shelley screamed long and loud, flailing her arms. The boat was pulling her down. She tried to push free of the boat or tread with her arms enough to keep her head above the surface, but it was futile. The boat kept sinking and pulling her down with it. The pond was now up to her chest, then her neck, then chin. Tears filled her eyes as she took one last desperate breath before going under.

Submerged and sinking in the frigid water, she couldn't believe she was going to die from such a freak accident. She still didn't understand how this had happened to her. But in her final moments of fear and anger, she believed that some form of evil had found her on the pond and done this to her. And that anger turned to full-blown rage when she realized she would never see her mom and dad again, never get to enjoy the rest of her youth, and never get to become a doctor in a hospital and save patients' lives.

She felt a muted thud as the boat hit the bottom of the pond. Her panicked mind grew focused when she realized this gave her one last chance to get free.

She planted her right foot on the bench and pushed with all of its strength while pulling the trapped foot with everything she had. The exertion let some air escape, and she felt the bubbles roll up her face toward the distant surface. She felt as if her chest were imploding. It was as if her lungs refused to accept that she couldn't just take a quick little breath, and the impulsive reflex just to open her mouth and inhale water was a maddening urge that she couldn't fight much longer. She gave a spastic jerk in the water. Nothing was left for her except the pain and the need to open her mouth and suck in her death. The cold darkness had her, and it wasn't letting go. She accepted that this was it—the precise moment that made the difference between life and death. If she had anything left to give, now was the time. So she crouched in the bottom of the boat, tensed the trapped leg, and pushed in one final effort. If she ripped the ligaments in her knee and ankle apart, so be it. The strain and pain built for a few more excruciating seconds ... and the trapped foot suddenly popped free.

Kicking frantically, and stroking with her arms, she hauled herself up through the water until her head burst through the surface, and she sucked in her first breath in nearly two minutes.

Coughing and gasping as she treaded water, she looked up at the pristine clarity of the stars, clear in the North Dakota night sky, glimmering in their perfect constellations. It was as if no atmospheric barrier existed between the Earth and the heavens. The fabric of the universe felt so close, she could reach up and almost touch it.

Then, without warning, her brief reverie was broken as a swarm or flock of creatures flew past overhead. Birds, bats, or something else. The blurred visual image and the rushing, hissing sound seemed to warn of some ancient evil in the pond or the surrounding wood. She sidestroked toward shore. A faint glow of light from the sunk flashlight beneath her jostled in the shifting, translucent water. She kept trying to look into it to see if there were any moving shadows. The snakes had disappeared when the boat went under, but she feared they were still out here somewhere.

One of her flutter kicks hit muck, and she realized she had made it ashore. She pulled herself up through the mud and onto the grass. Wet and cold, she now worried about hypothermia and pneumonia. She stumbled to her feet and ran back through the woods, toward home.

14

Rachel closed the rusty door of her Volkswagen Beetle and crossed the dark neighborhood street toward the big house. An array of jack-o-lanterns lined the porch, leering at her with their flickering gaze. She jogged up the steps, rang the bell, and waited. Two stained-glass diamond shapes in the door mesmerized her until the footsteps broke the silence. Then the door opened, revealing Jessica's excited face.

"Thank God you're here!"

"What's wrong?" Rachel asked, reading the affliction on her friend's face.

"It's Shelley—she almost died!"

"What!"

"Something really bad happened, and she almost drowned in the pond behind her house."

"Is she okay?"

"She's downstairs," Jessica said. Then she stepped forward and gave Rachel a strong hug. "We thought something might have happened to you, too."

"Me? Why?"

"Shelley's story is crazy. She said she saw things ... things that are hard to believe. And she believes that something might have been trying to kill her. You're the last one here, so we were getting worried. We tried to call and text you."

"Something tried to *kill* her?" Rachel asked, feeling a cold lump in her gut.

"That's what she thinks."

"I want to see her."

They walked through the living room, past an antique organ and a cabinet displaying blue collectible plates, through a small kitchen, to a descending stairway. Each wooden step creaked and groaned as they made their way down. In the concrete basement, a few bare lightbulbs dangled by their cords from the ceiling, illuminating the headquarters of their Ghost Hunting Club.

Shelley was sitting in the middle of the deep, cushiony couch with Aaron and Tommy on either side of her. Scott sat in a leather recliner next to them and was leaning forward to listen. Rachel walked briskly over to them, knelt down in front of Shelley, and took her hand.

"Are you okay?"

Shelley nodded, then sniffled.

"What happened?"

Rachel listened as her friend told her about a dark pond, a rowboat taking on water for no reason, a stuck foot, being pulled down to the bottom of the pond, and an almost miraculous last-second escape. And she listened to descriptions of moving tree branches that looked like clawing witches' fingers, and blood-red water with black snakes swimming in it.

Shelley began to cry, and Rachel hugged and held her.

"It wasn't an accident," Shelley said between sobs. "Something was *out there.*"

"You're safe now," Rachel said. She slowly let go, then rolled back to sit on the rug. There were two more old couches on the short ends of the rug, along with a large beanbag chair. A decades-old box TV was pushed into one corner on a rolling stand that had a DVD player and a stack of old movies on its lower shelves. The rest of the basement was unfinished concrete walls, storage shelves, and boxes.

"We'll just stay in tonight," Rachel said.

"No, I still want to go to the hospital," Shelley said.

"We should stay here," Aaron said. "There'll be other nights to look for Annabel."

"I'm not afraid," she said. "It was terrifying, but I'm dealing with it. I still want to go."

"We should just stay here," Rachel repeated.

"No, please," Shelley said. "My dad always told me that I would need to control my fears if I ever wanted to become a good surgeon someday. He said patients' lives depend on it. I have to go tonight. I can't ever let my fears control me."

No one spoke.

"Please," Shelley said. "I took the extra key without my mom knowing. We have all the equipment here. We're close to the anniversary of Annabel's death, and we know there was some sort of activity in the hospital last night. We need to go."

"I agree," Tommy said.

Rachel wasn't surprised that he should be the first to support Shelley. As a farm kid, Tommy was always confident when he spoke, and he rarely shied away from a challenge.

"It would be good to get readings so soon after last night's activities," Jessica said.

Rachel turned to see her already walking over to one of the four suitcase-size containers of ghost-hunting equipment.

"You sure you're okay?" Aaron said to Shelley.

"Yeah." She sniffled. "If I don't die of pneumonia. That water was *freezing*."

"Poor thing," he said, rubbing her back.

"Jessica's right," Scott said, leaning back in the recliner and looking at the containers. "We might get the best readings ever tonight. Maybe we should still go."

"Looks like it's about to storm," Tommy said, looking at his phone.

"Will that mess with the equipment?" Scott asked.

Seeing that Shelley seemed better, Rachel looked at the equipment. "You guys ever worry that we're going about this all wrong?" She had been wondering this more and more as her random visions kept growing more frequent and more potent.

"What do you mean?" Scott asked.

"The guy who encountered Annabel last night didn't have any of the equipment, but from what Shelley's mom told her, he had a real experience. We, on the other hand, haven't seen much in our four trips. Maybe all this stuff is scaring her away from us."

"We need to get readings or we can't prove anything," Aaron said. "But we don't have to turn it on right away. We can spend a little time looking around first. How long we gonna be there?"

"Couple of hours at most," Shelley said. "I don't think hospital security leaves the new building very often, but you never know when they might decide to walk the whole property and check on the old building."

"All right," Tommy said. "We should get over there before the weather gets too bad."

Rachel was still looking at the cases of equipment when everyone got up and started grabbing coats and flashlights and the laptop bags. The boys grabbed the cases and carried them up the stairs. But she couldn't stop thinking about her growing abilities. She had hinted that they didn't need the equipment, but it was what they were all used to. They didn't understand that there was probably another way to reach the dead. She was starting to believe that she'd had this gift her entire life. She didn't know what to call it—maybe psi or super-psi, or maybe some other variation of parapsychology or psychic ability. Or maybe she was just losing her mind. In any case, sooner or later she would need to tell the group the truth: that she just might be receiving cryptic communications from the same spirit world they were trying so hard to record on their plethora of modern ghost-hunting equipment. Sooner or later, she would need to admit that she was not like them.

But not tonight. She was not yet ready to be labeled a freak, not ready to become an outcast.

15

Jason was in the conference room, where he had spent hours reviewing the records detailing the write-offs for bad-debt expense. And with many selected patient accounts, he had seen the revenue system's print-out of patient billing activity. Molly was right: people were vanishing from the town. He saw names and social security numbers and dates of service at the hospital. He saw attempts to bill patients for balances due. And then nothing. Many had probably left town, but something didn't feel right. Molly said that crime had increased in Williston. What did that mean, exactly? What if something was happening to the migrant or homeless people in town? Would anyone notice? The hospital had written them off and moved on. He had to wonder, who else had written them off?

It was now past seven, and once again he was the last person in the old building of the hospital complex. He made notes for some follow-up questions to ask Molly about the reserves. After that, he found himself at a standstill until he could get more information. And he soon found his eyes turning away from his laptop and stealing glances at the book Peggy had lent him about spiritualism, mediums, and ghost hunting. How could he possibly focus on work when there was rumored to be a ghost that may start wandering the halls of the hospital at any moment. And this book with its stories from times past, with its promise of answers to questions as old as humankind—it was as if the book had cast some spell on him, giving him a voracious desire to drink of its magical knowledge.

He closed his laptop and pushed it away from him to make room for the book. Opening its cover, he flipped the first few pages with the eager wonderment of a child rising inside him.

He read about the Fox sisters in Newark, New York and their encounters with Mr. Splitfoot. He read about Emmanuel Swedenborg. He read about D. D. Home. And he read about *The Davenport Brothers* with their spirit box, and Leonora Piper and Eusapia Palladino. More than an hour flitted by, and the more he traveled through time learning about the extensive history of ghosts and spirit contact, the more the wind picked up outside the small windows. Another storm was coming. The latched handle rattled against the frame as if an invisible hand were trying to open it from the outside. He turned back to the book and read about the screaming skull of Bettiscombe House, the horrors for the doomed men of the haunted German U65 submarine, the Brown Lady of Raynham Hall, and the battlefield miracle by the Angels of Mons. The more he read of death, the more alive he felt. And he grew more fearless with each new purportedly true story of spirits and ghosts. The legends became real, the stories gained the weight of historical fact, and the accounts of witnesses consolidated into a consistent narrative of survival after death. He felt an itch inside him to learn more— even to experience firsthand the wonders he read about. He no longer feared the ghost of Annabel haunting the hospital. He had become far too curious to fear such dark, horrifying mysteries.

Suddenly, a heavy bang resounded in the hallway outside the conference room. Jason stared at the doorway for a long time, then closed the book and stood up from the table. The window rattled louder and louder with each cautious step he took toward the hallway. Having spent the past two hours reading about the history of ghosts and spiritualism, he wondered if he had been preparing himself to walk straight into certain death. He couldn't believe how bold he felt. He'd heard it said that people feared what they didn't understand. And he now felt he understood much more about ghosts and spirits, so some of that fear was gone. In all the stories and witness accounts he had read, he noticed one continuous theme about all ghosts and spirits: in the end, they all—

Bang! Bang! Bang!

The sudden noise came from the hallway. He stepped out of the conference room and stood in the square of light projected from the room into the hallway. The rest of the corridor was a shadowy abyss that flickered with sporadic lightning flashes through the windows of adjacent rooms.

Bang! Bang! Bang!

"I'm not afraid of you," he said, his voice shaking.

Bang! Bang! Bang!

"I know you just want to make contact. It must be important."

Bang! Bang! Bang!

"I won't run away. I want to understand; I want to help."

Bang! Bang!

Then silence. And then a long, horrific scream.

He covered his ears, but it didn't dampen the noise one whit. Somehow, the scream was not in the air but in his head.

"Stop," he pleaded.

It didn't.

"STOP!"

Silence.

He stared into the darkness of the hallway, trying to be brave while also watching for anything that might spring out at him.

Then, to his left, he heard a slow, soft hissing. He turned his head to look back into the conference room. The office chair he had been sitting in was slowly spinning around. He squared up in the doorframe and stared at it. The chair was making a rotation every few seconds. Then one every second. Then faster. As its speed increased, the hissing rose to a higher and higher pitch. Then another chair began to spin. Then another. Soon all nine chairs were whirling, spinning so fast they were almost a blur. They gave off the ominous sound of a machine about to overheat and explode. Then, as if pulled by invisible strings, all the chairs were suddenly yanked away from the table and crashed against the walls.

Jason stumbled back from the doorway and into the hallway. Still looking into the room, he saw that plastic pieces had broken off the chairs and scattered across the hard floor. The chairs had crashed like corpses onto the linoleum floor. The walls were now pocked with gouges and dents.

He could feel his eyes stretched wide in disbelief. Sitting in the hallway, he tried to focus on calming his heart. But even before he had time to settle down and catch his breath, he heard a new hissing, whirring sound from his right. Turning his head, he looked into the distant darkness of the long hallway's vanishing point. The sound was from far away, maybe around the corner or even farther away in this old building. Somewhere down there, another chair was spinning.

He stood and pulled out his phone to turn on its flashlight, but the phone had somehow powered down and wouldn't come back on. Nor would the hallway lights turn on. His instincts told him to run, but his curiosity told him to follow the bread crumbs ... Annabel's bread crumbs. After reading so much about the mysterious contacts between the living and the lingering dead, now was his chance to experience such unknown things firsthand. So he took one slow step forward, then another, moving farther into the void and toward the eerie sound of the hissing, whirling thing that was somewhere out there, waiting for him in the dark.

16

Rachel and her friends moved through the trees outside the old hospital wing. The boys were carrying the heavier equipment in their backpacks, while Rachel and the other two girls had the most expensive and sensitive instruments. A few lights were on, on the third floor, but otherwise the stone building looked dark and asleep.

The wind had been getting stronger over the past few minutes, and now lightning jumped from cloud to cloud only a few miles away. They needed to get inside fast or risk damaging the equipment in the rain.

As they reached the side door, Rachel heard a hair-curling scream from inside. It seemed to come from directly on the other side of the door.

"What the hell was that?" she asked, looking at the others.

"What was what?" Scott asked.

"Sounded like a scream," she said.

He shook his head.

"From inside," she added.

The others gave her the same confused stare as Scott's.

"No one heard that?"

"The wind," Shelley said. "Distant thunder."

"That's not what it was," she said, now wondering whether she had heard the scream or just sensed it. She couldn't always tell the difference between audible sound waves and psychic-wave transmissions.

Shelley stepped forward and inserted and turned the key.

"Be careful," Rachel said. "I think something's in there."

"Let me do it," Scott said.

"I've got it," Shelley replied. She turned the knob and opened the door.

Rachel watched as her friend vanished through the dark plane of the doorway. Lightning flashed in the distance behind her, casting brief, faint silhouettes around the door, like phantoms watching them. The others followed Shelley into the old hospital. Rachel was last in the procession, and as she closed the door behind her, a loud thunderclap made her start.

She turned away from the electrical storm erupting outside and followed the faint images of her friends moving down the unlit hallway.

This was the fifth time in as many months that their merry band of ghost hunters had broken into the old hospital in hope of documenting proof of Annabel's spirit haunting these halls. Moreover, they had been on twenty other ghost hunts at different locations across the Dakotas, as far south as the Badlands and as far north as Devil's Lake. In each case, the group had found various opportunities to obtain circumstantial evidence of ghosts, which was exciting for them and really served only to energize their efforts and commitment to continue their search for the world beyond the current plane of reality. But Rachel was different. She had seen and felt a dimension beyond temporal life, and while she didn't need proof of it, she did need to be around others who believed in such things.

As Rachel walked through the dark behind her friends, she was reminded of how lucky she was to have them. She had known Scott most her life because their families went to the same church. Only in the past year had their friendship begun to flirt with becoming something more. It had caught her quite by surprise and—for the moment—gave her pause. She didn't want to cross a line that might jeopardize their friendship, but every day it seemed harder to resist the magnetic forces of nature.

Tommy and Jessica had also been in Williston forever, and they would probably stay here forever, too. Tommy's family farm already provided him with the perfect means for building a life in the area, and it was hard for her to imagine him loving anything else as much as he loved farming. The work seemed hard for him to juggle with high school life—something he had already acknowledged by quitting football—but it had made him strong and tough. Jessica was tough, too. She restored cars for fun, which had always impressed Rachel. And although Jessica and Tommy weren't involved, Rachel thought they would make a great couple if they ever got together.

But the Ghost Hunting Club hadn't really formed until two years ago, when Shelley and Aaron moved to town during the same summer. Williston had been expanding then because of the oil boom. Shelley's mom was hired to oversee the growing hospital's finances, moving Shelley away from Portland and her father. She and Rachel had clicked right away, and Rachel admired how focused Shelley already was about going to medical school someday so she could become a surgeon. Aaron had been brought to town when his dad, a rising oil executive, had moved his family from Odessa, Texas, to oversee a major expansion in some shale-oil drilling operations outside town. Aaron was smart as hell, and it sounded as if he had been into science and tech toys all his life. At some point on that journey, he had discovered electronic ghost-hunting equipment and began accumulating an impressive collection over the years. After arriving in Williston, Aaron became friends with Scott, who also became fascinated with the idea of ghost hunting. Scott recruited

Tommy and Rachel. Rachel recruited Jessica and Shelley. And with these six members, the Ghost Hunting Club was born.

The brief light on the third floor that she had seen from outside was nonexistent down here on the dark first floor. Only the red exit sign above her, and the other at the end of the long hallway, provided any visibility, although their crimson glow seemed mostly to die within a few feet of the signs. Only the faintest light escaped, as if a fog lived within the dark building.

One by one, each member of the team turned on their flashlight, creating a dense glow around them, with narrow, discrete beams planking out through the thick air like the torches of deep-sea divers trying to penetrate an engulfing darkness. She didn't understand why they couldn't see more. Her confusion and concern only grew when Tommy flipped the switch to the hall lights, with no results.

"The lights don't work?" Aaron asked, his face orange above his light, like a kid about to tell a scary campfire story.

Tommy flipped the switch up and down a few times, then dropped his hand in defeat.

"We don't want the lights on anyway," Shelley said.

"Where should we set up this time?" Jessica asked.

"My mom said the accountant from Chicago saw Annabel on the third floor, near the old surgery room," said Shelley.

"We did the surgery room last time and didn't get anything," Aaron complained.

"I thought we were going to do the basement next time we came," Tommy added.

"That's right," Aaron confirmed. "In the boiler room."

"Yeah, I remember. But the old surgery room just had the sighting."

"We can do both. We'll break into teams and set up half the equipment in the basement and half on the third floor."

"Who goes where?" Jessica asked.

"I want to try the EVP recorder in the basement," Aaron said. "We haven't tried it there yet, and I've got a hunch Annabel spends most of her time down there. I think I can get our highest readings yet."

"A hunch?" Rachel asked.

"It's the boiler room. It's the creepiest area in this whole place. It's where I would hang out if I were a ghost."

"I'll go with you," Jessica said.

"Me, too," Tommy added.

"I want to try the third floor," Shelley said.

"Yeah," Scott said. "I want to use the Mel Meter to see if we can get any readings up there."

"I'll go, too," Rachel said.

A long, low whistle from the other end of the hallway startled them. Scott spun around so fast that his shoulder struck Jessica's chin, knocking her into Shelley, who dropped her flashlight. The sudden clank startled everyone a second time as the flashlight rattled around on the polished concrete until they were certain everyone in town had heard it.

"Sweet Lord," Shelley gasped, holding her chest as if to calm her racing heart.

"Ouchie," Jessica moaned, rubbing her jaw.

"Sorry," Scott whispered.

"What was that?" Tommy asked.

"My flashlight."

"No ... that whistle."

"The wind," Rachel said.

"It came from inside the building."

"Someone may have just opened a window or a door."

"But none of us did that."

"Someone else," Rachel said.

"Annabel?"

"No, another person. We might not be the only ones in the building."

"You really think so?" Tommy asked.

"It feels like someone else is here," she replied.

"I think it's Annabel," Jessica said excitedly, the sore jaw apparently forgotten.

"And you know what else?" Aaron said, the gleam in his eye captured by the flashlight's beam. "I think it came from the boiler room."

"You're terrible," Scott said.

"Maybe I should go to the third floor instead," Tommy joked. "I'm not really feeling the basement anymore."

"No. We need at least three to set up and operate the equipment," Jessica said.

"All right, guys," Shelley said. "Twenty minutes to set up the equipment in both locations." She looked at her watch. "Let's try to start recording by nine thirty. We'll try to get in at least an hour. What's everyone's curfews?"

"Eleven o'clock," Scott said.

"Me, too," said Rachel.

"Yeah, also eleven," said Aaron.

"No curfew," Jessica said.

"Midnight," Tommy said with a note of pride.

"Mine's eleven," Shelley said. "So we'll do as much as we can with our time."

"I can sneak back out after eleven thirty," Rachel said.

"So can I," Scott said. "After midnight."

"All right," Shelley said. "If we need to, Jessica can stay with the equipment when we go home, and wait for some of us to come back after our parents go to bed."

"I can't sneak out," Tommy said. "They'll hear me."

"It's okay," Rachel said. "We'll each do what we can. Hopefully, we find something soon, anyway."

"We'd better get moving," Shelley said.

They exchanged backpacks so each group had the right equipment for their planned setup. Then they broke into two teams of three and quietly went to work.

As she moved up the concrete stairs with Shelley and Scott, Rachel listened to the soft chatter of Aaron and Jessica and Tommy descending below them, until the sound ceased as if they had vanished forever into the subterranean shadows.

The hospital already felt different from during past visits. Perhaps because of her spirit-writing spell during class today, or because of Shelley's strange near-death experience, or because of the loud scream a moment ago that only she had heard. But the hospital felt colder, darker, more silent, and more dead than ever before.

She couldn't believe it, but something about all this suddenly felt wrong. Dangerous. Even wicked. She shuddered as she trudged deeper into the tomb.

17

Jason had followed the sound of a single spinning chair to this spot at the other stairwell at the end of the building. But instead of finding the source of the sound, he had met only sudden silence when he blundered upon this remote staircase. He was farther from the conference room than he had ever ventured at night. The storm had intensified over the past few minutes as he had followed this ... this *force* around the corner and into a different corridor.

Now, at the stairwell, he saw a glow coming from the next floor up. He had thought the third story was the highest level in the building, and it was with trepidation that he ascended the stairs into the blue light. Rounding the concrete banister, he found a wooden door cracked open at the top landing. A pale blue light emanated from inside, through the sliver between door and frame.

He pushed it open and stepped cautiously inside a storage attic the size of a basketball court. This fourth level was much smaller than the rest of the building and on the opposite end from the part facing the parking lot and the new building, which explained why he hadn't seen it before from the outside. It was filled with old wooden chairs and desks, some archaic medical devices that looked almost Victorian, an operating table with leather straps, and other equipment of Industrial Revolution vintage. Then he saw the source of the pale blue light: a full moon shining brightly outside despite the loud rain and thunder he heard from the roof. It was the biggest full moon he had ever seen.

Mesmerized, he approached the window, drawn toward the moon as the world around him evaporated from his mind. He could see the giant craters and pockmarks while the rock orb glowed as if it contained some warm energy source at its core. One of early humans' first illusions was that something so cold and dead could appear to radiate energy.

He stopped in front of the window, suddenly realizing that he was looking out at a clear night with no hint of the thunderstorm he still heard pounding the roof above him. It sounded like hail now, as another thunderclap left no doubt that the storm cell was alive and present. And yet, through the window he saw no trace of this violent weather. There was only peaceful countryside on the edge of town, bathed in moonglow and dappled with faint shadows.

Then his stare fixed on what he could see: a square farmhouse in the distance, with a steep hipped roof pointing up like an arrowhead. In a field behind it stood a few smaller buildings. The house looked quiet and peaceful on the sleeping landscape—until he saw two sharp, bright flashes in its top left windows. Startled, he stared in silence, trying to figure out what he had just seen. Then came another flash. Then a second pause before two more flashes. He tried to open the window's latch, but it wouldn't turn. The house was maybe a quarter mile away. He stared at it, wondering what the flashes were, fearing that they meant some trouble, some danger. Wondering what he should do, he kept staring, expecting to see more flashes, more activity. Then he noticed a blurred movement in the windowpane he stood before. A reflection. He was looking at the reflection of a woman standing directly behind him.

He froze. Her face was almost over his shoulder in the reflection. It so startled him that his entire body tensed up and he couldn't move. He couldn't scream or utter so much as a terrified whimper. He stared at the pale face for what felt like an eternity: the emerald eyes, the sad glimmer of tears streaking down her cheeks, and a mouth half open as if to whisper in his ear.

But no sound came, other than an artillery barrage of thunder from the storm still not visible out of this window.

He turned his head an inch, just enough for his peripheral vision to see no physical being behind him. Cautiously turning back to the window, he looked deep into the young woman's sad face. Her mouth moved a little, but still no sound came. Her eyes seemed to water, but he didn't know whether he really saw them tear up, or just felt it.

The moon began to fade, as if it were suddenly running low on energy. The house and the countryside fell under a heavy shadow, then grainy darkness. They began to fade away with the outside world.

The woman's image, too, began to fade. Her mouth moved again, and this time he thought he heard a sound, though he couldn't make it out.

"What?" he whispered. "Tell me."

She seemed to struggle, as if the more she faded before him, the worse pain she felt.

"Tell me," he pleaded. "I'm listening."

She was almost gone. Her mouth moved again, and he heard her whisper as she faded out. "Lies," she said, her face scrunching, as if begging to be understood. Then her reflection vanished into the windowpane's growing darkness.

"Lies," he heard her whisper again. "Lies, lies, lies."

And then there was nothing except his own faint reflection, looking out the window at the side of the new hospital building, pounded by rain and jumping out of the night in dazzling flashes of lightning. The countryside and the farmhouse were gone, along with the moon, but the woman's words were planted like a haunting nightmare in his memory.

18

Rachel stopped halfway down the hall and stared with wide eyes at the inside of the old operating room. The light was on, and a closed laptop was surrounded by piles of documents in the center of the conference table. But even more startling were all the broken chairs along the edges of the room, and the many dents and holes punched into the drywall.

"Oh, crap," she said.

She heard Scott slip the bag from his shoulder and set the equipment on the floor behind her. "Damn! What the hell happened here? So someone is still in the hospital. And it looks like they've lost their fricking mind."

"We should leave now," Shelley said. "If my mom finds out we were here …" Her voice trailed off as if the thought was too terrifying to complete.

"Maybe they went out to grab some food," Scott suggested. "Or a baseball bat and a wrecking bar to finish the job."

Rachel said, "It doesn't look like they planned to be gone long."

"What should we do?"

"Maybe we can hide somewhere and wait them out," Rachel offered.

"Someone needs to warn the others," Shelley said.

"I'll go," Scott offered. "You guys stay up here, find a hiding place—maybe see if you can get some baseline readings. But be careful." He then turned and ran back down the hallway.

Rachel picked up the backpack. She looked again at the conference room, still uncomfortable that it felt as if it had been abandoned only minutes before they arrived.

"This must be the accountant your mom said was visiting the hospital," she said. "The one that saw Annabel."

"It's some guy from Chicago. If he comes back and catches us, my mom will turn *me* into a ghost. Let's find someplace to hide ASAFP."

Rachel looked down to the end of the hallway. "Are any of these doors unlocked?"

Shelley swung the keychain in front of her face, like a hypnotist's talisman. "With this, they're all unlocked—it's a master key."

They rushed down the hallway, hesitating at every doorway until Rachel stopped halfway. She stopped by a door with a small window at head level. Putting her forehead to the cool glass, she made blinders with her hands and searched the darkness inside. A few green and orange lights pulsed from the outline of a desk, and the rest of the office came into view in shades of black and gray.

"This looks good," she said. "It's close enough to the old operating room to keep an eye on it, and close enough to the stairs for us to run out if we need to."

Shelley unlocked the door. Once inside, Rachel slid through the shadows around the desk and began unloading the backpack. Shelley locked the door from inside and joined her behind the desk. They used the dim red light stick from inside the pack to see inside the backpack without illuminating the rest of the room.

"What should we try first?" Rachel asked.

"Electromagnetic pulse emitter sensor," Shelley whispered, pulling the laptop out of her pack.

Rachel pulled out the case for the EPMS and set up its telescopic triangle mount as quietly as she could while Shelley fired up the laptop. They moved as silently as possible in the dim light, constantly aware that at any moment the accountant might discover them. Or, worse, Annabel might happen by.

19

Aaron leaned against one of two enormous hot-water tanks in the boiler room. Numerous pipes along the walls and ceilings snaked around the room. Even the old pressure gauge and thermometer from the boiler seemed to stare at him like wide eyes looking out of steampunk goggles.

He had set up the EVP recorder and was waiting for Jessica to get her laptop ready before connecting the main sensors. Tommy was busy positioning the infrared cameras in each corner of the boiler room. The basement level was a skeleton of abandoned windowless rooms that had been used for God knows what. Perhaps treatment rooms for patients. Maybe lab tests were performed in these cold passageways. This level would have been a good place to keep some of the creepier medical devices of the health-care industry of yore. The local economy in this region of North Dakota had grown in spurts during the boom-bust-BOOM of the shale oil development in the past decade. It meant a surge in tough oil industry jobs that could shorten a person's life expectancy. His dad had told him all about it when taking the job up here to lead a new drilling operation and planning their move from Texas two years ago. He figured that a lot of scary procedures had been done to a lot of sick or injured people here over the years. But one thing, he was certain of: the basement was where they had kept the dead bodies before burial.

A muffled thunderclap rumbled from what seemed miles away. Down here, it felt as if they were cut off from everything, even the end-of-days rage from the storm system outside the building.

Aaron cleared his throat with indecorous volume.

Jessica looked over at him.

He smiled. "Almost there?"

"Almost," she said. "It's taking forever."

"I have time to go exploring?"

"No."

"I'm just wondering where the old morgue is," he said, grinning. "We know it's here in the basement somewhere."

"The program's almost there. The main sensors are coming online now."

"But really, *where*?"

"Where what?" Tommy asked, returning from the deepest, darkest corner of the room.

"Where's the old morgue?"

"To hell with that."

"Don't you think we should find it and check it out, too? Seriously, why aren't we setting up there instead of here? What better place?"

"You said the boiler room was the place to be," Tommy said. "Besides, we need to have limits—you know, some respect for the dead."

"What if there's a ghost still trapped there?" Aaron replied. "One we could help. Like all those drifters that died here over the years. Wouldn't they want their spirits freed? Wouldn't that be respectful?"

"They're not drifters; they're migrant workers. Besides, you wanted the boiler room."

"And now I want the morgue, too."

"It's not a bad idea, actually," Jessica said.

"All right, I won't be long." Aaron strode toward the door while pointing back at Tommy. "Can you finish connecting the sensors once the system's online?"

"Got it."

"I'll be back in five minutes. If not, send out a search party."

"Yeah, right."

Aaron hurried out of the boiler room and into the dark basement hallway. Once the underbelly of a community hospital, it now felt as cold and eerie as an abandoned World War Two bunker. He turned his flashlight to full power, filling the long concrete passageway with an amber glow that exposed every strain and crack of peeling paint and patch of crud. The low rumbling from the boiler room faded behind him as he advanced into the unknown. The air here was cooler, draftier, damper. He tried every door he came to; none were locked. He scanned each room with his light, chasing the shadows from one corner to another, finding nothing but the remnants of a place that time had left behind.

He stopped at a wide double door, knowing he had found the old morgue. It opened with barely a touch of the knob, as if the room were as eager to see him as he had been to discover it. His flashlight flickered and died. He slapped it a few times, trying to jolt it back to life. No luck. He searched along the wall with his free hand until he found the light switch. But when he flipped it, it, too, was dead. He pulled out his lighter and flicked it.

Holding it at arm's length from his face, he inched his way farther into the large room. The flame gyrated, casting flickering light across the reflective metal tables used for draining the dead, getting identifications by family or friends, performing autopsies, or doing other shadowy procedures that the respectable world aboveground would rather not contemplate. Behind the two tables stood a wall of fifteen square stainless-steel doors in three rows. It looked a bit like a giant's version of an old library card catalogue. He wondered at the number of dead that had passed through this room before going underground or into the incinerator. Thousands, he guessed. This one room was as much a way station for the dead as anywhere in town.

"Annabel?" he asked.

Aaron moved closer to the wall, wondering what the chances were that any of the storage pods still contained a corpse. He had assumed they had a new morgue in the new hospital building, but he didn't know for sure. Maybe they were still using this morgue. The room was certainly colder than he had expected.

"Annabel?" he asked again.

He grasped the latch of the body drawer at chest height in front of him. As in tic-tac-toe, he was going for center square first. His hand moved in slow motion, as if anticipating at any moment a warning to stop.

But no warning came, and before he knew it, his fingers had wrapped around the cold metal latch. All he had to do was pull.

"Annabel?"

He snapped the latch down and pulled toward him. With a groan, the drawer slid outward, screeching as it neared the end of its sliders. He held the flame over it, but before he could look inside, the little flame blew sideways and licked his thumb knuckle. The pain was fast and sharp, and he dropped the lighter. The flame went out as it fell into the morgue box, once again throwing the room into darkness.

He froze.

Seconds passed as he listened for any sound and searched for any new smell. Spirits were sometimes known to bring horrendous scents with them when reaching out to the living. Or perhaps he could smell the corpse in the drawer, hidden by the pitch darkness.

But he caught no whiff of anything. There also had been no sound—not even of the lighter hitting the stainless-steel floor of the box, as if it had landed on something soft. The thought gave him a shudder.

He needed the lighter back.

Still blinded by the dark, he reached into the box. He had to extend his arm much farther down than he had imagined. Then he felt the sheet inside, covering something. He withdrew his hand and took a few deep breaths, trying to slow his racing heart and settle his spiraling fears. Then reached back into the box.

Feeling, searching, he found the sheet covering something soft. His probing finger brushed the lighter, and he grasped it. Lighting it again, he stared with annoyance at the single white sheet wadded in the center of the otherwise empty drawer.

"That's not cool, Annabel," he said. "You almost scared me to death."

Aaron closed the tray and looked around at the other doors. "I think we'll get the equipment and bring it in here. Give you a chance to communicate with us. Sound good?"

A soft pop came from the drawer at the top right corner. He raised an eyebrow and stepped back from the wall.

"Annabel? Is that you? Or did mice get into a box?"

Another pop came, this one more muted.

He stepped back farther, closer to the door. His instincts warned against opening it, but some force seemed to pull his mind toward it in ways he could neither resist nor understand. Then, just when he decided he must explore it, something hard hit him on the butt.

He screamed and spun around, only to be greeted by an even louder scream. Jessica had burst through the door, hitting him with it.

"Why'd you do that?" She punched him in the chest.

"You startled me."

"But don't scream like that!" She bent down and held her head as if afflicted with a sudden migraine. "Holy heaven!"

"Well, don't jump out of the dark like that."

"I had to find you. We think there's someone else in the building."

"We *think*?"

"Scott said they found work stuff still out upstairs in a room with lights on. And the place was trashed like someone had gone psycho."

"Crap."

"He came down to warn us. We're not sure if we should stay."

"Has anyone seen them?"

"No."

"So we're not really sure they're still here?"

"Rachel thinks they are."

"Where's she?"

"Still upstairs with Shelley."

"We shouldn't be separated anymore. Let's get everyone back together and just stay down here. Between the boiler room and this morgue, there's plenty for us to investigate in the basement."

"You find something?" she asked, shining her flashlight into the large room behind him. But the moment she did so, the beam flickered twice and went out.

He moved forward, gently pushing her back out of the room.

"What was that?" she asked.

"I don't know, but we'll figure it out later," he said. "Right now, we need to get everyone back together. I'm starting to hate the idea of those girls upstairs without the rest of us."

Halfway down the hall, both flashlights suddenly flicked on, prompting a startled yelp from Jessica.

"Holy Mother!"

"I know," Aaron whispered. He looked over his shoulder at the dark space behind them, trying to see the doors to the morgue. But the end of the hallway was cloaked in darkness. The doors were down there, maybe fifty feet away, but he knew better than to try to shine any light on them—at least, not until they could find Rachel and Shelley and return the group to its full courageous strength.

20

Rachel's face slipped to the side of the small viewing window in the door. She and Shelley had crouched behind the desk in the dark office as they booted up the laptop, listening for any noise from the hallway. Then she heard the quick, pounding footfalls of someone running down the corridor. Shelley had closed the laptop to extinguish even the faintest glow in the room.

Rachel angled her face so she could see the door to the old surgery room. The pounding footsteps grew louder, faster. Her breath fogged the base of the window. She checked to make sure the door was locked, then wedged a foot at the bottom for good measure.

The pounding rose in volume. And then, just when the sound of running feet became unbearably, maddeningly loud, it stopped, and she saw the blur of a figure dash into the old surgery room. Unable to see anything else, she removed her foot, unlocked the door, and opened it an inch.

"What are you *doing*!" Shelley whispered.

"Sh-h-h."

She listened to frantic shuffling sounds coming through the doorway less than fifty feet away. A snap and thump. Something zipped open, then zipped shut. Some tapping and thudding. Velcro ripping apart. A loud thump. Then the figure darted out the door: a young man with a laptop case slung over his shoulder. He spun and pulled the door closed behind him, then rushed back down the hallway.

"It's the accountant from Chicago," she whispered. "He's leaving in a big hurry!"

"Good," Shelley whispered back.

"I'm going to follow him."

"What? Don't!"

"Something's not right. He's moving like he's got the devil on his heels."

"Rachel, wait!"

But Rachel had already opened the door and entered the hallway. She jogged in the direction the accountant had gone. She raced after the fading clatter of his footsteps, dying to know why he was fleeing so fast. As she reached the east stairwell, she heard an outside door slam. It sounded two floors below her. Seconds later, she reached what must be the same door, and pushed it open into the storming night.

Rain splashed across her face as a huge lightning bolt flashed above the building. There the man was, running through the wet parking lot fifty feet away. A deafening thunderclap went off at nearly the same time as the flash, so loud that it felt as if someone had fired a cannon at point-blank range. She ducked instinctively. The man appeared just as startled as she, and actually fell down in the lot. Staggering to his feet and nearly falling again, he grabbed his computer bag from the wet pavement and kept running toward a white car that stood alone in the darkened lot.

She stood near the edge of the parking lot, drenched by the rain, watching him, searching for some clue to his strange behavior.

He slid the last few feet, bumping into the side of the car. Its lights had flickered to life a second before, as if it heard him coming. He yanked open the driver's door, tossed his computer bag into the far seat, and jumped in. The car shuddered, and the reverse lights came on. The front tires spun on the wet asphalt as the car reversed with the same frantic urgency that he had shown racing out of the hospital. And just as it stopped and the reverse lights went off, Rachel half saw something through the rain that sent a shock through every fiber of her being.

She stared through the curtain of rain at the license plate: *TLX 623*.

It was the number she had scribbled in her book during the brief trance she had entered during English class. Her eyes widened with the realization that someone or something was telling her that this number—this car, this accountant—was somehow important to everything that was going on.

She darted out into the parking lot as the car sped away.

"Wait!" she yelled, only half hearing herself in the storm. "Wait!"

But the car raced on, running the stop sign at the end of the parking lot and squealing out onto the main street. And off it sped into the night.

21

Jason tried to focus on the road as his thoughts kept spinning back to what he had witnessed at the hospital. His clothes were drenched, and his hair hung wet and dripping. Rain poured across the windshield faster than the wiper blades could slap it away, and the asphalt road had enough flowing water to look like a black river in the headlights.

The heavy rain had cast the entire town into near darkness. As he raced through the few blocks known as "downtown," he made no attempt to dial his forty-five miles an hour down to the twenty posted on the sign near the boutique flower shop. He had raced across the bridge over the railroad tracks. Not a soul was out in this storm—maybe not all that surprising for a Tuesday night even if Noah's flood weren't raging outside. He was heading in the direction of his hotel by the highway, but he wasn't really trying to go *toward* anywhere in particular. He just needed to get *away* from the hospital until he could process what he had experienced.

He saw the gray car at the last second and slammed on the breaks. Too late. A juvenile fear shot through him. He held his breath and looked in the rearview mirror for any sign of activity from the parked police car he had passed. It had been hidden on a side street. The rain on his rear window made it impossible to see anything at first. But then his heart sank as a distant ball of flashing red and blue lights appeared, stationary at first, then flying toward him like a heat-seeking missile.

He had dropped below the speed limit just after spotting the cruiser, but he was sure he had been going twice the limit.

He put on the hazard lights and pulled over.

Rain pounded the metal roof as he waited. The water rushing down his rear window created a kaleidoscope of images from the red and blue strobes flashing right behind him. Then a dazzling spotlight blazed through the rain, illuminating everything inside the car. Feeling naked and exposed, he hadn't realized until now how safe it had felt to be sitting in the dark.

He saw movement in the side mirror. Then another light hit him along the left side of his face. Squinting, he saw the outline of a tall figure standing outside his window. The flashlight cast a small yellow ring on the glass as it rapped three times.

He pressed the console button to lower the window. A sheath of rain splashed in, soaking a left sleeve already drenched from his dash across the hospital parking lot.

"Good evening, Officer," he said.

The man stared back at him with a tough, stony expression. He wore a black cowboy hat with a five-point brass star. A dark, slick rain poncho draped his shoulders, making him look a little like Clint Eastwood in a spaghetti Western.

"*Good evening?* Really?" the officer said. "You some kind of comedian?"

"I just meant that—"

"I know," the officer cut in. "You're just trying to be polite. But it would have been a lot more polite not to go racing through my downtown. It would have been a lot more polite not to be going forty-five when you passed me in a twenty zone. And you'd sure as hell have been more polite if you hadn't made me chase you down and stand out here in this storm. So I'll tell you right now that it's *not* a good evening—not for me and not for you."

"I'm very sorry, Officer. I'm in town for work and was just heading back to my hotel. The streets were deserted, and I just lost track of my speed. I'm not familiar with the area yet."

"No excuse for racing like that. Not in town. Especially not in weather like this."

"You're right, Officer." But before he could say more, his mind jumped back to the image of the woman in the hospital window. *Lies! Lies! Lies!*

"You okay?"

"What?" Jason stared at the officer.

"You don't look so good. You sick, or something? You look like you've just seen a ghost."

Jason laughed nervously, then swallowed and wiped his forehead.

"You had anything to drink tonight?" the officer asked.

"No, not yet."

"Please step out of the car, sir."

"Really?" Jason's face tensed as he assessed the cold rain saturating the dark world outside his car.

"Please step out." The officer stepped back.

Jason had learned in college that life always worked out better if one never hesitated to help law enforcement resolve a simple inquiry, while keeping any attitude well hidden away. He turned off the engine, opened the door, and got out. Water splashed across his face and seemed to stick to his clothes, making them feel heavier by the second.

"Stand over here," the officer said. He was pointing toward the front of the rental car. His arm was angled down, and a stream of water ran off his extended index finger as if he were a gargoyle shooting rainfall off the heights of a gothic church.

Jason obeyed.

"Now face this way, close your eyes, extend your arms outward. Good. Now touch your nose with your right index finger."

Jason did this, although doing it perfectly seemed harder than he expected, considering he was dead sober. In fact, he believed that in this moment he was probably the soberest person in town. For what could be more sobering than standing in the cold rain with a cop only ten minutes after seeing the live image of a woman who died a year ago?

"Okay. Now walk along the line towards me."

Jason looked down and saw only a shallow river of rainwater sliding past his leather shoes on the sheen of asphalt. "What line?"

"The white line. You're standing on it."

"I don't see it."

"Just walk towards me."

But before Jason had taken a step, headlights appeared behind the officer. The car had come fast out of the darkness but pulled over and stopped the moment it came upon the flashing lights.

"Hold up," the officer said, extending his palm while looking at the two round headlights now staring uncertainly at him.

Jason thought he saw the officer rest his right hand on his holstered firearm, but he wasn't certain. The sliding shadows were playing games on him.

The car just sat there, thirty feet behind the cruiser, the engine rattling as if in its death throes. He couldn't see inside for the headlights.

The officer waved for it to pass, but the car didn't move. Its engine was rattling louder now, as if it might drown in the rain.

"Don't move," the officer said to him. Then he stepped toward the car. "Turn off your engine and step out of the vehicle!" he shouted over the rain.

No response.

He circled out wide into the street to get out of the brightest part of the beam. He pulled the gun from his holster and held it down along the outside of his leg.

Jason instinctively stepped back to put the rental car between himself and the new arrival. He watched as the officer slid farther into the shadows in the rain. The engine shut off, coughing and bucking one last time as it succumbed to a merciful death. The door opened, and the driver rose out of the car. The officer's flashlight cut through the streaking rainfall to reveal the pale face of a teenage girl.

The three stood in silence, lashed by the rain, as if the heavens were furious at the world below.

Jason felt as if he were in a dream that made no sense. Only a little while ago, he had seen in the hospital's window things that he still couldn't process, and now he stood in the rain, staring at a police officer and teenage girl, both of whom had appeared as if from nowhere. He pressed a hand to the wet hood of his rental car for support. Icy water sluiced down every inch of him.

"Rachel Wynkoop? That you?" the officer shouted.

"Yeah," the girl yelled back over the rumbling thunder. "Is everything all right, Officer Connelly?"

The officer glanced at Jason and then back at the girl. "Yeah. Just a traffic stop. Mr. Rental Car here was going more than double the speed limit through downtown. But you shouldn't be out here—go home."

"Twice the speed along here isn't that bad," Rachel said. "That's still only forty miles an hour."

"It's far too fast for downtown."

"I do it all the time."

"You'd better not let *me* catch you doing it."

"He probably didn't ever see the speed limit sign. Rental tags. He's obviously not from around here. Weather like this … probably not his fault at all."

Officer Connelly looked at Jason. "I suppose you're going to tell me you didn't see the speed limit sign."

"I never saw it," Jason lied. "Too busy trying to see through the rain."

The officer glared at him, but this time Jason felt it was an act. From the beginning of their encounter, it had seemed as if the man might be messing with him—typical case of the local law having a little fun with an out-of-towner.

"Where are you from, Mr. Rental Car?" Officer Connelly asked.

"Chicago."

"You have connections with the Mafia?"

"What?"

"Al Capone. Those type. We don't need that kind of crowd here."

"I'm an accountant."

"Capone had accountants," Officer Connelly retorted. "Crooked ones."

"I'm not connected with the Mob. I'm with an accounting firm that does work for a large healthcare nonprofit. They own a lot of hospitals. They own Saint Catherine's."

Officer Connelly cracked a sudden grin. "Well, why didn't you say so? Saint Catherine's! I was born there."

Lightning forked across the sky, so close that Jason wanted to duck. Almost the same instant, an angry thunderclap rocked downtown.

"Holy sweet devil!" Officer Connelly barked. "We better get outta this. Rachel, you go straight home. Your curfew must be soon. Mr. Rental Car, you go to wherever you're going, but if I ever catch you going even one teensy mile an hour over the speed limit again in this county, you'll be cooling your heels in our nice little jail. Understand?"

"Yes, sir. Thank you, Officer."

Jason moved back toward the driver's side of his car, splashing through an unseen puddle in the dark. He glanced at the girl, who was still standing in the storm, watching him with a focus that unnerved him. Feeling Officer Connelly's eyes also on him, Jason ducked into his car and closed the door. He felt even wetter now that he was out of the rain and could feel how heavily his drenched clothes hung on him. Wiping his face with a soaked sleeve, he took a few seconds to collect himself. Then he started the engine and drove cautiously away, looking as much at the speedometer as at the dark river of road.

22

The man emerged from the shadows of a Chicago side street and limped down the sidewalk. His thick beard softened the bite of the wind buffeting the steel-and-concrete canyon. His wool fedora shaded his eyes from the L station's lights overhead. Other creatures of the night wandered the area: prostitutes, hustlers, dealers, vagrants, drinkers, and drifters. Cars slowed as they drove past, and eyes met—everybody looking to make a deal.

And the man was no different. What he wanted could be found only in this seedy area.

He limped past a dive bar, into a wide alley, and entered an old building on the right. Inside, he used the wobbly banister to haul himself up a long, narrow staircase. At the top, he followed the hallway to a Chinese mahjong parlor, where twenty men gambled at low tables covered with Bakelite game tiles.

He continued past them to the young woman in a frilled black and maroon gypsy dress. "I'd like to sit with Madam Bovell," he said. "Is she available?"

"She's with someone now," the woman said softly. "And two others are ahead of you after that. If you can wait, I'll put you on the list and you'll see her."

"I can wait," the man said coldly, his hat still shading the top half of his face while his beard masked the lower half. "I can wait as long as necessary."

*   *   *

Madam Bovell sat in silence while dozens of questions pounded inside her head. Her eyes were closed, but her mind was looking through all the space and time that her imagination could touch. She couldn't find the answers to any of the riddles posed by her dream vision and the word spelled out by the Ouija board: "stullwood." She had searched all over the web until she was inundated with information beyond her powers to assimilate. That single word took her to vacation beaches and prisons and wines and venture capitalists and fashion movements and science-fiction novels and Teflon skillets and everything else under the sun—everything except for anyone named Rachel Black.

Before the evening readings, she had sent out messages to some friendly acquaintances to organize a group séance at her apartment in a few days. With a group, the spirit hold would be stronger, perhaps allowing for better communication through the Ouija board.

She heard her next sitter enter the room. She had seen thirteen so far tonight—rather more than usual. Lately, more people wanted to contact the dead. Only four days before Halloween, this was her busy season. It could be a long night.

"Sit and be silent," she said.

The sitter sat.

She could tell that it was a man by the way the wooden chair creaked. Thousands of people had sat down in that chair over the years, and she had learned to gather a great deal about a person from that first sound.

But other than this, the man hadn't said or revealed anything. It was a fraught silence, which made her a little uneasy. There was no jittering or rustling or throat-clearing—not even the oh, so subtle nervous gulp—nothing that hinted at tension or anxiety, which was strange. This gave her a feeling of skepticism from this visitor—maybe even a sense of danger.

She concentrated further, looking beyond the sounds and smells of the man. Trying yet again to resurrect her lost powers, she relaxed and reached out with her mind to receive any transmissions from this man's subconscious or from any errant spirit that may have followed him here.

But she was getting nothing from this man and the space around him. She hadn't felt anything from tonight's other visitors, either, but her recent vision and the experience with the Ouija board had encouraged her to exert a bit more focus. She imagined the man's head, his stare, the synapses firing in his brain. She imagined she was searching his mind for impulses and links—to pockets of energy floating around him, to guardian angels, or to living spirits or clouds of emotions echoing in space long after a soul has departed.

But she felt nothing.

Still, something about this man seemed dangerous. Perhaps, he was one of those occasional weirdos who came here thinking she was an evil witch or a minion of Satan. She thought of the trapdoor under the table. She used it during many high-profile readings, to have objects handed to her or even to have actors crawl up through it and pretend to be spirits during fake séances.

She opened her eyes, hoping she hadn't tipped her hand.

"Hello," the man said.

She nodded in reply.

"I'm sorry," he said, feigning nervousness. "I'm not really sure how this works."

Liar, she thought, forcing a smile. His sharp eyes were those of someone who knew exactly how this worked. Perhaps, he was someone who went around trying to expose and maybe even hurt fraudsters like her. She must be very careful.

"You've come on a long journey to get here," she began.

"I live here in the city," he said with a grin.

"The journey has not just been tonight," she waffled. "Your life has been a long journey, and now it has brought you here."

"It has been long," he agreed. "As has yours, I'd imagine."

"You've lost someone," she said, making the careful guess.

"Hasn't everyone?" he replied coldly.

"Someone close to you," she continued. "I can feel their presence. They are here with us right now."

"Don't," he warned.

"They're trying to say something. There's something they want to tell you. They're glad you came here because they need you to know—"

"Don't!" He cut her off with a louder, sharper tone. "I know there is no one here except us."

"I feel another presence among us."

He shook his head. "It doesn't work like that. You know this. We are alone."

"Sir, I know it can be difficult to have faith, to believe the things that exist beyond our senses. But we must try to search for those we've lost, for some are searching for us. I know this."

"You *know* this?" he asked with disgust. "Let's see what you know. Can you tell me my name?"

"I cannot."

"With all the gifts you claim to have, you don't even know my name? Can't the spirits tell you? Or can't you read my mind and find it yourself."

"I can only receive and translate what the spirits tell me. I cannot just sense what your name is."

"You aren't anywhere near as good at this as you used to be."

"Excuse me?" she said, feeling a shiver of alarm.

"Have you lost your powers?"

"I think you should go."

"No."

"Please."

"Your power comes and goes, is that it? Or it used to, anyway. You haven't had it in a while, have you? So why do you keep doing this? Don't you realize how much harm you cause?"

She leaned forward, struggling to hide her terror of him. Was this the devil, come to collect her soul? Was it Death, come at last to show her the other side of the boundary she had danced around her entire life?

"You have many questions," she said, "but they can all be answered by the same simple truth." She leaned in closer to the three short candles lighting the room from the center of the table. "The world is a dark place. And it is only in the absence of light that we discover our greatest strength."

Then, before he could react, she blew out the candles in one breath, casting the room into darkness.

23

Professor Graves was startled when the room went dark. He felt the tablecloth move, pulling his elbows away from him. A rustling came from the other side of the medium's table, followed by the clap of something heavy that caused a brief vibration of the wood floor.

"Madam Bovell? Are you all right?"

When no response came, he dug his cell phone from his pocket and turned on the light. Her chair was empty. Panning the light across the room, he didn't see her anywhere. He pulled up the tablecloth and saw a trapdoor. With some discomfort, he crawled forward and lifted it enough to find a steep wooden staircase to the floor below.

"You've gotta be kidding me," he muttered.

Crawling back out from under the table, he hobbled to the door and hurried down the hallway. He went through the open waiting room, past the gypsy and the Chinese men playing mahjong, down the building's staircase, and out onto the narrow city street.

Steam billowed from manholes, creating isolated vaporous apparitions that blocked part of his view as he scanned the area for the woman. She was his age. He couldn't believe she would move fast.

Then, between two steam geysers near the end of the street, he saw the silhouette of a woman hurry around the corner. She was heading toward the main street.

Praying it was her, he began a fast hobble toward the corner. He tried to ignore the pain firing from his left knee. Each hard step he took probably meant an additional session of physical therapy. But he couldn't let her get away.

Reaching the corner, he leaned against the brick building and searched the street, which seemed surprisingly busy for the late hour. Across the intersection, he saw her climbing the steps towards the L train platform. He could hear the rumble of an approaching train.

"Oh, no," he groaned. He would never make it to the platform in time.

Glancing left, he saw a yellow taxi approaching. He hobbled into the street, whistled, and flagged it down. The cab jerked to a sudden stop as the train passed overhead. He slid into the back. "I'll give you a hundred bucks if you beat that train to the next station."

"You're on!" the cabbie announced, as if he had been waiting all night for the challenge. He stomped on the accelerator, thrusting Dr. Graves back into the seat.

As they sped away, he craned his neck to look out the rear window at the above L track. The back of the train was sticking out from the platform—it hadn't yet left the station. His vantage point didn't give him a view of the actual platform, so he couldn't be certain that Madam Bovell had gotten on this train. But she had been desperate to escape, so she would likely jump aboard the first train to arrive. He knew Chicago's rail system by heart, and there was only one station the train could go to next.

The cabbie had Grand Prix skills, racing around slower cars while honking in near-constant chirps. Dr. Graves held on to the headrest in front of him with his right hand, and the seat belt with his left. They raced a block up Clinton Street before turning onto Lake Street, which took them under the rail yard running along the river. They continued across the river, sped through two yellow lights on Lake Street heading into the downtown business district, and zipped past the glass tower buildings. The engine growled and screamed as the cabbie gunned it, eased up, and gunned it again. Zooming through intersections, they bottomed the cab's shocks on the dips. It felt like a speedboat slamming over the waves. Finally slowing after a few more blocks, the cab darted into a parking structure, near the narrow concrete stairs up to the next station's platform.

Dr. Graves slapped a ready Benjamin into the cabbie's hand. "Thank you, sir. Use the money to help find your way to Daytona. I hear NASCAR calling you."

He crawled out and started up the steps. A train was approaching above—from which direction, he couldn't tell. His knee was killing him, and his heart was hammering as if it wanted out. He reached the top stair just as the train from the last station raced past him. He hobbled frantically along the platform as it stopped. The rear door was the only one he could reach before the train took off again, and it was still fifty feet in front of him. No one else was on the platform, and he wasn't sure the conductor could see him. He moved as fast as he could, closing the gap. But then he heard a ding and a hiss as the doors began to close. He reached it just in time to desperately stick his arm inside, jarring the sensors and, finally, causing the doors to open again with a protest from the electronic bell.

Stepping inside, he caught his breath as the doors closed and the train began to move. He then took off his false eyeglasses and peeled away the fake beard from his face. Stuffing them in the overcoat pocket, he then took off the fedora and tucked it under his arm, inside his coat. Having finally completed the transformation back into his true self, he started through the train, searching for Madam Bovell.

24

Madam Bovell stared nervously as the closing door hesitated, reopened, then finally closed. As the train began moving forward, she glanced at the transit line map near the ceiling. She would follow this route for three more stops before it felt safe enough to get off.

The car was half full of people, which felt like a lot for this time of night. But she welcomed the crowd. Even though she had escaped the man, she still enjoyed the feeling of safety in numbers. She must wait at least a few days—maybe even weeks—before going back to her parlor. Maybe this was a good time to skip town for a while. Go to Lily Dale and sit with other mediums. Perhaps they could help her learn more about her vision.

She looked across the car at her reflection in the window. She hadn't been to Lily Dale in years, not since the scandal. But she still had friends there who could help her. And her home here wouldn't be safe anymore. Maybe all of Chicago had become too dangerous for her. Maybe whatever had happened tonight was somehow connected with her vision. A warning. She had never believed in coincidences.

A man sat on the bench opposite her, facing her, obstructing her reflection in the window. He stared at her, and staring back, she recognized him.

For what felt like an eternity, they looked at each other in silence. She couldn't understand how or why this man was here. This man who had ruined her career thirty years ago, forcing her to scavenge for a living in back-alley séance parlors ever since. She knew that he still lived in Chicago, still worked at the university, but how had he suddenly come to be on this train, on this night, sitting right in front of her, staring at her?

And then she understood. He held up a fake beard, pulled a fedora out from under his coat, like the magician he used to be, and smiled sheepishly.

"You?" she gasped.

He nodded.

"No," she said.

"Yep."

"Why?"

"I had to see if you had your gift tonight."

"Tonight?"

"Yeah."

"Since when do you believe that I have ever had my gift on any night?"

"Since yesterday."

She hesitated. "Why are you here?"

His countenance turned expressionless. "I was told to find you. At least, I think it's you. I don't know who else it could be."

"Told by whom?"

"I'm not really sure. It was a message, and to be honest, this all feels a little like a foggy dream to me."

"A dream …" She hesitated. "What, exactly, did the message say?"

"Just two words: 'Find her.'"

A light-headed fuzziness swirled between her ears, followed by a throbbing pressure.

"Are you okay?" he asked, crossing to the seat beside her.

She tried to recover from the sudden spell, wishing she had something to eat or could lie down without drawing attention.

"That's all I know. *FIND HER.*' I was visiting my son's tombstone when a strong wind knocked a bunch of hazelnuts from a tree. As I watched, they rolled to the base of his tombstone and spelled out the message."

She covered her mouth with her hand. Then, after looking around, she lowered it and leaned into him. "I had a strong vision that woke me around two in the morning today."

"Of what?"

"I was falling. And a gray woman was there. A spirit. I'm supposed to find someone."

"Who?"

"Someone named Rachel Black. I was told to find her."

"Find her ..." Dr. Graves repeated.

"Are you a believer again?"

"I don't know."

"You believe the message was from your son?"

He exhaled slowly. "The father in me wants to believe it was from him. But the investigator in me knows there are many other possible explanations. It could have been a hallucination, someone's hypnotic trick, or even—if we accept them—the doings of another spirit or entity that is not my son."

"And you thought the messenger wanted you to find *me*? There was no indication it meant this Rachel Black I was told to find?"

"I assumed it was to find you. You see, you were already on my mind earlier that day because of something else that was strange. An article in a London publication reminded me of you, of those séances you used to have on Halloween with hundreds of people at once."

"That was a very long time ago," she said.

"I know. But there is a big group that's going to try something like that this year in India. And a group of researchers are going to observe it. Apparently, they did it last year, too, with some interesting results."

"Define 'interesting.'"

The train slowed as it neared the Clark/Lake station. Most passengers moved to the doors, ready to exit at the hub.

"What kind of results?" she repeated.

"The bad kind," he said. He stood and held out his hand. "Come on. There's an Irish pub near here. What I'm about to tell you will be much easier to hear with the comfort of a whiskey."

25

"The report was titled *Reopening a Gateway to Hell*," Dr. Graves said after taking a drink.

"Charming," Madam Bovell replied.

He nodded. The walls of the Irish pub had dark wood dividers sticking out between tables, creating pockets of privacy amid the crowd of patrons. They were sitting opposite the fireplace. A four-person folk band—concertina, fiddle, bouzouki, and penny whistle—was playing "Lannigan's Ball" in an open area just past the horseshoe-shaped teak bar at the heart of the pub.

She sipped her whiskey. "And the researchers are going to India?" she asked.

"Yes. To a village called Murgo. It's in Kashmir, up in the Himalayas."

"For Halloween?"

"Yeah."

"To make contact with the devil when he appears at midnight?"

"That's their plan," he said, making Venn diagrams on the tabletop with his glass. "Heaven help them if they succeed. They found witnesses of a sighting a year ago."

"Tell me," she said, taking a rather longer sip. This Irish whiskey wasn't bad at all. The penny whistle had just handed off the lead to the fiddle, keeping the rapid, frantic melody going.

"Last year," Dr. Graves began, "over three hundred people gathered at a cemetery in Murgo on Halloween, to see if the devil would appear at midnight. And apparently, he did. Witnesses claim that the devil danced with other risen spirits that had been wronged in life."

"And this hadn't happened before?" she asked. "This gathering?"

"Not on this scale. There had been small groups over the years—mostly kids. But this was a flash mob, like the tens of thousands that used to appear suddenly in the streets of London outside rumored ghost sightings in the late 1800s."

"And so you believe the story?"

"All three hundred people swore they saw the devil."

"That doesn't mean they did," she said. "They could be lying. They could be delusional. Maybe they all drank the same Kool-Aid."

"*All* of them?"

"It could be a fraud. A prank. A group hoax on the world."

"After Halloween last year, six of them went blind."

A player started on the bodhrán drum, adding an eerie thumping to the fiddle's slicing, jarring panic. She set her glass down and stared hard at him for a few seconds. "This is a fact?"

He nodded.

"You're positive."

"The researchers verified it in their report. Within twenty-four hours after the devil's dance, six of the three hundred lost their sight."

She took the last of her drink and looked away from him. A line of vintage stained-glass amber swag lamps hung from the wooden planks over the bar. The light glowed in reflective patterns off the etched glass and mirrors behind the bar.

She said, "I need some more whiskey."

"I'll get two more," he said, then left the little table and lurched toward the bar.

She looked down at the maplewood table, lost in the swirls of varnished grain. She recalled her last large séance, at an old theater house in upstate New York long ago, and then became terrified over the séance planned in India. Pain from her past was on the horizon, moving fast like an approaching storm. Alcohol was her shelter.

Dr. Graves returned with two more tumblers and a pair of black whiskey stones in each. As she took the fresh drink, she noticed how his eyes were fixed on her before they ducked away as if afraid of being read. She sensed an unspoken tension in him—a hidden burden that weighed on him.

"What is it?" she asked.

"What is what?" he answered, all innocence.

"Your eyes betrayed you," she said. "What were you thinking?"

His face sagged and his gaze drifted down toward the table. He seemed frozen for a few seconds. Then his lips tightened and he looked up at her with sad eyes. "I'm sorry," he said. "About what I did to you back then ... however many decades it's been ... exposing you at that séance in front of all those people."

"It's not your fault. I was a fraud."

"But I know what I took from you when I did that. I didn't do it because I was trying to hurt you. I was just doing what I thought was right. But I'm sorry about the pain it caused you."

"That was a long time ago."

"Still, it has bothered me for a long time. I should have reached out to you years ago and told you. Please don't get me wrong. I still feel that I did the right thing … It's just that the older I get, the more haunted I am by those whom my investigations have harmed."

A burst of laughter erupted from the bar, which was lined with apple-cheeked men and glowing women. Everyone seemed to be talking at the same time, each telling some long, rolling saga that involved at least three generations of Irish. But for the sidewalls to their little snug, Dr. Graves and Madam Bovell might not have been able to hear each other.

"How many mediums have you exposed over the years?" she asked.

"More than I can count," he said. "But it was always you who bothered me the most. Your reputation was stellar. I had actually hoped when I attended your séance that you might be the real thing. And even afterward, I wondered if maybe, somehow, you were … if I was somehow wrong to expose and discredit you. But I know what I saw—what you did—and I knew I had to say something about it."

She felt her eyes tearing up as the memory and feelings of that night resurfaced. "I don't blame you," she said. "You see someone commit a fraud, and it's only natural to then question and doubt everything that person has ever done. I just wish it hadn't happened."

"But why did you do it? Afterward, I read that you still claimed to have paranormal abilities. Was that just an attempt to continue the illusion?"

"No. I really did have abilities."

"Then why resort to fraud and parlor tricks if you were the real thing?"

She stared at him, seeing shadows slide across his hard features as patrons moved between the table and the stone fireplace. Could she really trust him with the masked secret of all true mediums?

"The gift was not always present," she finally said. "It was random and unpredictable, like a dream. Sometimes, I could receive communications, and sometimes I couldn't. But people expected me to be able to do it every time. They paid for it, and my reputation would pay for it if I couldn't deliver. Ten percent of the time, the gift was there, and I could do a proper reading—I could make contact. But I had to be prepared to use fraud the other ninety percent of the time, or I would seem too unreliable as a medium and would fail professionally. Most of the famous mediums in history were the same way. It was like an athlete doping. The pressure to perform is very strong."

He sat back in the tall wooden chair, his hands gripping the curved edge of the little round-top table. His mind was clearly working through what she had said. "Is that why there are so many mediums who have been shown to achieve incredible, inexplicable feats one day and are caught in an act of simple fraud another day?" he asked. "The Davenport Brothers, Henry Slade, Florrie Cook, and Madame Blavatsky were all top names as either séance or stage mediums—and they all were exposed as frauds. Even Eusapia Palladino was caught in the act, while other times she performed miracles of sight and other astounding psychic achievements, under controlled settings that no one could explain. Only D. D. Home and Leonora Piper died with untarnished reputations."

"Yes," she said. "We are at the same time fraudsters and authentic spirit mediums; it just depends on the night."

"But that can't be true for all who claim to be mediums and psychics," he said. "You do believe that most are charlatans with no psychic abilities at all, right?"

"Of course. The world is full of con artists. The way I always think of it is that only ten percent of those who claim to have gifts truly have them—and even those people can access their gifts only ten percent of the time."

"But if that's true for you, then why did you fade away so quickly after I exposed you for trickery? Surely you could have posed a comeback with new displays of spirit communications."

"My gifts were already fading fast when you exposed me. By the time you were able to label me a fraud, I really had no ability left to prove otherwise. I was finished on the big stage of mediums and spirit contacts. Since then, I've just performed small readings and shadow séances in the forgotten alleys of life."

"Why didn't you move on to something else?"

She thought for a second. "It was all I knew. And also, I think I kept hoping that my gifts might one day return."

"And now you say they have?"

"I don't know yet. Something has definitely happened. And my vision of the gray woman also means something. But I don't understand it yet." As she said this, her eyes drifted to the embellishments in the table's side panel. She half wondered whether the elaborate Celtic symbols etched into the dark wood were some secret mystical message she might intuitively decipher if only she concentrated hard enough. Everything seemed to be calling to her. Formerly dead objects now tingled with energy.

"But this is the first time you've felt anything like this in decades?" Dr. Graves asked solemnly.

"No. Over the years, I've sometimes felt as if my gift were still there. I mean, I know that the spirits are still there. I know that many of them want to reach out to us. They want to have contact with the living. Some don't. Some just move on, perhaps searching for those who died before them. But some want to stay in touch with the living. It's hard, though, for them to communicate with us. Not many of the living are good receivers. It can be frustrating to spirits when they can't communicate clearly. Messages can get jumbled, misunderstood, or just go unnoticed. But most spirits are patient. Most are just trying to help us."

"Most? Is that what you believe?"

"I know they can't all be good. Some are angry. I felt that when I was younger. Those are the only ones we should fear. Most of them are ghosts, not spirits. Ghosts are unstable emotions trapped in a location or attached to an object. Spirits don't haunt places or people; ghosts do. But they are relatively few. Maybe only one in a hundred thousand become ghosts when they die. The rest become spirits. Something horrible has to happen in a person's psyche at the moment of death for them to become trapped as a ghost. And they can certainly be very dangerous, but they rarely have real contact with the living. They are like sharks in the open ocean, while the living swim at beaches. Death is a big ocean, and very rarely will the sharks swim into shallow waters near the living swimmers along the shore. Shark attacks are rare compared with how many sharks and people there are. They just don't come in contact with each other that often. It is the same with ghosts and the living."

He rubbed his face with his hands as if splashing water on himself. Then he said, "Do you have any interest in coming with me to see the devil's dance?"

"On Halloween?"

"Yes."

"You're going to *India*?"

"No. There is another cemetery much closer that folklore has linked to the one in India. The English researchers are all going to India to the source of last year's gathering. But no one is going to the other location. I don't think many are even aware of it anymore. Old-school paranormal researchers from the SPR like me are a dying breed. But the article got me thinking, and I've decided that someone should go to the other location. I'm planning to report my experience and findings to the group afterward, in case it helps them."

"So where are you going?"

"It's a small cemetery in Stull, Kansas. There's a church there next to the ruins of an older church. The cemetery is one of the seven gateways to hell, so they say, like the location in India. Some have referred to it as the Demonic Church."

Madam Bovell's eyes were wide. "What did you say?"

"The Demonic Church."

"No! Where in Kansas?"

"Stull. It's a very small town."

"That's the word I got from the Ouija board. *Stullwood*."

"Really …" He looked pensive. "That obviously can't be a coincidence. But it's not named Stullwood. It's just Stull."

"Maybe the name changed long ago?"

"Maybe."

"It's definitely no coincidence," she said. "But they were only single letters, one after another. Maybe I misinterpreted them. Maybe instead of one word it was two: 'Stull' and 'wood.' Is there something special about wood in Stull? A famous carving? An old wooden bridge? A haunted stand of trees? Anything?"

"There's an infamous piece of stone rubble from a fallen church in the cemetery, but nothing I'm aware of that's to do with wood."

"There must be something—in the cemetery, maybe. A marker? A symbol carved into the church's fireplace mantel if it has one? Something?"

"Maybe. But I think the cemetery is known mostly for its stones. The pile of stone rubble from the fallen church. The new church built out of stones to replace it. It's in the Kansas Flint Hills."

"There must be something there."

"Only one way to find out."

Madam Bovell paused long enough to center her mind in its spinning drunken current of activity. An Irish jig was energizing the already lively ambience of the pub. Half the patrons were singing with the band. A large, pasty barman with thinning hair stood with a grin, his thick arms crossed over his impressive belly. Everyone had turned their attention to the battle between concertina and fiddle, and the building beats of the frame drum.

Fate had given her half the answer to her vision's riddle. And she believed that it would provide the other half. She took another drink of whiskey and smiled at the man who had helped destroy her career. "Let's go to Stull, Kansas," she said over the chaos. "Not on Halloween. I can't wait four days. My vision couldn't wait. Let's go right now. Let's book the next flight. I've always wanted to see what the devil looks like. Maybe he'll know where I can find this Rachel Black."

The music got louder, and the tipsier patrons along the bar began stomping to the song like a wild, ancient people dancing around a fire. And both the professor and Madam Bovell sat back and soaked it in as if they had found the last place on Earth that death and darkness had not yet penetrated.

WEDNESDAY

If there was ever a place that should have ghosts, this was it.
—Stephen King, *The Shining*

26

Tommy gently closed the screen door on the back porch so it wouldn't slam and wake his parents. The predawn air was cold. The sun wouldn't be up for another hour, but he had work to do.

He walked away from the porch, moving along the hard dirt between the house and the barn. A fifteen-foot light pole in the center of the patch gave enough illumination for him to see where he was going, though he could have done it blindfolded. He spent most mornings before school doing his work. And someday, when school was behind him, he would continue to do this until he was too old to work the farm.

He walked around the barn to the two larger white buildings beyond. This part of the farm was where most of his family's income now came from. And it was the part of the farm where Tommy saw the most opportunity for growth—the part that he was most excited to expand someday when he took charge of the family business.

The two buildings had low-pitched gabled roofs and were each forty feet wide and five hundred feet long. He opened a side door to the near building and stepped into a small room. Inside, he used hand sanitizer by the door before changing into the blue pants and jacket hanging on the wall. He pulled a new white hairnet cap from a supply box on the shelf. Putting it on, he then slipped on the pair of rubber boots standing by the second door. Turning to the glass-faced red computer housing box mounted on the plywood wall, he read the readings. Both temperature and humidity looked good. Then he looked at the housing box next to it to see which switches were lit to indicate which fans were running. As usual, the computer system had everything under control.

He went back to the second door, dipped each boot into the pan of white disinfectant solution, then opened the door and stepped into the darkness.

After closing the door behind him, he just stood in the dark, enjoying the cavernous space he could feel surrounding him. A soft shuffling came from the black void in front of him, with numerous scratching sounds in the dirt floor, and hundreds of muted throaty, squawking sounds.

He knew that they could sense him here, that they were waking up.

He looked at his watch and saw that he had thirty more seconds. Feeling for the dispensary in the dark, he squirted hand sanitizer in his palm and rubbed his hands together thoroughly to kill any errant germ spores he might have picked up in the past minute. Then he heard the mechanical clicking and knew it was time. He looked up and watched as the computer slowly turned on a hundred hanging lamps to gradually focus the fifty thousand black and orange eyeballs staring at him.

He never got tired of that first morning image of this place. It was one of the reasons he knew that he would always love being a farmer. So many kids in his high school class were already talking about their plans for college so they could move on and get some big fancy life in Chicago or out in California or Seattle. A few wanted to head all the way east to Boston or Washington or New York. But he knew that the best life was right here. He would go to North Dakota State and study agriculture and maybe also get a business degree, and then he would come back to use that knowledge to run and even expand the family farm. His mom had said that in addition to giving him an education, college was the best place to find a wife to bring back home, and he was okay with that plan, too.

But he didn't have everything figured out. There were major concerns on the horizon that worried him. Even his passion for farming couldn't ignore the worrying headwinds that any young farmer faced in a modern America. So much had changed since his grandparents started the poultry farm over half a century ago. Even his parents found the modern business environment a rapidly changing landscape. It was fast becoming a new world with new rules that hurt the prospects of small and midsize family farms across the country. Big corporate farms were consolidating the business. Fewer from his generation were choosing to go into farming than from past generations, and challenges from all sides beset those few intrepid souls who did. Climate change, trade conflicts, sinking commodity prices, large upfront investments in equipment, and even poorly designed inheritance taxes on land-rich but cash-strapped families all created challenges for an industry that was already one of the toughest in America. And as much as Tommy loved the work and challenges of running the family farm, he worried that industrywide factors outside his control might eventually cheat him of the work and life and opportunities enjoyed by past generations.

He walked out onto the loose dirt and litter that covered the floor of the poultry house. As he moved, the hundreds of chickens nearest him tracked him like loyal pets. Twenty-five thousand chickens were under this long roof above him. At five and a half weeks old, they were nearly fully grown now, but he remembered when they had been only a day old and were delivered from the nearby hatchery in crates and dumped onto this floor as cute little yellow chicks smaller than his fist. He had needed to be extra careful back then just to avoid stepping on the little sprouts as they wandered around chirping incessantly.

But the dozens of hanging lines of feeders and poultry nipples—managed by the computer—had delivered all the feed and water they needed to grow. So the hordes of little yellow fluff balls had fed and fed and fed. And had they ever grown! In just five and a half weeks, they had gone from the size of his fist to the size of his head. And they weren't yellow now, but golden brown with dashes of black and red.

As he walked among them, he watched for any telltale signs of sickness. He had spent so many years working his family's poultry farm that he could usually tell what was going on with any of the birds just by looking at how they were behaving. If they were sick or hurt or stressed, he would be able to tell. They each had different personalities, and he would get to know many of them during the six-week harvest cycles before they were ready to be delivered to the processing plant that had bought them from his family. In that time, he would get to know them almost as if they *were* family.

Of course, they weren't technically family; they were livestock. And ultimately, they would be sold as a commodity to a large agricultural company's processing plant, where they would be hung upside down on a conveyer belt, stunned unconscious by a mild electrical current, pulled past a long blade that severed their jugular veins and carotid arteries. Then a long line of machines would pluck their feathers, cut off their heads and feet, suck out their organs, and then slice their carcasses into pieces before cleaning and separately packaging them. It wasn't pretty, but it was part of the business, and it fed the country.

Tommy noticed a group of chickens all standing still, staring at him. It was a strange behavior, appearing almost as if it were coordinated, and he couldn't remember ever before seeing it.

"You guys okay?" he asked. "Huh?"

They just kept staring at him.

"Okay, okay," he said. "I know it's early." Then he chuckled to himself. Talking to the chickens was part of the charm of the work, and he was fairly certain it helped keep them relaxed.

He walked down the wide space between the two long lines of feeder pans hanging six inches above the ground every ten feet, connected by the feed piping that stretched the length of the building. Above the feeders were the lines of lamps with their wide silver covers that made them look like an invasion of miniature flying saucers stretching back into the distance. The air was warm, its temperature also carefully controlled by the computer, based on the chickens' growth stage at the time. They were big enough now that the house was getting pretty full. The chickens in the other house were only three weeks old, so they weren't filling up that place nearly as much as here. But these birds still had space to move around.

A few steps ahead of him were some of the short crates he had turned upside down at the recommendation of the last inspector, who said it would make the chickens happier if they had a few limited places where they could jump up and sit to look down on the others. Tommy's dad had been so amused by the idea that he had even disinfected one of their old troughs, brought it in, and set it upside down near the crates so that some of the chickens could take a turn being kings of the hill. Tommy thought it ridiculous, but his dad got to enjoy his goofy ideas as long as he was still officially in charge of the farm. But his dad had taught him the family business well, and Tommy was excited for the day when he would become responsible for running everything.

He looked back and was startled to see twice as many chickens standing motionless and staring at him as before. With all the thousands of other chickens continuing to walk aimlessly in near-constant motion, it was unnerving to see so many in this one growing cluster stand so unnaturally still—and do so while staring so intently at him.

As he stared back at them, he suddenly felt the eerie sensation that they could somehow read his mind—and, in reading it, could see the future that he knew was in store for them. A future in which he would deliver them to their slaughter so that he and his kind could feast on their flesh.

And as he watched them, he saw more chickens stop their aimless meandering and join the growing group that now focused on him with such dark intensity.

A gust of wind rattled the metal roof above, turning his skin to gooseflesh. It felt as if some cold force had been outside the building the whole time and was just now finding its way inside.

One chicken jumped and flapped its short wings frantically, as if sensing a predator. Then another chicken leaped up in the air and gave a hellish squawk, as if an unseen force had just jabbed it with something sharp.

"Whoa, girl. What's wrong?"

The wind picked up and was now shaking the corrugated roof, and he thought he even saw slight movement from one wall. And now even the hanging lamps and feeder pans were swaying violently, as if he were aboard a ship in heavy seas. And as the lights swung, the shadows of chickens shrank and shifted while other shadows grew monstrous, menacing beaks and claws.

A cluster of a few hundred chickens suddenly darted away from the far wall. At first, he thought they were spooked by a new creaking from the wall, but when they stopped alongside the main flock and joined in with intense stares at him, he realized that they had wanted to get closer to him. Looking around, he saw that he was now surrounded by a large ring of chickens, and they all were staring at him with fierce eyes while jumping up and down and flapping their wings and emitting squawks that sounded like ghastly screams.

"Easy, girls. It's just a little wind."

A sharp pain jabbed the back of his calf, just above his Achilles tendon. Whirling about with a yelp, he saw a chicken looking up at him. It had a small splash of blood on its beak.

"Hey! What the hell!"

The chicken made a low gurgling sound that resembled a growl. He had never heard anything like it from any bird. And he had never been pecked on the leg—certainly not hard enough to draw blood.

The chicken took two quick steps towards him, then stopped when he flashed a hand down at it. "No!" he snapped. "Stop!"

The chicken growled again and moved spastically back and forth as if it was having some sort of seizure.

A soft scratching sound came from behind him, and he felt another stab, this time in his other ankle.

"Damn it!" he growled, spinning around to see another chicken that had drawn his blood.

At this second strike, a crescendo of low gurgling growls rose up from all the chickens. And in that moment they felt as dangerous to him as a pack of hyenas. Something had driven these birds collectively insane, and with the violent wind harassing the building, he had the sudden fear that some ancient evil had surrounded them. Something had come and poisoned the birds with knowledge of the fate that *he* was preparing them for.

"Whoa, whoa. Easy, girls."

The circle around him tightened as the chickens took a few steps closer. Some of them had stopped growling and taken to hissing. At least, he *thought* the hissing was coming from them. It could be just the rising wind outside.

Something stabbed the back of his knee. Then another. In the corner of his eye, he saw a chicken leap up and jab his thigh. Another jumped and beat its wings enough to rise up and rake claws across his forearm.

He winced and turned away, only to find a dozen more gang-rushing him and pecking viciously at his shins. Crying out, he tried to back up, but his heels hit more rushing chickens behind him, making him lose his balance and stumble to the floor.

The second he was down, the chickens swarmed him. Painful pricks and jabs all over his body sent him into a whirl of terror. His first instinct was to curl into a ball and shrink as far as possible into the thin jacket. But this only seemed to infuriate the birds. He felt them climbing on him and scratching him with their claws and pecking him with their hard, pointed beaks. He rolled as he had been taught to do should his clothes catch fire, but so many of them were swarming him that he couldn't shake them off for long. One got under his jacket and clawed its way up to his neck and seemed to be going for his eyes. It pecked hard and just missed, hitting the bridge of his nose before he grabbed it with both hands and wrung its neck.

The growling intensified. He felt a sharp pain in the back of his neck, as if claws had sliced exposed skin. Reaching behind him, he grabbed a tough chicken leg, and flung the bird away.

He rolled onto his knees and elbows, shrugged the jacket up to cover his head, and rose up on his toes. He was now certain they would kill him if he couldn't escape.

He was too afraid to look at the exit. Even slightly exposing his face might give one of them the chance to peck out an eye. But he had a good sense of the direction and distance to the door. Fighting through increasing pain, he lunged forward. Each step was a struggle as the vicious birds continued to attack him. Most plowed into his lower legs, but he felt some jumping and flapping up enough to scratch and peck as high as his arms and covered head. He stumbled, stepping on a few of them. Then he tripped and fell forward, landing on them as they kept up the horrible squawking, clawing and pecking more furiously than ever.

He must risk his eyes if he was to have any hope of spying an escape path. Rising to his knees, he saw a dense swarm of savage, bloodthirsty chickens wild to tear him apart. It was said that birds descended from flesh-eating dinosaurs. Looking around him, he had no reason to doubt it.

Feathers were floating in the air. His limbs burned from hundreds of cuts. The door was still fifty feet away. He would never make it that far before they pecked and clawed him to death. He threw the jacket back over his head and scrambled on all fours until his forehead bumped the trough. He blindly reached out, tipped it over, and crawled under it.

Now protected inside the metal half-cylinder, he checked that every part of the rim was touching the ground. He couldn't let them start working their way under the edges and inside this shell.

Secure for the first time since this nightmare began, he took a few seconds to breathe and assess the pain he felt all over his body. He felt as if he had been rolling around in an acre of prickly pears. But just as he began to calm down, he heard dozens of hard pops. Then hundreds. It sounded like hail on a metal roof, but it was chickens, smacking their hard beaks against the steel trough.

Crawling on all fours, he pushed the trough along the floor. He didn't think they could get to him as long as he stayed under it. He still had no idea why this was happening. It felt as if some evil force was at work. The wind had been too violent before the attack, the air too cold and stale, and the chickens had suddenly become too wild as a unified force.

The popping and pounding against the trough was so loud that it must be doing real damage to the birds. In the faint light inside the trough, he saw the bloodied ground as he continued to push across the building. He even saw a few pieces of what looked like broken beaks. The chickens were killing themselves for a chance to kill him.

Closing his eyes, he kept pushing. He had to be near the door.

He saw little chicken feet with their sharp little claws sticking out between the trough and the floor.

Then he felt and heard the trough bang against the metal side of the building. He prayed he had gotten himself within a few feet of the door. It was time. Planting his feet, he stood up under the trough, raising it with him, and threw it away from the wall. Then, as the chickens went completely berserk upon seeing him again, he grabbed the door handle beside him, yanked it down, and jumped back into the small room he had entered from.

Before he could get the door closed, a dozen chickens made it into the small room with the mounted computer boxes and sanitation supplies. Tommy grabbed some cardboard cartons containing spare rubber boots off the shelf and tossed them at the charging birds. Then he opened the door to the outside, staggered through it, and slammed it shut.

Only two chickens had made it all the way outside with him. Screeching and pecking, they flew at him. But he kicked one and stomped the other, ending their madness and their lives.

At last, with nothing trying to kill him for the moment, he fell back to the grass. A blood-orange sunrise was peeking over the horizon and illuminating the big cottonwoods that shaded the farmhouse where his parents were probably still sleeping. A muted rapid pounding came from the door of the poultry building. Even now the chickens weren't stopping. He had no idea what to do about it. Probably they would all need to be killed. Today.

Looking down at his cut and bleeding hands and arms and his holed and torn pants, he started shaking. His face hurt, too. What kind of mass insanity could have made the chickens act that way? Thinking back on the horrifying experience, he swore he had sensed something from outside just before the chickens turned on him. And thinking about it, he wasn't even sure that the growling had come from the chickens. It almost seemed as if something else had been in the room—some force that had poisoned everything before bedlam erupted.

A scream came from the farmhouse.

Jerking his head, he saw his mom looking at him from the back porch. "Tommy!" She opened the door and ran toward him. "Baby, are you okay?"

She must have seen his face. He could only imagine what he must look like covered in blood and chicken manure.

"I'm okay, Mom! I'm fine! But don't go in there! Something's wrong with them!"

"Oh, Tommy! What happened?"

His father was now out the porch door and trotting toward them.

He didn't know what to tell them or how to describe what had happened. And he certainly didn't know how to explain that something had come onto their property that he believed was pure evil.

27

Jason had just finished dressing and was about to leave his hotel room for work when he heard a knock at his door. Opening it, he was surprised to find the girl who had helped him during last night's traffic stop.

"Hi," she said.

"Who are you?" he asked with genuine curiosity. "And how did you know what room I'm in?"

"I'm Rachel," she said. "And let's just say I had a feeling this might be your room."

"What?"

"By the way, you're welcome for last night. If I hadn't helped you, you'd be making chalk marks on a wall in the downtown jail."

"It wasn't that bad, but still ... thank you. I do owe you one. But really, who are you?"

"You were in quite the hurry to get away," she said, ignoring his question. "What did you see in the hospital?"

The question stunned him into silence.

She stepped forward, and her emerald eyes seemed to look into his darkest secrets, as if to reveal all the things in his life that he kept locked away from coworkers and friends and family. Something about her made him want to surrender and trust in ways he hadn't, with anyone, in a long time. He couldn't explain it, but it felt as if she was already in his head. There was something hypnotic about her voice.

"I saw a woman in a window," he said. "In the reflection. Standing behind me. But she wasn't really behind me—she wasn't really there at all—but still, in a way ... somehow, she was there."

"You *saw* Annabel?" she almost spat in amazement.

"You know her?"

"Everyone does. But no one's actually seen her since her death."

"You're sure?"

Rachel nodded. "She hasn't shown herself to anyone."

"Why not?"

"I don't know."

"Then why appear to a complete stranger from out of town?"

"I don't know. But there must be a reason."

"A reason?" he asked vacantly, slipping his grip on the door. It tried to close and stopped when it hit him in the leg. He remembered Annabel's face behind him and saw the painful, terrifying movement of her blue lips. "She said, 'Lies.'"

"Lied about what?"

"No. She said the word 'lies.' She said it three times: 'Lies, lies, lies.' What does that mean?"

Rachel shrugged.

"You believe me?"

"Yes," she answered.

"Who are you?"

"Can we talk in your hotel room? It feels weird standing out here in the hallway."

He hesitated. "How old are you?"

"Seventeen. You're worried about letting me into your room? We're just talking."

"I know, but maybe it would be better if we stayed out in the open. Do your parents know where you are?"

"My parents are dead. I live with my adoptive parents, and they think I'm at school—which, by the way, I do need to get to in thirty minutes."

"Let's go downstairs," he said. "There are some couches in the lobby."

They walked down the wide, long corridor that stretched toward the center of the third floor. From there, the elevator took nearly a minute to lower them to the lobby. The stairs would have been faster. They walked through the small lobby. Stickers of cartoonish ghosts and witches and vampires decorated the wall behind the front reception desk. Three empty couches formed a half circle around the fireplace with a silent television on the mantel, showing the morning business news. They sat on the middle couch.

"We need to figure out what Annabel wants with you," Rachel said, forgoing any kind of small talk.

"With *me*?" The pointedness of her statement surprised him. He still didn't feel as if he had been selected for anything.

"She's been in that hospital for almost a year, and you're the first one to actually see her," Rachel said, almost bouncing on the couch as she scooted closer to him. Whispering, she continued, "We need to figure out why she chose you. What makes you so special to her?"

"I've never heard of her before this week."

"She picked you. There must be a reason."

He raised his hands as if to show his innocence. "Maybe I'm just the first person to work really late in that part of the hospital."

"Many others have been in that hospital. Some at night. I'm in a ghost-hunting club, and we've been there four times before this week. Once, we even stayed out until two in the morning. We got some crazy readings on our instruments, but we never actually saw her."

"Well maybe ..." he cut himself off as a middle-aged couple rounded the corner from the small room where the continental breakfast was happening. The man munched a half-eaten bagel while his wife brushed something off his beard.

Jason continued in a softer voice once the couple had passed and were out of earshot. "Maybe this is happening because it's so close to the first anniversary of her death. Her husband killed her on Halloween. That's only three days from now."

She gave a pensive nod. "I do think there is a connection to Halloween, but I also think it's more than that. What if she's latched on to you somehow? What if you and she have become psychologically linked?"

"Psychologically linked? How could that be possible?" *Listen to yourself,* he thought. *How could that be possible?* was a ridiculous question. How could *any* of this be possible? How could ghosts even exist? How could this be real. Having fun with ghost stories was intriguing and scary and entertaining, even exhilarating. But to believe, to truly believe that people could float around after death and meddle with the living—it was ridiculous. Yet lots of people did believe in it. There had been stories and accounts of sightings since the beginnings of history. The book he had received yesterday claimed that about half of all people in the world believed in ghosts—about the same percentage as believed in some form of God. Perhaps, ghosts were tied to religious belief. Perhaps, all varieties of the afterlife were connected in ways that he could never comprehend. Perhaps all of it—God, the devil, angels, demons, spirits, and ghosts—was part of the complex puzzle pursued by scientists and religious adherents in the quest to understand the cosmos and the spiritual unknowns of life and death and matter and energy in a multidimensional universe.

"Psychological links," Rachel said, "are believed to be the essential element that distinguishes a ghost from a spirit."

"I don't understand."

"Death comes in many forms: peaceful or painful, fast or slow, expected or unexpected, deserved or not. These factors all play a part in the soul's reaction at the moment of death. In most cases, the soul is able to cope with the end of its connection to the body at the exact moment of death—even in the most painful and shocking and tragic deaths. And in those moments, the soul becomes a spirit in another realm, though some spirits discover ways to move between realms, to communicate with the living through a living person's subconscious or dreams or through someone who's fallen into a trance state."

"But I was conscious when I saw her."

"She's not a spirit. She's a ghost—an apparition, a specter, a phantasm, but not a spirit. In rare cases, a soul can become twisted at the exact moment of death, so twisted that it can't pass on to the next realm. There's too much negative emotion at the time of death, too much anger and hatred or too much sadness. And so the soul becomes trapped in the echo of the emotion, bound to suffer its effects for years or decades or centuries— however long it takes for the echo's energy to dissipate. Some say it can never fade and that ghosts become trapped for all eternity."

"And you believe all this?"

"I believe in these truths as much as I believe that you and I are sitting here right now."

He rubbed his face in an effort to ward off the morning weariness that pressed on him. It had been too many nights since he last slept well. He had been in this town for only a few days, but this place had been bad news from the beginning, when the Flight of Death terrified him during his arrival. And then there was Annabel. His head hurt, and his body felt weak. It was as if this town were slowly poisoning him.

"How do you know so much about ghosts and spirits?" he asked before drawing a deep breath to prepare himself for whatever she would say next about this dark maze of death that he had somehow blundered into.

"We read a lot of books and articles online," she said. "We've all joined a few different ghost-hunting communities online, including the SPR."

"Society for Psychical Research," he said, recalling its countless mentions in the book.

"None other," she said. "It's the oldest and most prestigious group for investigating ghost sightings, hauntings, or spirit contacts."

"There really is a whole world out there of people devoted to this stuff, isn't there?"

"It's important stuff. People want to contact loved ones after they're gone. They want to know what really happens in death."

He felt like he was sinking into the couch, so he shifted forward and placed more weight to his elbow by leaning on the armrest. He could sense time becoming an issue—she had school, and he must get to work. But he had so much more he needed to understand, and even if this girl didn't have any answers, it was a relief just having someone to talk with about the unknown.

"So what does a group like yours suggest we do about Annabel?"

"We've been trying to capture evidence of her presence ever since we started hearing stories of her haunting the hospital." The girl's eyes widened as if she had just remembered something. "That was just eleven months ago. Before they finished the new wing, there were a few reported encounters with her—strange sounds, rapping, things moving. And they were all from patients in hospice care or in critical condition in the ER. I think they only sensed her because they were near death."

"I'm hoping that's not why I saw her."

A sudden rapid clacking sound startled him. To his left, a gangly fellow in a dark blazer pulled his rolling suitcase across the tile floor. The hotel was waking up.

"And you think she specifically targeted me?" he asked, trying to mask his growing unease.

"There are many others she could have reached out to but didn't."

"But what would she want with me?"

She shrugged, seemingly out of answers.

"Well, let's break it down like a simple formula," Jason said. He still wanted to believe that logic ruled the world. "Let's say she really does exist as some type of ghost. Her husband murdered her on Halloween last year, and the anniversary of her death is this Halloween—only three days away. He caught her in bed with their neighbor and killed them both. That's why she's traumatized. She actually died in the hospital, so that's why she's trapped there in some heightened emotional state. At the exact moment of her death, her mind and soul were tormented—far more disturbed than the average person at death. And now I'm here working late by myself, in the same room she died in, near the anniversary of her death. And suddenly she's trying to contact me."

He clapped his hands, drawing a glance from a passerby. "So that's it! She's just asking for help! She needs us to help her soul escape this trapped state that she's been in since her death."

"It may not be that simple," Rachel said.

"Why? How would we go about freeing a trapped soul? How can we save her?"

"If that's what this is, we would need a special séance." She looked almost fearful.

"Like what? An exorcism?"

"No, that's only for when a person is possessed by a demon. The Catholic Church has a special division of priests that investigate and perform exorcisms across the globe. In recent years, the number of possessions worldwide has increased, and with it the need for exorcisms. Every year, hundreds of priests attend an annual exorcism conference at the Regina Apostolorum in Rome. But this isn't a demon; it's the ghost of someone who once lived. And we'll need to conduct a rare type of séance to have any chance of reaching her—of helping her."

"*How* rare?"

"Very. I haven't read about any like it in years."

"Well, how do we do it? What do we need?"

The trace of panic reappeared on her face. "I need to think about it," she finally said. "It may not be possible." She stood up as if suddenly upset. "I'll get back to you when I know more."

"Well, when might we do it? On the anniversary of her murder—on Halloween?"

"No," she snapped with uncharacteristic aggression. She paused, then added, "Bad things happen on Halloween."

"Well, I gave you my cell number. I'll be either at the hospital or here. Please don't take too long to get back to me. I'm not sure when she might try to contact me again."

"I'll call you later today. Don't do anything without me, okay?"

"All right. Thank you."

She gave him a concerned look, and he got the feeling she was keeping something from him. As if sensing his perception, she forced a smile before turning to leave for school. But it was already too late. In that brief worried glance, he had felt a portent of coming danger.

Twenty minutes later, he was driving to the hospital for another day of work. But the job was the last thing on his mind. All that he had learned from the accounting staff at the hospital, all that he had read about the spirit world in the ghost book, and all that Rachel had said rushed and tumbled in his swirling thoughts. And against that ghostly backdrop, he saw in his mind's eye Annabel, whispering behind him, "Lies … lies … lies …"

28

"What is fire?"

The chemistry teacher's booming deep baritone added gravitas to every sentence he spoke to the class.

"Well, I ask again, what is fire, really?" Mr. Becraft said.

A kid somewhere behind Rachel said, "It's the burning of wood and other stuff."

Mr. Becraft pointed at a sign hanging above the whiteboard, which read, "Even fools are thought wise if they keep silent." The biblical proverb had become a de facto motto in his classroom, and a warning for students to think before they blurt.

"Fire," Mr. Becraft said, "is the rapid oxidation of a fuel source in the exothermic process of combustion." He stepped to the side of his tall lab desk, which sat like a toppled monolith between the periodic table and the rest of the classroom. "Combustion converts oxygen into carbon dioxide and water vapor, releasing energy because weak double-bonded molecules are being converted into more strongly bonded molecules. This released energy creates heat, which ignites more fuel. As long as a fire has fuel and oxygen, it will continue to burn. And in an uncontrolled environment, it will spread and grow."

He reached over the chemistry lab table and turned the stopcock on a Bunsen burner. A soft hiss issued from the opening. He then took the flint lighter from the table and sparked the gas. A deep blue flame popped up.

"Fuel and oxygen," Mr. Becraft said. "If I turn off the gas and starve it of fuel, the flame will die. If I put a container around it that was sealed air-tight, the fire would eventually use up all the oxygen and die even if I kept the gas flowing. If I throw water on it, it will take away the heat being generated from converting weaker-bonded to stronger-bonded molecules, thus preventing new ignition of unused fuel and ending the combustion process—and it would die."

He brought his face closer to the flame and gazed at it with a look of wonder, as if discovering his passion for science fresh for the first time. And at this moment, Rachel sensed in him a thought that went beyond a basic love and understanding of chemistry. She sensed his mind imagining the reaction of fuel and heat with oxygen, the thermodynamics of combustion at the level of elements on the periodic table, the bonding structure of elements, and how they changed within the chemical reactions occurring in fire.

Then his mind turned back to the classroom—as did *her* mind.

"So," Mr. Becraft said, turning off the gas and killing the flame, "go to your stations with your lab partners and work through the experiment on the handout."

Everyone got up, and the activity shifted to the twelve lab tables occupying the other half of the room.

Shelley was the only other person from the Ghost Hunting Club in the class, and Rachel briefly considered telling her about the telepathic episode she had just experienced reading Mr. Becraft's mind. But since it had nothing to do with Annabel, she decided against it.

"Ready to do this?" Shelley asked as they walked together to their lab table after grabbing white coats and protective goggles from the wall.

"I thought we're not supposed to play with fire," Rachel said, feigning a smile.

"Looks like today's the exception."

They sat at their lab station and began working through the handout instructions. They lit the Bunsen burner, then used tongs to hold various items over the flame and note the color the different elements produced. And for a while, Rachel lost herself in the fun of performing these experiments with her friend. But as time passed and Shelley readied the next item to test, Rachel felt herself drawn to the flame. At first, she saw it the way Mr. Becraft had seen it: with a scientific understanding of the chemical reaction's effect on the bonds holding chemical elements together. Then she could almost feel the cosmic energy of the fire, as if it was something she could make a connection with, as if it might somehow be controlled by a telekinetic alteration of the energy produced in the rapid oxidation of the fuel. She became entranced by the sudden idea that she could form a physical barrier of psychic energy between the flame and its fuel for a brief moment, thereby interrupting the reaction and killing the fire. She gazed into the flame, sensed where it came to life against the flowing gas, envisioned a barrier of energy between flame and gas. Then, to focus her mind and direct the energy of her thoughts, she tapped her fingertips together.

And the flame went out.

She froze, staring at the Bunsen burner and the invisible gas still whispering from the nozzle. Even though she had felt she could do it, she still couldn't believe that it had happened.

"Did you really just do that?"

Rachel turned off the gas and looked up to see Shelley staring at her.

"I think I did."

"How?"

"I can't explain it." This was one of her worst fears: that her gifts would reveal themselves as she grew stronger, her friends would see her as a freak, and she would be alone again.

Shelley leaned in closer. "You did it with your mind?"

"Yes."

Shelley glanced around and then turned back to her. "Can you do it again?"

"I don't know. Do you think I should try?"

"You *have* to try. I don't think I'll believe what I saw unless I see it again." She turned on the gas, reached out with the flint lighter, and sparked a new flame.

Rachel took a moment to calm her racing heart. She closed her eyes and took deep, slow breaths. Imagining the fire, she tried to sense the energy from the flame. And there in the darkness of her own making, she found the chemical changes taking place through combustion. Once again she touched the edge of the reaction with a concentrated force of her own. Then, holding this force as she had before, she opened her eyes and pushed it forward.

And in that instant, every flame in the room went out.

"Hey!" a student exclaimed from a few lab tables away.

"What the …?"

"Mr. Becraft …"

"Holy crap," Shelley whispered.

"Sh-h-h!" Rachel hissed, alarmed at how much stronger her force had been than the small action she intended.

"What is it?" Mr. Becraft said, looking up from a book. "What happened?"

"The fires went out," a student answered.

"Is the gas still on?" he asked.

"Yes."

"Then everyone, turn off your gas, wait sixty seconds, then turn the gas back on and relight the jet," Mr. Becraft said, returning to his book.

As the other students returned to their experiments, Rachel and Shelley just stared at each other.

Finally, Shelley left the other side of the table and sat on the stool beside Rachel. Leaning in close, she whispered, "How was that possible?"

"Not a clue," Rachel replied.

"That's bull. You know *something*. You have to tell me."

"Look," Rachel said under her breath. "Sometimes I can feel things in my mind that others can't. You know this. But lately it's been getting stronger. And it's not just the *feelings* anymore. I can affect things, too. I mean, I've never actually affected anything before now, but I've been feeling as if I could. This time, I felt the fire and I imagined pushing something between it and all the fuel and oxygen around it."

"Like an atmospheric vacuum?"

"Yeah, I guess it was something like that."

"What else can you do?"

"I don't know," Rachel said.

"You have to tell the others in the group."

"I don't want to talk about it with anyone. I don't even understand it." She was struggling to keep her emotions in check. The last thing she wanted to do was tell her friends about all the things she had been experiencing: the screams from Annabel, the flashes of thoughts from others, the automatic writing that had come to her from God knew where, which ended up being part of the license plate to a guy's rental car. It was all too much. She just wanted to have a fun, normal life. She just wanted to enjoy her youth. She just wanted a little more time before this thing she felt growing inside her came out and changed her life forever.

"You have to tell the others," Shelley repeated.

"I can't." She felt tears welling in her eyes.

"You have to. Whatever this is, you can't face it alone."

Rachel felt as if a cold bucket of water had just been thrown on her. In a flash, her entire perspective had changed. Shelley was saying that the others in the group needed to hear what she was experiencing—not just because they might have a right to know, but mainly because they would want to stand with her in her struggles. Kids were quick to joke and laugh at others, and slow to empathize with unconventional struggles. But Shelley's words made her realize that maybe, finally, she needed to trust her friends with her deepest, darkest secrets.

She just needed a little more time before taking the leap.

They both turned back to the handout before anyone noticed that they weren't doing the assignment. But it was hard for Rachel to focus on the elementary chemistry experiment after what she had just experienced. And she sensed that it was hard for Shelley to focus, too.

29

Jessica put her fork in the center of her plate after taking her last bite of lasagna. She wiped the corners of her mouth with the cloth napkin and laid it next to her plate. "That was delicious, Mom. Best meal I've had this week."

"Don't sass me," her mother said from across the small kitchen table.

"Oh, I'm not. You make a real mean lasagna. You sure you're not part Italian?"

"I'll show you *mean* if you keep wising off at me."

Jessica grinned. "May I be excused?"

Her mom turned her head away just enough so she could look sideways at her with a dramatic glare. "I haven't heard about your day, yet."

"Nothing to hear."

"Uh-huh."

But her mom's expression didn't change. Jessica knew a lot of other kids who could get their moms to believe all manner of fibs and half-truths, even out-and-out lies. Those moms were a little too trusting or else just too tired to wangle the truth out of their kids. But Jessica's mom was the youngest of all her friends' moms, which might have been the reason she was neither gullible nor tired. Her parents had been high school sweethearts. They had gotten pregnant with her their senior year and married the summer after graduation. It messed up any college plans they might have had, but Jessica somehow didn't really see either of them as being the college sort, anyway. But that was a long time ago. At one point, she had wondered if maybe she was responsible for the demise of any big youthful dreams her parents had once entertained, but she quickly realized that none of it was her fault. They were the ones who got careless when doing the hanky-panky. All she had done was get born.

"I told you everyone's coming over later, right?" Jessica asked.

"Who's 'everyone'? Shelley and Tommy and Rachel?"

"And Scott and Aaron."

"Another ghost club meeting? Again?"

"Would you rather us go out in a field somewhere and experiment with drugs and stuff?"

Her mom put her hands up. "Hanging out here is fine. Just don't open any portals to demon worlds without giving me a heads-up, okay? It's hard enough keeping the basement clean as it is."

Jessica smiled. "Heard from Dad?"

Her mom nodded. "He called earlier. Just got to Pennsylvania. Heading to Florida after. Thinks he'll be back middle of next week. He's sorry he's gonna miss Halloween."

"That's okay," Jessica said quietly. "Does he think he'll be back for a while when he returns?"

"He thinks at least a week," her mom said. "Maybe even two weeks."

"Cool," she said. There was so much more she wanted to say, but it wouldn't do any good. Her dad was doing the best he could. She just wished the three of them could spend more time together, especially since this would be her last year at home before moving away to college.

"When are people coming over?" her mom asked.

"Couple hours. I was going to work on the Chevy for a bit, first."

"Your dad will like that. Can you wash the dishes before you start wrenching? I'm going to do some laundry downstairs before your friends get here."

"Please don't leave any underwear lying around," Jessica joked, as they got up from the table.

She took the dishes to the sink, and after ten minutes of scrubbing and rinsing and drying and putting away, she was ready to begin what was always the best part of her day. Rushing to her bedroom, she changed into her old ripped jeans and gray T-shirt. Then she raced out the back door and went to the freestanding garage at the end of their long side driveway.

"Hey, beautiful," she said as she entered the garage through the side door and flipped on the lights. A tremor of excitement shot through her every time she stepped into this little cocoon and beheld the half-restored baby-blue 1957 Chevy Bel Air. The car had no tires and sat on four tripod jack stands.

To Jessica and her dad, it was one of the most beautiful American cars ever made, and it had been their pet project for much of the past summer and fall—when her dad was home, anyway. As a long-haul driver for a Minneapolis-based trucking company, he spent half of every year on the road. And Jessica always tried to do a little work on the car every day he was gone, so she could surprise him when he got home.

She walked around the Bel Air, surveying the progress and envisioning the stunning potential of the finished car. "You are going to turn heads all over town," she said.

Touching one of the round headlight casings, she wondered what part she should work on next. She decided it would be a good time to start doing a coat of undercoating near the left side panel she had welded to the body mount yesterday.

The garage was rather a mess. She hadn't bothered to clean up her tools yesterday, so the work space around and under the Chevy was cluttered with thick cords from the droplights, random bits of rust from the body work, wrenches, bolts, a side panel, cutting tools, buckets, rags, and a few specialized toolboxes.

She walked to the other side of the Bel Air, picked up the bucket of undercoating, set it on the floor by the left side, and pushed away a toolbox so she had room to work. Then she lay down on her back on the creeper and rolled under the car. She reached above her head and moved the orange droplight. Its cord wound across the floor, to the wall outlet near the garage door. She had to whip the cord to get it away from the little wheels on the creeper. Then she switched on the droplight and set it on the floor beside her to illuminate the Chevy's undercarriage.

Putting on the protective eyeglasses she had clipped to her shirt, she was ready to begin. She removed the brush from its case and began applying the undercoating to the area near the siding she had attached yesterday. With an hour before her friends arrived, she had enough time to coat the area. Then she could spend the rest of this week's garage sessions doing rust work on the body, give the panels a fresh coat of baby-blue paint this weekend, and then clean up the garage before her dad came home next week.

A low whistle came from wind sweeping over the roof outside.

As she began working, she smiled at the thought of how impressed her dad would be once he saw how much she had done while he was on the road.

The wind picked up, brushing tree branches against the outside of the garage. The sudden sound rattled her, and she stopped to listen more closely. The walls of the garage seemed to buckle. The roof moaned as if some outside force were trying to push it down. Then the garage door rattled.

She listened with growing concern under the Chevy. She had spent more hours in this garage over the years than she could count, but she had never heard the wind make such haunting sounds.

A loud crash came from the far corner. Startled, she jerked upward and whacked her forehead on the rear axle. It smarted. Then another crash came from another corner—this time, the recognizable clatter of steel tools clanging across the concrete floor. Trying to blink away the pain, she didn't even look in the direction of the noise.

Just then, a loud, creaking sound came from all around her. At first, she thought the entire garage was collapsing, but then she saw the Chevy start sliding to her left. Glancing sideways, she saw to her horror that the tripod jack stands were bending under the weight of the car and were starting to fold over.

"Oh, God!" she gasped, grabbing the axle to sling herself and the creeper out from under the Chevy. But before she could pull sideways, the car fell down on top of her.

The wind continued to batter the garage with what sounded like hurricane-force winds. A hanging rack came loose from the wall and toppled onto the worktable where she had been cannibalizing a spare carburetor for parts. A small cardboard box of drywall nails spilled out by a tangle of cords.

The chaotic sounds exploded all around Jessica, but she couldn't see anything. She felt the undercarriage of the Chevy pinning her down, but it hadn't crushed her—not yet, anyway. It was pushing down on her hard enough that she could take only shallow breaths, and her head was pressed sideways against the creeper with no room to move. Willing her eyes open, she saw the side door to the garage through the narrow space between the Chevy's undercarriage and the concrete floor.

She could move her arms, but that was it. She caught sight of one of the jack stands, which had folded completely over on itself, but its base was still strong enough to hold the car nearly a foot off the ground. The other three jack stands must have collapsed down to their bases, too. Thank God the bases had held, or she would be dead.

She could inhale only about half a lungful, but it was enough for a surprisingly loud cry for help. She was competing with the gale outside, so it would be hard for her mom to hear her from this small detached garage. And she feared that her mom might still be doing laundry in the basement, where it would be impossible to hear her cries for help.

She could feel the car pressing her harder, and she shuddered at the thought that the jacks were collapsing farther. If the Chevy was continuing to push closer to the ground, then she might have only minutes to live.

She fought again to slide out from under the car. But the various parts of the Bel Air's undercarriage had her bracketed on all sides. Even though she was still on the creeper, its little wheels couldn't even roll her to safety without some part of her head or body getting lodged against the left tailpipe or spring mount or rear cross member or some other part of the metallic briar patch protruding from the undercarriage. She tried one more time and yelped with pain as something squeezed her knee and something else caught her hip and something else pinched her chest.

If she could just slide off the creeper, she might have enough space to slip out. She managed to wriggle enough to slide the creeper halfway down so that her back was on the concrete. As she did this, she heard more moaning from the crushed jack stand closest to her head. Desperately she tried to slide out from under the car, but she couldn't get her waist past the nearest side and cross members of the chassis. Then the moaning intensified, and one of the jack stands must have bucketed further, for the

Chevy dropped another few inches, this time pinning her directly against the concrete. She whimpered in pain, helpless against the ton and a half of car that was slowly squashing her. Jessica screamed again, but there was no help. Tears filled her eyes as she was forced to confront the idea that this was actually going to kill her, that her life was about to be so unfairly cut short, and that her mom would be the one to eventually come out to this work garage and would find her crushed and lifeless body pinned under the car.

Her left hand touched a cord and closed around it as if it were a lifeline. She could crane her neck enough to see the left-rear wheel. Doing so, she scraped her forehead on the metal hook holding up the left tailpipe. The protruding hook cut her forehead, but she fought through the pain long enough to turn her head all the way across so she could look left and up over her head.

Just then the Chevy shifted again and dropped another inch, pushing into her chest and abdomen. She screamed with all her strength, panicking at the inability to take a full breath. So this was the numbing pressure of being crushed to death. Before she died, the Chevy's hard undercarriage would break her legs and chest cavity, cause internal bleeding, and rupture organs. The building pressure hurt more with each passing second, and she soon went from praying she might somehow live to wishing she would just die.

She screamed again and again as hysteria overcame her. She closed her eyes and cursed the world, then wailed again, knowing that her cries were trapped inside the small, hard confines of the garage, where no one could hear them. Then, gradually, her weakness calmed, her screaming stopped, and her breath slowed. Death was coming, and she would greet it the way that only the long-dying can: with acceptance and even—at the very end—gratitude.

She opened her eyes, expecting to see her first glimpse of heaven or whatever awaited her on the other side. But looking over her head, she saw something else: the orange droplight cord that snaked across the room to the wall outlet near the garage door. And ten feet away, entwined in a loop of the cord, was her dad's spare scissor jack.

Hope sparked in her. This one little long shot set off a vivid dream of escape. It was now so potent in her imagination that achieving the nearly impossible became her obsession.

Tightening her grip on the cord, she gave it a cautious tug. The tangle of electrical cable drew closer to her, dragging the scissor jack with it. Ignoring the pain from the rest of her body, she reached over her head and pulled again. The jack drew closer, but this time it tipped sideways and threatened to fall off the pile of cable. And the jack's crank, also caught in the tangle, slid off and clanked to the concrete between her and the jack. She gasped at the fragility of her new dream of salvation. Because the crank had landed in front of the tangle—which still held the jack—she could get both if she was lucky. And to have any chance at surviving, she needed both. More carefully now, she pulled again, then again, each time inching the jack a little closer to her. Eight feet ... careful ... seven ... breathe ... six ... pain ... five ... focus ... four ... breathe again ... three ... hope ... two ... dream ... one ... got it! She almost cried with joy as her fingers curled around the near edge of the jack's base. She pulled it and the crank under the car and went to work.

Still reaching over her head with both hands, she tipped the jack upright and slid it under the left rail of the chassis. Then she spun the jack's threaded rod with her fingers until the top reached almost to the Chevy's chassis. She then slid the crank arm into the end hole on the threaded rod.

With both hands stretched out over her head, toward the left-rear wheel, she managed to grasp the end of the crank and hold it in place with her left hand. Then her right hand could do the cranking.

It took some doing, and she prayed the remaining jack stands would hold until she could create enough space to get out. The tight space meant she could leverage the crank arm up only about ninety degrees for a partial rotation; then she must pull the crank from the hole, turn it over, reinsert it, and give another twist.

It was hard to get much force on it while pinned on her back. But this was the only escape she could see, and she would give it everything she had left. So she pulled the crank arm down with the little room she had. It was hard to move, but not impossible. And as the scissor arms pulled infinitesimally closer together, she felt the pressure on her chest ease up a little. But just as the pressure on her lessened, a deep moan came from the jack stand farthest from her, on the front right. So along with her first glimmer of real hope, she had also been given a warning that something was still trying to kill her. The violent wind that had marked the arrival of this terror no longer seemed like some natural meteorological effect. No, this was something else, something dark and ancient and evil, tied to the realms of death that their ghost-hunting group had been naively daring to show its face. Well, here it was, tonight, in this garage, trying to squash her under a three-thousand-pound car.

She must be delirious. Were these wild thoughts of terror visited on all those whose fate it was to die slowly? She had to ignore the groaning of the weakening tripod stands and focus on the one thing she could control. She pulled the crank arm out, repositioned it in the threaded rod, and pulled down again. The Chevy eased off her some more while the sounds of metal fatigue grew more unsettling. She took a breath, extended her arm, and repeated the step. Then she did it again. And again. With each increment, the pressure on her body lessened, while her pain increased as the numbness left. And each time, the metal around her creaked as if everything was going to buckle inward and smash her like a pumpkin on a train track.

Her tiny increments of progress with the jack had accumulated enough to relieve the worst of the pressure on her chest and ribs. Shrugging her shoulders and wiggling her hips, she tried to move. And for the first time in a nightmarish eternity, she slid over an inch. Then another inch. She kept skirting and wiggling and sliding until her lower half was sticking out from under the car. Another minute of shimmying and wriggling, and she was out.

Hysteria returned the moment she was out of danger. Her skin tingled, her head was light and dizzy, and her hands shook. It all had been a bad dream, a blurred experience of terror that had consumed her until she escaped and reclaimed the life and future that had so nearly been stolen away. Her eyes fixed on the Bel Air with the innocent-looking baby-blue paint. Outside, the wind picked up again. And once again the dark thought crept back into her mind that all this was the work of some menacing force they had awoken with their attempts to contact the dead.

"Annabel?" she whispered. "Was this you?"

The garage rattled and shook, and the wind whispered back some indecipherable reply that made her feel cold and alone and very lucky to have escaped death. Just then the car crashed down onto the concrete. Jessica shrieked, stared at it for a second, then put her face in her hands and sobbed.

30

"I can't believe they all died," Dr. Graves said.

"I can't believe they all once lived," Madam Bovell said.

He looked at her.

"Seriously," she said. "Look how big it is. It's almost unbelievable that there was a time when they lived on the Earth."

"Honestly," Dr. Graves said, "it's a miracle there is any life left on this planet."

They stood together in the center of Chicago's O'Hare International Airport, looking up at the fossil skeleton of a brachiosaurus towering above the flow of travelers.

"My knowledge of prehistory is terrible. I can't remember if humans were ever alive at the same time as dinosaurs."

"That *is* bad," Dr. Graves said. "There was a big gap between them and us. Humans didn't appear on Earth until sixty-odd millions of years after the dinosaurs went extinct. I don't remember the actual number."

"Sixty million years?"

"Something like that."

"Can you imagine?" she said. "So much time." She pointed at the giant fossil. "They were here and then they weren't. Then sixty million years go by. And then, just like that, there were humans on Earth."

"Darwin wouldn't say it was *just like that,*" he replied.

"Well, of course. But to think that we came from somewhere, *anywhere,* is incredible. Our being here at all is nothing less than a miracle."

"The miracle of life," he said. And upon saying it, he felt light-headed, as if some unseen entity had just cast a spell on him.

"Are you okay?" Madam Bovell asked.

"I think I've been standing for too long. Do you mind if we sit down somewhere?"

They walked to a seating area maybe fifty feet from the fossil. Sitting down, he took slow, relaxed breaths while staring at his cane's silver wolf handle.

"You're not having a stroke, are you?"

"I'm fine. I just need to rest."

"Our flight doesn't board for another few hours," Madam Bovell said. "We can stay here and rest."

"Sounds good," he said, slouching back in the chair so that it supported his head. "I'm just going to close my eyes for a little bit."

He heard her mumble something in response. His eyelids had fallen like a theater curtain lowered on a stage, and he was already drifting into another world buried deep within his mind. Theater curtains. A stage. He remembered these things from a life long past. He was standing on the stage behind the curtain, waiting for this barrier between himself and his audience to be removed. And when it finally rose, he was bathed in spotlights and applause. He stepped forward with his cane and waved his black top hat at the crowd. Then he sidestepped to his beautiful assistant, and she snugged handcuffs over his wrists as a large glass box was lowered from above the stage. But as he looked out into the crowd, he was startled to see his son, David, sitting in the audience with a stony expression—ten years before he was even to be born. Then came a blinding flash, and he was on a different stage seven years later, in a black robe, walking toward an older man who stood at a microphone, holding out a leather diploma case symbolizing his doctorate in psychology. But as Graves looked out into the crowd, he again saw David sitting with a dead expression. Another blinding flash, and he was in a dark room, sitting around a large round table as a famous medium performed a séance for a group of wealthy patrons. He had just seen how she was cheating them. His background as a professional magician and psychology professor gave him all the necessary tools to unmask charlatans preying on the vulnerable by "contacting" the spirits of deceased loved ones. But as he stood up from the table to point out the slight-of-hand he had witnessed, he saw David standing in the shadows behind the young Madam Bovell. Another blinding flash, and he was in a bright room next to a large hospital bed. His legs weakened when he saw David lying in it, asleep to the hum and whir of the monitors. He stared silently at his son, unable to believe that such an innocent, happy little boy could be given such a cruel fate. He fell to his knees and wept, with his head pressing against the hard side rails of the bed. Looking up briefly, he saw a second David standing in the doorway, staring at him with the same stony expression. Dr. Graves lowered his head and banged it against the metal rails once, twice, and again, until there was a flash. The fourth time, his head hit the metal armrest of his chair in the airport. He jolted upright with open, watery eyes and saw more travelers walking underneath the dinosaur fossil.

"Hey. Wow. You okay?"

He turned to see Madam Bovell staring at him with concern. Then he covered his eyes and shook his head to bring his focus back to the present. Without looking, he reached out and grabbed her wrist. "How long was I asleep? Are we going to be late for our flight?"

"No, we're fine. You were only out for about twenty minutes. You okay?"

He rubbed his head, still trying to shake off the memory of the dream. "How long until our flight?"

"We board in about an hour."

"Let's go to our gate. I can't sleep anymore, and I don't want to stay here."

They got up and walked down the wide concourse in the direction of their departure gate. He walked tall with his cane, wheeling his luggage behind him through the flow of people. He tried to appear strong and confident so Madam Bovell wouldn't worry about him. But with every step he took, he had to force his gaze to stay on the floor, for fear that if he looked up, he might catch a glimpse of David, staring at him from somewhere in the crowd.

31

Jason parked on the quiet neighborhood street and turned off the headlights. He checked the address on the text message. The driveway was full of cars. He got out and followed the walkway to the long front porch decorated with glowing jack-o'-lanterns and cobwebs with giant spiders and ghoulish faces lurking in the shadows.

He rang the doorbell and stood waiting, surrounded by the terrors of his childhood.

The door opened, and a pleasant middle-aged woman in a bushy orange sweater beamed at him.

"Is Rachel here?" he asked awkwardly. "She gave me this address."

"She doesn't *live* here, but I think she *is* here. All the kids are downstairs. I'm Jessica's mom, Nancy. Who are you?" She extended a hand with long, glossy red nails.

"I'm Jason."

"How do you know the kids?"

She had asked the question nicely enough, but he couldn't miss the trace of suspicion in her eyes. After all, what kind of creepy guy wanted to hang out with high school kids ten years younger than he?

"Well," he said, deciding on an even mix of truth and lie. "I live in Chicago, but I'm in town doing some accounting review work at the hospital. Somehow, the kids heard I have some experience with paranormal investigations, so they asked me over to see their setup."

"What sort of experience?" she asked, appearing more intrigued than suspicious.

She seemed the "cool mom" type. His first clue probably should have been that she hosted the kids' ghost club meetings.

"I saw a ghost once," he said.

Her eyes lit up. "What did it look like?"

"Just what you'd imagine: translucent, but right there in front of me."

"Come on." She flashed him a skeptical look. "I don't believe it for one minute, but they will, so come on in. They're downstairs."

She waved him down the hallway and opened the last door on the left. "Try not to encourage them *too* much," she said. "I'm still hoping this is a phase they'll grow out of eventually."

"No one wants their babies to grow up to be ghost hunters—is that the idea?" he asked with a smile.

"Precisely."

As he started down the stairs, she closed the door behind him and went back to whatever mothers did while juveniles had ghost hunter sessions in their basements.

With each step down, the chatter grew louder. They hadn't seen him yet because of a shelf half full of boxes that stood between two support poles, mostly blocking the view. There were six high school kids: three boys and three girls. They were in the far corner of the basement, in the only part of this concrete cave with places to sit. Three of the ghost hunters sat on the ratty couch, one on a sagging recliner, one on a beanbag chair, and one on the large Persian rug. Equipment lay scattered all about. It looked hi-tech yet strangely old, as if it was equipment from the eighties.

"It just collapsed for no reason," said one of the girls to Rachel. Her voice was cracking. "I heard this violent wind outside, which rattled the garage. Then the car came down on me. I barely managed to get the jack that saved me. I'm *still* shaking!"

"Did you tell your mom?"

"No, I don't want her to know about it. It didn't just fall on its own. I think something pushed the Chevy down on me. And I think it was Annabel. Just like what happened to Shelley in the pond. And I have no clue how to explain that to my mom."

"I didn't tell my parents about the chickens," said a boy with the broad shoulders of a wrestler or a linebacker. "They found me, so they know I was attacked, but I didn't tell them how bad it really was in the poultry house. Those chickens would have killed me if I hadn't gotten out of there."

"And you think *that* was Annabel, too?" asked a tall boy.

"It sounds the same as what they described. A sudden, violent wind right before everything went bad. After that, the chickens turned into wild little psycho killers. It was as if something evil had arrived."

Jason had been listening long enough that it now felt uncomfortably like eavesdropping. "Hello?" he announced, leaving the stairs. "Rachel?" He walked around the shelves and into the open room.

"Jason!" Rachel said. "Welcome! We've been talking about Annabel. Come over and meet everyone."

"Hi," he said, waving uncomfortably. This was already starting to feel like a mistake. He felt awkward after seeing just how much younger than he everyone was. He certainly didn't remember looking so young when he was in high school.

"I told everyone in the group what you told me, so they're all up to speed. Now we just need to decide what to do next. But first let me introduce you to everyone." She started pointing at different people. "This is Shelley—you know her mom, Molly, from the hospital. This is Jessica—it's her house. This is Tommy. This is Aaron. And this is Scott. Everyone, this is Jason."

"Hi," Shelley said. Jason could see Molly in her, especially the pronounced chin and sharp brown eyes.

"Greetings," Aaron said. He sounded a little nerdy, though his slender height would have caught the imagination of any basketball coach.

"Yo," Tommy said in a detached tone, as if waiting to reveal more of himself until he had taken the measure of this newcomer. His face looked all scratched up, which gave his stare a certain intimidating aspect.

"Welcome," said Jessica, the only one to step forward and shake his hand. She had a strong grip.

"What's up," Scott said, glancing at him briefly, almost suspiciously, before turning his blond head to look back at Rachel.

"Hello, everyone," he said. "So you guys have been investigating Annabel's ghost for a while now? Any idea what we're supposed to do?"

"We were hoping you could tell us," Jessica said. "You're the one that talked to Annabel."

"I didn't talk to her. I saw her, and she showed me a farmhouse that I assume was her home on the night of the killings. And she kept repeating the word, 'Lies.'"

"But don't you have some idea of what we're supposed to do next? She was obviously trying to tell you something."

"No idea," he said. "Isn't this what you guys do?"

"We try to capture evidence that a ghost is present," Aaron said. "We look for heat readings, EVP recordings, infrared activity. We're looking for scientific data proving the presence of paranormal activity."

"But what about the *why*?"

"The what?"

"The *why*," he repeated. "The thing that explains why she's still here after her death. Don't you try to communicate with her?"

"We ask questions when we're recording, sure. But it's mostly just to get a response—any kind of response. We never get actual *answers*."

"You never try spirit communications?" Jason asked, shocked.

"You mean like a séance?" Jessica asked. "We can't do that."

"Why not?" Jason asked.

"We can't just sit in a circle and start talking to ghosts," Scott said. "You need to have a medium to lead a séance."

Shelley turned to Rachel. "Tell them."

The room went silent as everyone turned to Rachel. And Jason saw in her face a blend of shame and fear.

"You have to tell them," Shelley pushed.

"I ... ah," Rachel started. "I can sometimes sense things."

"What do you mean?" Aaron and Jessica asked in unison.

"I can sense things from people. And sometimes I can hear or sense things from what I believe are spirits or ghosts."

"This is a joke, right," Aaron said.

"What are you saying?" Scott asked.

"I, um ..." She froze.

"She has gifts," Shelley said, jumping in. "They started about a year ago and have been gradually getting stronger. She has psychic abilities. Telepathic abilities. She can even do some telekinesis."

"What are you talking about?" Tommy asked.

Rachel looked as if she might cry. Her eyes got red, and her chest heaved as if she were having a panic attack.

"Seriously, what are you talking about?" Aaron said.

"She can do things," Shelley continued. "I saw her do something in chemistry class today that was impossible. She's been keeping it secret because it scares her and because she's worried we won't understand it."

"You're worried about *that*?" Scott asked.

"Yes," Rachel said, choking back tears.

"Why?"

"Because *I* don't understand it! I don't know what's happening to me! I don't know why it's happening, and I don't know what it means."

She stepped back from the others, leaving the circle, and sitting in the far sofa chair. She pulled her knees in close to her chest, hugging her legs, and stared at her jeans. She looked like a hurt animal.

Everyone else was speechless.

Jason stepped forward, surveying the group. A week ago, he would never have believed any of this talk about Rachel's abilities. But in the past few days, he had read authentically documented accounts of Swedenborg, D. D. Home, Leonora Piper, Eusapia Palladino, and Helene Smith—all of whom had been observed in controlled settings by some of England's most renowned professors of physics and psychology and other developing sciences during the last half of the nineteenth century. Any one of those many stories had the power to make a skeptic believe in the efforts of ghosts and spirits to reach out to the living. He had read proclamations of belief by such respected minds as Sir Isaac Newton, Mark Twain, and Sir Arthur Conan Doyle. He had read of Thomas Edison's hope to develop a machine that could capture and record the voices of spirits. Jason was convinced that there had been a few legitimately gifted psychics and mediums in the past, who could indeed communicate with the dead. He thought back on Rachel somehow sensing what he had experienced in his Annabel sighting. And in that moment, he realized he completely believed that Rachel possessed all the gifts and abilities they claimed. And with this brave faith came an obligation to help the girl.

"I understand why you wouldn't want to tell people," Jason said, looking at Rachel. "They'd think you were crazy. Maybe you yourself were even a little concerned you were going crazy. And even if they did believe you, they would treat you differently, and probably not in a good way. At the very least, they would treat you like an outcast. And people might even fear you and what you can do, perhaps even responding with violence. Humans are genetically wired to reject those who are different from themselves. It's an ancient cultural survival technique going back to tribal societies, and mankind's history over the past few thousand years hasn't shown much evolution in that regard."

He could sense that everyone was at a low point, that Rachel was still struggling, that the group and their electronic ghost toys were not prepared to truly investigate the illusive *why* hidden behind Annabel's haunting activities. And if he was honest with himself, he was not at a good place in his own life to see this through. He barely knew Rachel and had only just met the others. He was not a leader. And Annabel had made a mistake in choosing him as her contact. He had his own problems, and he had a life he needed to get back to in Chicago.

He walked over and knelt beside her. "Look, Rachel, you're going to be okay. From what I've read about people with gifts like yours, it can be a great blessing. The world is much more accepting about it these days. It's because of the isolated culture we live in, with people watching more and more television or using devices on social media instead of actually spending time with other people. Everyone is lonelier now, emptier, more unfulfilled. Everyone is looking for answers, and when you get older, you'll have the option of using your gift to help people find those answers. And they'll love you for it."

"You're leaving," she said, sadness washing over her face.

He looked at her, realizing she had just read his mind. "I'm sorry, but I have to go. I can't get involved in this—in whatever Annabel is doing. I thought I could, but I can't. And you shouldn't get involved, either. It will just hurt you."

"What if I don't have a choice?"

He took her hand. "I pray that you do."

Then he stood and looked at her one last time. "If you ever need someone to talk to, you can call me anytime. I don't want you to feel that I'm abandoning you. I just can't get any more involved in this, so close to when I'm leaving town. I hope you can understand this."

She nodded but then broke eye contact and stared back down at her knees.

He turned to the others. "I'm sorry," he said. "Good luck."

Then he walked back to the stairs, up the steps, and out of the house. The cold night hit him the moment he was on the porch. As he clumped down the porch steps, he could almost feel the jack-o'-lanterns leering at him with looks of anger and disappointment.

And with each step, he felt more ashamed.

32

It had been twenty minutes since Dr. Graves and Madam Bovell passed through Lawrence and drove into the Kansas night. According to the GPS, they had arrived in Stull, but nothing showed in their headlights except a small church set well back from the road. The landscape was hilly with dense woods, restricting what they could see. Just past the church, a single streetlamp revealed a dirt lane running left off the country road. A couple of houses fronted the dirt road, but otherwise there was no sign of life anywhere—no house lights or cars or any other activity. The area looked vacant and abandoned. Whatever town may have once existed here, it now seemed to have vanished.

Then, to their right and across the country road from the church, they saw a modest-size cemetery that rose up the side of a low hill. Bounded by a short chain-link fence, it certainly didn't look imposing or scary. A cemetery, a little church, and a couple of houses on an empty country road—nothing to hint that this was one of the seven gates to hell.

"This doesn't look like what I imagined," Madam Bovell said. "It's not creepy or gothic or anything. Just dark and empty. Tranquil, even."

"I was thinking the same thing. Just a quiet old cemetery on the Great Plains in America's heartland."

"Are we sure this is it?"

"GPS says it's Stull. I just thought there would be more of a town."

"Maybe everyone's in the cemetery," she said. "Maybe *this* gate to hell opened up and swallowed them all."

He pulled off the country road and parked in the shadow of the church, out of the dim glow of the streetlamp. He tried to see the cemetery in the rearview mirror, but now the streetlamp seemed weaker and no longer reached into the darkness across the highway.

He then looked at the church.

"Legend has it," he said, "that a witch was hanged from a tree in the cemetery. Later, the townspeople built a stone church, right there amid the graves, to ward off her evil spirit. That was in 1867. About thirty or forty years later, lightning struck and burned the church down except for the stone walls. The ruins were abandoned, and a new church was built outside the cemetery in the early 1900s. *This* church." He gestured to the building. "The ruins of a burned, abandoned church in a graveyard became the perfect place for calling up the devil. He is said to appear every year on Halloween. The walls of the church ruins are said to bleed when he visits."

"Halloween's only three days away," Madam Bovell said. "Let's hope the devil doesn't come early this year."

Dr. Graves grunted and opened his door.

They walked across the gravel parking lot, toward the dirt road. "No cars anywhere," she said. "Doesn't anyone use this road?"

"Interstate Seventy is just a mile away and runs almost parallel to this road. We might not see another car all night."

"Maybe Kansans are smart enough to stay away from places like this."

"Apparently, University of Kansas students have been trespassing into this cemetery in droves since the mid-seventies. Quests for demonic encounters became all the rage after *The Exorcist* became a huge best seller in 'seventy-three and a blockbuster film a year later. And because this quiet hamlet had old legends tied to witchcraft and Satan, high school and college students were bound to get wind of it. They got high. Threw beer bottles at the stone walls of the ruins to see whether it was true that glass wouldn't break against it. They knocked over tombstones. Camped out all night. Did God knows what else."

"Sounds horrible."

"Yes, it does. But the fad ran its course. Interest in demonology isn't what it was back then. And as you said, we're still days from Halloween, so if we're lucky, we're the only living souls in the cemetery tonight."

They crossed the road and arrived at the waist-high chain-link fence. The cemetery seemed to be shaped like a rectangle, and they were on one of the long sides. He didn't know for sure, though, because the ground sloped up and away from the road and vanished in the thicket of trees and shrubbery that surrounded the rising wave of tombstones.

Madam Bovell passed her flashlight across the fence. "I know you're not expecting me to climb over this."

"It's only three feet high," Dr. Graves said.

"It's not going to happen. Find a better way for me to get in there. I'm not some college kid."

"All right, let's look for an entrance."

They walked along the front of the cemetery, following the fence until they found a gate. He shined his flashlight on the big yellow padlock holding the swivel bar in place on both sides of the fence.

"This is ridiculous," she said. "What's the point of putting a lock on something that most people can just jump over?"

"To make sure it's clear to people that they're trespassing," he replied.

"Ridiculous," she repeated. "Well, I can't imagine this lock will be a problem for you, Mr. Houdini."

"I don't practice anymore," he said.

"Since when does a natural magician need practice? I'm sure you've conquered much more difficult tricks than this onstage."

"I don't have my kit."

"Will this work?" She pulled a bobby pin out of her hair.

"A bit old fashioned, don't you think? It will help, though. I don't suppose you've got a nail file you can pull from that hat, too."

She reached into her pocket, pulled out a penny purse, opened it, and took out a short gray nail file. "Presto!"

"Impressive," he said, taking it. "You do realize this is much more illegal than just trespassing? This makes it breaking and entering …"

"Don't tell me you've never broken into a cemetery before," she chided. "A man with your reputation … didn't the *New Yorker* once call you 'the Indiana Jones of paranormal research'?"

"It was *National Geographic,*" he said.

"She wants us to go in there," Madam Bovell said.

"Who?"

"The gray woman."

The air was cold. His eyes wandered above the low fence and across the silent tombstones dotting the hillside. All of it was waiting for them in the shadow of a dark cloud sliding across the nearly full moon.

He knelt and stuck the nail file into the cold lock, pushed down on the chamber slide, and used the bobby pin to jimmy the hidden tumblers off the inside of the lock. A click announced his success, and the lock popped open. The gate swung out and away from them as if some unseen entity were now inviting them inside the graveyard.

"Houdini would be proud," she whispered.

He stepped back, bowed, and gestured for her to enter. "Ladies first."

"Letting me enter the grounds of Lucifer before you—such a gentleman!"

She entered the cemetery and moved slowly between the rows of headstones. He followed. Their shoes brushed the wet blades of grass, making a faint hissing sound with each step. A copse of trees stood near the top of the hill. He surveyed each twisty branch in the moonlight and wondered where a witch might have been hung.

The wind picked up, pushing thousands of dead leaves between the tombstones and up the hill toward them. The few large branches creaked and moaned in the blustery wind. It felt as if the cemetery were coming alive around them.

"Where's the old church?" he whispered, continuing his slow climb up the slope.

"I don't know. Don't see it."

They reached the hilltop. Dr. Graves looked out at the land below him: the tombstones, the few buildings and houses that seemed to make up the entire town, and the moonlit trees and fields beyond the quiet hamlet.

"There is no evil here," he said. "This is not a gateway to hell. The devil has never been to this place."

"You sure?"

He looked at her and saw the heavy outline of wrinkles deepen on her face. And then and there he realized she was a little disappointed at the idea, that she actually wanted something unnatural in this place—even if it was the devil himself.

"You think people in this part of the country would live right next to a cemetery that was haunted—a place the devil visits regularly?"

"It doesn't look like the town's doing that well."

"Doesn't matter. A lot of these small towns aren't doing well. But some people still live here. And that's how I know it's not evil."

"Well, evil or not, this place must hold the answers to my vision," she said.

"Then let's find them."

He turned on his flashlight and slid the beam of light across the ground. His light stopped on an open patch of grass without any graves. He held his light on the spot and saw that most of the leaves blowing up the hill were stopping right there, as if pushed or pulled by some unseen force.

"I think the old church fell down," he said.

"Or they tore it down," she added.

"Who's 'they'?"

"The townspeople."

He looked at her. "With pitchforks and holy water?"

"I would guess a backhoe," she said with a grin.

He smiled. "In any case, looks like it's gone."

"What's that?" Madam Bovell asked.

"What's what?"

"There," she said.

In her flashlight beam, he saw a tombstone that had been split in two by the roots of a massive pine tree. The trunk itself looked at least fifteen feet around, and the tree had to be one of the oldest and biggest trees in the area—perhaps even the state. And the split tombstone belonged to a married couple who had both died in 1879.

"Have you ever seen anything like that?" Madam Bovell whispered.

"Never in my life."

She stepped next to him and reached out to touch the tree. "It feels warm."

He touched it and felt only the ambient cold. "How warm?"

"Very. And I think it's getting warmer."

"You feeling all right?"

"There's a glow," she said.

"From the tree?"

"No, from over there. You don't see it?"

He followed her eyes to the grass opening beside the trees, near the new pile of leaves, where he figured the old church may have once stood.

"What is it?"

"You can't see it?" she asked without shifting her gaze from the direction. Then her face beamed and her eyes teared. "You can't see it."

"What?"

"I'm receiving something. A green outline, a glow, like an emerald-colored fire or light. Aurora lights."

"In the sky?"

"On the ground. A structure. An echo of the old church. There's a woman now standing in front of it. It's her. My God, it's her."

"From your vision?"

"Yes."

Graves saw nothing but empty shadows and shades of night. "You'd better not be conning me."

"She's walking away. She wants me to follow her."

He caught the distant flashing light in the corner of his eye. A single police car had stopped on the road alongside the cemetery. It hadn't made a sound when arriving.

"Damn it," he grunted. "We're busted."

"I must follow her." Madam Bovell walked away from him and toward the far side of the sloped hill.

"We don't have much time," he said as he watched the officer push through the fence and splash the area with a powerful flashlight. Red and blue flickered brightly from his cruiser, giving an odd strobe effect to the distorted silhouette moving through the graveyard.

"I think she wants to show me something," Bovell said.

"Hello!" the officer yelled. "Show yourself!" He was lumbering up the other side of the hill, heading straight toward them, as if he already knew right where any trespassers would go.

"He's going to stop us," Dr. Graves said. "His light will be on us any second now."

"If I lose this connection, I may never be able to reestablish it," she said. "After we're caught, we'll never have another chance here at night. She's going to show me what we came here for. We just need a little more time."

"We don't have it."

"She's passing through tombstones. She's pointing. Her mouth is open. She's glowing brighter. My God, do you see any of this?"

"Not a thing."

"Stop right there!" the officer yelled as his light caught them from a few hundred feet away. "I said stop! STOP MOVING!"

"Go," he said to her. "Finish this. See what she's pointing at." And as she moved farther into the darkness before him, he turned to the officer with his hands up. "Is that you, Satan!"

"Oh, Christ," the officer spat. "Stop right there."

"Prince of Darkness, tell me my path! Guide me!"

"I'll show you your path," the officer answered, now only fifty feet away. "I'll take you there myself. Now, down on your knees with your hands behind your head."

"Yes, Lucifer! Yes, O great Mephistopheles! Speak thy bidding!"

The officer removed a pair of shiny handcuffs from his belt. "Where's your friend going?"

"To talk to the witch."

"Uh-huh. Do you have any weapons on you?"

"I have the power of dark magic."

"Okay." Stepping behind him, the officer put the handcuffs on him. "Do you have any sharp objects in your pockets."

"No, my lord."

"You know, no matter what we do, we still get you crazies that keep coming to this cemetery. Why can't you all just leave the good people here in peace?"

Dr. Graves didn't reply. He felt as if his distracting act was wearing thin. But he still must give Madam Bovell as much time as possible.

"Where's this witch-seeking friend of yours?" the officer asked, standing up straight after searching his pockets. The flashlight beam lit up distant tombstones. Dr. Graves watched as it froze on the back of Madam Bovell's head, which was hunched over unnaturally among the shadows.

"There she is," the office said. "Don't you move, sir. Ma'am! Stand up, ma'am! Fun's over! Hands in the air!"

"You're not Satan!" Dr. Graves said, standing. "You're not him!" Then he began hobbling away, jarring awkwardly past gravesites with his hands still cuffed behind his back.

"Sir, stop! STOP!"

He heard the officer gaining on him, and the clank and clatter of the equipment on his duty belt. A strong hand tightened over his shoulder, and he was tackled to the wet grass.

"Sir, I need you to settle down!"

The officer rolled him onto his back, and he saw that the man was holding a canister of pepper spray near his face.

"I'm calm, Officer," he quickly said. "It's okay. I'm calm. It was just a joke. I'm sorry."

The officer did not look amused. "A joke?"

"We just wanted to see the old church. I had heard the legends. I'm a paranormal researcher of psychical phenomena, from the Psychology Department at the University of Chicago. I'm writing a book on haunted towns in the Midwest."

"You're a ghost professor?" The officer loosened his hold but kept the pepper spray ready.

"Well, yes."

"Then you should know better than to enter a cemetery at night without permission from the groundskeeper and local authorities."

"You're absolutely right, Officer. This wasn't planned well. I'm truly sorry."

"We prosecute all incidents of trespassing at this cemetery. No exceptions. You wouldn't believe the trouble kids have caused over the years. But a man of *your* age should be ashamed."

"Oh, and I am, Officer. Terribly embarrassed. Deeply ashamed."

Dr. Graves leaned forward and let the cop help him to his feet. After being tackled, he was feeling every day and hour and minute of his age.

"You're not going to cause any more trouble?"

"Absolutely not, Officer."

"I've still gotta take you in."

"I understand."

"And your friend, the witch hunter—she won't cause any trouble, either, right?"

"She's as peaceful as a butterfly."

"Uh-huh. Anyone else we're missing out here?"

"No. Just her and me."

"Let's go get her, Professor."

The officer held Dr. Graves's shoulder, guiding him across the slope as his flashlight's beam jiggled over the top of tombstones until the round yellow glow rediscovered the back of Madam Bovell's head. She hadn't appeared to move in the past minute, and Dr. Graves wondered whether she had fallen into a trance state. There was no telling what may have happened to her mind if she really had made contact with the dead in this place.

"Ma'am, put your hands where I can see 'em!"

The officer lumbered around a broad granite tombstone, pulling the professor with him.

Dr. Graves wondered whether the spirit of the gray woman was still here, standing or floating right in front of them, watching them from her green glowing aura that only Madam Bovell could see. The officer had no idea that he may be disturbing the communications of the dead.

Now in the same row of graves as Madam Bovell, they moved slowly toward her. The officer's light slashed across her, revealing nothing of the void behind the lank hair that veiled her face. Still motionless, she knelt, as if in prayer, before a charcoal-gray tombstone.

"Ma'am, are you okay?"

No response.

"Madam Bovell?" Dr. Graves spoke.

She turned slowly and looked at him, her teary eyes bloodshot in the cop's light.

"She's here," she whispered.

"Ma'am, you have to come with me. You're both trespassing and are under arrest. I'll read you your rights at the car. Do you need help getting up?"

"She's here," she repeated.

"Come on, ma'am." The officer released his hold on the professor and took another pair of handcuffs from his duty belt.

As the policeman stepped forward, the light slid off her and to the grass by her knees. She hadn't even acknowledged the officer's presence.

Dr. Graves thought she needed help, that the officer could use assistance getting her to her feet. But just as he took a step forward, the light slid across the grass and cast a bright glow on the gravestone. A chill ran through him when he saw the name "Elizabeth Black" engraved into the glittering granite, and below that "Beloved Mother of Rachel Black."

"She's here," Madam Bovell whispered again. "She's right here. She's standing right here in front of us. And she needs our help."

33

The police cruiser drove along the dark road through the Kansas Flint Hills. Dr. Graves and Madam Bovell were handcuffed separately in the back seat, facing the metal grate segregating them from the front seats. The officer sat silent behind the steering wheel. Madam Bovell also seemed lost in thought.

As they crossed Interstate 70 on a small overpass, Dr. Graves couldn't believe the string of headlights below them. He wouldn't have expected anyone else to be out here in the sticks at night, but here in view were hundreds of cars, all heading the same direction.

"Why's there so much traffic?" he asked.

"Game five of the World Series was in Kansas City tonight. Royals just tied the series yesterday. These are fans from the game, driving back to Topeka or Manhattan or wherever."

"Who won?"

"I don't know," the officer said. "I was watching it at the station, and it was tied in the eighth when I got a call about suspicious activity in the cemetery."

"Oh. Sorry."

"You should be," the officer mumbled. "You know, there's a minimum fine of a thousand bucks for trespassing in that cemetery, for each person caught. Hope it was worth it."

"Well, I'm just happy we didn't bump into the devil," Dr. Graves said.

"Is that why you people come here?"

"Not me."

"What about you?" the man asked, his eyes shifting in the rearview mirror to Madam Bovell.

"I came here for Rachel Black ... and, I think, also for Elizabeth Black."

"And why are you so interested in them?" The officer's voice had an aggressive edge, as if he found her words especially irritating.

"The tombstone said Elizabeth's been dead thirteen years," Madam Bovell said, ignoring his question. "Did you know her?"

"No. I grew up in Council Grove. Only been in this area five years now. But I've heard about Elizabeth Black and her mother, Margaret."

"Margaret? What have you heard?"

"Just the stories ..."

The cruiser slowed and turned right onto a smooth asphalt highway that looked as if it had been paved in the past week. The double yellow line, brightly illuminated in the car's headlights, stretched infinitely away from them, into the darkness.

Within a minute they had passed a large green sign that read, "Welcome to Basalt, Kansas - Population 991." Entering the town, they drove half the mile that was Main Street, and turned into the back of the county police station.

The officer turned his head slightly and spoke into the radio handset strapped to his chest. "Tim, what's your twenty?"

A crackle came through the police radio, followed by a loud voice. "I'm out at the Allen Ranch. Someone broke through the fence near the K Forty-Seven junction."

"Who won the game?"

"Don't know. It was tied in the ninth when I got the call from Bob Allen."

"Jiminy Cricket!"

"I know."

"Well I've got two criminal trespasses for night lockup. Arriving at the station now."

"Where'd you find 'em?"

"Stull Cemetery."

"Damn kids!"

"These two ain't kids. Older than me. From Chicago, they say."

"What?"

"Yep."

"Need assistance?"

"Na, they're no trouble. Come back when you're done. And tell Bob and Susan I said *hello*."

"Ten-four."

The officer killed the engine and opened the door, awakening a chorus of electronic dinging before he yanked the key out of the ignition. He helped Dr. Graves and Madam Bovell out of the car and escorted them toward a large yellow brick wall with a metal door in the center. The cold, impassive eye of a security camera above watched them. The warped metal door frame shrieked as the officer yanked it open with violent force. He led them down a concrete hallway to a pair of empty jail cells.

"We'll do lockup first, and then each of you will get to make your phone call."

He took out a set of small keys and stepped behind Madam Bovell to unlock her cuffs. Then he opened the door of bars to the first cell and waved her inside. He closed the door and locked it. Then he turned to Dr. Graves, but his eyes widened when he saw the professor holding out his handcuffs, dangling from his index finger.

"How in the hell did you get those off?" the officer asked, visibly shocked.

"Once upon a time, I was a magician."

The officer snatched the cuffs from him and pointed him toward the open door of the next cell. "Get in there!"

Dr. Graves shuffled his feet into the cell.

The officer closed and locked the door with a key the size of a fork. Then he stared at Dr. Graves through the bars. "A magician, huh?"

"Long time ago."

The officer held up a hand, dangling the cuffs. "But these are not trick handcuffs."

"I was also an escape artist."

"You gonna try to get out of this cell, David Copperfield?"

"Do you want me to try?"

"Nope."

"Then I won't."

"Good, 'cause if you did, I might have to shoot you." He hesitated, then glanced back and forth between his two prisoners. "Let me grab some papers to start your files. After that, I'll get both of you to your phone calls."

Then he vanished down the other end of the hallway.

Dr. Graves looked at Madam Bovell and winked.

She smiled and said, "Houdini would be proud."

He sat on the concrete floor of his cell, with his back against the iron bars that separated them. "You never did thank me for convincing you to come to Kansas."

"No, I didn't."

He chuckled, then grew silent and serious. "What did you see out there?"

"The gray woman," Madam Bovell answered, lowering herself to the ground and leaning back against the opposite side of the same bars. "She was there."

He felt the cushion of her back pressed against his through the bars. "What did she look like?"

"She was surrounded by a green aura. It swirled around her like a gas, like liquid in zero gravity. And once she got behind the tombstone, she began to float."

"Did she say anything?"

"Her mouth moved slowly as if she was speaking, but there was no sound."

They heard the officer returning down the hall. "Okay you punk kids," he said, "you rascally teenagers. Time to scan your fingerprints and make your phone calls."

"Excuse me, Officer," Dr. Graves said, "but do you know how Elizabeth Black died?"

The officer had just come into view with a clipboard and keys. His mouth dropped at the question. "Are you kiddin' me? You're still on that? Listen here Mr. Cop-per-field. You need to be focusin' on your legal situation, not some mother-daughter witch legend from decades ago."

"Witch?"

"Black magic. They say she was the real deal. But all the rest of the stories I heard were about her mother, Margaret. She's the one whose stories scared me when I was a kid growing up. Margaret was a big legend in these parts back in the mid-sixties through the early eighties. I mean, we heard stories about her when I was in high school, and I was living all the way out in Council Grove then. Word wouldn't have traveled that far unless she was a big deal."

"You're saying they were *real* witches?" Dr. Graves asked.

"You didn't know?" the officer asked, openly shocked. "I thought that's what you came here for. Why the hell else were you at her grave?"

"Elizabeth Black spoke to me in a dream," Madam Bovell said.

The officer dropped the clipboard and took a few steps backward as his face turned strangely pale. He glared at her without a word as the wall clock ticked off a dozen seconds. Then, after the man's mind seemed to fight off whatever had troubled it, he turned a stern gaze to Dr. Graves.

"You said you were paranormal researchers from a university."

"We are."

"Researchers that are receiving visions? You're lying."

"Look," Dr. Graves said. "I had a sign to contact her," he said, gesturing to Madam Bovell, "and she had a vision to come here. We have a history together. Not a good one, either. We're not even sure why we're here. We just know that we're supposed to be here. And it relates to the name Rachel Black."

"I don't believe in this type of stuff," the officer said.

"But you used to," Dr. Graves guessed.

"When I was young and foolish and bored—maybe. As a kid—maybe. But not anymore."

"I was the same way," Dr. Graves said. "I believed. Then I stopped believing."

"But now you believe again?"

"I'm starting to."

"Well, that's your problem, sir. Not mine. I don't believe you saw anything except maybe whatever you wanted to see. Delusions to feed your imaginations. Nothing more. And I don't believe any of those stories are true about Margaret or Elizabeth Black."

"But you know someone who does," Madam Bovell said.

He hesitated. "People tell crazy stories. No one really believes them."

"Someone does," Madam Bovell said, her eyes now closed as if in deep concentration. "Someone around here. Someone you know."

"I'm not helping you with this. People like you have been disturbing Stull for too long."

"Wood," Madam Bovell said, eyes still closed. "Janice Wood."

The officer glared at her with a stoic veneer over his frustration. "Who are you people? Con artists from Chicago? You better leave Janice alone."

Madam Bovell opened her eyes and turned to Dr. Graves. "That's it! That's how we find Rachel Black. Stull Cemetery and Janice Wood. Stull and Wood."

Dr. Graves couldn't believe what he was hearing from her. As in the cemetery, he found himself considering that maybe she was conning him from the beginning. Other than the message at his son's grave, he hadn't really seen anything. She had been the sole witness to everything. Had she pulled him into some phony quest she had made up for him to follow with her? Had she researched Stull in advance, identified the men who might patrol the cemetery, discovered names of eccentric people in the community, like this Janice Wood? Was all this nothing more than an elaborate hoax to con him into believing that she was once again an authentic medium? Him, her most damaging critic, conned into professing that he had been wrong thirty years ago and that she truly was the real deal. Had *he* been the target all along?

"What are you doing?" he asked her.

"Our answers are here." She shifted back toward the officer. "Please, we need to speak with Janice Wood."

"No."

"How did you get the name?" Dr. Graves asked her.

"I heard it … in my mind … from his mind, I think. It was in the air, permeating everything … like a fog, or sunlight."

Dr. Graves felt his face tighten. He hadn't expected this from her and was trying not to slide back into his habitual stern skepticism and cold disbelief. It had felt so good to regain faith in something he had once lost and didn't want to lose again. But he could feel it slipping away.

"You have your gift again?" he asked.

"Something has returned."

"Is it growing?"

"No. It's barely there. Almost nothing. But I feel it." Her face had a joyful glow that could be found only on the other side of an ocean of pain. She had been a brilliant con artist and charlatan, but his gut told him to take one last gamble on her.

He put his hands on the bars. "You have to let us speak with this Janice Wood."

"That's not going to happen," the officer said. "What is going to happen is me fingerprinting you both, you making your allotted phone calls, me processing your trespassing charges, you spending the night in jail, me taking you to the courthouse tomorrow, you paying the thousand-dollar fine each, and *me* escorting *you* across the county line."

"I want to use my phone call to ring Janice Wood," Madam Bovell said.

"We're just trying to solve a mystery, Officer," Dr. Graves said.

"Or maybe prevent a death," Madam Bovell said.

"*Really?*" Dr. Graves asked her.

"Really."

"You're trying to prevent a death?" The officer cocked an eyebrow. "Where? Here?"

"Somewhere in North or South Dakota."

"Right."

"Please, Officer … Barlow," Dr. Graves said, reading the name tag below the badge, "just let us make our calls."

"Well I can't stop you from making your calls. It's your right. But Mrs. Wood is old, and if I find out that you did or said something to cause her distress, I'll charge both of you with additional counts of disturbing the peace. Do we understand each other?"

"Yes, Officer," they said in unison.

He stepped forward, jingling the keys as if to ward off evil spirits before unlocking their cell doors and escorting them down the hall toward the phone bolted to the concrete wall.

As they walked, Dr. Graves noticed the officer shaking his head and muttering to himself. "What is it?" Dr. Graves asked, trying to be friendly.

Officer Barlow looked at him with an amused expression. "I was just thinking about how interesting my job is. Tonight, I caught an escape artist and a mind reader trying to contact the ghost of a witch, in a cemetery, just three nights before Halloween. Every Halloween, we have to deal with people trying to do things in Stull Cemetery, but I was just thinking that the circus came a little early this year."

Dr. Graves chuckled, still hoping to get on the officer's good side. But he couldn't help believing that however crazy things had been tonight, it was nothing compared to the horrors that lay ahead in their quest. But in the back of his mind, he found himself starting to doubt what Madam Bovell had told him. The ghost of a witch in the Stull cemetery? Really? He hadn't seen anything. Was there any chance she had *imagined* what she supposedly saw in the cemetery? Was there any chance she had made it up for some hidden agenda? Was there any chance that all this was one big hoax?

Within the maelstrom of confusion, he closed his eyes tightly, thought of his son, and tried to keep his fickle faith alive.

THURSDAY

We were cut off, really, together; we were united in our danger.
—Henry James, *The Turn of the Screw*

34

D r. Graves drove behind the police car, pushing through the thin cloud of dust like a plane cutting through clouds. At times, the car would almost vanish in front of them. There were occasional snaps of rocks thrown up from the tires and clattering against the rental car's underbelly. Madam Bovell stared silently ahead through the dusty windshield.

"Is he taking us to the far edge of the world?" Dr. Graves asked.

"I like it out here," she replied. "It's peaceful."

"You've been in the city too long," he said.

"So have you," she said. "I'd almost forgotten how calming nature's open spaces can be."

He smiled and glanced out his side window at the field stretching off into the tall grass of the rolling Flint Hills.

"By the way, how the hell did you get out of those handcuffs last night?"

"Magic," he said.

"No, seriously," she said. "I know you're a former magician and escape artist and a big Houdini fan and all that, but after all we've been through, you can at least tell me this one secret."

"No, seriously, it was magic."

"Really?" She rolled her eyes.

"Well, in a manner of speaking, yes, it was magic. You know, of course, that Houdini was one of the greatest escape artists of all time. He actually had a trick where he would escape from any type of handcuffs. He did it by studying every model until he could look at them and know how their tumblers worked and what type of key they used. At one point, he even made a trick belt for himself that had keys and picking tools hidden inside a secret compartment that he could slide open with his elbow."

"So you have a secret belt?" she asked.

"No, but I have this watch," he said, jingling the silver watch on his left hand. "Houdini was buried in Queens in 1926. The bust at his gravesite was damaged in the mid-seventies, and for a long time there were no funds set up to take care of the site. Finally, the caretakers of the Houdini Museum in Scranton convinced the Society of American Magicians to manage the restoration of his grave. I made a nice contribution to the fund, and they gave me this watch as a gift."

He held the steering wheel carefully with his left hand while sliding his right index finger along the watch's bezel. Pressing his nail into a small ridge, he slid out a thin sliver of metal. "And because the Society never misses a trick, the watch conceals a thin shim pick that you shimmy between the ratchet and the teeth of cuffs. Then you can slide open cuffs. If they're double-lock cuffs—which most are—then you have to pick the double lock first, which you can do with this pick, up here." He moved his fingernail along the case of the watch to pull out a small pick with a little hook on the end. "This goes in the keyhole and carefully rotates clockwise in the mid level to release the double lock. Then you can use the shim to push the locking mechanism off the teeth. The whole thing takes a minute or two if it goes right. I never really get to use it, but it's a great showoff piece when I meet other magicians."

He took off the watch and handed it to her.

"H. H." She read the inscription on its back. "Very cute."

"It tells time, too," he said with a grin.

Brake lights peeked through the dust. He slowed. As the murk around them thinned and settled, he saw they were turning into a gravel parking lot in front of a large stone church. Its white limestone gleamed in the sun.

"What do you think she'll tell us?" Madam Bovell asked, seeing they had arrived.

"I don't know. The truth, I hope."

She pointed at the church. "Whatever it is she plans to tell us, she wanted to make sure that God is witness."

They left the car and walked with Officer Barlow to the large double doors with Gothic inlays. They went inside. The strong wind they had been fighting outside whistled as it wrapped around the church.

A wide central aisle sloped downward through a sea of oak pews to the elevated altar with a pulpit, a choir section, and a communion table decorated with Leonardo Da Vinci's rendition of the *Last Supper*. And behind it all and above and looking down was a suffering crucified Christ.

Dr. Graves looked at the giant figure of Jesus and wondered, as he often had, whether someone was looking back at him. The blue eyes and thinly bearded face had an air of sorrow and peace. Many surely took comfort seeing their savior bear such a burden, just as they bore difficulties in their own lives—just as Graves, too, had suffered since the loss of his son twenty years ago.

"That's her," the officer said.

Dr. Graves turned his teary eyes away from Jesus and searched until he found the small silver-haired figure sitting with bowed head.

He and Madam Bovell left the officer waiting at the back of the church and walked down the aisle, sidling between the pews toward the woman mouthing an inaudible prayer.

They stopped a few feet from her and waited respectfully to be discovered. She finished her prayer with a whispered "Amen" just as a gust of wind outside gave off the eeriest moan yet. And with this, the woman opened her eyes to find them hovering there.

"Mrs. Wood, I'm Helen Bovell, and this is Professor Donovan Graves. It's very good to meet you."

"It's very good we met," the woman replied. "Very good. Very, very …" She stopped and scratched her cheek. "So much is open. So much is unfinished. Someone had to come."

"What is unfinished?"

"The dead. They are not dead."

"I'm sorry?"

"The dead are not dead. No … not dead."

Dr. Graves glanced back at the officer, who was eyeing them coldly from across the rows of pews.

"We need to keep her calm," he said to Madam Bovell.

"It's all right, Mrs. Wood. We're here, and we want to help. Like you said, so much is unfinished. Help us finish it. Please tell us about Margaret Black and anything you might know about her daughter or granddaughter."

"Margaret … Oh, she was very powerful," the woman said, nodding. "Very, very powerful. And so was her daughter," she added, raising an instructive finger. "Elizabeth … We called her 'little Lizzy.'"

"Powerful how?" Dr. Graves asked. He reminded himself that this was a woman nearly a hundred years old, holding on to her oldest memories, from when she was most full of life, for the more recent memories were the least exciting and hence the first to be discarded by the weakening mind.

"Powerful how?" he repeated. "Like magical powers?"

"No, no. She was powerful with the Lord." She turned and stared intensely into Madam Bovell's eyes and whispered, "She could call the angels. She could *talk* to them."

"Did you witness this?" Madam Bovell asked.

"Oh, yes. At Mr. Winfield's house."

"What happened at Mr. Winfield's house?"

"That's where we would meet," she said. Her eyes widened as if one of the best moments of her long life had suddenly flashed into her mind.

"Who would meet?" Madam Bovell asked, placing her hand gently on the woman's slim, bony shoulder.

"Our *group*!" Her voice rose higher in almost a squeak, and her brow furrowed as if she were surprised they didn't already known the answer.

Dr. Graves reiterated Madam Bovell's question. "What group? We haven't heard about it. Please tell us."

"It was just our group," she said. "We met most Friday nights at Mr. Winfield's house. Only ten of us were invited. Plus Mr. and Mrs. Winfield. Margaret Black made it thirteen. She led the sittings."

"These were séances," Madam Bovell said understandingly. "Home circles. Hosted by the Winfields. And Margaret Black was your group's resident medium to the spirit world."

"Oh, yes."

"And she could connect with the dead?" Dr. Graves asked.

"Oh, yes, so many dead. Dozens every Friday night. From all over the world. And from all eras. Time and distance meant nothing. So many dead. So many souls searching for the living. The living need only look for them." Her bony arm jerked, and she grabbed Madam Bovell's wrist. "The dead are not dead!"

Madam Bovell looked at her with compassion. "I know."

Mrs. Wood smiled. "Not dead."

"What happened to Margaret?"

"She's passed on," Mrs. Wood replied.

"She's dead," he said.

"Not dead."

Dr. Graves grinned politely. "Not dead, yes. Sorry. She's passed on."

"Yes," the woman replied.

"How did she *pass on*?" he asked.

"The devil took her," she said, placing a finger to her lips. "The devil didn't like her talking to angels, so he *took* her."

"How did he take her?"

"During a séance. It was dark. We were all holding hands at the table. Thirteen of us, but only Margaret was speaking to call the spirits. Once a spirit made contact through her, the rest of our group could ask questions. We were waiting in silence, holding hands and trying to give off positive energy to help her attract drifting spirits. And then, finally, after maybe half an hour, she sat up straight. Her chin lifted, her breathing turned deep and loud, and she said, 'Hello.'"

She smiled as her eyes closed.

"We all said hello back. Then Mr. Winfield asked, 'To whom are we speaking?' 'Gabriel,' the voice answered through Margaret. 'Is this the Angel Gabriel?' another asked. 'It is I,' the spirit replied from Margaret's mouth."

Her head wavered as if she had briefly found joy in the memory. But just as suddenly as this brief bliss appeared, it vanished. Her countenance sank, as if a shadow had fallen over the joy of that specific moment in her memory.

"But then *he* came. Before Gabriel had spoken another word, *he* came to destroy her."

"Who?" Dr. Graves asked.

"The devil!"

Madam Bovell clasped both hands to her mouth. "You reached the devil in a séance?"

Dr. Graves would have dismissed the claim if it had not been for the ghostly pale painted across both women's faces.

"The devil was there … with us … in the room … speaking through Margaret Black."

"Speaking through her?"

"Yes."

"The devil? Not some minor demon instead? Not some poltergeist?"

"It was not some lesser evil. It was the worst of all damnation. It was the devil." Mrs. Wood shrank back and recoiled from the hymnals and Bibles in the slot shelf on the back of the pew in front of her. She seemed ashamed before God, as if she deserved to be kicked out of the church and shunned by all the faithful.

"What about Gabriel?" Dr. Graves asked.

"He was gone. Margaret jerked upright and became even taller at the table, as if levitating a few inches off her chair. When she spoke next, her voice had changed, and it became horrifically clear to all of us that it was the devil."

"What did he say?"

"He said, *'Sin will corrupt all. And temptation will make all sin.'* Then there was an unholy animal growl, and the voice said, *'I will tempt and corrupt all, and all will follow* ME *and forsake* HIM.'" She gazed toward the altar with a thousand-yard stare, her expression frozen in time by the horror she was reliving. "And then she died."

Madam Bovell's eyes widened. "Margaret Black died *during* a séance?"

"The devil killed her," Mrs. Wood whispered. "He took her life on Halloween. She collapsed forward onto the table. There was nothing we could do. And that poor little girl of hers saw it all."

"Little girl?" Madam Bovell asked.

"Her daughter?" Dr. Graves said. "She was there?"

"Yes," Mrs. Wood said, her hand shaking as she reached forward, pulled a Bible from the pew, and clutched it to her chest.

"How old was her daughter?"

"Four."

"And she was at the séance?" Madam Bovell asked, horrified.

"She was not part of the group. She was hiding in the next room and had apparently been spying through a keyhole. Margaret and her daughter had been staying in Mr. and Mrs. Winfield's guesthouse since the summer. She hadn't had much, and once the Winfields realized her gift, they asked her to move onto their property. They were passionate spiritualists. The girl was supposed to be in bed asleep. But instead, she saw everything." She clutched the Bible tighter. "I can still hear her screams."

"What happened to her daughter?"

"The Winfields adopted her. No one knew who the father was, and there were no other known relatives."

"She was raised near Stull?"

"Yes, on the Winfield farm."

"Was the cause of death ever determined?" Dr. Graves asked.

Mrs. Wood looked at him with confusion. "I told you, the devil killed her."

"Yes, but … never mind. Did the Winfields have any more séances?"

"They couldn't," Madam Bovell said. "Not without a medium."

"No, they couldn't," Mrs. Wood confirmed. "And they didn't want to. None of us did. Not at first, anyway."

"So you did have more," Dr. Graves said.

"Many years later. Only when Lizzy was old enough."

"Oh, no, you didn't," Madam Bovell breathed.

"Lizzy wanted to," Mrs. Wood said.

"The daughter?" Dr. Graves clarified.

"Yes."

"Why?"

"Because she had the gift, too. She was even stronger than her mother."

"How old?" Madam Bovell asked sadly.

"She showed signs at thirteen but didn't become powerful enough until she was sixteen."

Madam Bovell shook her head. "After what happened to her mother, how could you let her perform séances?"

"How could we stop her? She had the gift."

"How many séances did the group have with her?"

"Oh, hundreds."

"And they were productive?" Madam Bovell asked.

"Yes. They were always successful."

"All of them?"

"Yes."

"She never once failed to make contact with the dead?"

"Never." The woman smiled. "Lizzy could find them so easily. And it wasn't just the dead. She could also enter the dreams of the living."

"And you're sure it couldn't have been tricks?" Dr. Graves asked. He was thinking of fraud, but couldn't use the "F" word with someone so obviously a long-time believer in such mysticism.

"No tricks. She was the real thing. The stuff we heard in those séances left no doubt in the minds of the sitters. She had a spirit contact that was as strong and connected to her as any medium could hope for. It was certainly part of why she was so powerful."

"What did her spirit contact call itself?" Madam Bovell asked.

Mrs. Wood beamed, showing only her second real sign of joy since they had met her. "It was her mother. Her mother had found her through the other realm and was now her spirit guide through the different dimensions of the afterlife."

"Incredible," Madam Bovell said. "A mother-and-daughter pair. One medium guiding another from across the great beyond."

Dr. Graves watched Madam Bovell become caught up in the woman's story, perhaps even believing those elements that could never be confirmed. This worried him.

"And the daughter was stronger than the mother," he said as encouragement to continue.

"Little Lizzy had a gift beyond anything we had ever witnessed," Mrs. Wood said. "And we've been to Lily Dale! We've sat with the great mediums there. But our Lizzy was more powerful than any of them. We believed she could become the greatest medium since Leonora Piper—maybe even since D. D. Home or Swedenborg."

"Did she ever go to Lily Dale?" Madam Bovell asked. "Did she ever meet with the mediums there? What did they think of her?"

"She never went. She wanted to. She was planning to. But then …"

Her eyes glazed over as if she had fallen into a trance.

"Mrs. Wood?" Madam Bovell asked, touching her shoulder.

Dr. Graves leaned in and looked into her face. Not a muscle moved, and her gaze remained locked on some unknown place far from the safe confines of the church. He waved his hand before her eyes, which he soon regretted because it attracted the officer's attention.

"Mrs. Wood?" he asked, now realizing that time was short as the officer slid his way across the pews.

"Little Lizzy died," Mrs. Wood whispered, tears forming in her eyes. "In a séance, just like her mother. Also on Halloween. She's buried in Stull Cemetery right next to her mother."

"My God," Dr. Graves said.

"We saw Elizabeth's grave last night," Madam Bovell said. "But we didn't see Margaret's or any other family members around her."

"They knocked it down," Mrs. Wood said. "College kids drinking and smoking drugs—they knocked it over. They broke Margaret's tombstone, and no one would fix it. They all thought she was a witch."

"I'm so sorry," Madam Bovell said.

"The devil killed them both," Mrs. Wood said, her face contorting. "First Margaret, then—twenty-three years later— little Lizzy. Poor child. Oh, Lord, you let the devil kill our little Lizzy. Please help her. Please protect her. She's in so much danger. I beg you, Lord."

"What in Christ's name is going on over here?" Officer Barlow snapped, arriving in a huff.

"Did you know that both Margaret and Elizabeth Black died on Halloween?" Dr. Graves asked him.

"Oh, whoa, whoa. Okay, I said you could talk to her, but I warned you not to upset her. She's ninety-two, for Christ's sake."

"The devil's going to kill her, too," Mrs. Wood said.

"Okay, this is over," Barlow said.

"Kill whom?" Madam Bovell asked. "They're both dead."

"The devil is going to kill little Lizzy's daughter. The devil is going to kill Rachel."

"Where is Rachel?" Madam Bovell asked the woman.

"She was sent to an orphanage in Kansas City for a few years," Mrs. Wood answered. "Then she was adopted by a married couple living in Williston, North Dakota."

"Williston?"

"Yes."

"Do you remember their names?"

She nodded. "Wynkoop."

"Oh, my God," Madam Bovell said, her face brightening. "We've found her! We've actually *found* her."

"The devil will kill her," Mrs. Wood warned. "He killed all the others. Every one of them. And Rachel is the last one left. The last one." She started to weep. "And after she's gone, there will be no one left who can talk to the angels."

Her sobbing poured through the sanctuary, bouncing off the hard surfaces designed to amplify praise and joy and worship. And when Dr. Graves lowered his gaze from the ceiling, he thought he noticed a change in the crucified Christ behind the altar. It was the eyes on Jesus' pained expression that had changed. They were no longer blue, but brown, and they now looked shiny and wet and alive. And they seemed to be watching him with compassion, as if trying to tell him something that, even after all these years, he could not understand.

35

The midsize jet bobbed in the high winds as it descended on the isolated runway. It wobbled before leveling out just in time for the tires to hit the concrete at what had to be near maximum shock. Not until the engines screamed in an aggressive reverse thrust did the terror of the past few minutes leave Dr. Graves.

"It's called the Flight of Death," said Madam Bovell beside him. "I heard some men talking about it while you slept."

"That's a horrible name."

"Not as horrible as if it had lived up to it," she said, nudging him. "I don't know how you could have slept through any part of that flight."

"I was dead tired. Not everyone can sleep in a jail cell as well as you."

The jet came to a stop, and the seatbelt light turned off with a ding. One of the pilots emerged from the cockpit in his pressed dark-blue captain's uniform and pulled the inside hatch to the cabin door. Nothing happened for a few seconds. Then a thump sounded as the door popped out and swung open. Dr. Graves watched the first passengers get off while most waited in a motionless queue as people struggled to extract the bags they had stuffed into the tiny overhead compartments before takeoff.

Eventually, he and Madam Bovell walked down the blue airstair and breathed in the cool North Dakota autumn air. Ten minutes later, they had moved through the regional airport's small terminal, claimed their rental car reservation, and were rolling out of the parking lot in a shiny yellow Yukon that made him feel even more conspicuous and out of place in the barren landscape.

"What do you think she'll be like?" Madam Bovell asked.

"She's just a kid," he replied. "I imagine she'll be like any other teenage girl."

"Her parents are gone. She's never really had any family of her own blood."

"She has her adoptive parents. You're making it sound like she came from a wolf pack."

"Her mother had the gift. So did her grandmother. And now she's living up here in this isolated place. It's as if someone's trying to keep her hidden away from the rest of the world."

"She's just a kid."

"A third-generation seer … Imagine the power she must have, the things she can do."

A gust of wind hit the Yukon from the side, pushing them just over the white line. The tires whined loudly as they rolled across the grooves cut onto the shoulder.

"Maybe she doesn't have the gift," he said, steering back into their lane.

"I'll bet you my life she does."

He found her confidence annoying. It was not so easy for him to believe these things. Decades of exposing frauds had made him equally weary of people's eagerness to believe the incredible. He was skeptical of any medium he had not yet proved to be a charlatan. And yet, despite this fading but lingering doubt, he had begun this journey with a renewed sense of wonder. He had pledged to his son's eternal soul that he would try one last time to approach the world of the dead with an open mind, just in case there was a window through which the living might truly communicate with them.

"It may be too early for her to have developed the gift even if she was born with it," he mused. "Most of the strongest mediums in history didn't show signs of their gifts until their late teens."

"She's seventeen, so she's right at the age when the changes could be occurring," said Madam Bovell. "That might be why her mother is sending us to her. She may need our help."

"You told Officer Barlow we're trying to prevent a death. But that was a lie, right? You never before mentioned anything about that."

"I don't know if it's true or not," she said.

"But you said it to Barlow."

"I don't think this is just about helping the girl understand her gifts. There's been a strong, desperate feeling to the visions—a frantic urgency in the messages. I think something really bad is about to happen, but I don't know what. I said 'death' to get Barlow's attention. And maybe that's what is in front of us. Or maybe we're needed to help her with something much worse that she'll be facing. Hell, maybe *she's* the threat and we need to stop her before she does something bad."

"Like what? Hurt someone?"

"Maybe. Or maybe she tries to help someone she shouldn't help. Maybe she inadvertently unlocks something evil with her powers. Maybe she tries to communicate with a dark spirit without realizing it, or ..." She paused, frozen in thought.

"Or what?"

"Or a demon pretending to be the spirit of someone else— someone good who died tragically. A demon that might trick her into magnifying her influence between two divided realms."

"So we find her, and then what? How do we know what to do?"

"I don't know," she answered.

"Can you read her?"

"Maybe. If she has a gift, there might be too much interference. Her mind could be receiving signals from other forces, making it difficult to sense her thoughts. Psychics receive signals from the living, and mediums receive signals from the dead. I used to do both to some degree. That gift has returned a little these past few days. But I'm not sure how effective I'll be against someone like her."

"So we just hope she believes us?" he asked.

"I think she will already have seen things she doesn't understand. Maybe dangerous things. She might be terrified at this very moment, alone and scared of things inside her mind. As a teenager, my first vision terrified me."

He took an exit ramp toward an old gas station. Parking in front of an outside display of blue washer-fluid bottles, he walked past a handwritten message taped just above a fuel pump, which said "*Prepay Inside.*" A little brass bell dinged when he pushed open the glass door. Inside, a thin bearded guy sat behind the counter, hemmed in on all sides by a display of lottery tickets and cigarette cartons.

"Got a pay phone?" Dr. Graves asked.

"Outside on the right. Takes quarters."

"Can you make change?"

The man slowly set his newspaper aside, then even more slowly typed the register's keys with one hand while holding out the other for the exchange. Dr. Graves placed two dollars in the man's open palm.

"It has a Williston phone book?"

"The whole region. Where you from?"

"Chicago."

"I got a nephew there," the man said dryly. He placed the quarters in Dr. Graves's palm. "There you go."

Dr. Graves went outside and stuck his head into the car, saying, "I'm going to try her adoptive parents. See if we can't arrange a meeting."

"Thought you couldn't get a signal," Madam Bovell said.

"There's a pay phone on that side of the building." He pointed with his thumb.

"You gonna tell them why we're here?"

"No, not the truth. But I've got an idea." He chuckled. "You'll love it."

He walked around the corner of the building to the weathered pay phone bolted to the concrete wall between two rustic restroom doors. A phone book was chained to it, but the wind picked up and slapped at the pages as he fought to find the one with Rachel Black's adoptive parents. Luckily, there was only one listing for Wynkoop. He dropped a few quarters in and dialed the number.

36

Madam Bovell's feet hurt as she walked up the steps to the light-blue farmhouse. At least, it looked like a farmhouse, though she saw no barn, no stables, and no livestock pens. But there was a lot of land.

She let Dr. Graves ring the doorbell while she looked down at her feet, anxious to meet the girl she had been building up in her mind all day.

The door opened and revealed a middle-aged couple who beamed at their visitors with the legendary Midwestern trust of America's happy heartland. The man was big, with broad shoulders, pale skin, and a grizzly beard which made his smile feel even warmer and more inviting. Madam Bovell sensed right away that he had a taciturn nature and that she and Dr. Graves could trust him with their secrets. The woman had a florid face and hair that reminded her of the fleece on a black lamb. She had uncountable freckles that seemed faded from age. But the couple's most telling feature was the way she held the man's arm: sweet and lovingly, yet a little too tight. She feared that something from the outside world would enter their lives and threaten the little piece of paradise they had worked so hard to build over the years. Madam Bovell could sense all this even better than she could see the visual cues.

"Professor Graves?" the man asked in a gruff voice.

"Yes, how do you do?" Dr. Graves stuck out his arm and shook their hands in a rigid movement. Then he tilted his palm toward Madam Bovell, like a magician presenting a new spectacle. "And this is my colleague Dr. Bovell, one of the best researchers from our Economics Department."

The couple beamed more widely, and Madam Bovell tried not to cough as the air left her throat. He hadn't told her she was getting such a prestigious background, and she only prayed she could fake it.

Her revived gift felt as strong as ever. She could sense that the couple were everything they appeared to be: good people with kind, welcoming hearts.

"I'm Rosemary Wynkoop," the woman said. "And this is my husband, George. Please come in."

The house was clean and homey. The tiled entryway opened into a large living room with two sofas facing each other across a beautiful maple coffee table. A box piano stood in the corner, behind floor-to-ceiling windows that looked out to a small gully on the other side of a grassy backyard. Opposite the windows, a wide opening led into a large kitchen and dining room. Other than the sofas, all the furniture looked like antiques, though Madam Bovell sensed a long family tie from the objects, as if they all had been together for generations. She could sense echoes of memories tied to the objects.

"Can we offer you something to drink?" the woman asked. "Coffee? Lemonade?"

"Coffee would be great," Dr. Graves said.

"Me too," added Madam Bovell. "Thank you."

The couple moved in lockstep to the other room, leaving their visitors alone.

"What are you smiling at?" Dr. Graves asked her.

"Was I?"

"Yes."

Madam Bovell felt her lips pulling back even farther and realized that she had let her guard down and must have been grinning foolishly since stepping into the room.

"My abilities are getting stronger," she whispered. "I can't explain it, but I haven't felt like this in decades. I thought it was lost forever. But something's happening to me. This journey is doing something that I can't understand. Even this room and the objects in it are calling to me." She felt her eyes watering.

"But are you feeling okay? Should I be worried?"

"I feel wonderful."

"Okay!" said the wife, returning with a silver tray holding three coffee cups and two small porcelain jars for sugar and cream. Her husband followed her in with a red can of soda.

They sat down on the sofas—Dr. Graves and Madam Bovell on one, and the Wynkoops on the other—with the silver tray positioned neutrally on the coffee table in between. They each took a cup and sipped their drink while waiting for someone to speak.

"Well, thank you for inviting us into your house and allowing us to ask you some questions," Dr. Graves finally said.

"Oh, it's our pleasure," the wife said. "This is all very interesting."

"Yes, very interesting," the husband echoed.

Dr. Graves smiled. "I'm glad. And it's very helpful to us." He shifted on the couch to turn and look at her. "Dr. Bovell, would you care to begin?"

She wanted to slap that smug grin right off him. It was one thing for him to concoct a fraud against these nice couple, but it was just devilishly cruel to also use the opportunity to push her into the deep end of his pool of lies.

"Oh, I think it's fine if you begin," she replied.

"But you said you wanted to start things."

The couple measured her with their eyes, but she could sense they weren't suspicious. "Really, no one wants to *start* with me," she joked. "I insist *you* begin."

"Very well," Dr. Graves said with a charming, victorious grin. He turned back to the couple. "George and Rosemary— may I call you that?"

"It's our names," the husband said dryly.

"Yes. Very good. George and Rosemary, please tell me when the economic troubles started in this area."

"'Bout a year ago, when oil prices tanked," George said.

"Before that," Rosemary corrected. "It started years earlier— when oil prices went *up*."

"I guess that's true," George conceded.

"What happened—in your own words?" Dr. Graves asked.

"Prices were high when these big oil companies discovered the Shale Oil all across this part of North Dakota," Rosemary said. "And they built a large operation from nothing, in no time—like they was the US Army puttin' up bases in the deserts during the I-rack War. I mean, in the matter of just *months,* these companies had come in and built drilling operations all over the place, and huge refineries and trucking depots and new rails and pipelines. New hotels were built all over town for all the nice businessmen and engineers that kept visiting to check on projects. Executives and other VIPs built nice new houses in nice new neighborhoods just to stay in the area from time to time while supervising the progress. Other businesses grew to supply the oil industry work and support all the new people comin' here. Money was flooding into the local economy. Buses full of migrant workers from all over the country arrived every day— remember a lot of the rest of the country was going through hard times, especially blue-collar workers that had lost manufacturing jobs."

"Things were crazy," the husband summarized.

"And then home prices went up a lot!" she said.

The husband grumbled in frustration.

"Your home's value went up?" Madam Bovell asked.

"Everyone's went up," she answered. Her husband was now shaking his head slowly in growing irritation.

Madam Bovell didn't need to sense their emotions this time, because they wore them on their sleeve. They looked defeated and helpless when tapping into their memories. Still, she could sense a flush of negative brain waves faintly emanating from the active neural network the same way someone would sense humidity or a foul odor in the air. The reception was clear enough to change her own mental state, making her slightly angry as she absorbed their buried frustrations. But she couldn't understand it. Why would they be angry that their home's value had gone up? Didn't people jump for joy when their home equity jumped? She worried that she was underqualified to pretend to be an economics professor, and worried more that she would reveal her fraud with the next question. But she had to ask it.

"Isn't it good that your home values went up?"

"God no!" the man said.

"We're not planning to move," the wife explained. "This is our *home*. We don't have much extra money, and suddenly our property taxes and insurance rates doubled. That's real money!"

"Real money just flyin' out the window!" the husband proclaimed.

"I see," Madam Bovell said. "I'm sorry."

"Not your fault," the wife said. "Just a lot of people decided they wanted to rush into this area for oil or opportunity, and it's changed our town too much, too soon. People that grew up here don't even recognize it anymore. It used to be such a nice place. We didn't used to have homeless, but now there's a lot of it. The city passed new ordinances, but that just caused other problems. Didn't used to be any crime, either. But now bad things can happen here. It's sad. And it's scary."

Just then the front door opened, and a teenage girl came in.

Both Madam Bovell and Professor Graves perked with excitement. Here she was: this girl who just might possess more power than any medium in a hundred years. The professor chided her for jumping to such conclusions, but she could feel that this girl was the one. She had suspected it from the clarity of her first vision in thirty years. She had sensed it from the certain bold movements of the Ouija board—an instrument that was weak and unreliable in most hands. It hadn't been just this girl's mother driving Madam Bovell to find her. Part of Madam Bovell believed that this girl had also been psychically pulling on her.

And she looked just as her mother did in those pictures they saw in Kansas, taken only a few years before the woman's death.

"Rachel," the wife said, "please come on in. We have guests."

Rachel stepped into the room, stopping behind a blue cashmere La-Z-Boy at the head of the coffee table. She hesitated for a moment, the way any high school student might if suspecting they were at risk of being pulled into a long, boring conversation with a bunch of grown-ups. But then, as if seeing no way around this unexpected encounter, she dropped her backpack and slumped into the cushiony chair.

"Hi," she said.

"This is our daughter. Rachel, these are researchers from the University of Chicago. This is Professor Graves. And this is Professor Bovell. They research the effects of economic changes around towns like ours. Oh, how did you phrase it?" she asked, looking at Dr. Graves.

He cleared his throat and pronounced his fictional title in his most nonfictional, professorial tone he could muster. "The Psychological Effects on Traditional Tribal Communities from the Abnormal Economic Fluctuation caused by Volatile Outside Parties: A Case Study of Williston, North Dakota, during the Oil Shale Boom and Bust."

"BRAVO!" the wife said, clapping. "It sounds so much more impressive when you say it."

"So what do you want from us?" Rachel asked defensively.

"We just want to talk, dear," Madam Bovell said.

"About your lives here," Dr. Graves added. "The more we can learn, the more we can understand this particular case study—and the better we can explain this unique phenomenon."

"Sounds kind of invasive," Rachel observed.

"Oh, no, honey," the wife jumped in. "They just want to know our story and the town's story so they can help others that might later go through the same thing."

"It's okay, Rachel," the husband said. "You don't need to participate if you don't want to. We can answer all their questions."

"Actually, we would love it if you stayed," Madam Bovell said.

"It would add a lot of value to our research to hear a youthful perspective," Dr. Graves added. "There will be a side to this community that you'll understand better than adults."

"And in turn, you'll help get Rachel a scholarship to your university," the wife said half-jokingly.

"We can certainly work on that," Dr. Graves said.

"All right," Rachel said. "What do you want to know?"

I want to know if you understand who your mother and grandmother were and what they could do, Madam Bovell thought. But she said, "How old were you when you realized the town was starting to change?"

Rachel flinched, hesitating as if a little stunned or confused by something. Her expression showed a strong, sudden interest in Madam Bovell—enough to make the hairs stand up on Bovell's neck.

"Go on, Rachel," the wife said. "Answer her question." Then, turning to the visitors, she said, "She's not usually shy."

"About thirteen," Rachel said, still focusing on Madam Bovell. Her eyebrows furrowed slightly, and her expression intensified with such subtlety that Madam Bovell wondered whether anyone else had even noticed the change. And then, without warning, Madam Bovell felt a slight pressure behind her eyes, as if a migraine was forming. She looked down and pressed her fingers to her temples, relieved that the pressure had vanished.

"You all right?" Dr. Graves asked.

"Yes. Just a sudden ache. I'm fine."

"Have some more coffee," the wife said.

"Thank you." She looked up and saw that Rachel was now watching her with a relaxed, almost apologetic expression.

I'm sorry.

The words whispered to her from the back of her mind, like a distant voice cutting through the silent void of a dark tunnel. The words had come just as she made eye contact with Rachel. It had been decades since Madam Bovell felt such a powerful thought transference. This was much stronger, much clearer, than the fumbling snippets she had sensed from Officer Barlow's mind last night. She had received the exact words in a distinct voice: a woman's voice ... Rachel's voice. Had she read Rachel's thoughts so clearly? Or had Rachel initiated the communication by speaking into Madam Bovell's mind? If it was clairvoyance, then Madam Bovell's gift was continuing to revive in growing strength. But if it was telepathy, then it was not her but Rachel who was displaying the power. Never in Madam Bovell's life had she witnessed someone with the ability to project such clear thoughts into someone else's mind.

There was only one way to discover which had occurred.

'Is that you?' she thought, still looking at Rachel.

'Yes,' she heard from within the recesses of her mind. Yet it seemed strange that Rachel's expression never changed: no hint of a smile for the wonder she was performing, no visible strain

on her face. If anything, this girl in front of her appeared worried. Madam Bovell wondered whether there might be perhaps a third explanation: maybe after all these years in séances, she was starting to lose her grip.

"You're not crazy," Rachel said out loud.

The adoptive parents had been listening to Dr. Graves talk about something, but now everyone stopped and looked at the teenager. Madam Bovell dropped her jaw and subtly shook her head while staring at her.

Rachel, who had been matching Madam Bovell's studious gaze for the past thirty seconds, now pulled her eyes away and scanned everyone else. "You're not crazy," she repeated, "to think that it's been hard for people in this town to deal with so much change."

"What's been the hardest part for you?" Dr. Graves asked.

She glanced quickly at Madam Bovell before her eyes shied down to the coffee table. "You can see the future in small towns, because small towns don't change much. And when they do change, it happens slowly over a long period. And that helps one know a place really well, which makes it feel like home. But when something from the outside world comes into town and causes rapid changes—new people, more buildings, different interests, more class division—it makes it hard to feel like it's still your home."

"She's right," her adoptive mother said. "When a place starts changing so much, it's hard to imagine what it will be like in the future. And that makes everyone here worried."

"But things are supposed to change," Madam Bovell said. "They're supposed to grow. To evolve."

"But I just want things to stay the same," Rachel said.

"I'm sorry, Rachel," Madam Bovell replied. "I understand these things as well as anyone and better than most. And these changes you're experiencing around here—I can tell you: things will never again be the way they were before. But you'll be okay. You'll learn to live with the things that are happening. In fact, experiencing these changes will make you a stronger person."

Her adoptive parents nodded, and the conversation turned back to Dr. Graves, pushing forward with a dozen additional questions for the family that he seemed to be making up on the fly.

But even as the discussion moved forward, Madam Bovell soon felt a slight pressure against her temples, then a tingling across her forehead. And then the distant voice murmured again in the back of her mind. *'I need to talk to you.'*

Shifting her eyes away from the adoptive parents, Madam Bovell once again found Rachel staring at her with deep concentration.

37

"She knows," Madam Bovell murmured as she walked away from the front door with Dr. Graves. The adoptive parents and Rachel had said goodbye to them and stepped back inside the house.

"Knows about her mother and grandmother?" he asked.

"No, I'm not sure about that. But she knows we're not who we say we are—that we're not here to research economics. She said she needs to talk to me."

"To you?"

"To us."

"About what?"

"About what's happening to her."

"Wait. When did she say all this?"

"She didn't *say* it. She thought it."

"You read her mind?"

"I think she read mine. And I think she then put her thoughts into my mind."

He stopped by the car. "A thought transference?"

"Yes."

"Telepathy?"

"That's what I think."

"From an untrained, inexperienced teenager?"

"She's special."

"Let's get in the car. They might be watching us."

In the car, he put the key in the ignition but didn't start the engine. "If she doesn't know why we're here, how could she know she wants to talk to us?"

"She said she *needs* to talk to us. *Needs,* not *wants.* Maybe she's had dream visions, too. Maybe she's in trouble."

"She read your mind?" he asked in disbelief. "If that's true, does that mean she knows what everyone around her is thinking?"

"It was more of a conversation through the mind. I didn't get the feeling that she was seeing any thoughts that I wanted to hide from her. She could see them only because I chose to open them up to her. Maybe it's because my mind is so experienced with spirit communications that she could communicate with me the same way spirits do. If that's it, then her potential to communicate with spirits could be stronger than anything the world has seen in a long time."

"You're jumping to a lot of conclusions," he said.

"I'm telling you my intuition. I think we just met someone who could become a very powerful medium."

He looked visibly irritated by her self-assured prophesying about the girl. Then his face relaxed, as if in resignation. "So what now? We found her; we came here; we met her. What do we do next?"

"We go back to the hotel and wait. She wants to talk to us in private. She'll find us as soon as she can get away."

"Okay. How soon until that happens? I'm starving."

"We'd better get takeout so we can get back to the hotel pronto. Something tells me this is urgent enough to her that she'll find a way to be there within the hour."

"She know which hotel?"

"I'll tell her now." Madam Bovell looked back at the house and saw the narrow outline of Rachel looking out at them from an upstairs window. She closed her eyes and thought of the big blue sign in front of their hotel. She held the image for at least ten seconds before turning her thoughts to the number three hundred: three hundred, three hundred, thinking it over and over until she felt the car moving forward.

Opening her eyes, she saw the distant figure of Rachel step back from the upstairs window, disappearing from sight. But then, just as the car turned away from the house, she saw the white curtains in the window flutter side-to-side three times.

Sitting back, Madam Bovell felt a smile spread across her face. And she knew that Rachel could feel it, too.

38

Aaron looked up from his homework at the kitchen table. His dad had just come back inside from lighting the propane grill on their back deck.

"Sure you don't need any help?"

"No, thanks," his dad said. "You keep working on your school assignments. I'm planning on your good grades saving me a fortune when you get scholarships."

"All right. Just don't forget I offered."

His dad went around the counter, washed his hands, and began slapping together the hamburger patties. Aaron turned back to his AP physics textbook and reread the highlighted summary of Einstein's Theory of Relativity. There was a lot to unpack from the theory. Even though he only half understood it conceptually, it was still an exhilarating read. While he tried to envision how gravity could warp time, his dad was carrying a plate of seasoned patties back toward the sliding glass door to the deck.

Trying to ignore the prospect of tasting a warm, juicy burger in his near future, he committed himself to a few more focused minutes on his studies. He dropped his eyes and stared at an artist's rendering of a black hole. Below it was a three-dimensional grid that sank in the middle to illustrate the power that a dying star has when it finally collapses into itself.

A deep grumbling noise rose from outside as a strong gust pushed through the backyard trees and rattled the sliding glass door. Aaron looked up in time to see his father's graying hair whip around wildly. Something about the forceful gust made Aaron a little queasy. It was so sudden and violent, it didn't seem quite natural, and now it continued to rattle the glass door like an invisible intruder trying to get in.

Then he heard a muffled pop as the lower doors on the grill blew open in a fireball from inside. He saw his dad stumble backward and fall to the deck. He lay motionless after hitting the back of his head on the cedar planks.

"Dad!" Aaron jumped up from the table and yanked the sliding door open. Then he saw that the lower front of his dad's jeans had caught fire. He rushed back to the dining table, yanked off the tablecloth, and rushed back outside. Throwing the tablecloth over his dad's legs, he patted down around the shins until the fire was out.

But then, just as he started to relax, he heard a deep hissing behind him. Turning to look back over his shoulder, he saw the tall orange flame dancing inside the under shelf of the grill—right at the top of the propane tank.

With no time to check on his dad, he sprang to his feet and raced to the grill. Bending down to look inside the shelf casing, he saw that the flame prevented him from reaching inside to twist the valve shut. And as long as the valve was open, a strong stream of propane would continue to rush out of the tank. Something must have gone wrong with the tank's regulator or the hose hookup. And now, with no way to turn off the gushing propane, the flame would continue to heat the tank, building the pressure of the gas inside until the tank exploded.

"Aaron!" His mom stood in the doorway with a frozen panic on her face.

"Call nine-one-one!" he yelled.

"Oh, God! Robert!" She was looking at his dad.

"Mom! Call nine-one-one! Hurry! Tell them we have a propane tank fire on our deck that we can't put out. We need the fire department fast. This thing's going to spread to the whole house. And Dad needs an ambulance. Hurry!"

As she shuffled to her cell phone on the counter, Aaron raced around her and grabbed the small white fire extinguisher from under the kitchen sink. As he rushed back toward the deck, he saw his younger brother, Ricky, running up the basement stairs.

"What's going on?"

"Pull the outside hose around to the deck," Aaron said. "And turn on the water."

"What's happening?"

"There's a fire on the deck. *Hurry!*"

"Where's Dad?"

"Just do it!" Aaron raced back outside. He pulled the pin from the extinguisher, pointed the nozzle at the flame, and squeezed the handle. The foam sprayed in the direction of the tank, but it was difficult to see into the ball of fire, to find the exact spot to hit with the foam. He changed to a sweeping motion to suppress the flame enough that he might then smother the source at the tank's apex. The flame receded, and he thought he was close to getting it out, but then a louder hiss issued from the tank. The tank had heated enough to break open the pressure release valve. And with the PRV now opened, the propane gushed at a much faster rate. The flame immediately rose to his own height, reaching from the grill and nearly touching the eaves.

Aaron couldn't believe what he was seeing. In no time at all, their evening had gone from just another casual dinner prep into this uncontrollable, compounding horror that was maybe seconds away from destroying his family's home. The flame was now monstrously big, and he could feel the small kitchen extinguisher growing lighter.

Then, to his confusion and horror, he thought he saw a face in the center of the flames. The heat was pushing him back and making it difficult to keep his eyes on the fire, but he was certain he saw the outline of something looking out at him from inside the curling blue and orange inferno.

The extinguisher died. And just as the last of the foam dripped out, a long flame shot out of the fireball and wrapped around his wrist like a tentacle that wanted to pull him toward the face. A sharp, intense pain felt like a thousand little teeth piercing his skin. He dropped the extinguisher and lunged away from the face and the grasping tentacle of flame. Falling next to his father on the deck, he no longer wanted to fight this evil thing that had found his family in their home. He just wanted them to escape with their lives.

Scrambling to his feet, he hooked his hands under his dad's arms and dragged him across the edge of the deck. He prayed nothing would reach out and try to grab them. When he got safely to the stairs, he dragged his dad down the steps and out into the yard.

Just then Ricky came running around the house with the long, green garden hose. Water was spewing out of it. Aaron could hear sirens screaming in the distance beyond the backyard trees. Placing a hand on his dad's chest, he felt the subtle rise and fall.

"What happened to Dad?" Ricky said.

"I'm not certain. He hit his head, but he's breathing. Go back around the house and make sure Mom got out."

"What are you gonna do?"

Aaron picked up the hose. "I'm going to try to save our home. If that tank keeps getting hotter, it will eventually explode and burn down our house."

He pressed his thumb down over half the hose's open end, increasing the water pressure enough to get a thin thirty-foot spray. He aimed it at the deck and hit the grill with a long arc of water. He had no chance of putting out the large gas fire, but it could help lower the flames and—most importantly—cool down the propane tank before it could explode. And occasionally, he would divert the spray under the eaves to keep them wet.

In the corner of his eye, he saw his brother race off into the night to find their mother. Their father moaned behind him. But he couldn't even glance away from the fire. The flames had pushed up to only a foot below the eaves.

He heard multiple sirens now. He felt relief that help was coming, mixed with the very real fear that they would get here too late. If fire got to the roof, it would quickly spread through the insulated attic, and the house would be lost.

He sprayed more water under the eaves, but then he had to turn the spray back onto the tank. Water and fire mixed in an unholy chaos of hisses and puffs and roars as the gas pushed the blaze ever closer to the house.

He heard the first screaming siren arrive on the other side of the house. Flashing red and blue lights were now reflecting off the top of the giant oak tree in the front yard.

"Hurry!" he yelled, desperate for them to understand that they had less than a minute before this turned into an unstoppable inferno.

The fire reached up and brushed along the bottom of the eaves. A flame licked the side of the house. The firefighters were going to be too late. After everything he had done to hold shut this gate to hell, help was going to be just a few seconds too late to prevent his home from kindling into a burning, raging nightmare. And Aaron could do nothing more than watch in horror.

"Hurry! Please!" he yelled to no one. "It's about to spread! Please! Someone! Back here! HURRY!"

He took a step closer to the house and adjusted his thumb, widening the spray enough to splash thin streams of water on both the house and the propane tank at the same time. It gave a few moments' relief before the flames pushed up even stronger. It was as if some unseen force were turning up the gas flow, countering his desperate struggle to save his home.

The grill tipped sideways as one of the plastic wheels melted. An autumn wreath hanging near the sliding door caught fire. He could see the paint under the eaves start to bubble.

"Hurry!" he yelled into the night. His dad was moaning louder now behind him. The sirens had multiplied, as had the flashing lights now painting the gnarled branches reaching above the house.

He heard shouting on his right and looked to find movement in the darkness. Reflective stripes came swinging out of the dark. The rustling of heavy protective gear grew louder until a firefighter appeared. Another firefighter rushed from the inside of the house, through the kitchen and out onto the deck. The man was equipped in dark yellow coveralls and jacket, with a large fire extinguisher strapped to his back. Aaron watched with relief as the man squared up with the grill and released a steady burst of white chemical over and around the fire. The man kept hitting the top of the propane tank until the flames pulled back, shortened, and died away.

Aaron fell to his knees in exhausted relief. Another firefighter rushed up the deck stairs, unhooked the propane tank, and carried it down and out into the center of the backyard. Aaron could hear gas still escaping from it, hissing like some evil creature of the night. Two other firefighters emerged from the dark corner around the side of the house. He felt a cold wetness at his knees and looked down. He had lowered the hose, and water was pooling in the soggy grass. He recovered from the shock enough to crawl over to his father.

"Dad, you okay?"

"What happened?" his father asked. He was still lying on his back and blinking his eyes as if trying to take in the world around him.

"Dad, there was a fire. Do you remember being at the grill?"

"A fire?" Startled, his father tried to sit up.

"Whoa. Hold on, Dad. It's all right. The firefighters got here in time. It's out. Everyone's fine. The house is fine. But you hit the back of your head, so you need to be checked out. You're also going to have some burns on your shins. An ambulance should be here soon, and they'll know if you need to go to the hospital. In the meantime, you shouldn't move until they get here. You can sit up, but that's it. Okay?"

"I'm fine."

"Dad, I mean it. You could have a concussion or worse. Please just sit and wait."

"How'd it happen?"

"I don't know," Aaron said. "A leak around the valve or hose, or a problem with the tank's regulator." But even as he said this, he thought of that face in the fire, and the flame lasso that had reached out to grab his wrist. He pulled back his sleeve and saw a faint mark like a bracelet around his wrist. But the mark didn't look like a burn. It looked more like a thick scar that was very old, as if he had had it for years.

"So everything's fine?" his dad asked, staring at the house and looking confused as two firefighters walked up. "Thank God."

Aaron's wrist stung, but a second later, the pain vanished. He held it and looked back at the house and the charred grill, the blackened wall siding, and the burnt wreath. He thought again of that face of twisted rage living in the flame. "Yeah, Dad, everything's fine," he lied.

"Thank God it's over," his dad said.

His wrist stung again.

Aaron nodded at his dad, but he knew it wasn't over. He couldn't believe that a mere fire extinguisher killed what he had seen living inside the flame. And he had to warn someone—anyone who would believe him. Anyone who had room in their universe for the possibility of an evil from beyond this natural world.

He had to wait for the paramedics, to get his dad checked out. And then he had to warn his friends that Annabel's rage and power were growing and might soon surpass their worst nightmares.

39

Before this trip to North Dakota, Jason had never done an unethical thing in his career. So he was surprised at how easy it had been to spend so much of his time at work focusing on the mystery surrounding Annabel instead of finishing up his audit project. But he had continued to plug away reviewing the accounting records. Something that still puzzled him was the undeniable correlation between the hospital's high uncollectible patient balances and the rumors of vanishing migrant workers and homeless people. But explaining why people were disappearing wasn't part of his job, and he couldn't think of any likely reason other than that people were just leaving town abruptly without telling anyone. He needed to stay focused on his assignment and wrap up the audit. But it was hard to concentrate. Even though he had already gathered enough information about the accounting records to form his final conclusion, he realized he might need to finish his report next week, back in Chicago. But for now, it was hard to stay focused on work.

"Lies. Lies. Lies." The words whispered in his memory.

Even though he had meant what he said to Rachel about not being able to get more involved in her club's ghostly investigations, he just couldn't get the words out of his head.

Lies. Lies. Lies.

Maybe they were the last words Annabel had heard before she died. Maybe her husband had yelled them at her before he murdered her and her secret lover.

Lies. Lies. Lies.

Maybe these words had been rattling around in her head for the last week of her life as her conscience succumbed to her infidelity. Maybe she had been planning to tell her husband about the affair. Maybe she had been planning to end the affair or even her marriage.

He rubbed his temples, sensing the early tingles of a migraine. It was no good just guessing at everything. He needed to clear his mind and approach this problem the same methodical way he would piece together the puzzle of a financial crime. The truth was that he had very few facts about the murder. Everyone he had met in town seemed to have their own ideas about Annabel's marital problems, but it was time to learn more about the real question: what was the actual story behind Annabel's marriage and her affair?

He would start with the Internet and its wealth of good and bad information.

He typed "Annabel Heller" and "Williston, ND" into the search engine. The instant the results appeared on screen, his mind sharpened. Leaning over his laptop, he was instantly glad he had left the hospital early. The last thing he needed was to leave a trail on the company's hospital network that he had browsed numerous articles about this gruesome murder. The headlines alone chilled him.

- DOUBLE MURDER WHEN HUSBAND FINDS WIFE CHEATING.
- HUSBAND DEAD AFTER KILLING WIFE AND HER LOVER.

- INFIDELITY AND MURDER IN WILLISTON.
- POLICE GUN DOWN NORTH DAKOTA MAN WHO MURDERED WIFE AND NEIGHBOR.
- THREE DEAD IN BLOODY CRIME OF PASSION.

Jason clicked on the link to the top article. Gooseflesh crept across his skin when the screen changed to reveal two faces of the dead staring at him. His hand shot to his mouth. A man and a woman, side by side in one photo, both with beaming smiles of the best that life and love can give two people. Happy days, no doubt, before darkness destroyed their lives.

"What happened to you?" he whispered. The couple in the photo stared back at him in haunting silence.

Looking at the woman's face, he was both excited and terrified at the similarities between it and the figure that had spoken to him in the hospital vision.

Lies. Lies. Lies.

Was it their marriage that was a lie? Was it their fiction of a loving relationship? Such secrets, if they existed, would be so buried in the hearts of the dead that no one would ever discover them now.

But she wants me to know. She wants me to discover the truth of her life. She wants me to understand her secrets.

He looked at her husband in the picture. He had a big smile and looked as if he had been laughing at something when the photo was snapped. Jason could see the strength of the man: his square jaw and strong cheekbones, piercing blue eyes, and even the bulges of muscle under his T-shirt. Strong arms that were wrapped around her.

He scrolled the article without reading it, searching for any more pictures. Halfway down the piece, he found two more: one of a large house somewhere in the countryside, the other of a man's body facedown in a dark pool of blood on a wood floor.

What happened to you? How could the couple have gone from that first photo to such a horrifying end? He realized that the husband must have loved her in a fatally twisted way to be driven so mad upon finding her in bed with another man.

So who, really, was to blame? That was the secret.

He looked at the picture of the house again. It looked familiar. It was a view from the front, but as he twisted it in his mind, he focused on the shape of the roof, with its many gable accents and dormers, and the thick woods surrounding it within a larger open field in a valley. It was the same house that Annabel had shown him as he looked out the hospital window on that stormy night. A vision of something from the past.

"Lies, lies, lies," he whispered, trying to remember exactly as she had sounded. "This is your house, Annabel. That's where it happened. You want me to go there? Is that it? You want me to find your lies?" He paused. "Or your husband's lies?"

He found the address of the house in the article, wrote it down, then went back to the top and read the full story.

A 911 dispatcher received a call from the Hellers' house at nine thirty on Halloween night. The call was quick, with just the sound of the phone clattering to the floor before the line went dead. The dispatcher put out an emergency message on the radio, and the police arrived at the remote country home ten minutes later, where they engaged a gunman and shot him. The gunman died at the scene. Two victims—a woman and another man—were found naked in bed together, both shot and unresponsive. But when paramedics arrived, they discovered that the woman had a faint pulse. They rushed her to the hospital in Williston, where she died.

Jason took a deep breath, trying to shake off the horror he imagined from that night last Halloween. He read a dozen more articles. The neighbor whom Annabel had been having the affair with was a mid-thirties divorcé named Gary Weston, whose small farm was down the road from the Heller house. There were only a half-dozen other homes in the area, all of them separated by vast farm fields and patches of trees.

Jason returned to the first photo of the house and remembered its isolated surroundings in the vision Annabel had shown him. "You were all alone out there," he said. "You and Gary, when your husband caught you. No one to help you. No one to know what was about to happen. You called nine-one-one, but they couldn't get there in time. You were too far out of town."

He rubbed his temples and blinked his eyes.

"Why didn't you try to run?" he asked. "Because you were afraid for Gary? Because you thought your husband wouldn't really do it?"

He stared at the address written on the paper. Then he turned back to the photo of the house as a strange and sudden urge to go there invaded his mind. "What happened out there?" He hesitated, as if wondering whether she could somehow hear him even though he was not in the hospital. "Did you drive him to madness—a madness that led to your own murder?"

He propped his head in his cupped hands. "What do you want me to do?"

But even as he asked the question, he felt the conflict rising within him. He had spent most of his life suspicious of what people called love. He knew what had first jaded him. When he was young, his parents had seemed to love each other as if they lived in a fairytale. He remembered them, sometimes after dinner, dancing to country swing music in the living room. He remembered the countless babysitters on the nights they went out together. How happy they had once been together, and how comforting it had felt when they loved each other.

But he also remembered how his father changed after his mom's affair came to light. Jason hadn't understood what was happening at the time—only that his parents yelled at each other and his mother cried and his father hit the wall before crying, too. And after that night he could tell they didn't love each other anymore—at least, not the way they once had. They never danced again. They had a talk with him to try to explain things, but all he remembered was that his mother was moving out. That was how he knew it was her fault. And that was when he learned that true love was no more real than a jolly bearded man who flew around the world in one night on a sleigh pulled by wingless flying reindeer, and climbed down every chimney delivering billions of presents.

He looked at the picture of the house again and felt the sudden urge to go for a drive. He grabbed the car keys and the paper with the address and left his room. Taking the stairs to the hotel lobby, he saw two people walking into the building through the sliding doors. The man had on a worn brown suit, and the woman was in showier garb, like some modern-day Molly Brown. She made eye contact, which he wouldn't have thought twice about if not for the way she raised one eyebrow at him as they passed. It was as if he had something written on his forehead, which she had only half glimpsed as their paths crossed. The fleeting encounter bothered him enough to stick in his mind as his current mission pulled him forward. He left the hotel, jumped in the rental car, and was soon following GPS directions down a lonely dark highway.

40

Strange feelings had been surging through Madam Bovell in waves since she arrived in North Dakota. Most dominant was her excitement over meeting Rachel. But she could sense much more to this town than one girl with off-the-charts psychic abilities. There was a strong presence of spirit energy. She had noticed it even before the plane touched down a few hours ago. It was as if the town were founded on intersecting ley lines— those ancient, invisible pathways of earth energy that crisscrossed the planet and, according to lore, were often connected with hauntings and unusual geomagnetic disturbances. Or perhaps some extreme event in the town's past had left a powerful spirit concentration. But what worried her most was the sense that deep within this cloud of spirit energy lurked a heavy presence of evil.

Dr. Graves pulled into the parking lot, and they walked together in silence to the hotel entrance. As they passed through the automatic sliding glass doors, a young man was walking toward them, and in passing he looked up and made eye contact. In that instant, she received a flash from his mind: a surging mix of excitement and fear, as if he was on his way to do something dangerous that part of his conscience was warning him not to do. It was such a strange and intriguing feeling, she couldn't contain her surprise, which he clearly noticed in that fleeting shared glance. But his momentum kept him moving, and he vanished out the door behind her and into the parking lot.

They took the elevator to their neighboring rooms on the third floor.

"You think she'll come here tonight?" Dr. Graves asked at the door to his room.

"Yes."

"Want to talk about how we're going to do this? How we're going to tell her everything we've learned about her family's past—assuming she doesn't already know?"

"Yes. I need a few minutes in my room. Then we can wait for her in your room and figure this out."

She entered her room and sat down on the bed. She needed time to catch her breath and think.

Something was bad in this town. She could feel it more strongly now than even just an hour ago.

She wondered whether to mention anything about the darkness she felt hanging over the town, then decided not to say anything just yet. She needed a little more time to understand exactly what she was sensing. Her gifts seemed to be returning with more strength the closer she got to Rachel. Perhaps, the next time they met, she would receive some illumination on why she and Dr. Graves had been called to this remote place. And maybe she would learn something about the mysterious evil that hung over the land.

41

Rachel fought to control the excitement bubbling inside her. Hunched over her plate at the dinner table, she chewed her green peas without hearing a word of her adoptive parents' conversation. She was still immersed in her experience with the woman who left their house forty-five minutes ago.

She had captured thoughts from others before. It had started a couple of months ago, at the beginning of the school year, but it was never more than a few words at a time, and always tied to a strong emotion.

I like you. You're nice.

Get outta my way. I'm better than you.

Cute shirt.

Teacher's pet.

Punk.

They had been strong thoughts, unmasked and offered to her. Eye contact was usually involved, but not always. She had realized early on that for her to hear them, the person had to be focusing on *her*. That was why it always felt more like *receiving* their thoughts rather than hearing or reading them. She couldn't just close her eyes and listen in on what everyone was thinking.

There had to be a lowering of the psychological guard, an invitation almost, as if the person didn't care whether she knew what they were thinking. An unmasked facial expression, but on the inside, that only she could see. It was like a weak radio wave.

Of course, no one ever caught on that she had received their thoughts—until this woman.

But the woman had known and had used that knowledge to communicate back and forth with her. The woman was like her, although Rachel could sense that her gifts were weak. She had felt only a slight tingling from the woman's attempted intrusion, but it was enough for Rachel to amplify her own abilities beyond what she had thought possible. It both excited and terrified her to think that her gift was growing and might even become so strong that she couldn't control it. What if it eventually overwhelmed her?

And those fears and curiosities made her antsy to escape the dinner table and find this woman who may be the only one with the answers to her questions.

Shoveling the last bite of tuna casserole into her mouth, she chewed three times and swallowed. "I'm finished," she said. "May I be excused? Jessica wants me to go over to her house and work on our presentation for AP English."

"What's it about?" her adoptive father asked while chasing down an elusive pea with his fork.

"Everyone's giving a presentation on a different Edgar Allan Poe story. Jessica and I were paired up and assigned 'The Murders in the Rue Morgue.' We give it tomorrow afternoon and just need to practice it a few more times."

"Sounds scary," he said.

"Worse—it's *terrifying,* and I don't want to be up too late working on it."

He nodded. "Then you're excused."

She jumped up from the table and grabbed her empty plate.

"Call if you won't be back by ten," her adoptive mother said.

"—Count on it," she promised, too excited to argue about curfew.

Minutes later, she was out the door and driving her beat-up old Beetle toward the hotel.

42

Jason turned off the highway and drove along a dirt road in the dark countryside. A fleet of storm clouds blanketed half the sky and would soon swallow the large moon and few remaining stars. His eyes darted between the soft glow of his phone's GPS app, and through the windshield at the dark shapes moving past just outside the reach of his headlights. There were no other cars. The newspaper articles had said that only a half-dozen farms were within a few miles of the Heller house. There was nothing illegal about driving at night down dirt roads in the middle of Boondock, East Nowhere, but because the place was so empty, he worried that some nearby resident might find headlights around the Heller house suspicious—which might prompt a call to the police. He had no idea whether anyone was living in the house, though it seemed likely now that almost a year had passed since the killings. It would be best if he could find it without delay and drive by to satisfy his curiosity. If no one seemed home, he might even stop and get a closer look at the house Annabel had shown him in the vision that now haunted him so.

His heart skipped at the sight of a dead animal on the side of the road. Something fairly big—a raccoon or coyote or whatever roamed these parts—curled up right where the shoulder met the tall grass.

Following the final GPS instructions, he turned onto another small road and felt a surge of excitement as the display showed a virtual car nearing the end of its virtual journey. He was now within a half mile of the farmhouse, which should be on his left. The land was uneven, in one of the few rolling wooded landscapes he had seen in the area. After driving through flat, open countryside for so long, it felt like entering a different world.

The first thing he noticed when he arrived at the turn to the long, gravel driveway was the large mailbox with "HELLER" on top. It seemed wrong that the sign was unchanged since the killings. Something didn't seem right, yet he couldn't turn back now. He pulled the car into the long curving driveway and killed the engine even before the house was in view. It must be hidden behind the thick stand of pine trees just ahead.

He saw no light through the trees, although he didn't know how far the house was set back from the road. A surge of nervous excitement rushed through him as he opened the door and stepped out onto the gravel. Closing the door as quietly as he could, he walked along the driveway with one slow step after another, trying to find a gait that would muffle the crunch of gravel beneath his shoes. A low roll of thunder echoed from miles away. He followed the driveway into the trees. The moon was giving off enough light to cast an anemic glow on the gravel while the surrounding foliage remained shrouded in darkness.

And then, as if a magician's curtain had been whisked aside, the dim outline of the house came into view. The drive opened into a gravel area in front of the big farmhouse. No vehicles were in sight, and no lights were on inside. The front porch was long and dark against the house. No lights were on even outside the garage. The only illumination was from the moon, which hung above and behind the steep hip roof above the two main floors.

But just as he looked up to take in the eerie grandeur of this classic farmhouse, the storm clouds drifted across the moon, and everything sank into darkness.

Standing nervously in the void, he listened one last time for any sound of life before getting his cell phone out and turning on its flashlight. But this was in some ways worse than the moon's glow, for while his light brought great clarity to his immediate surroundings, it made the vast spaces outside its reach even darker than before.

Taking a deep breath for courage, and another for what was surely stupidity, he went up to the house and stepped onto the creaky front porch. The wind was picking up, and the pine trees began swaying back and forth as if they had now come alive by some unnatural agency. One treetop even bent far enough to rake the wall up near an attic window, scratching rhythmically at the upper siding.

Somehow, he sensed that the house was empty. Beyond the absence of any cars or lights, and lack of movement from within, he also sensed a sad emptiness from this place. It was like finding the ruins of a thriving village whose people had vanished for unknown reasons long ago. He felt he understood the happiness that had once filled this place before that tragic, fatal night. Whoever owned this house seemed content to let it go to ruin.

Shining his flashlight along the porch, he was startled to find the front door cracked open. It was as if the house were daring him to enter.

"Hello?" he called. "Is anyone here? I've run out of gas and need to call for help. Anyone here at all? I need to use your phone. I'm coming in, okay? I'm coming in!"

It was stupid, he knew. Since cell phones, who needed to borrow a house phone to call anyone? Still, he had to announce *something* just in case someone was inside.

The door creaked as he pushed it the rest of the way open. Using the flashlight, he found the light switch on the wall and flipped it up. Nothing happened. He flipped it down and up again. The power was off. Perhaps a storm had caused it, or perhaps the utility company had cut it long ago. Either way, he wasn't remotely interested in searching for the breaker box to check, for it was probably somewhere in the basement—about the last place he wanted to explore.

"Hello?" he yelled once more. At this point, he actually hoped someone would respond from the darkness so that he wouldn't be alone in the house with whatever horrifying memories haunted it. But the only answer he got was a flash of lightning and the thunderclap that rattled the windows.

He slid the phone light's beam back across the entryway, watching as the shadows fled like phantoms into doorways on the left and right, down the hallway that bisected the house, or up the narrow staircase to the unseen floor above. It had already looked like a big house from outside, but the inside felt even more expansive.

He stepped through the doorway on the right. His light played over the furniture in the room, each piece covered by a white sheet. It unnerved him that the place had been mostly gutted, and the rest made to look like a sheeted phantasm from a Victorian ghost story.

He stepped among the sheets, eyeing each one carefully for any hint of movement. This place had not been lived in since Annabel's murder.

He moved into the next room. It was larger, with a huge fireplace of gray stones, and a ring of what looked like chairs and sofas covered in more white sheets. Above the covered furniture was a gorgeous antique-looking chandelier that sparkled in his flashlight beam amid the floating dust motes. He suddenly felt a wave of sadness wash over him, magnified by a loneliness he couldn't begin to describe except to say that it seemed to come from outside himself. The emotion overcame him like a bolt from the blue. His imagination tried to fill in the missing bits. The chandelier, which he envisioned shining brightly as the lovers danced beneath it, now hung in shadow. Perhaps it wasn't just something in this room that had filled him with sadness. Perhaps, the house itself was mourning the tragedy it had witnessed.

He continued to the next room—a study—then a dining room and a kitchen. He was growing more comfortable with the shadows, though he never forgot that he was trespassing in a cursed place that had seen horrible crimes.

Having come full circle, he found himself standing by the front door once again. He looked up at the dark, narrow staircase. The murders had occurred somewhere up there. He said a brief prayer, swallowed his fear, and started up the creaky old steps.

The wood sagged under his modest weight and groaned as if it were a living thing responding to an unwelcome stimulus. The next step creaked louder, as if the house were now protesting his ascent to some forbidden place. The wooden banister felt ice cold against his palm. He felt a little light-headed, as if each step up took him another thousand feet higher. He asked himself what in hell's name he was doing here, and couldn't form a rational answer. This little adventure had gone well past satisfying his curiosity. He had hoped only to find the house, see it from a distance to prove to himself that the murder story was true, and feel the reality of Annabel's life and death in a way that one never could just from reading old newspaper articles. This was a woman's life, and for whatever reason, he felt driven to make a personal connection. This woman had found him in death. No, not found him—*chosen* him. She could have contacted any number of people going in and out of the hospital, but she had chosen him. And he had felt the pressure of that choice the moment he arrived outside the house: the pull to go inside and discover a secret she needed him to find.

As he neared the second-floor landing, his light revealed a bleak wooden hallway that stretched perpendicular to the staircase. In front of him was a barren wall with a round patch outlined below a single nail hole, showing that a picture once hung here. The entire hallway seemed to have been stripped of everything. The dust motes floating in the air now seemed to stop, as if time itself had frozen. They hovered in front of him for a moment, then gradually drifted toward his phone, as if attracted to the light. But then they slid off to his right, as if something was pulling them down the hallway.

He took the last two creaky steps and turned right in the hallway. Holding his phone light low, he followed the thousands of drifting white dust particles.

Halfway down the hallway, a faint gurgling behind him made him jump. Whirling about, he shined his light into the brooding darkness. Nothing. Somewhere in the distance, the gurgling continued, then stopped. Lightning flashed a shadow of twisted branches outside the far window at the other end of the hallway, and for a brief moment the spindly silhouette looked like monstrous claws. Looking forward again, he saw more dust particles than before, drifting toward the dark doorway at the end.

He continued down the hallway to the end and stood in front of a closed door. The dust motes had drifted to the wood floor and then disappeared under the door.

More lightning flashes flickered with a strobelike effect along the walls, followed by the loudest, most violent flurry of thunderclaps he could recall.

But just at the very end of the thunder, he heard the loud bang of a door slamming shut. He tensed and froze. The noise had come from below. Someone was in the house. He covered his light and stood rigid in the darkness as the veins in his neck throbbed. He waited for another sound, for any indication of where the unknown new arrival might be in the house. He expected at any moment to hear creaking on the stairs. A minute ticked past as the storm intensified. After another minute, he started to wonder whether the storm had caused the sound. Had he perhaps opened a door without closing it during his walkthrough of the first floor? And why would anyone come into the house and slam a door? It must be nothing more than the wind. Had to be. Still, he was crazy to have come here—and crazier to *still* be here. He would leave soon, he promised himself. But first, he had to see what was on the other side of this door.

He reached out and touched the doorknob. It was freezing, colder even than the stairway banister. He turned it and let the door slowly creak open. Stepping inside, he found a large empty room with white walls and a pair of large windows looking out on both the front and back of the house. It must be the largest room on the second floor, and he now realized exactly where he was. There was really nothing one could do to prepare for standing in a place that had seen murder—a double murder, he reminded himself, for Annabel's husband had killed both her and her lover. And he had done it right here in this very spot.

He leaned back against the wall, taking slow, deep breaths. The thunder was now almost continuous, rolling in waves across the dark landscape as the rain came down faster and harder on the farmhouse.

"This is where it happened," he said out loud, imagining that Annabel was here listening to him. "This is what you wanted me to see?" He moved his light across the empty room. "But I don't know what I'm supposed to look for ... what I'm supposed to discover."

His eyes fixed on an area of the wood floor by the back wall, between the window and the open door to the master bathroom. This space in between would have been the logical spot for the bed. "My God, it happened right *here*." Suddenly, the house moved. He felt it. It was so unexpected that it pulled his imagination away from the past and attuned his senses to his present surroundings. It was a fresh warning of danger. As he watched, frost grew along the edges of the windows. The walls moaned, and a sharp creaking came from the hallway behind him. The air pressure changed, too, making it hard to focus. His head spun with vertigo. The room was now quite obviously shaking. The floor was unsteady. The boards of the hardwood floor shifted slightly, but enough to give the impression the entire house might soon fall into a sinkhole into the ground—maybe drop all the way down to the pits of hell.

"Annabel!" he shouted, not knowing whether anything he felt was real. "Stop this! Stop it! Please!"

But the vibrations only increased. The floorboards rattled audibly. Chips of paint flecked off the walls.

He took a step back, realizing that he had no influence over what was happening. He had made a mistake trusting Annabel. He could no more control her than he could control a tornado, could no more befriend her than he could a rabid dog.

One of the floorboards behind him had popped up enough to catch his heel as he stepped backward. He fell hard on his butt. The floor rattled aggressively around him as if the entire house were being pulled apart. A dark crack formed at the base of the doorjamb and ran up it, splitting the wood.

Clambering to his feet, he ran from the room. He sprinted down the hallway, slung himself around the banister newel, and raced down the stairs in sheer panic. He missed the bottom step and stumbled, smacking into the base of the facing wall across the landing. He had managed to spin enough so that his right shoulder and back took most of the blow. He needed a second to recover, but terror got him back on his feet to continue his desperate flight.

Scrambling to the front door, he flung it open and darted onto the front porch. But just as he left the house, a sharp flash of lightning brightened the night and revealed the wet, intense face of a tall man right in front of him. Shocked, Jason screamed as he collided with the man, sending them both crashing over the porch railing and into the mud.

Jason tried frantically to get up and run. But he slid in the mud, falling back to all fours. And as he struggled to get up, he saw the dark-shadowed silhouette of the man slowly grow until it towered over him. The man grabbed him by his upper arm and dragged him out of the mud puddle and onto a nearby patch of wet grass. Muttering and growling, the man flipped him to his stomach and pinned his arms behind him while jamming a knee into his back.

Jason fought helplessly, terrified that his life would end at any minute by stab or a broken neck or any number of other ways that he was now powerless to stop. But just when he was about to beg for mercy, he felt the hard metal tightening around his wrist, followed by the words, "You're under arrest, you bastard. You have the right to remain silent …"

The rest of the man's words turned into meaningless syllables as Jason grasped what was happening. He had never been arrested for anything, never even remotely been in trouble with the law, so this was both humiliating and shameful. But all those feelings were dwarfed by his relief that the man wasn't some lunatic about to kill him and that he had escaped whatever demonic presence was inside that nightmare of a house.

The man pulled him to his feet, and when he turned around, he got his first good look. It was the same police officer who had pulled him over two nights ago.

"You?" the cop said. He was covered in mud and looked mad as hell.

"Oh, Officer! Thank God! It's not safe here! We have to go! Now!"

"What are you doing here?" The cop's tone was hard.

"Look, man—sir—we have to get out of here fast."

"Are you alone?"

"What? Yes! Officer, we have to *go*!"

"Why is it not safe?"

"Didn't you hear all that?"

"Hear what?"

"The house!"

"Is someone in there?" The officer turned his head and glared up at the dark structure in the pounding rain.

"The house was shaking! Boards were rattling! Windows vibrating!"

"You on drugs?"

"No—what? No!"

"It's a bad storm," the cop said before the next thunderclap. "And this is a bad place to be." He spun Jason about, facing away from the house, where a police cruiser waited in the dark on the gravel driveway, rain drumming on its roof. "And you're trespassing."

The officer frog-marched him down the driveway, to the cruiser. Jason kept his head down to shield his face from the cold rain and to watch his step in the dark. When they reached the car, the officer opened the back door and helped him inside. Jason had a hard time sitting with his hands cuffed behind him. The officer closed the door. Jason had a few seconds alone to look through the welded grate dividing the front and back seats, past the rivulets of water running down the windshield, at the imposing bulk of the house, and the strange shadows that kept shifting and morphing like a live Rorschach test with each flicker of lightning.

The cruiser's front door opened, and the loud growl of the storm jumped in volume. The officer got in, made eye contact with Jason in the mirror, and swore. They both were muddy and dripping wet, and Jason didn't really know what to say. He had never been in the back of a police car before.

The officer shook his head and groaned. It was so unexpected and—especially within the confined space of the police car—aggressive, that it scared Jason. Then the man took a deep breath and looked again at him in the mirror. "It's been a long day," he said. "And then I get a call about some car lights stopped near the old Heller house. So I gotta come out here, on a night like this, and figure out what's going on."

Jason was silent, looking up at him in the mirror.

"So, Mr. Hardy, tell me. Just what the hell *is* going on?"

"I was just driving around ..."

"Don't lie to me!" the officer said, raising his voice, and for an instant Jason saw real rage on his face. "If you had stopped in front of any other house, I might believe you. But not here. So you'd better tell me exactly what you're doing unless you want me to hit you with every violation I can hang on you—starting with assaulting an officer."

"That was an accident. I didn't see you until the last second."

"It looked intentional to me."

"What?"

"You'd better start explaining," the officer said, and it was clear by the way he raised his eyebrows that this was the last chance Jason was going to get.

But Jason couldn't tell him the truth, for it would look as if he had lost his mind. But he had to tell him something, and the lie had to be close enough to the truth that he could say it convincingly. Cops were practically psychic when it came to sensing a lie from a suspect.

Lies, lies, lies. The words rang again in his head.

"I heard about the murders that happened here last Halloween. The wife murdered by her husband. The neighbor murdered, too, because he was caught in bed with the wife."

"Annabel," the officer said softly. "Her name was Annabel."

"You knew her?"

The officer nodded. "It's a small town. Everyone knows everyone."

Jason realized he needed to be even more cautious in his lies. "I was told the story by people at the hospital. It just sounded so crazy. A small-town crime of passion. I was in my hotel room going stir crazy, just wanted to get out of the room, didn't know what to do in town, so I just thought I'd go for a drive. Thought the countryside might be fun since I spend so much time stuck in Chicago traffic. But I didn't really know where I should drive to."

"So you looked up the address where the murders happened," the officer said sadly. "You thought you'd come check it out, like it's some sort of tourist attraction."

"I'm sorry," Jason said. "I didn't mean any offense. I was just looking for something to do."

"But you didn't just drive by. You stopped. You broke in."

"I didn't break in," Jason said. "I stopped because no one seemed around. I went in because the door was open, and no one seemed to be in the house. It's like it was abandoned."

"It *is* abandoned," the officer said. "The door was open?"

"It was cracked open. Still, I know it was stupid to go inside. I don't know what I was thinking."

The officer nodded as if at least partly understanding the motivation. "You were acting like a damn high school kid; that's what you were doing. You're not the first person we've caught out here. The others got warnings, but for you it's different."

"How?"

"You're from out of town, for one thing. I don't know you or what kind of real intensions you might have. But the locals—we know them, so we can cut them some slack. And the others were kids. You're older and should know better. And you assaulted me."

"I said that was an accident."

The officer was now staring forward out the windshield, in the direction of the house. He fell silent, as if lost in a deep memory. Then he said, "She was a good person, you know. Annabel. Don't believe the way the papers made her out. I knew her since we were kids. She didn't deserve what happened to her."

Jason remained silent.

The officer wiped his drenched face with the inside of his shirt. "All right, Mr. Hardy. Here's what we're going to do. Driving recklessly Tuesday night: strike one. Trespassing tonight: strike two—a *big* strike two. Now, I'm sure a fast-paced city boy like you must go stir crazy in a quiet place like this, but you need to get a handle on yourself. I'm going to let you go, but I swear to God, if I even see you jaywalking after tonight, I'm going to haul you before Judge Heitz and let you explain to him all the things you've been doing in *his* county since you hit town. You understand?"

"Yes, Officer. Thank you."

"Yeah." The officer started the engine, turned the car around, and drove back down the long, winding gravel driveway. The windshield wipers beat quickly, sounding like a racing heartbeat and lending an added sense of fright to the storm still raging above. Rolling past the pine trees that lined the drive, the officer stopped the vehicle next to Jason's rental car near the mailbox.

He got out, opened the back door, and helped Jason out into the rain. As the man fussed with the handcuff key in the wet night, Jason saw the biggest, brightest bolt of lightning yet jag sideways above the trees, in the direction of the house. And a second later, in the same instant that the thunder banged like a rifle shot in his ear, he felt again the alarming vibrations around him that he had experienced in the house.

The handcuffs came off. "I'll follow you back to town. Now, go."

Jason walked straight to his rental, too embarrassed and humiliated to look back at the officer. As he got in the car, he remembered how the second floor of the house had shaken. What had he done to cause the disturbance? For he believed that he had awoken something dark and dangerous in Annabel's spirit, but he couldn't understand why. He was certain she had wanted him to come here, to discover her lies. And what dark power had shaken the house in a way that, while terrifying to him, went unnoticed by the officer who was right outside.

He put the car in gear, whipped a U-turn on the county road, and drove slowly toward the main highway back into town. And despite all the distractions of the unrelenting rain and the many haunting secrets of this dark night, he still had to focus on driving carefully. He tried to ignore the watchful headlights following behind him all the way back into Williston.

43

"She's here," Madam Bovell said to the professor.

Sitting at the desk in his hotel room, he paused in his writing to look up at her. "How do you know?"

"She just told me."

He dropped his pen onto the journal. "Please try not to show her how excited you are."

"Too late," she replied. "I think she can already sense it from both of us."

"We need to be careful until we know what we're dealing with in her."

"She's the most powerful medium the world has seen in a long time," Bovell answered, stretching her legs out farther on the sofa. "I can feel it. And she's so young—she's only just beginning her journey."

"If that's true, it's all the more reason for us to be careful," he warned.

There came a soft knocking at the door.

"'Suddenly there came a tapping,'" Madam Bovell whispered, looking at him with wide, playful eyes. "'As of some one gently rapping, rapping at my chamber door.'"

The professor nodded as a slight grin betrayed his amusement. "'Quoth the Raven, "Nevermore."'" He looked up at her again. "Just remember why we were sent here. Something wanted us to find her. She may need our help. She may even be in danger."

"I haven't forgotten," Madam Bovell said. "Now I'm going to let her in."

As she walked toward the door, the professor closed his journal and leaned back at the desk. He hadn't been given a glimpse of this girl's mind the way Madam Bovell had. He hadn't seen her do anything that convinced him she was as powerful as Bovell hypothesized. But he did have to admit at least one thing to himself: he no longer found himself categorically dismissing the intentions of others to make legitimate contact with things beyond the reality that most experienced. He no longer wanted to prove them all con artists. For the first time in decades, his professional skepticism was blinded by hope—which, before this journey, had all but faded into the deep, dark night.

With an open, eager mind, he wanted so much to believe in what the mediums were always selling. He wanted to reach out to the dead—perhaps even find his son and see what existence he may have found in the afterlife. He wanted to journey into the magical spiritual world that blurred between the vibrant *now* and the timeless, eternal realm of death. And if there was any chance that Madam Bovell and this girl could somehow lead him into that mysterious abyss, then he would follow.

*   *   *

Rachel watched the door pull away from her, and the woman's warm, lively visage take its place. The man was farther behind her, sitting at a desk at the other end of the long hotel room.

"Thank you for coming," the woman said. "Please do come in."

Rachel walked past her and dropped her backpack on the couch. "Who are you both, really?" she asked, foregoing the niceties. "You can start with your real names."

"I'm Dr. Donovan Graves, professor of psychology at the University of Chicago and former president of the American Society for Psychical Research."

"And I'm Madam Helen Maria Bovell, medium; expert in crystology, Kirlian photography, and board and card readings; and former senior spiritualism guide at Lily Dale."

Rachel felt gooseflesh creep across her tingling skin. If these two were telling the truth, they were the real deal in the world of paranormal research and spirit contact. Every ghost hunter in the world knew of the British Society for Psychical Research, where ghost sightings and spirit contact investigations were born a century and a half ago, and its sister society later founded in America. And just as famous was Lily Dale, a community in upstate New York with the largest concentration of psychics and mediums anywhere in the world. Even Rachel's little troop of amateur ghost hunters had read countless articles online about these organizations.

And here in front of her were two people from the tops of those ranks—if they were telling the truth.

She looked down, trying to sense their feelings and emotions, their energy. From the woman, she felt warmth mixed with anxiety, and maybe even worry or a tick of fear. From the man, she got tension, hesitation, uncertainty—and pain. Nothing aggressive from either of them. They were like adventurers: open and brave and full of hope.

"You came here for me?"

"Yes," Madam Bovell answered.

"Because of what I can do?"

"Yes."

"How did you learn of me?"

"That's a long story," the professor said.

"I had a dream," Madam Bovell offered. "A vision."

Rachel could hardly believe this was happening. A vision that had led these two to find her right at the moment that her gifts were beginning to bloom, and right when she was desperate to understand what made her so different from everyone else.

"What did you see in this vision?" she asked.

"I was falling," Madam Bovell said. "It was night and I was dropping through the sky. Then I saw a woman in gray. She was falling next to me and looked at me and told me to find you."

"Just like that?" Rachel questioned.

"We made a few stops along the way," the professor said. "Everything leads to you."

"Why me?"

"Your gifts," Madam Bovell said. "You're more powerful than you realize."

Rachel didn't know how to respond. She stared at the woman, then looked away, to the mirror above the narrow dresser cluttered with hotel visitor magazines and a half-unpacked purse. For an entire year, she had kept secret the things she could do. But now it seemed that the truth of her abilities was spreading like wildfire: first to Jason, then to Shelley in chemistry class, then to the rest of their ghost-hunting club in Jessica's basement, and now to these two newcomers. When would it stop? When would her life just go back to the way it had been before these changes?

"What do you know about your family history?" the professor asked.

"They're all dead," Rachel answered.

He nodded without breaking eye contact. "What else?"

"My mother was my only family still alive when I was born. She died when I was four. I have no memories of her. The only thing I have of hers is an old religious book by Pope Gregory, and even that has only one small memento from her—an underlined passage. Everything else of my mother's is gone. I was sent to an orphanage in Kansas City for a few years before I was adopted and moved here. I don't really have any clear memories of my life before Williston."

"Nothing?" Madam Bovell asked, probing as if she knew there was more. "No memories of her at all?"

"I have dreams sometimes," Rachel said. "I see things in them. Fragments of memories, maybe. They remain only for a second or two, lingering when I wake up, and then they're gone."

"Do you know how she died?" the professor asked.

"A blood clot," Rachel answered. "She was playing cards at some friends' house when it happened. A note in my orphanage file said she died right there at the table, in the middle of their game. Apparently, I was present when it happened."

The professor looked sad and glanced at Madam Bovell.

"Rachel," the woman said. "We've been trying to discover who you are for the past few days—ever since my vision. Our path took us to Stull, Kansas, where you're from. We found your mother's grave and spoke to someone who knew her. Did you know your mother was a medium? Did you have any idea?"

Rachel felt a little unsteady and sat on the cushioned ottoman in a calm movement, conscious that she was being observed. "A medium?" she said, staring at her open palms as if looking for clues. "I felt something ... I suspected, maybe. Once my own changes began last year, I pretended she might have been, but I didn't know for sure. I didn't actually ... She really was?"

"She had great abilities," Madam Bovell said. "And so did your grandmother."

"So it's not an accident," she said. "The things I can do—I'm not some sort of freak."

"No, you're not," Madam Bovell said. "Don't ever let anyone tell you that. You're gifted. And you're very special."

"What can you tell me about them?" she asked in a soft voice—a polite request bordering on a plea.

"They both lived in Stull," Madam Bovell said. "And they both were well-known mediums in the area. Your grandmother had performed hundreds of farmhouse séances. During the seventies, after *The Exorcist* became a best seller and then a major movie, the idea of exploring the spirit world became a mainstream interest once again. College students from the University of Kansas flocked to Stull hoping to join your grandmother's séances. But a séance is always conducted with a small, select group, invitation only, and when your grandmother couldn't indulge mere thrill seekers, the college students began having all-night ghost-watching parties at Stull Cemetery. Especially around Halloween. Soon, rumors of the devil appearing at the cemetery started making the rounds, and the events became a self-fulfilling legend."

"Our ghost-hunting club has read about Stull Cemetery," Rachel said. "It's known as one of the seven gates to hell. They say the devil goes there twice a year to visit the grave of a witch who was a former lover."

"They say a lot of things about Stull," the professor huffed. "None of it true."

"But what is true," Madam Bovell said, "is that not long after this started, your grandmother died during a séance."

"How?"

"They say a brain aneurysm."

"Same as my mother," she said, suddenly uneasy.

"That's what they said in the news articles. But someone we spoke to who was part of that séance had a different story to tell. And it involves the devil."

Rachel shuddered. This last comment allowed a memory to surface from the deepest crevasses of her mind. Over the past six months, during so many dreams that increasingly felt like visions, she had sometimes sensed another presence near her:

intruding into her dreams, observing from the shadows as she explored the hidden realities of the world.

"The devil," Rachel whispered. "What role could that creature have in this?"

"Some think it was the devil that killed your grandmother," Madam Bovell said. "They say that the devil felt her powers and didn't like that she had such strong abilities to bridge the worlds of the living and the dead."

"Do you believe that?" Rachel asked, wishing to sort facts from lore in her family history.

"Not at first," Madam Bovell said. "The devil doesn't usually come up in accounts of séances. Almost never, in fact, and even when it does, we tend to find credibility issues. However, it was said that your grandmother had greater depth than most mediums. Most just open their minds up like radio-wave receivers, waiting to catch open signals of spirits passing by or hovering in the vicinity. A bit like fishing from a boat in a big ocean. But your grandmother may have had the ability to reach farther than her peers. Not just to those spirits who are trapped in a place, unable to move on. And not just to spirits that have moved on to heaven yet can briefly return to Earth to watch over loved ones they left behind. Those are the kinds of spirits most mediums can make contact with. But your grandmother … She was special. They say she could—at times—make contact with spirits trapped in hell. And this, I believe, would have gotten the devil's attention. This might have driven him to kill your grandmother during such a séance."

"Kill her how?"

"The point of a séance is for people to contact those in the spirit world. To hear those spirits speak, which they can do only through a living person, using that person's lungs and diaphragm and vocal cords to form sound waves of words. They do this by tapping into the electrical signals in a person's mind, temporarily taking control of that person's consciousness. Mediums are ordinary people born with an extraordinary ability to sense and receive these energy signals through receptors in their neural network. They then translate the signals into brain-wave activities that convey understandable information to the consciousness. These are gifts passed down through genetics, but usually the genetic codes are turned off or lie dormant for many generations, so that even a strong collection of the specialized genes will only rarely result in the passing down of a usable gift. So children of gifted mediums almost never display any gifts themselves. And in all recorded history on the subject, there has never been an authenticated instance of a sequential third-generation medium of remarkable talent. Never, until now."

Rachel looked up from her lap. "I'm still not sure I understand how my grandmother died."

"She was conducting a séance with twelve others at a farmhouse near Stull. It was a group that met every Friday night to try to communicate with the dead. Someone owned the farmhouse and was the host of the weekly event, and your grandmother was their resident medium. A witness from that night told us that your grandmother fell into a trance and was channeling through her spirit guide when suddenly, candles around the room flared up. A breeze blew around the room even though all the windows were closed, and your grandmother suddenly arched up. They said she was actually floating out of her seat. She said some things that freaked out the group. And then in a sharp, loud voice, she said, 'Diabolus.' Then she collapsed and died."

"'Diabolus' means 'devil'?" Rachel asked.

Madam Bovell nodded. "Latin."

"She was thirty-seven when she died," the professor said.

"Ten years older than your mother was when she died," Madam Bovell said.

"Which is ten years older than I am now," Rachel said. "Seventeen," she whispered. Then, looking at the woman, she said, "Am I in some sort of danger?"

"Maybe," Madam Bovell replied.

"How did my mother die?" Rachel asked, too nervous to look either of them in the eye.

"The same way as your grandmother."

"During a séance?"

"Yes."

"She was in a trance?"

"Yes."

"Did she say anything before she died?"

"She said, 'Diabolus.'"

Rachel felt her heart beat harder—not faster, just harder. The strong pounding started in her chest, but the heavy pulsing now seemed to swell the veins in her neck. Her throat felt squeezed as if invisible hands were choking her. And the harder it was to breathe, the louder she heard her throbbing heart.

Her lost gaze drifted down to the brown and green diamond-patterned carpet. She had to focus on breathing, on vanquishing the invisible fingers tightening around her throat, on easing her disturbed, heavy heart.

"We're sorry to tell you all of this," the professor said. "We understand it's a lot to process. And we're here to help in any way we can."

She traced one of the carpet's diamond patterns with her eyes, around and around each side, finding a rhythm in her mind that finally vanquished the choking pressure and calmed her heart.

"Have you ever tried to contact the dead?" Madam Bovell asked.

"I've never been in a real trance," she said. "I don't know how to do that. But the dead have tried to contact me when I sleep. One spirit in particular. Her name's Annabel, and she was murdered by her husband last Halloween."

Madam Bovell exchanged glances with the professor. "Do you know what she wanted?"

Rachel shook her head. "She haunts the Catholic hospital."

"Haunts it *how*?" the professor asked, tilting his head and lowering his voice on the last word. It was the first hint of suspicion she had gotten from him.

"There are dozens of stories of encounters involving her and patients at night—usually patients near death. But the stories about her only involve sensations of warmth, or things moving or strange sounds. None of these patients ever said they actually *saw* her, though it's possible some may have died in the night before they could tell anyone." She pinched her lower lip, still hesitant to reveal her own long-held secret. Finally, she added, "I've been hearing her screams in my sleep since just after her murder."

She looked up to read their reactions. Madam Bovell was nodding silently with moist, understanding eyes. Dr. Graves was leaning back a little in his chair, the fingers on his left hand tapping on the desk in an indecipherable pattern, as if restlessly playing a piano part in his head. His right hand fiddled with a pen that he kept rolling along a pad of paper.

"It's all right," he said. "What else?"

"Some of my friends and I have a ghost-hunting club, and we've tried many times to make contact with her at the hospital at night. We don't do séances or anything like that, but we use ghost-hunting equipment like EVP recorders and EMF meters and night-vision cameras."

"Any luck?" he asked.

"Some strange readings, but nothing we can make sense of. However, we're only a few days away from the first anniversary of her death, and this week there have been some frightening things happening across town."

"Like what?" Madam Bovell blurted before Rachel could finish. The woman now wore a look of horror on her pale, sagging face.

"Four of my friends from the ghost-hunting club have had brushes with death in the past few days." She paused, recalling each of her friends' fear as they recounted their near-death experiences. "Shelley almost drowned in a pond. Tommy was brutally attacked by a mob of chickens on his farm and barely escaped. Jessica was nearly crushed to death when a car collapsed while she was working under it in her garage. And I just got a call on the way over here that a malfunctioning propane tank at Aaron's house caused a gas fire that put his whole family in danger. These were all freak accidents, and thank God everyone survived, but each was a close call with death. And each reported seeing or hearing strange things during the scariest moments. Unnatural things. It was as if Annabel had somehow done these things … as if she was trying to kill them."

"Her, perhaps," Madam Bovell said. "Or perhaps, something worse."

"Worse?"

"What you're describing about your friends—it doesn't sound like it would be Annabel. A ghost is usually stuck in one place, though sometimes their presence can attract ancient negative forces. These can form a cloud of evil around a disturbed ghost and can grow and spread beyond the place that the ghost haunts. It's quite rare, but it might be more likely in this town because of you. Dark forces found and killed your mother and grandmother, and now those same evil forces may be trying to find you. Even though you've never been in a séance, it may have sensed your presence in this town through some connection it made with Annabel's ghost."

"So why would it try to kill my friends instead of me?"

"I don't know. It may not yet know exactly who you are—exactly which one of your group is *you*. It may still be trying to zero in on you."

"So my friends are still in danger?"

Madam Bovell's eyes were now red and watery. "All of you are in danger. You most of all, but your friends, too … and maybe everyone in this whole town. From the moment I arrived, I've sensed that something evil has been unleashed here."

Rachel buried her face in her hands. "All because of who I am and what I can do." She could feel her hands and legs shaking. "How do we stop it?"

"There's only one thing we can do. We need to contact Annabel. And we can do that only through a séance. We need to find out why she is still here. And we need to try to get her to move on to the afterlife, and hope that her leaving removes any evil that may have found you and this town because of her."

"What if she won't leave?"

"We'll deal with that if it happens."

"What if you're right and there is another evil force here, but we can't get rid of it?"

"Then we'll deal with that, too."

"Won't a séance put me in more danger?" Rachel asked. "You said my mom and grandma …"

"I think we're beyond those choices now," Madam Bovell answered. "Whatever is trying to find you, be it Annabel or something else, it's already on your trail. We need to confront it now, before it succeeds in killing you or someone else. And I'll be leading the séance, so you should be more protected than your mom and grandmother were when they died leading séances. But we need to do it NOW. If Annabel's death anniversary is only a few days away and things keep getting more dangerous, we don't have much time."

"There's something else," Rachel said. "She's shown herself to someone—a businessman from Chicago who's visiting the hospital for work. He's here in town right now. Staying in this hotel, actually. He saw Annabel for the first and only time just a few days ago. Tuesday night."

"Oh, that is interesting," Madam Bovell said.

"He says Annabel is trying to show him something. He thinks she has a secret she's trying to tell him."

The professor took a deep, audible breath, then said, "Yes, that is indeed interesting."

Lightning rickracked across the black sky outside the window, followed by a rolling, thunderous boom. Rachel thought of her mother facing the devil in the final moments of her life. And her grandmother, doing the same before her. If those stories were true, it felt inevitable that she must soon face the same fate. But she told herself that her situation was different. Her mother was somehow helping her from the other side of death. And her mother had sent these two strangers to help her against the devil. This was a challenge by the greatest evil the world had ever known. A struggle that maybe she could avoid.

She turned away from the storm and marched toward the hallway door. She grabbed the door handle and looked back at the room. "You said you could help me contact Annabel."

"Yes."

"Then come on. We don't have time to waste."

44

Jason lay in his bed and stared up at the pale blue shades on the ceiling of his hotel room. An all-night café was across the street, and the light from its neon sign crept faintly through his window as the storm spat and grumbled from above. But a more chaotic storm was rumbling in his mind. He couldn't shake the image of the empty bedroom shaking like a cold dog, rattling the floor planks, warping the walls, breaking windows, and cracking the doorjamb as he fled the room. The unseen, tormented power haunting that place was not the Annabel he had encountered in the hospital. It was as if the house itself had awakened a rage in her. She was clearly affected by the place of her murder. Or perhaps, he feared, her rage was directed at him for some failure to discover whatever secret she was trying to reveal to him.

He didn't know what to do. He was too shaken up from the experience even to consider returning to the farmhouse, yet he didn't want to give up trying to help her. He was at a loss.

Perhaps, he wondered, he had taken this foolish pursuit as far as he could. He was at risk of damaging his career if he didn't wind up the audit. And after tonight, he was beginning to fear for his sanity should he pursue this any further. Perhaps, it was time to walk away from this while he still had that option.

A knock came at his hallway door. As his peripheral vision picked up a lightning strike in the distance, he turned his eyes away from the ceiling and stared at the door. Maybe he had imagined the sound. Ten long seconds passed. Then came another, more forceful knocking at the door. It reminded him of the fierce pounding at the farmhouse. He felt a shiver of dread. Had Annabel somehow followed him here?

He sat bolt upright, startled that anyone would be at his door so late.

The knocking grew louder, more urgent.

He got out of bed and stumbled barefoot through the dark, wearing only his sweatpants and a white T-shirt. Through the peephole, he had a fisheye view of Rachel's face, flanked by an older man and woman. He was tired and so stressed from his nightly encounter with Annabel's rage, he had trouble mustering up the will to open the door—especially since last night, when he told Rachel he had to quit the ghost investigation. But he remembered the energy Rachel brought to her pursuit of the unknown. And he remembered his promise to listen if she was ever having troubles.

He grasped the door handle. He owed both Rachel and Annabel this much, but nothing more. He would listen to what she had to say. And then, tomorrow afternoon, he would get on a plane back to Chicago and his life.

He opened the door.

Rachel's face gleamed with eager excitement. "Jason! I know you said you're done. But things have changed. Now we know how to get the answers we've been seeking."

"Who are your friends?" he asked.

"They know how to contact Annabel! They have experience with contacting the dead."

"I still don't think I can be a part of this."

"We need you, Mr. Hardy," the older woman said. "You're the one that Annabel has chosen to trust."

"You need me for what, exactly?"

"A séance."

"What, like people sitting in a circle and trying to talk to the dead?"

"It's a bit more complicated than that," the woman replied. "A séance is a channeling of positive energy to attract spirits drifting in dimensions hidden to the living, and receiving and transmitting their messages through the conduit of a medium and her spirit guide."

He raised his eyebrows at Rachel. "Where did you find these people?"

"You know that Annabel is real," Rachel said. "I know that you know. And you also believe that she is trying to tell you something. And these two can put us directly in contact with her."

"Through a séance?"

"Yes."

"Where?"

"The hospital. The old operating room—the room you work in. The room she died in."

He stepped aside and waved them into his room. "When?" he asked after closing the door.

"Tomorrow. After dark."

"Friday night," he mused. "The night before Halloween. The night before the anniversary of her murder."

Rachel nodded. "Everything that has happened since her death: all the hauntings at the hospital, all the stories, the ghost hunts by my friends, your sighting of her, the vision and discoveries of Madam Bovell and Professor Graves ..." She gestured at her two companions. "All of it leads us to whatever will happen tomorrow night."

"To what secrets lie beyond the grave," he said.

"Yes. We will open up a channel with Annabel, and for the first time, she will be allowed to say whatever she has been so desperately trying to communicate for the past year. And she'll be able to say it in her own words."

"And you think she'll reveal her secrets to us?" he asked. He thought about the rage he had witnessed from Annabel at the farmhouse, and wondered just how much they should fear the answer.

"I think she's dying to tell us," Rachel said. "I think she's trying to claw her way out of the grave to reveal whatever secret is preventing her from moving on. Maybe we can free her. I don't care what she may have done—she doesn't deserve to be trapped any longer."

Listening to her words, Jason knew he couldn't abandon her now. All his survival instincts told him to quit exploring whatever dark secrets Annabel had in life that had been silenced by her death. Perhaps that was death's real function: fate's way of burying secrets that should remain so. But as much as he wanted to keep his flight tomorrow and just run away from this, he couldn't ignore Rachel's invitation to communicate directly with Annabel. For the only thing worse than facing danger would be to run from it and be haunted by unanswered questions the rest of his life.

FRIDAY

Perhaps it has us now, this house, perhaps it will not let us go.
—Shirley Jackson, *The Haunting of Hill House*

45

Jason watched as the blood-red hand climbed the left half of the clock's face, making one small cut in time after another as it mercilessly approached the terrifying moment that he had pledged to take action against the dead. And with each second that ticked away, his thoughts flashed through another reason why he was making a big mistake. Click … *Death is a one-way door that the living shouldn't try to open.* Click. *Revealing Annabel's secret won't be good for anyone.* Click. *They're toying with dark forces they don't understand.* Click. *A Trojan horse.* Click. *Pandora's box.* Click, click, click.

Then, as the time reached the top of the evening hour, the slender red second hand seemed to hang on to the "12" for an extra tick before continuing on its way. But even that minor oddity triggered an anxiety that he had been trying to fight off while awaiting the countdown to the night's terrors.

But now it was time. No more waiting, no more hoping for delay. Time to walk the plank.

He got up from the table and went out to the hallway, moving down it and checking each room for any sign of life. Most lights were off since the skeleton staff had left before five o'clock, and even the night cleaning crew had vanished by seven. After checking his floor, he raced up and down the stairs, jogging through the other floors, shouting for anyone remaining in the building. Between breaths, he even yelled out a few times, "Hello! Is anyone here? Anyone!"

Satisfied and out of breath, he returned to his conference room after five minutes and, with a little thrill of youthful rebellion, flicked the light switch off and on five times—a smoke signal to his new tribe. Then he turned the light off and sneaked through the darkness to the small window. Peeking outside, he saw a platoon of shadows creeping along the parking lot, advancing on the hospital. It made him think of the zombies in *Night of the Living Dead.*

He turned and rushed back out of the room. Clomping down the concrete stairwell, he reached the side door just as a head filled the entire view of the small wire-reinforced window. He swung the door open on Scott's grinning face and mop of blond hair.

"Come in," Jason said. "Everyone, come in before someone sees you."

He was looking for Rachel and soon found her, hidden in the middle of the pack. The whole ghost-hunting crew was here. And at the back of the group, he saw Madam Bovell and Professor Graves.

"Do you know everyone?" he asked them as they reached the door.

"We met them in the parking lot," Madam Bovell answered. "They seem like good kids."

"They tried to bring their ghost-hunting equipment," Dr. Graves said as if it was the most ridiculous idea he had heard in ages.

"A séance is a spiritual event, not a mechanical one," Madam Bovell explained. "We need peace and openness and positive group energy to attract spirits and channel their messages.

Treating it like a science experiment would have been counterproductive."

"Well, I'm glad you set them straight," Jason said, smiling.

After they entered the building, he stuck his head out the door. The black asphalt of the empty parking lot matched the dark sky full of shadowy soot-colored clouds blotting out the stars. He had parked his rental car in the larger lot of the new hospital building in an effort to hide the nocturnal activities in the old wing. The others had done the same. The wind was picking up strength, pushing hundreds of curled dead leaves across the parking lot in such a frantic clatter that at this distance, under the lamps, they looked almost like a horde of small rodents coming at him.

He ducked his head back into the building, pulled the door shut, and made sure it was locked. Turning around, he saw eight faces.

"You'd better lead the way," Rachel said. "In case someone else is still in the building."

"Right," he said, starting up the stairs. "Let's stay quiet until we get into the room."

Unlike the darkened first and second floors, the third floor hallway was awash in light. He led the silent troop down the long, bright corridor.

Stopping in the doorway, he found the conference room exactly as he had left it. Recalling the shock of his first experience with Annabel, when she had tossed chairs all around the room, he had half expected to find the place in disarray. But this time, there had been no paranormal activities in his absence, and he imagined Annabel instead watching them with curiosity and reserve.

"This is it," he said for the benefit of Madam Bovell and Professor Graves. "The room where she died."

"Then this is the best room to have the séance," Madam Bovell replied.

"I've shut my laptop down like you asked."

"Good," she said. "We'll also want to remove all electronic devices from the room to minimize signal interference."

"It's the back office of a hospital," Jason lamented. "There are electronic devices and wi-fi throughout the building."

"Can you turn them off?"

"I'd be afraid to. I'm not sure how the networks interact with the main hospital, and I don't want to do anything that might make the IT system go down. It could affect patient safety."

"Well let's at least remove any portable devices from this room. All cellphones. Your computer."

Jason slung his computer bag over his shoulder, unplugged the network phone on the conference table, and collected everyone's cell phones after they powered them down. Carrying them down the hall, he put them in a corner of the break room. Returning to the conference room, he found Madam Bovell directing its transformation. They had slid the conference table into the center of the room and covered it with a black velvet cloth that draped to the floor. Nine chairs were evenly spaced around the table. Shelley and Aaron were taping black construction paper over the small windows.

"Anything else I can do to help?" he asked Madam Bovell.

"No. We're almost ready to start."

He walked over to Rachel, who was standing alone in one corner.

"You still sure we should do this?"

"I am," she said in barely more than a whisper. "But I'm nervous."

"The lady seems confident."

"She's nervous, too," Rachel said. "She's worried about me."

"Why?"

"My mom and grandma both died during séances, and this is my first one."

"People can *die* during these things?" Jason kept his voice down because Tommy was near them, placing brass candlestick holders along the baseboards at the edges of the linoleum floor. Jessica followed, placing tall white candles in the holders.

"No, it's not really a risk for people. But my mom and grandma were special—like Madam Bovell but apparently even stronger than her. It was their strength that got them killed. They were both in a trance state leading séances when they collapsed and died."

"Then you'll be fine," Jason said. "Madam Bovell is leading this thing. If anyone's at risk tonight, it's her."

"I'm worried that something bad is going to happen— something we're not considering. It's just a feeling."

"Well I don't like that at all," he said, glancing around the room. "Should we cancel?" Jessica was halfway through lighting the candles, which had a remarkable effect on the room's ambiance, transforming it from stuffy conference room into Gothic hideaway. Still, he didn't want Rachel feeling pressure to continue if she didn't feel safe.

"We have to do this," she said. "Forces have pulled us all together to be right here, in this place on this night. All to contact Annabel. I don't like it, either, but we have to do this."

"Do you want me to sit next to you in case something goes wrong?" Jason asked.

She seemed to ponder this for a second, then shook her head. "Could you sit across from me? That way I can see you more easily—to signal you if I think we're in trouble."

Professor Graves walked over to them. "We're going to start soon, but Madam Bovell wants everyone to leave the room first. She needs a few minutes alone at the table."

Rachel helped Jessica finish lighting the candles while Shelley and Aaron packed up the extra paper and tape from blacking out the windows. Jason walked toward the hallway with the professor. When everyone was out, he looked back into the room and saw Madam Bovell, sitting alone at the black-shrouded table. She had placed a white crystal ball about six inches in diameter on a separate cloth in the center of the table. Her eyes were closed, and her pale skin seemed to glow in the dim red light from the special bulbs that Scott and the professor had installed in the corners of the room.

"What's she doing?" Jason asked.

"She's preparing herself," the professor said. "Some mediums feel they need to meditate before a séance, clearing the mind of worldly thoughts and emotions, centering themselves to sense the tenuous connections between our reality and the spirit realm."

"You've known her a long time?"

"Professionally, I've known her for thirty years, but I think we would consider our friendship only a few days old."

"And this is normal for her?"

Dr. Graves seemed to hesitate, breaking eye contact with Jason. It was as if he suddenly felt uncomfortable in the cool, bland hallway with its old linoleum floors.

"For the past thirty years," the professor said, "Madam Bovell has been a con artist. She claims she had lost her gift, but her reputation still allowed her to earn a living, though not a good one. I think she had other reasons, too. I was a skeptic, so I didn't think she ever had the gift, and had always been conning people."

"Are you guys gonna screw this up?" Jason asked. "'Cause I don't know if the two of you are real or not. But I'm telling you, Annabel *is* real."

"Mr. Hardy, like you, I too have seen things in the past few days that makes me question things I had once been certain of. Tonight is about atonement for many faithless years. Maybe even redemption. We're not going to screw it up."

Jason took one last glance into the room before the door closed. And what he saw was mesmerizing. Madam Bovell sat at the table with her arms stretched on either side of the crystal ball, her head lowered above it, with her wavy black tresses and many gold necklaces hanging down like protective curtains.

They had left her alone in the room to grapple with whatever dark forces thrived in this haunted place. But the moment the door closed, he heard a tormented cry and moan from the other side. Startled, he reached for the doorknob. But Dr. Graves grabbed his wrist, stopping him. His alarmed look at the professor got him only a stern glare and shake of the head for an explanation. The moaning continued for a moment longer, then ceased abruptly. He had no idea what, exactly, Madam Bovell was doing on the other side of the door, but the unnerving—and potentially unholy—severity of what they were doing suddenly hit him in a way that frightened him as never before. Had he underestimated the dark forces they were messing with? This was no mere parlor trick anymore. They were really about to reach out to the dead, and in that act, they might be inviting secret horrors into their lives. As the professor released his wrist, Jason stepped back from the door.

46

Madam Bovell closed her eyes as everyone left the room. She needed to steady her mind before any séance could begin. Up until now, she had shown all the confidence of a seasoned spiritualist so that everyone would follow her lead. But now that she was alone, she opened her eyes and stared with growing apprehension at the murky ball of quartz. It had been nearly thirty years since she led a true séance with a group of sitters—thirty years since the combined power of positive thoughts had propelled her into the spiritual realm. And thirty years since she last made contact with her spirit guide: Godfrey Bale.

She touched the crystal ball, feeling its smooth, cold surface. What were her chances of receiving Godfrey Bale after such a long break? Since spirit guides were channeled through a medium only after the medium fell into a trance state, she had never even met or conversed with him. Past sitters had to describe her spirit guide to her after a séance ended and she woke from the trance. They told her that her voice had deepened while she was in a trance and that she had spoken slowly with a strange accent, her voice announcing itself as Godfrey Bale. And this Godfrey Bale had claimed to be a head servant from a great house in Ireland and had died in Dublin in 1836.

"Maybe now you can find me again, Godfrey," she whispered.

A strong breeze rattled the line of small windows behind her. She knew it wasn't a response to her question. Spirit guides could be channeled only through a medium's trance state. But she also didn't believe in coincidences. Something was out there.

She rose from her chair and approached the blacked-out window. Pulling back a corner of the paper, she peeked outside. Some bright lights from the new hospital shone brightly across the dark yard. The sides of the building were angled in a way that didn't present a straight-ahead view inside. And at that distance, with these small windows blacked out, it would be almost impossible for anyone in the hospital to see inside this conference room.

And yet, something was out there.

She heard a muted deep groan coming from the other side of the dark glass. The wind pulsed against the window, like the ebb and flow of waves, or the beating heart of some sleeping beast. The dark stand of trees was barely visible in the night, but she could see them rustling violently, as if something was shaking them.

She stared past the reflection of her worried face and watched the rampant, jerking motions of the outside world. Something was not right. It wasn't just Annabel. There was something else in this place—some form of evil that had found its way here and now hovered over the entire town.

What if she couldn't do this? What if it had just been too many years since she led a group of sitters through a séance? What if she couldn't make contact with Godfrey? What if there was more at stake here than any of them realized?

The window rattled harder, and the deep groaning became a growl within the howling wind.

The dark mass of two large clouds floated below the nearly full moon. As she gazed at them, they almost seemed like giant black eyes, glaring down on her with rage and foreboding. She stepped back from the window, aghast at the sudden image of a wild beast that had appeared in her mind. Rachel had told her that wind had been the common prelude to each of the near-death experiences described by the teens in the past few days. They had recounted their stories to her in the parking lot while awaiting Jason's signal to approach the hospital. Shelley had described a strong gust across the pond before her rowboat filled with water and pulled her beneath the surface. Tommy had heard the wind shaking his poultry barn before the horde of chickens attacked. Jessica had heard the wind howling outside her garage before the car fell off its jacks and almost crushed her to death. And Aaron had experienced a sudden gale-force gust just before the fire that could have killed his dad and nearly burned their house down.

And now this same ferocious wind was circling the old hospital, rattling the window as if some ancient evil were trying to claw its way into the room.

The cloud eyes flattened, as if narrowing their malicious stare. Then a sudden pop exploded from the window, and a star crack appeared in the tempered glass only a few inches from her eyes. Then cracks radiated outward from the penny-size star.

"Stop!" she commanded, pulling back the black paper from the windowpane. "Stop this!"

But the cracks continued to divide and spread, turning the glass into a white spiderweb of fissures. She had to stand here, strong and steady against this unholy horror that was transforming the smooth, innocuous glass into something rough and ugly and sharp—something ready to break and fly in and cut her soft flesh and slice the veins in her neck and throw sharp shrapnel into her tender eyes.

From one of the deep pockets of her shirt, she removed a hemp bag the size of her fist. Unwinding the string wrapped around its neck, she opened it and pulled out a quartz crystal the size of her pinkie. She placed it on the windowsill. Then she took out another crystal and set it by the first. Then she put down another. Then another and another, until she had a dozen sparkling rock crystals lined up along the sill.

Even before she had finished placing them all, the expanding cracks slowed, then pause. Then, incredibly, the cracks receded back to the star fracture at the center, which shrank into itself until it had vanished. The windowpane was once again smooth and flawless. Even the wind had calmed. The glowering pair of cloud eyes had divided into many smaller puffs that drifted like dark little boats across the sky.

She felt calm flow back into her. Whatever evil hovered around this town seemed to have drifted away from the hospital campus for the moment, but there was no way to know how much time they had before its return. She decided not to mention anything to the others for fear that it would shake up the peaceful, positive state of mind essential for the séance. The stakes were higher for this session than for anything else she had ever done in her life. But she couldn't let fears and negative thoughts and painful memories cloud her mind. She needed to stay positive and relaxed.

Leaving the window, she returned to her chair at the table. She closed her eyes and listened to the energy in the room.

"Annabel, if you are present, if you can hear me, we have come with good intensions, wishing only to communicate with you. And, if we can, to help you. We are not here to harm you, so please do not harm us."

She held silent for nearly a minute, allowing the room to absorb her words and intentions.

More time passed, and she sensed no response. But she hadn't really expected one. She had to keep reminding herself that for many years she had possessed nothing resembling a gift, and even the resurgent abilities she had enjoyed in the past few days were starting to weaken like a dimming sunset. She hadn't told Dr. Graves, but she could feel it leaving her again ever since she met Rachel. And while she could not be certain, she worried that this could be her last night to use her resurrected gift before it faded away forever.

It was time to begin before her strength dissipated. She closed her eyes and called to Rachel.

47

"She's ready for us," Rachel said.

Professor Graves looked at her for a second as if to say something, then seemed to change his mind. "Okay," he replied. Then he raised his arms and, like a coach on the sidelines, waved everyone over. "She's ready for us. Remember, open-mindedness, curiosity, and positive thoughts will all contribute to a concentration of good vibes designed to help Madam Bovell attract a spirit into her trance-state consciousness. Sit in male-female order around the table, hold hands, and don't say anything unless a spirit announces itself. And even then don't say much."

"You've done this before?" Shelley asked.

"Well, in a manner of speaking."

"What does that mean?"

"I've sat in hundreds of séances, but a lot of them were frauds performed by charlatans."

"How many is a lot?" Jessica said.

"I was able to prove most of them as false claims, con-artist acts, or 'magic' tricks. And those I couldn't prove, I still suspected were frauds—just clever enough frauds to escape my detection."

"Weren't there any you thought were real?" Aaron asked.

"None," he said. "But tonight is different. Tonight, I'm willing to believe."

Rachel was first to the door. The metal handle felt warm to the touch—her first indication that Madam Bovell had already done something to alter the energy in the room. She opened it.

The woman sat motionlessly at the table, facing the door and staring at her with shiny dark eyes. The walls had a crimson glow. She stepped gingerly through the embracing dimness. It was like moving through a foggy mist. The others followed in silence. Nearing the table, she heard the deep, rhythmic breathing of Madam Bovell.

She sat diagonally from the woman at a triangle point. Jason sat at the third imagined point lightly drawn on the round table. Dr. Graves sat at the chair beside Madam Bovell. Everyone else filled in the remaining seats, alternating between boys and girls.

"Please hold hands," Madam Bovell said in a soothing voice. "Focus on positive thoughts. If you like, you may pray silently. You may keep your eyes open if you wish. I'm the only one who must keep my eyes closed, to maintain a trance state. In times past, sitters would sing church hymns while a trance medium found the spirits. But times are different now, and I'm guessing none of you know many hymns by heart. So silence is best until Dr. Graves indicates that the group may communicate with whatever spirit chooses to join us. Now, please, remain silent."

Without moving her head, she glanced to her right and made brief eye contact with Rachel. Then she leaned back, closed her eyes, and seemed to slip into a trance.

Rachel watched the woman effortlessly create a self-induced altered state of consciousness. She had read about people using hypnosis in psychotherapy sessions, but she was amazed that a person could basically hypnotize oneself.

A tension hung in the air, and Rachel realized that something had changed within her. She felt a sudden focus and alertness, and a tingling of everyone's thoughts that were reaching her mind. Without looking at anyone, she could tell who in the group was most afraid, excited, or skeptical. She felt anxiety from the professor, which surprised her because he had so far been calmer than anyone. And she felt excitement from Jason, which she understood because he had already had a few encounters with Annabel and must be thrilled finally to have witnesses and reassure himself that he wasn't insane. But what Rachel had not expected was to be able to sense, to a degree, what was happening inside Madam Bovell's mind. A firestorm of cosmic signals lit up the woman's neurons. She was actually feeling the woman's subconscious awaken to the dimensions of multiple physical worlds.

A dizziness washed over Rachel as she felt Madam Bovell slip into a trance state. It was nauseating, and she worried it might make her sick. But then she sensed a change within the woman's mind, as if something else was waking up … as if someone else had just arrived in the room.

Madam Bovell slumped toward the table. She held the awkward-looking position for a moment, then slowly sat up straight, rigid, with her eyes still closed.

"Good evening," she said in a husky voice very different from her own.

"With whom are we speaking?" the professor asked.

"Godfrey Bale, my good fellow, at your service," the voice replied. "It is so good to be with you again, sir. It has been what you would consider a long time."

"Yes, it has," the professor said. "Nearly thirty years. But not to you?"

"Time does not exist where I am."

"And where are you?"

"I have returned to greet you, called here by an old friend."

"But you haven't answered her calls for many decades. Why now?"

"This is the first time I have heard her since that long-ago time. If she has called since then, she has not been heard."

"But she is heard now. Do you know why?"

"There is a girl here who is amplifying Madam Bovell's gifts. But that will not last long. Soon, the girl will learn to focus and will no longer radiate so much of her power to others."

Rachel could sense the professor's glance at her before he turned his attention back to the tranced medium channeling this unseen entity.

"We're trying to contact a spirit that we believe is in this building," Dr. Graves said. "She may be trapped. We don't know. Can you contact her? Can you guide us to her?"

"Annabel Heller," the tranced medium answered. Then Madam Bovell's face contorted into a mask of agony. "She is here. In this room. Such pain. So much suffering. Love and sorrow. Injustice and anger and hate. Trapped rage. So many secrets. So much loss. Behold. Beware."

Madam Bovell's body had stiffened upright and looked almost as if it had risen an inch or two off her seat, as if levitating.

Dr. Graves stiffened as well. He didn't seem to have expected this. "What can you tell us about Annabel?"

"She has secrets," the voice said. "Dark secrets."

"Can you tell them to us?"

"No."

"Can she tell us?"

"Maybe."

"Can we speak with her?"

The voice didn't reply, but Madam Bovell's shoulders fell, her face relaxed, and her entire body seemed to lower an inch. Rachel felt another change in the woman's brain activity—a strain removed briefly before being replaced by a new strain more burdensome than the last. She felt a strong pull, an unexpected empathy, toward this new entity. It was somehow familiar to her, this multidimensional force concentrating inside Madam Bovell's mind, forming, preparing to manifest itself. Just as it had done in so many of Rachel's dreams during the past year.

"She's here," Rachel whispered. In her peripheral vision, she could see Jason's face looking at her, but she dare not take her eyes off Madam Bovell. A cold darkness had clouded the medium's face, drying up any color from her skin. Her lips tightened as her cheeks tensed. Sinews drew taut.

"Everyone, stay calm," the professor said in a low, hushed voice. "Try not to be frightened. Fear may provoke her. To maintain a strong connection, we need to give off positive energy."

But Rachel could sense the others sliding toward terror. She tried to follow the professor's instructions by envisioning the field of wildflowers she had hiked through last summer near Devil's Lake. She closed her eyes and saw the purple clover and pasqueflowers and bright yellow daisies splashed across the rolling meadowland, surrounding her with color and life. Then, on the trail a hundred yards ahead, she saw a figure. A woman in dark rags, her long black hair tangled and heavy, and a pale, expressionless face stared at her. Abruptly, the sun vanished and the sky darkened and a wave of cold gray washed over the land, sucking all the color from the fast-wilting flowers. The woman stretched her arms forward as if reaching to grab Rachel with her long, gnarled fingers. She walked forward, closing the gap.

Rachel opened her eyes. Startled and sweating, she found the others sitting around the table, just as they had been a moment earlier. But Madam Bovell, still in a trance state with eyes closed, now had a mischievous smile on her face.

The new expression sent a chill across Rachel's skin. "She doesn't want us to have positive energy," she whispered. "She doesn't want us at peace. She wants us disturbed." She glanced at the professor. "She wants us frightened."

"That doesn't make sense," Jason said. "She wouldn't try to open communications with us just to terrify us. She could have just kept haunting this hospital if that's all she wanted. You didn't see what I saw. She's trying to talk to us."

"He's right," Aaron said. "She doesn't need a séance to disturb us. She must be trying to communicate with us."

"I'm telling you, something's wrong," Rachel warned.

"Everyone, quiet, *please,*" the professor said. "I must be the only one to talk until we've established a strong connection. Many things could explain Rachel's concerns. It's even possible that Madam Bovell has attracted more than one spirit."

"She's exceeding her capabilities right now," Rachel said. "I can feel it. Something strange is happening. She's being taken over."

"Do you know by whom?"

"Something familiar, I think. No, something cold. It's close now. It's here."

Just then a whisper came from Madam Bovell, and a cold vapor escaped her lips.

"Mr. Bale?" the professor asked.

Madam Bovell's skin looked as if it had aged ten years in the past ten seconds. Creases lined her face, tinted by the red glow of the lights. Her eyes opened and fell in a lazy, weak gaze on the table. Her head tilted sideways, and her mouth opened in a hideous, distorted shape as if half her facial muscles were paralyzed from a stroke. Then she whispered a single word: "*Lies.*"

"Who is this?" the professor asked. "With whom do we speak?"

"Lies ... Lies."

"It's Annabel," Jason said.

"Shh-h," the professor whispered. Then, louder, he repeated, "With whom do we speak?"

A groan rumbled from Madam Bovell's mouth. Her body appeared rigid, her face stony, her lips cold and dead. But from those blue lips, sounds reached out from beyond the grave. *"Ann-a-bel."*

"We welcome you, Annabel," the professor said. "We welcome you and wish to listen to you. We desire to communicate with you."

"De-si-i-ire," the voice said. It was slow, but somehow higher pitched than Madam Bovell's voice. Younger but tired, sleepy, weak.

"Yes," the professor said. "We wish to communicate with you."

"De-si-i-ire. Death. Lies."

"You wish to tell us about death?" the professor asked.

No answer.

"You wish to tell us about *your* death?" he said. "We know how you died. We know that it happened in this room. Is that why you have remained here?"

No answer.

"Why have you remained, Annabel? Why have you not passed on?"

The blue lips moved. *"Mur-mer,"* the voice gasped painfully.

No one else said a word, though some looked around in confusion. Rachel had no idea what to expect from this, nor any idea what the communications were supposed to be like during a séance. It involved much more psychic strain than she had imagined. It wasn't easy traversing between dimensions, multiple realities, or whatever plane of existence separated Annabel's spirit from the living. But Rachel could sense with every grain of instinct in her body that this voice was not Madam Bovell the trickster, or some twisted dissociative identity disorder buried deep within the old medium's mind. No, this voice was another entity altogether, one that Rachel could sense a bond with—a bond formed through many visions she had experienced on dozens of sleepless nights over the past year. Nights where she had sensed the haunted cries of this tormented spirit who had suffered God-knows-what pain to force her pleas for help to be heard across this barrier between the living and the dead. This spirit that had pulled against the currents of death to warn the living of her dangerous lies. This spirit of sadness and beauty and a young life lost.

"Why have you not passed on?" the professor said, repeating his question.

"*Mur-mer,*" Annabel moaned again.

Rachel didn't know how long these fits and starts would continue before they started getting real answers, but the professor had warned everyone to be patient. He had told the group that séances could often go hours without anything ever happening.

"Please, Annabel, trust us," the professor tried. "We only want to help. Why have you not passed on?"

"*Mur-mer,*" Annabel repeated.

And on this third utterance, Madam Bovell's arms began to shake, sending muffled vibrations through the table. Half the group jerked backward in a startled reaction; the other half were too shocked to move. The red lights now flickered and dimmed like candles guttering in the wind. A cracking of glass came from the dark window behind her. A faint, pale glow, barely visible at first, seemed to grow from the center of the crystal ball on the table. A strange, icy breeze trickled through the room, even though all the windows and doors were closed and no sounds came from the vents.

A violent energy was pushing and pulling at the room, as if this were a ship in stormy seas.

"*Mur-mer,*" Annabel groaned.

"Everyone, stay calm," the professor said loudly enough to be heard over the many scary distractions going on around them. "Stay positive, or we'll lose her."

"Mur-mer. Mur-mer."

Rachel noticed dozens of little balls of light floating over the séance, near the ceiling. But no one else was looking up. "Do you guys see this?"

"See what?" Jason asked, following her gaze upward.

"Those lights," she answered.

"What lights?"

"Mur-mer … mur-mer … mur-mer."

"We're losing her!" the professor almost had to yell to be heard over the growing commotion. "Everyone, stay positive. Stay engaged. Annabel, don't leave us! We can help you! Stay with us!"

"What's happening?" Jessica yelled.

"We're losing her!" the professor answered. "She can't hold Annabel! She's not strong enough!"

"No one sees those lights?" Rachel asked excitedly. Now more than a hundred spheres of light hovered high overhead, higher even than the ceiling, spinning slowly as if she were watching a time-lapse image of the Milky Way or some distant nebula.

"MUR-MER!"

The voice had taken on a shrill, screeching quality that pulled Rachel's gaze away from the lights floating above her. And when she looked at Madam Bovell, she found the old medium's eyes now open and staring directly at her. But they were no longer the woman's eyes: they were now pale blue, glowing orbs. And as Rachel looked into them, she felt a dizzying pull— and feared that she herself was now falling into a trance.

"Oh, God," Rachel said, her eyes locked on to the powerful, hypnotic gaze.

"What's wrong?" Jason asked, though his voice sounded faint and far away.

She was drifting away from this room. Away from everyone else. Annabel or some other force was pulling her away from this reality and toward the floating orbs above. Another world was opening before her, just as the one she knew seemed to be disappearing through a vanishing hole behind her. She could faintly hear Jason yelling something at her, but his voice was muted by the growing, blinding stars and the thunderous galaxy she was floating into. And as she rose into this gravity-defying dream, she heard clearly the two syllables that Annabel had been repeating.

With her last conscious breath connected to the real world, she spoke it even though she feared they could no longer hear her: "Mur-der! Mur-der! Mur-der!"

48

Jason could only watch as the séance went off the rails. Madam Bovell was pounding the table in a slow but consistent cadence. The lights had dimmed unbidden, a cold breeze from nowhere had blown out the candles, and a window had cracked for no apparent reason. All eyes had been on the medium until Rachel started spouting a bunch of excited blather about orbs of light floating above the table. Jason had followed her gaze but saw nothing.

"What lights?" he asked her over the commotion.

Her eyes were darting between the space above the table, and the shaking Madam Bovell. He looked up and saw nothing but the dark red glow of the ceiling catching the dim light around the table. Looking back to Rachel, he saw her staring in horrified wonder at the ceiling, her mouth and eyes wide and her head jerking spastically as if trying to follow sudden movements on the ceiling. He looked up again and still saw nothing.

The table began to shake, and Jason felt Jessica's grip tighten on his left hand.

"Is this normal?" Aaron whispered.

"Quiet, please," the professor said.

"Something's not right," Tommy said, his chicken-scratched face looking especially disturbing in the low red light. "We should stop."

"I'm scared," Shelley confessed, and Jason could see her hands trembling.

"Everyone, *please* stop talking," the professor begged. "Silence and positive thoughts, please." Then, as if to set a proper example, he closed his eyes and lowered his head.

But only Scott and Aaron took the cue. Tommy's eyes were fixed in terror on the vibrating table. Shelley had closed her eyes, but she squeezed them so tightly that Jason would bet she wasn't relaxing in positive thoughts. He tried to breathe slowly and deeply, but the damn table was now jumping enough to make loud clunks and bangs. The clatter got louder and faster and more violent until the table finally settled into a subtle humming vibration.

"*Mur-mer,*" the voice from Madam Bovell said.

Rachel's head jerked up as if someone had slapped her. Her eyes looked glazed, and she seemed to be falling into some sort of daze or—he realized with horror—a trance. He considered jumping up from the table to grab her and pull her out of the room, knowing that a trance was the one thing in the world that she feared would kill her. But he, too, was paralyzed.

"Oh, God," Rachel murmured, as if drifting off to sleep.

"What's wrong?" Jason yelled to her, hoping she could hear him. "Rachel! What's wrong?"

Her face steadied and relaxed, but only to the extent that Madam Bovell's had when first falling into a trance. And then she spoke the single word, "*Mur-der! Mur-der! Mur-der!*"

And as Rachel did this, Madam Bovell awoke and fell to the table, sobbing uncontrollably.

"Are you all right?" the professor asked in a panicky voice.

"Something's happening to Rachel," Jason said.

The professor jerked his head to look at her.

"What's happening?" Jason demanded.

"Annabel is with her now," the professor answered.

"How's that possible? Rachel isn't a medium. The spirit isn't supposed to talk through anyone other than Madam Bovell."

"We were having trouble communicating with the spirit. Maybe she has chosen Rachel."

"Is it going to kill her?"

"What!" Scott gasped.

"No," the professor snapped. "Don't even suggest that! Everything will be fine if we just stay positive and open. Spirits can sense our energy levels, good and bad. We must remain positive and calm."

Jason stopped asking questions. He had to trust the professor because he didn't know what else to do. All he could do was watch. And in this moment of helplessness, he found himself saying a short, silent prayer for Rachel's safety, for there seemed no better time to ask for God's help than when staring at the awesome forces beyond death.

He prayed and hoped for Rachel's safety while watching her face shift and twist as if she were dancing with Death itself.

49

Rachel walked on a black, frozen sea. Stars reflected off the gleaming surface, and she looked up to marvel at the billion diamonds flung across the black vault above her. Despite the infinity of stars, most of the area around her was a dark void that gave an impression of distant, eternal nothingness. Astrophysicists explained that this was due to Hubble's discovery of the ever-accelerating expansion of the universe.

Rachel had no idea where she was or what had happened to the others. But her many questions seemed more trivial as she continued to explore this strange environment. This was not a dream or some deep subconscious recess of her mind, or even the outer reaches of some other galaxy far from the spinning Milky Way. Was this death? She was too fascinated by her surroundings to worry about the possibility that she may have died. Black liquid objects were now moving around her. Was this another dimension? Her mind seemed at a loss to process or even imagine an explanation of what she was witnessing.

As she walked forward, she realized that the stars were slowly drifting toward her from their deep-space heavens. Amazed at the illuminating beauty of these orbs, she kept walking in hopes of not disrupting their steady flow as they continually contracted into a massive sphere around her. As the first few dozen lights approached, it was clear that these were not stars in the universe. She gently reached out, and almost wept with joy when one of the bright orbs rested in her palm. It gave only the barest tingle of warmth, but the feeling went well beyond sensations on the skin, for what was physical and real in the world was not physical and real in this realm. She knew not what to call this place except "another realm," for a realm it was, and no lesser word captured its nebulous, bending space.

The light orb flickered in her hand like a living thing. But it was not living, for death had passed it on to this place, where it lived on as if born anew. But new it was not, for this same light had occupied a living space of flashing neurons before passing back into its earlier energetic state. It was very confusing, yet so simple. It was the soul of a person who had died and now lived forever in this interstitial twilit realm.

Rachel's eyes filled with tears at the beauty that she felt in this moment. The life beyond life. The defeat of death. So much glory and truth washed over her in this glimpse of what lay beyond the mystery of death that she was overcome with ecstasy.

What was this place? Where had she arrived? What had brought her here? Was there any way back? Did she even want to *go* back?

She remembered the stories of her mother and grandmother, both dying at séances while in trances. Was *that* what this was? Was she dying? Was she being led away from the physical world forever, in the same way her mother and grandmother had been taken away?

The stories said the devil had taken them. This didn't feel like that. But she had to wonder.

More of the light orbs reached her. Like little creatures, they settled on her arms and shoulders and chest and head. All these lives touching her from beyond the greatest, most inexorable barrier she could imagine. And suddenly, a shock wave of memories assailed her. Swing sets in sandy city parks. Children laughing. A state fair. A Thanksgiving dinner with a family. Endless splashing at a city pool. A thrilling scene of a Hollywood film in a dark theater full of silhouetted heads. A snowball fight. A first dance. A first kiss. A last goodbye. Scattered wrapping paper around a fir tree. A thousand marriages. A thousand children. Laughter. Love. The best memories of a thousand lives stuck to her and bonded with her own living soul in this rare moment of understanding across the realms—an understanding that only one in a hundred million could know.

And she was that one.

She was one of the few who could understand this realm. And she was one of the *very* few who had ever found their way to this place without dying.

What a miracle. What a gift.

What a responsibility to the living and the dead.

She looked up and beamed a beatific smile at the hundreds of millions of orbs now drifting toward her from the ever-unfolding eternity beyond all worlds.

What a gift she had! What a responsibility! She understood this now. And her tears of wonder blurred all the dancing, bobbing lights into one exquisite glow.

50

"Everyone, please keep holding hands—don't break the circle!" the professor said. He could hardly believe it, but it seemed as if Annabel had jumped from Madam Bovell to Rachel, leaving Bovell hunched over and exhausted on the table, and the girl in a sudden trance state. "Are you all right?" he asked Bovell.

She looked half dead as she struggled to raise herself off the table. Her face sagged, and her glazed eyes cast about in confusion. "What happened, Donovan?" she croaked.

"Godfrey Bale returned," the professor said, "and he introduced us to Annabel."

"He did?" A smile grew on her drowsy countenance.

"Yes, but contact was lost after a few minutes. Annabel couldn't maintain the link with you—but she found another way." His eyes darted toward the stiff, motionless figure of Rachel, locked in the shadows of the dim red lights.

Madam Bovell's gaze drifted to Rachel. When she saw the state of the girl, her mind seemed to snap awake. "How long has she been in a trance?"

"About a minute."

"She isn't ready for this."

"Is it safe to wake her?"

"I don't know. It's better if she returns naturally. But we should try to wake her if she hasn't come out of this on her own in the next four minutes. Since this is her first time, it could be dangerous if she remains in a trance state for longer than five minutes. Does anyone have a watch with a light?"

"I do," Jason said, releasing his hands from the circle to mark the time. "One minute down. I'll tell you when it gets close to five minutes."

Madam Bovell turned back to Rachel. "Annabel, can you hear me?"

"Ye-e-es-s-s," the voice from Rachel said.

"Do you know where you are?"

"Ye-e-es-s-s."

"Did you call us here?"

No reply.

"Did you call *me* here?"

"No-o-o."

"Did you call to anyone?"

"Ra-a-ache-e-el-l-l. Ja-a-aso-on-n-n."

"Why did you call to them?"

"HE-EL-LP-PH." The phonetic sounds blew across the room in a startling, unnatural gurgle.

It sent a sharp chill down the professor's spine. His eyes were locked on Rachel, studying her in detail for any hint of what might happen next. For now, he was content to let Madam Bovell continue the questioning, but he feared what this intrusive encounter could be doing to the girl.

"How much time?" he asked.

"Two minutes left," Jason said.

"Help?" Madam Bovell said to the spirit. "You want our help? How can we help?"

"No-o-o mo-o-ore li-i-ies-s."

"No more lies. Okay. We can help you. What lies? Help us know what lies."

"Ninety seconds," Jason said.

"What are the lies, Annabel?" Bovell repeated. "Please tell us."

"Lies, lies, LIES!" the voice said. "Murder. Lies."

"We don't understand, Annabel," Madam Bovell said.

"Lies led to her murder, which led to more lies," the professor guessed.

"Is that it, Annabel?" Madam Bovell asked. "Please help us understand."

"Lies. He-e-e i-i-is-s-s tra-a-apped by-y-y lies."

"He is trapped by lies," Madam Bovell repeated. "Who is trapped? Annabel, who is trapped by lies."

"Thirty seconds," Jason said.

"Annabel, who is trapped?"

But Rachel's face was changing, tightening, twisting in pain. She arched up suddenly, and her fingers clawed at the table. Then her voice changed into something softer and higher-pitched. "Papa?"

Professor Graves felt his heart collapse within him. An icy chill shot through every vein in his body. His mind swirled in dizzy, overwhelming memories from a time in his past that lived far from this room, from this night, in the most guarded vaults of his mind.

"Papa?"

It can't be. Not here. Not now.

"Papa? Please?"

Don't torture me, God. I beg you, don't torture me like this.

"Papa? Papa?"

The professor closed his eyes, knowing he had to face it. Even if it proved once again to be nothing more than a fraudulent false hope. But maybe this was different from the last time.

Maybe this time, the hope would be real. "Yes, I'm here. I'm here."

"Time's up," Jason said.

"We need to wake her," Madam Bovell said.

"Papa?"

"Wait. Not yet," the professor said, almost believing.

"We need to bring her out of the trance now," she warned.

"Just a little longer. Please." Then he turned back to Rachel's tormented face. "David?"

"Yes, Papa."

He could feel tears welling up and then spilling over his lower lids. "Is that really you?"

"Yes, Papa. You got my message, Papa."

He covered his mouth with his left hand. The only one he had mentioned the message to was Madam Bovell, and he didn't think she had mentioned it to Rachel. Still, he had to be certain he wasn't being conned somehow. "David, do you remember your favorite place to go? The place we would sometimes go on Saturday mornings?"

"The fire station, Papa. The firemen would let me sit inside the fire engine, behind the steering wheel."

He tensed in an effort to hold back the sobbing convulsion that was fighting to overtake him.

"Don't cry, Papa."

"We need to wake her up," Madam Bovell insisted. "Waiting any longer could be dangerous."

He nodded but couldn't make himself to move toward Rachel to wake her. For so long now, he had hoped to be with his son again. He had dreamed that there was life after death and that his son somehow had a life in it. And that they would someday meet again. And now here it was. *What* it was, he didn't know. But just knowing that it existed was already more than he had ever dared to believe.

"Are you with your mother?"

"Sometimes, but not now. I'm with *you* right now."

"We have to wake her," Jason said, getting up from the table.

"Wait, please."

"No."

"Papa, you have to help her."

"Who? Rachel?"

"Annabel."

"What do you know, David?"

"You have to help her. Her secret has to be known."

"What is her secret?"

"She won't say."

"Then how can we know her secret?"

"You are not the one that needs to know her secret."

"Then who needs to know it?"

"He does."

"Who's he?"

"He needs to know her secret. He needs to know soon ... or more bad things will happen."

"David, I don't understand what that means."

"Papa?"

"David?"

"Papa, are you still there?"

"I'm still here, David. I can still hear you. I love you. I love you and your mother so much. I miss you both so much."

"Papa?" Rachel's chair tilted back from the table as all the dim red lights in the room suddenly flashed wildly.

Jason darted around the table and dived like a beach volleyball player to keep her head from hitting the floor. Jessica started shaking until Tommy put his bandaged arm around her.

Dr. Graves felt a swirling, dizzying joy mixed with the weight of suppressed sorrow. His sweet little boy was still out there. His David still existed, and in a state that was perhaps better than anything Dr. Graves could have imagined. And somehow, his son had found him.

Lowering his head to the black velvet tablecloth, he wept.

51

Rachel saw the reflected galaxies shake as the black ice beneath her trembled and turned into sparkling black sand. Now she stood in a dark desert that extended as far as she could see in all directions. The bright little spheres silently drifted up and away from her. She felt nothing at first. Then a gale-force wind knocked her off her feet. On her hands and knees, she sensed the growing vibrations in the air. Looking up, she watched the orbs of light speed away from her, back toward the heavens.

"Wait!" she yelled. "Please don't go!"

But as they grew more distant with each passing second, she faded into a darker, shadowy realm. A cold wind swept across the sand, which had felt warm and inviting only moments earlier, when the lights hovered around her. Now everything was dark except for a pale blue object growing on her right. She had first noticed the color reflecting off the sparkling black sand. Turning, she saw the back of a woman walking away from her. The woman hadn't been there a second ago but was now walking away. And Rachel could sense that she, too, was an orb of light that had somehow materialized into this human form.

"Wait!" Rachel called out. "Why have I been brought here? Why have I been chosen to see this? What am I supposed to do?"

But the woman kept walking.

"Annabel?" Without the strength to stand up, Rachel began crawling through the sand on her knees and hands. "Please! What should I do?"

But the woman kept walking.

"Please," Rachel begged. "I'm lost! I don't know who I am, what I'm supposed to do … who I'm supposed to be!"

The woman stopped.

"Please, don't go! I need your help!"

The woman turned around, her pale face glistening in the blue light that she emanated. And when Rachel saw the face, she knew that it was not Annabel. But still she knew it—better than any face she had ever seen before. These were the same eyes she saw every time she looked into the mirror. Her same high cheekbones. Her same dimples. The same wry curve of the lips.

"Mother?" she asked, already knowing the answer.

Her mother mouthed a few words, but no sound made it to Rachel's ears.

"Mother!"

A swirl of blue vapor rolled up along her mother's legs, growing brighter as it clouded her body. And just as it reached the face, her mother's spirit reached out more determinedly and mouthed more words. This time, they came to Rachel as a distant whisper: "Be strong. Be strong."

Then the vapors wrapped around her mother's face, turning her into a large ball of soft light that quickly contracted into a smaller, brighter orb. It hovered in front of Rachel for a few seconds before being drawn up and away by the distant gravitational pull of the other souls.

"MOTHER!"

But her pleas were useless against whatever force was pulling them apart.

She soon found herself alone in the dark desert, beneath an infinity of souls, still glimmering above her yet as distant as galaxies.

Then everything turned red and she found herself looking up at the hovering faces of Jason and Madam Bovell and Shelley. She was back in the hospital's small conference room, lying on the floor. A storm was raging outside.

52

Madam Bovell stood over Rachel and stared down in awe. She could still remember her first journey into the spirit world all those decades ago. She had stood on the edge of a mountaintop with icy clouds sliding below her, and tiny lights moving around her. And she had known that the swarming tiny lights were individual souls. She even got a glimpse of the vast dimensions that held the dead after they traversed beyond life. Now, as she watched Rachel trying to sit up, she realized that this poor girl had been thrown abruptly into one of these dimensions, too. And by that fleeting visit to a realm of the afterlife, she would be forever changed and must now find a way to walk again among the living.

"What did you see?" Shelley asked.

"My mother," Rachel said, her face damp and flushed.

"How well did you see her?" Madam Bovell asked.

"I was … very close," she panted, sucking in a fresh breath after every few words. "I could see her face but I couldn't touch her, couldn't hear her … at first."

Madam Bovell knelt beside her. The linoleum floor was cold and hard. Aaron had turned the lights back on, washing out the dim crimson glow. She touched Rachel's forehead and felt a warmth that would normally suggest a raging fever. But she knew the aftermath signs from personal experience.

"Your body has been through the wringer," she said. "You'll be weak for a moment. Look at me and breathe slowly. Don't try to move or talk. Calm … calm. That's it, breathe … Wait for the dizziness to wash away … There you go, good job."

Rachel's eyes had been filled with panic, then discomfort, then relief. Madam Bovell pulled a purple silk handkerchief from her pocket and dabbed Rachel's face. "Feeling better now? Okay. Now you can tell us about your mother. Did she say anything to you?"

"She tried to speak," Rachel said softly. "Before she drifted away, her last words were 'Be strong.' But I couldn't hear her first words; I could only see her lips move. It looked like she said, 'The hospital,' but it was shorter than that."

"You think it started with an 'H'?" Shelley asked.

"Yeah. I can still see her mouth moving."

"The house," Jason said, abandoning his feet to sit beside them. Their private powwow had grown to four, with the professor and the other kids clustered around them, mesmerized.

"The house?" Madam Bovell asked.

Jason nodded, looking almost pale. "Where Annabel lived. She died in the hospital, but she was shot in the house."

"'The house,'" Rachel said, her eyes widening. "Yes! I think that's it. 'The house. Be strong.'" She closed her eyes. "My mother wants me to go to the house. And she's warning me to be strong."

"Why the house?" Shelley asked.

"Because that's where the secrets are," Jason said.

As he said this, the lights flickered and the wind rattled something outside the blacked-out window. Everyone seemed to hold their breath, as if Annabel might materialize at any second.

Tommy had his arm around Jessica, as if to merge their courage. Dr. Graves just looked exhausted, drained.

"Do you have any idea what happened here when you were in the trance?" Jason asked Rachel.

"She won't know," Madam Bovell said.

"What happened?" Rachel asked.

"Annabel talked to us," Madam Bovell said. "She told us *he* is trapped by the lies."

"Who's '*he*'?" she asked.

"We don't know."

"If the secrets are kept at the house, then that's where we'll find the answers," Jason said. He turned to Madam Bovell. "What do you think?"

"We can't do another séance here tonight," she replied. "Too much energy has already been drained from this place for now. The house, though—it may give us fresh energy. Maybe Annabel will be able to communicate with us better there."

"I thought she would only be able to haunt one place," Rachel said. "The place where she died."

"That's usually how it works," Madam Bovell said. "But there are a few historical instances of ghosts attaching themselves to objects or people instead of places. Maybe there is some connection between the hospital and the house that allows Annabel to move between them." This was quickly becoming the most complex and intriguing haunting she had encountered—and also the most urgent. "We should go there tonight. Tomorrow is the anniversary of her death. We may not have much time to discover her secrets."

Jason looked at her as if he was going to be sick. "It's kind of a scary place to go to at night."

"You've been there?" Jessica asked.

"Yeah. Haven't you?"

"No," she said. "None of us have. It's supposed to be possessed by evil now. They say the next of kin can't even sell the place."

"None of you have ever been out there?" Jason asked, perplexed. "Not even you?" he said to Rachel.

"It was easier to sneak into the hospital," Rachel said. "We had a key, so it didn't seem as illegal. And this is where all the sightings occurred. No one's been out to the Heller farmhouse."

"Well, I think we need to go out there," Madam Bovell said, having made up her mind and now trying to make up theirs, too. "Annabel still wants to tell us something. And I think she wants to tell us tonight."

"What time is it?" Rachel asked.

"Just before ten o'clock," Dr. Graves said. "When is everyone's curfew?"

"We all have pacts with our parents," Jessica answered. "They trust us and support our ghost-hunting club, so we have no hard curfew on Friday and Saturday nights as long as we're all together."

"Okay, so let's go to the farmhouse," Dr. Graves said.

"We got to fix this place first," Jason said. "You two should rest a bit," he said to Rachel and Madam Bovell. "You, too, Professor. The rest of us can have this room back to normal in five minutes."

The youngsters went at it with the skill and efficiency of a production crew. Tommy and Jessica wrapped the velvet tablecloth around the crystal ball and packed it away in Madam Bovell's bag. Scott whispered something to Rachel. She nodded, and he started rounding up the extinguished candles, which had rolled all over the room during the séance. Jason collected the red lightbulbs and their wall plugs while Shelley and Aaron peeled the blackout paper from the windows.

Madam Bovell realized that Dr. Graves had left the room. She stepped out into the corridor. Just before the staircase at the end of the passageway, a strange sensation washed over her. She stopped dead near the top step leading down into the shadows. She felt a heaviness in the air and a sudden drop in temperature that hung on the very spot where she stood. She slowly turned her head to look around for anyone or anything that might be near her. A deep bass vibration rattled through her, paralyzing her with a spike of instinctive fear. She saw nothing, but she could feel a disturbance in the air. Some conscious entity was here, near this very spot—perhaps right beside her. With a quickened heartbeat, she inched forward until the toes of one foot overhung the top step. Something was here with her at this very moment, watching her.

She moved down the stairs with a cautious hesitation on each step. At the bottom, she inched along the wall. Peeking carefully around the corner, she saw a figure curled up in the shadows along the edge of the floor, eerily motionless. It raised its head and turned toward her with wet, shining eyes.

"Who's there?" the silhouette asked.

Madam Bovell sighed with relief on hearing the professor's voice. "Donovan, it's me. Are you okay?"

He sniffled and sighed. "I wasn't prepared for that."

"To talk to your son?"

"I never thought I'd get the chance. I'm not sure I even fully believed it was possible." He sniffled again. "He was so little when he died," he said, his voice cracking. "He used to be scared at night, when it got dark. And for some stupid reason, I kept thinking about how, if there was an afterlife, how scared he must be in it all alone without me. I didn't know whether he would be with his mother. I didn't know where he would be ... or if he would even be *anywhere.* All these years, I kept wavering in my beliefs, thinking he was in heaven, or maybe some cosmic soul drifting as energy without any ability to comprehend existence, or maybe even to have vanished forever into bleak nothingness. I wavered constantly between hope and despair, belief and doubt."

He began to shake. "But he lives on in another way … in another place, with his mother. And he *understands*. He understands *life*, and he's *not* scared." His voice cracked. "And he remembers me … He thinks of me."

She stepped across the dark hallway and sat against the wall, facing him. "You really didn't know he had made it into the afterlife?"

"How could I know?"

"But he found you," she said, smiling. "He gave you the message at the cemetery."

"I didn't know for sure who or what helped me at the cemetery. But, yes, he found me." He took a deep, audible breath.

"And he wants us to help Annabel."

"Yes, why couldn't he tell us what she needs?"

"They tell us what they can," she replied. "We can't know what challenges they have communicating from the beyond."

"You were right about Rachel," he said softly. "You were right to be excited about her."

She stood and offered him her hand.

Taking it and slowly getting up, he said, "You know, these kids are just having some excitement, exploring a fun way to spend a few idle moments of youth. They haven't seen the world that we have. They don't understand how important this night might be for humanity. If we find a way of *proving* to the world that life exists after death, think what it would mean for humanity. Completing the research of Gurney and Podmore and Myers and Crookes and countless others. Millions of hours of the men and women exploring death throughout history. Millions of hours of séances, ghost hunts, paranormal investigations, academic research, and prayers. All searching for the one answer to the most elusive question in history: what happens to us when we die? And tonight, we may actually find that answer to one of the great abiding secrets in the history of humankind."

"Annabel's secret?" Madam Bovell mused. "The secret of what lies beyond death?"

"All these spirits want us to discover Annabel's secret," Dr. Graves said. "Have you stopped to think about why that might be?"

"It must be connected with Rachel, too," Madam Bovell said. "The odds of this happening in a small town that just happens to have someone like her in it—those are the unlikeliest odds."

"I agree," he said. "Rachel must play a big part in this. She may even be the focus. I now believe that all those answers may be waiting for us at the farmhouse."

"The night before Halloween."

"And the night before the first anniversary of Annabel's death."

Madam Bovell nodded.

"We should be terrified," he added.

"We should," she replied. "But I have faith in the spirits. I have faith in their guidance."

"I have faith, too," the professor replied. "I now know that death *will* reunite me with my son and wife. Come what may, I am now certain I'll see them again. And with that knowledge comes the courage of gods."

The professor patted her on the back, then squeezed her shoulder. It was the first time he had touched her so affectionately, and it made her feel as if they had completed their journey into friendship over the past three days. This man who had been her archenemy for decades had become the person in the world she most trusted. And it gave her courage knowing that she would have a true friend at her side as they closed in on Annabel's secret and whatever dark forces it had unleashed on this town.

53

Jason was rattled by the eerie pop and clatter of gravel kicking up against the bottom of the Jeep. They were rumbling through the dark, back toward the farmhouse he had visited last night.

He sat in the back seat. Rachel was in the front passenger seat, and Scott was driving.

"I mentioned I came out here last night," Jason said, breaking the silence.

"Yeah, you said you wanted to see it."

"I didn't just drive by," he confessed. "I stopped. And I went inside."

She turned around and stared at him. He looked at her, and in the dashboard light he could see she was alarmed.

"It doesn't look like anyone's lived there for a while," he continued. "Not since the killings, I guess. Hardly any furniture. It's dark, and it's creepy. But there is something still there."

"What do you mean, *something*?" she asked.

"A force of some kind."

"Annabel's spirit."

"I guess so, but she's aggressive at the farmhouse. It's not like at the hospital. There's a violence to her. An anger—a real rage."

"It's where she was shot," Scott said. "She's just closer to the bad memory there. I'd be angry, too."

"I don't know," Rachel said. "In all my dreams of her, she seemed sad. And before I fell into the trance during the séance, I also sensed her sadness when she was connected to Madam Bovell. I think Annabel has suffered greatly and she's tormented by some overwhelming sadness, but I don't get the sense she's angry."

"You didn't see what I saw," Jason said. "When her spirit is in that house, she gets mad as hell. And we need to make sure everyone in the group understands that."

"Did she try to hurt you?" Scott asked.

"I don't know, but she scared me. I wasn't going to wait around to see how far she'd go. The entire house was shaking, and not like in an earthquake when a slipping foundation shifts everything. This was a violent force shaking every individual thing in different ways: a door frame split, boards in the floor slapping up and down, windows cracked—while other things didn't even move at all. One wall bowed in and out while another didn't budge."

"Aaron will want to get the equipment out for this," Scott said.

"I don't think that's a good idea," Rachel said.

"We might see something really spectacular."

"What's he talking about?" Jason asked.

"Ghost-hunting stuff," she said.

"It's not just *stuff*," Scott said. "A FLIR thermal cam, a Rook EMF meter, a full-spectrum POV cam, and an Olympus EVP recorder. Aaron's got *good* stuff."

"You really believe that stuff works?" Jason asked.

"Yeah, man. It's scientific. Different light spectra, sound frequency, particle disturbances. We can record things that we see and hear, and we can also capture things we wouldn't have known about without the equipment. If we really want to discover what Annabel's secret is, we should set up the gear. It will help us figure out what she's trying to tell us."

The Jeep turned through a long curve on the dirt road, leading the three-vehicle caravan through the darkness. Somewhere up ahead, the farmhouse waited near a patch of black trees. The sky was spotted with small, brilliant white stars, and the Milky Way was again visible in staggering detail that he could never see in the all-obscuring city lights of Chicago. Looking up at the heavens, he thought of night camping with Nicole on Lake Michigan last month. He recalled them standing at the edge of the shore, listening to the lapping water, and looking up at the night sky in search of stars to claim for themselves. He picked Sirius because it was the brightest star in the sky and flickered with twinkling light. She picked her star, which he realized was Venus. But she loved it so much, he didn't have the heart to tell her it wasn't a star. They had held each other and kissed, and he really thought he was falling in love. That night, they made love in their tent while nature's mood music played all around them. They had been dating since last spring and had had a good run before she ruined their future. Now all he had left of her was a scattering of happy memories poisoned by her betrayal. And he realized now that the portent of their end had been there since that night: her star hadn't been a real star at all, and his star, Sirius, twinkled only because it was really a two-star system that just looked like a single star, and one of those two stars was a dying white dwarf. Her star was a fraud, and his was a dying illusion. They were not star-crossed lovers like Romeo and Juliet. Not even close. They had lost faith and betrayed each other and proved to him once and for all that true love existed only in the minds of artists and dreamers. In real life, it was a sickness—a disease that only led to people hurting themselves and others. Just like Nicole, just like his parents, and just like Annabel and her murderous husband.

"What's wrong?" Rachel asked, turning again to look back at him.

He pulled his awareness back from the heavens and past memories and looked at her. "You getting inside my head again?"

"Sorry," she said. "I don't know how to control it. Who was she?"

"Someone from my past. It doesn't matter."

"Okay. I'm sorry."

"Don't worry about it."

"Hey, guys, is that it?" Scott asked.

In the headlights, the gravel road curved left and faded into fog. The dark, jagged bulk of trees stood in the sliding headlights. Then a faint glow of faded white paint appeared like a phantom ship on a black sea.

"That's it," Jason said. "That's where it all happened."

"And that's where her secret hides," Rachel added.

As they pulled into the driveway, Jason saw the porch rail, still broken where he had collided with the police officer. The cop had given him a stern warning last night. Jason didn't even want to imagine how much trouble he would be in if he got caught trespassing again.

His eyes scanned along the front of the farmhouse, rising up the facade to the window of the bedroom where the killings had happened. He wondered what Annabel would have done if he hadn't fled. Would she have killed him? Would she have continued shaking the house until it collapsed? Then a new thought occurred to him. What if she hadn't been angry at all? What if she had just been trying to shake the truth out of this place, to reveal her secret?

He suddenly regretted running from the room like a coward last night. He suddenly felt ashamed.

He opened his door, stepped out on the gravel, and looked at the house. It was dark and quiet, as if none of last night's craziness had ever happened.

"Remember me?" he whispered. The house didn't respond. "I'm sorry I ran away last night," he continued under his breath. "I won't let that happen again. And I've brought friends. We all want to discover your secret. We all want to know the truth of your life—of how you lived and why you had to die so young."

He stared at the house, looking for any reaction to his return or his whispered words. An icy breeze brushed past him, then stilled, then blew again, then stilled, then blew, until it felt less like the night air and more as if the house were *breathing.* At the first-floor window nearest him, one of the dark drapes was shifting slightly. When the last car from their caravan finally neared the house, its headlights hit the window, causing a reflection much brighter than Jason had expected. And then, to his bewilderment, the reflected light in the window flashed wildly at him: FLASH-FLASH ... FLASH ... FLASH-FLASH. Then the window went black, as if nothing had occurred.

It was the same flashing pattern he had seen in his first vision of the farmhouse—*this* farmhouse. The vision Annabel had shown him at the hospital three nights ago, just before her pale face appeared behind him in the reflection and whispered, "Lies ... lies ... lies ..."

And now that he was here, she was showing him again.

But why?

He felt a tingling on his left forearm, as if a largish insect were crawling along his skin under his shirt. Flinching, he slapped and brushed his arm with urgency until the feeling died. He sensed new movement in his peripheral vision even *before* looking back at the house. Cautiously, he raised his gaze and saw that the drapes had stopped swinging in the window near him, but now the drapes at the second-floor bedroom window were moving slightly from side to side, subtly, a few inches either way, as if someone had just brushed them while trying to look out.

Someone or something was in the house watching them.

What if Annabel had never been trying to show them anything about any secret? What if, instead, this whole time she had been desperately trying to warn them of something? All the others seemed to believe that Annabel wanted them to come to this house. But they had never been here before now. Only he had felt the rage inside this bad place. Only he had witnessed the wrath that awaited, hidden inside this abandoned house of death. And now only he was worried that they had made a terrible mistake coming here.

54

As their car headlights pulled into the gravel driveway, Dr. Graves saw Jason step back from the house and bump into Rachel. Something was wrong. Something seemed to have spooked the guy.

"What is he getting out?" Madam Bovell asked.

Dr. Graves turned his attention from Jason to Aaron. The kid was pulling some large objects from the bed of Tommy's truck. "He thinks he's going to set up their equipment."

"The ghost-hunting stuff?"

"Yeah," Dr. Graves replied. "Why the hell would he do that? Didn't we explain at the hospital why that was a bad idea?"

"But that was because we didn't want equipment to disturb a séance," she said.

"Aren't we doing one here?"

"Are we?"

"I thought we were."

"No, I don't think so."

"Why not?"

"Because we already spoke to her tonight and learned to come here for our answers. I don't think she wants to tell us anything here. I think she wants to *show* us something. Maybe using their equipment isn't such a bad idea."

"You can't be serious. Wouldn't a séance be better?"

She looked at him. "Donovan, you need to stay focused."

"I am."

"But you're not. You're thinking of your son. You want to speak with him again. But that can't be our focus tonight."

Dr. Graves looked down. "He did have information for us. Maybe he can still help us."

"I promise you, when we're done with our mission here, I'll work with Rachel and we'll help you reach your son again. But right now we need to focus on Annabel and whatever it is that she's trying to show us."

He got out of the Yukon and shuffled his feet into the dark gravel scattered along the driveway. The others from Tommy's truck walked past him toward the farmhouse. He took a few steps forward, then stopped short at the strange isolated *ting* he heard beneath him. Looking down, he saw, illuminated in the Yukon's headlights, a single pine needle lying on the fine gravel. It spun a little clockwise, then back counterclockwise, then a little clockwise again—like a compass confused by overlapping magnetic fields in the sci-fi movie he had watched alone last month, on David's birthday.

Or maybe he hadn't been alone after all.

Just when the needle finally stopped spinning back and forth, another needle flew past him, tinged off the headlight, and landed on the first one. He stared at them both for what seemed an eternity, a dryness forming in his mouth. Another needle pinged off the edge of the headlight and joined the first two. One more made it a foursome.

The eerie memory of the clustering hazelnuts at David's tombstone flooded his thoughts. *FIND HER.* The message from David that had started him on this journey.

He heard rustling in the air and looked left and up. What must have been hundreds of pine needles flipped and spun lightly through the air, heading toward him, then past him, then alighting on the gravel, in one large pile atop the now buried four.

He stared at the pile, waiting, knowing that David was not yet done. Eventually, gradually, the pine needles began to shudder and shake, vibrating like sand during an earthquake, shifting and sliding until the needles had clustered into five separate piles. Then, slowly, they continued to vibrate as they started forming what promised to be five letters.

Watching as the letters formed with excruciating slowness from left to right, he identified the first letter as "D."

David, he thought with a smile, guessing the message and its sender.

But the next letter was "E."

He frowned. *Death?*

The next letter—"V"—revealed itself like a sinister grin.

No, he thought. *No, no.*

An "I" formed.

No, no, no ... please, God, no ...

But before the last pile could form the last letter, a violent gust disrupted the collection of pine needles and blew them away into the dreadful night.

55

Rachel stepped around Jason and approached the farmhouse. The headlights from the three cars cast her thin shadow on the clapboard siding. She opened her mind to any signals from the spirit world. And echoes of death were what she sensed. But unlike the hospital, which had a mix of pain and sorrow and acceptance and even peace, this house was filled with hatred and rage.

"So this is it?" Madam Bovell said, looking up at the house. "This is where the crime happened?"

"Yes," Rachel said.

"But it's more than that," Bovell mused out loud. "This is where she lived. The articles about the murders said that she and her husband had lived here for nearly a year, moving in just after their wedding."

"What do you suppose went wrong between them?" Dr. Graves asked, walking up behind them.

"We're just trying to figure that out," Madam Bovell said. "She cheated on him, and he murdered her. They were married less than a year."

"Think that's her secret?" Dr. Graves asked. "Think we're supposed to figure out what went wrong in their marriage—why she was unfaithful to him?"

"That is the mystery no one can figure out," Rachel said. "I remember the way the town talked after the murders. People said they had never seen a couple more in love. They had known each other since childhood, were sweethearts since high school. Things had been tough out here when oil prices dropped. Homelessness increased because migrant workers that had come up from the south lost their jobs. The local economy was hurt when out-of-state investment dried up. Then agricultural prices fell because of trade wars, which hurt farmers like the Hellers. The paper said that Annabel and her husband were having financial troubles and that he had been able to get one of the few part-time night jobs in the oil fields to earn a little extra money. But no one knows why she began an affair with their neighbor. They don't even know how long it had been going on. But they know how it ended: he came home and found her in bed with the man and killed them both. People blamed her for the murders as much as him. They blamed her for betraying him and for putting him in that situation. After the funerals, vandals spray-painted 'whore' on her tombstone. The Chief of Police had to warn of a big fine. But still, that's how the entire town remembers them now: her as a whore, him as a murderer."

A moan came from the house as a gust of wind swept across the land. It backed everyone up a step and kicked up leaves. Rachel's hair whipped across her face. The sudden gale ceased after ten long seconds, but during that time the moaning sounds had continued in an unnatural wail.

"What was that sound?" Rachel asked after the wind had stopped. "Was that the house?"

She could hear the fear in her own voice.

"That tree rubs against the house," Jason answered, pointing left. "It did that last night, too, before the storm arrived—before the trouble began."

"We should get inside," Madam Bovell said.

A patch of dark clouds slid in front of the full moon, casting the farmhouse into darkness. As they stepped out of the headlight beams, Rachel turned on a small flashlight. So did Jason. Madam Bovell seemed to enjoy the darkness and made no effort to alter it.

"Could use a little help here," Aaron said.

Rachel looked back at the truck. Scott, Tommy, and Aaron were starting to carry some of the dozen large hard plastic cases from the truck to the front porch. She went to help them. Jason did, too. Madam Bovell remained near the house, and as Rachel watched, she touched the siding with her palm.

"You've got to be kidding me," Dr. Graves said as he reached the truck and lifted one of the cases. "This is heavy as sin. What do you have in here?"

"That's our main ghost kit," Aaron said proudly. "It includes three full-spectrum POV cams, two Rook EMF meters, a Mel Meter, an EVP recorder, and a laser grid scope."

They stepped cautiously onto the front porch. If Rachel had been alone, she might not have had the courage to take another step. But with this brave band of investigators, she found herself ready to face the darkest demons of this house.

The front porch creaked as if each of their steps caused it pain. Her light caught a broken section of the wood railing.

"I did that last night," Jason said.

Rachel was first to the front door. "The handle's warm," she said.

Jason looked down and froze. "That's not right."

"What?" Rachel asked.

He stared at the bottom of the door.

"What?" she repeated.

"I ripped it," he whispered.

"Ripped what?"

"The screen at the bottom of the door. I'm sure I tore it running out of here last night."

Rachel studied the door. The screen looked fine. She bent down and pressed her hand against it. "It's not ripped anywhere," she said. "It's actually in really good shape."

"Someone fixed it," Jason said.

"You sure it actually tore?"

"I'm positive."

Then, without another word, he turned and walked away. Rachel followed him to the edge of the porch.

"What is it?"

"I fell through here last night," he said. He pointed to the muddied dirt a few feet below.

"What's wrong?"

"What do you see there?" he asked.

"I don't see anything."

"Exactly," he said. "Where's the wood? It should be right there. There were pieces of it everywhere."

"Someone picked it up?" she asked. "Someone was out here since your adventures last night?"

He stepped back and looked again at the railing. "I don't even think this is right," he said. "The gap—it's too narrow. We broke through a lot more than this."

"We?"

"Yeah, the police officer and I."

"What police officer?"

"You know him. Same guy that pulled me over Tuesday night. He got a call that someone was out here with a flashlight. That someone was me. He arrived right when I came blasting out the front door. I didn't see him until it was too late. Smacked right into him on the porch, and we both fell back through the railing. That's how it broke. But I'm telling you, it broke a lot more than this."

"What are you saying? Someone cleaned up the area below, fixed the screen door, and started fixing this railing?"

"I don't know," he said. "I mean, yeah, I guess that's what I'm saying, but why would anyone do that? And *who*?"

"The cop?"

"Why would he care?" Jason said.

"Then maybe someone else," she said. "Someone that takes care of the property. Someone we don't know about."

"Maybe," he said. "I just can't believe someone's been here since last night." He shined his flashlight below again on the patch where he had fallen. "And the way the repairs are half completed—it just doesn't look right."

She heard someone step up behind them.

"Hey," Scott said, "we'd best keep moving. It's going to take us a while to set up."

"Come on," Rachel said, placing her hand on Jason's shoulder. "Let's get inside. Annabel's waiting for us."

56

D r. Graves hit the light switch and nothing happened, so he shined his flashlight along the bare living room walls, just off the entryway. The only objects he saw were covered in white sheets. He assumed that the rest of the house had also been stripped of all mementos or decor that held any echo of the couple's memories.

Death and time were erasing all that they had ever been.

He had lived long enough to see this effect on many occasions. Life was so full of joy and energy. Death was a dark void—painful and sorrowful at first, but after a while it became even crueler in the relentless process of forgetting.

What kind of troubles did these young lovers have? What went wrong?

What kind of woman betrayed her husband?

What kind of man murdered his wife?

What kind of evil infested these walls?

A loud clattering burst through his awareness. He whirled about, half-expecting to find the devil with a dozen leering imps ready to shred his soul. But it was only Aaron and Tommy, dragging a heavy crate of equipment up the stairs. And in that moment, the long box reminded him of his son's small casket from many years ago. At the funeral, he had wanted to stand up and speak about how amazing his son had been during his brief life, but in the end he couldn't do it.

And now he found himself facing that haunting memory again with each strike of the crate on the steps. It was as if this house contained an evil that had burrowed deep into the hidden recesses of his mind to torment him with the most painful memory of his life.

"You okay?"

He turned to find Madam Bovell next to him.

"You all right?" she repeated. "You look like you've seen a—"

"I'm fine," he replied.

"You ready to go upstairs?"

"To where the murders occurred?"

"Yes."

He nodded. "Why wouldn't I be?"

"You just seem off."

"Yeah, sure, maybe I am a little off. Why not? Maybe it's because everything about this is off. What am I missing here? All these things connecting! All these different spirits and events bringing us all here right now. This group! What could possibly be so important for all these elements of fate to draw us here? What are we really about to face up there? Annabel? Something worse? Something evil? A demon? The devil itself?"

"We're not going to face the devil," she said.

"Wait a minute," he murmured, leaning in close. "I know you don't believe that. You've been hiding something since the cemetery in Stull. I could tell, but I didn't say anything. I thought you'd tell me when you were ready. Something scared you out there. And I saw that expression again when we first arrived here and you touched the house. But you can't keep it to yourself any longer. You've got to tell me. I've got to know before I go any further. I need to know what you're hiding."

"I'm not hiding anything," she said. "Nothing that I know for sure. Look, something did happen at the cemetery that I haven't mentioned. But it was just something I felt. That's all. Just a feeling."

"What feeling?"

"A bad feeling. I'm not really sure."

"Try to describe it."

"A darkness, maybe. A living coldness. Like something was there, watching us from within the night. Like a beast in the shadows. But it was an intelligent beast. It understood who we are. I just felt it, you know, like the way you just know certain things in dreams."

"Was it hunting us?"

"Not hunting, but maybe tracking us."

"Did it follow us to North Dakota?"

"I don't know. Maybe. If it's even real. It's probably just in my mind."

"You don't know?"

"It's just a feeling. I thought I felt it again at the hospital right before the séance. Briefly."

"And you felt it again here?"

"I don't know. Maybe."

"Should we tell the others?"

"And what, exactly, would we tell them? I don't know what it means—if it even means anything."

They stood at the base of the steep staircase to the darkness above. He heard a soft creak overhead and told himself it was just the wind pushing against the house.

Rachel and Jason came through the living room from the back part of the house.

"See anything interesting?" Madam Bovell asked.

"The backyard has been mowed recently," Rachel said. "Like in the past few days. And the patio looks good, too. Everything's well maintained."

"Except for the flowerpots along the edge of the yard," Jason added.

"Yeah," Rachel said. "The edges of the yard look terrible. So does the garden. But the yard itself has been cared for. Someone has definitely been coming over and spending time here."

"Strange," Madam Bovell said.

"Very," Dr. Graves added.

A sudden banging startled them. Dr. Graves felt a jolt, but it was just Aaron, pounding down the stairs.

"Tommy's setting up the thermal cam," Aaron said. "I'm going out to grab the Nightcrawler ghost kit. Might set it up in the basement. I could use a hand, Professor, if you're not too busy."

"Well, I think we were all going to head upstairs," Dr. Graves said.

"Won't take long."

"Oh, go on," Madam Bovell said. "It'll be good for you to see what a real ghost hunter does."

"Don't get me started," the professor deadpanned. "Fancy electronic machines won't get any closer to witnessing spirits than if we just unplugged everything and opened up our minds."

"Go on," Bovell urged. "Help the kid out. You should be encouraging the next generation of paranormal investigators. You're not going to live forever, you know. You may want them to try to contact *you* someday once you shuffle off this mortal coil."

As the others moved up the stairs, he followed Aaron back out the front door. "Okay, kid, let's go get the rest of your electronic toys."

They reached the truck, and Aaron stepped on top of the rear wheel and jumped up into the back bed. Lifting four cases from the large tool compartment along the cab, he slid each one to the lowered tailgate. Jumping over them, he landed on the ground, spun around, and wrapped his arms around two of them.

"Can you grab the other two?" he asked.

Dr. Graves stepped past him, grabbed the last two cases by their handles, and pulled them off the tailgate. Surprised by their weight, he struggled briefly before lowering them to the ground. "Good God, what's in these?"

"The TG-One-Six-Five thermal cam, a few three-sixty pucks with IR light sensors, a Rook EMF meter, and a few of everyone's favorite REM-ATDD Mel Meters."

"Are you speaking English?" Dr. Graves exasperated.

"It's science, Professor. *Modern* science."

"You ever consider that all this electronic stuff might actually be scaring ghosts away?"

"I thought it worked the other way. Aren't *ghosts* supposed to scare us away."

"Fear is a two-way street."

"You make it sound as if ghosts are afraid we'll intrude into their world."

"Maybe they are," the professor said. "They may understand the reality of Einstein's theories better than we do. Maybe they have good reason to be afraid."

"And I suppose now you're going to tell me Einstein was really just researching ghosts with all his work?"

"Well," the professor said, "Einstein believed in multiple dimensions and energy transference and the relative warping of space and time. If you don't think the spirit world fits perfectly into all that, then you're as bad as the religious zealots who rejected Darwin when he first published *On the Origin of Species.*"

"Did Darwin believe in ghosts?"

Dr. Graves smiled, pleased as all professors were anytime someone proposed an interesting question with an interesting answer. "No, actually, he didn't. But his research partner did."

"What other scientists believed in ghosts?"

"Well, historians don't agree on it, but many say that Sir Isaac Newton did. Some say Edison did, too, and he once remarked he had planned to invent a device that could be used to communicate with spirits, though who knows if he was serious."

"So if all these scientific minds in the past were looking for ghosts, don't you think they'd approve of us using our equipment to get measurements of activity?"

"I think the paranormal investigators of that time, like Hodgson and Hyslop and Carrington, would have been very skeptical of claims that your equipment provides authentic, valuable readings of ghost activity. They exposed a lot of frauds and gimmicks in their day. And other researchers in the late nineteenth century—Myers, Gurney, and Podmore—published a multivolume book titled *Phantasms of the Living,* which compiled a monumental record of ghost sightings. In that book, they interviewed people and documented over seven hundred sightings of ghosts. They then determined that nearly ninety percent of those were unreliable accounts. They were skeptical scientists—they weren't looking for something to confirm their preconceptions or hopes. They were seeking the truth, whatever that may be, and they were more likely than not to dismiss things as unsubstantiated false claims."

"And the other ten percent?"

"Those, they concluded *actually were* authentic witness accounts of ghosts or other phantasms."

"So they were skeptical but open-minded," Aaron said.

"That's exactly how they were."

"Approaching everything through the scientific method."

"Yes."

"Then you should do the same."

"How so?"

"You shouldn't dismiss our ghost-hunting equipment just because you have no experience with it. You should approach it with an open mind. See it in action. Be skeptical. Be careful in your observations and cautious in your conclusions. But be open-minded, like those great scientific paranormal researchers from the past that you so admire."

Dr. Graves grinned. "Okay, kid. I'll give your toys a chance."

"They're not toys," Aaron said. "They're the most advanced ghost-hunting tools on the market."

Dr. Graves chuckled. "Trust me, kid. The fact that there's even a market for ghost-hunting equipment should make you suspicious of this stuff. People have been trying to profit from spiritual scams since even before London's Cock Lane ghost was exposed as a fraud in the Seventeen-Sixties."

"You know, for a ghost hunter, you're one hell of a cynic."

"I'm not a ghost hunter. I'm a paranormal investigator—and one who has seen a thousand frauds and false prophets."

"Well, at least I was right about the cynic part," Aaron said.

The night wind strengthened as they manhandled the equipment across the gravel. A hollow whistling rose and fell from the stand of trees left of the house. The branch in need of pruning kept on slapping against the house. The dark clouds looked ready to cut loose. There was something magical about this place: the strange heat radiating from the house, the icy rain and violent wind across the uneven land, and the pale driveway stretching into the black void behind him—where he kept looking over his shoulder half-expecting to find some ghostly figure standing behind him. Each time, he saw nothing, but he couldn't shake the feeling that something was there staring at him.

He carried the cases up the squeaky front steps. Following Aaron along the front porch, he noticed something strange: none of the white paint was peeling off the house. For that matter, none of the paint on the patio was peeling, either. Hell, it didn't even seem old.

"Are you kids sure this house is abandoned?"

"Sure, we're sure," Aaron said. "Why?"

"Something feels off. I've been on a lot of investigations in abandoned houses. Ones that were rumored to be haunted. But none of them looked like this. This is too well maintained. Something's not right here."

"I'm pretty sure it's abandoned."

"Yeah, I'm not so sure."

"Don't start getting jumpy on me, Professor. The first place we're going to set up equipment is in the basement, and I don't need you making that place any more unnerving than it will already be."

"Just keep your wits about you, kid, because we may not be the only ones here tonight."

"See? That's what I'm talking about. It's not helpful, you saying things like that."

"Kid, this work isn't for the faint of heart. Just keep your eyes open."

57

"So this is the room where it happened?" Rachel said. She had felt it the moment she stepped into the couple's bedroom. So many emotions mixed in overlapping echoes. She could sense the happiness that once abided here, and the laughter and the passions and the fears and pain and anger and sorrow. It was all here. But like a dozen radios in the same place playing different stations, it was impossible to decipher. There was no narrative to be found, no harmony—only chaotic, overlapping echoes of the past.

"This is where it happened," Jason confirmed.

Rachel walked to the center of the room and knelt. She had felt a sharp pain in her belly, and a brief, twisting sensation in her head. Then it passed. "This is where the husband died," she said.

"I think it was over there, actually," Jason said. "I saw the photo in the news article."

She looked to see him pointing toward the area by the bathroom door opposite the entrance to the hallway. "No," she said. "He died right here."

"It's strange," Shelley said, "to be standing in a place where something so horrible happened."

Rachel could see the confusion on her friend's face. She had to remind herself that aside from her and Madam Bovell, no one else could even begin to understand this house. Rachel had been hearing Annabel's screams for nearly a year. And now she was feeling a tingle of energy in the musty air. Something was here with them in the house, but she didn't know whether it had followed them here or just lain in wait.

Whatever it was, she could feel it hiding from them, watching them explore the room. She hoped it was Annabel, but it could be whatever dark force Annabel may have attracted to the town. She thought about Aaron's description of the sudden grill fire that had threatened his family. She thought of the dozens of cuts crosshatching Tommy's face from the homicidal chickens. She looked at Shelley, who had joined Jessica near the bathroom door, and recalled their near-death accounts.

She closed her eyes and shuddered. Something was here, moving in or around the house, and it was getting closer to them.

A few hard gusts rattled what sounded like loose siding outside the window facing the backyard. Rachel stepped to it, cupped her hands around her eyes like horse blinders, and pressed her face to the cold glass. She looked out over the dark field that stretched as far as she could see in the thin moonlight. The wind was picking up, and a massive reef of black clouds was marching across the sky and just beginning to edge over the nearly full moon. Then her eye caught something below in the field. About a hundred feet past the yard, she saw a blurry image of a figure standing motionless in the field. But just as she glimpsed it, the dark clouds crawled over the moon, and the rest of the field and the figure vanished.

She stayed at the window. Searching the night, she found nothing. The human shape could have been a scarecrow, an elongated puddle reflecting the moon, or any of a thousand other perfectly natural things. It could have been natural, sure, but she was sensing another presence here with them, and it could be coming from the field.

The wind hissed past the window. The pressure had changed in her ears, and she felt the need to yawn and pop them.

Pulling back from the glass, she saw the reflection of Shelley and Jessica behind her, still standing near the bathroom. They both were looking at her as if eager to hear about whatever she had seen outside. She was about to say something to them when the bathroom door slammed shut, sending a loud bang through the room. Both Shelley and Jessica jumped and screamed as they darted to the other side of the room. They hugged each other and cursed loudly enough to frighten off any unseen critters creeping about in the walls or attic.

"What the hell was that?" Shelley finally gasped.

"Pressure change from the wind," Rachel said. "A draft slammed the door."

"A draft, my butt," Jessica said. "I heard that same moaning sound before my Chevy collapsed onto me. It's here. Whatever *it* is, it's here in this house."

"It was only a door," Madam Bovell said. "We need to stay calm. Positive thoughts only."

The two girls stared silently at the woman, and Rachel was about to tell all three that she thought each was correct on some level. But before she could say another word, she felt a dizziness overcome her. A black cloud crept into her peripheral vision and soon closed in and veiled the room from her. All she could see was the tight darkness shrouding her. She was now lying on her back in a confined place. She couldn't even fully stretch out her arms or legs. It was like being enclosed in a coffin. She reached up and banged her fists on the lid. A steady hum and vibration surrounded her, but she felt it strongest beneath her. She screamed and banged on the lid and screamed louder.

But she couldn't escape this prison.

Where had the others gone?

Where was the house?

Where was *she*?

Before she could even guess at answers to the many questions tumbling through her mind, she felt the vibrations easing until they vanished. Then a gentle rocking, followed by an engine dying, a car door closing, heavy crunching footsteps walking around her, a key scratching metal, a click and pop, and then the large trunk she was inside opening up and exposing her to cold rain and the towering figure that reached down for her with large, hairy hands.

She closed her eyes and screamed, and when she opened them again, she was back inside the farmhouse, in the bedroom. Madam Bovell and Shelley and Jessica were huddled around her, holding her, reassuring her that everything was okay. Jason was near the window.

"What happened?" Rachel asked frantically, still panicking. Her hands and arms were shaking. She was sitting on the wood floor, though she couldn't remember how she got there. And she was now in the center of the room instead of by the window.

"You freaked out all of a sudden," Jessica answered.

"Where did you go?" Madam Bovell asked softly. She had pressed her palm to Rachel's forehead as if checking for a fever, but then she closed her eyes as if trying to see what Rachel had seen.

"Someplace dark and confined," Rachel said. "I was trapped. Something was keeping me there, and then it came for me. Large hands—claws—reached for me out of the storm."

"A vision," Madam Bovell guessed. "Maybe even of the near future."

"It wasn't of the future," Rachel proclaimed. "I could feel it happening right now."

"But you're *here* right now," Jason said, stepping toward them. "You're not trapped anywhere. You're safe with us."

"But somehow, I am trapped, right now as we speak. I can't explain it, but I can feel it. Something has me right now." She started crying.

"We can't always understand what the gift is trying to tell us," Madam Bovell said. "But you *are* here with us right now. Your mind may have left us briefly, but your body was always safely here."

"It felt so real."

"I know, honey. But you can't always control or force these things. If a vision isn't clear, then you can't let yourself become overwhelmed with fear or speculation. Give it time. If it's somehow important, then whatever connection you had with it will often come back again with more strength and clarity."

Shelley and Jessica each extended a hand down to her. She grabbed them and let them pull her to her feet. Her eyes slowly drifted back toward the window. It seemed to be whispering something to her. Cautiously stepping over to it, she looked out into the dark backyard. Her breathing quickened when she saw the figure again, this time standing at the edge of the backyard and looking out into the field. She couldn't tell for sure if this was what she had seen before, but it was more pronounced and no longer in the field. The moon was still obscured, so only the faint light from the house fell on the human figure. It looked tall and strong, and its stillness made it seem eerily threatening.

Footsteps came running down the hallway, and Scott appeared in the doorway. "Did I hear screaming?" he asked.

"We had some scares," Shelley answered.

"Where's Tommy?" Jessica asked. "I thought you two were together."

"We were," he said, "but he wanted to take a quick look at the field."

"Why?"

Scott shrugged. "Farmer stuff, I guess."

"Yeah," Rachel said, gazing back down at the figure in the backyard, still looking out into the field. "I see him out there."

More footsteps came up the staircase and down the hallway.

"Are we getting this party started yet, or what?" Tommy said as he walked into the room.

Rachel jerked her head from the window to see them. Everyone looked at Tommy, then at her. She looked back out the window and stared at the backyard. The figure that was there only a few seconds ago had vanished, in its place only the growing fog of her rapid breath on the window.

58

Aaron flipped the switch at the top of the basement stairs. Nothing happened. He flipped it down and then back up. Still nothing.

"What did you expect?" Dr. Graves asked. "All the power in the house is out."

"I was just hoping," Aaron said. They had set up a few portable lights on the first and second floors but hadn't thought to spare any for the basement. "You still have your flashlight?"

Dr. Graves snapped his fingers and said "presto" just as a flashlight beam came to life. It cast a long, wide shadow of Aaron going down the stairs, his head silhouetted on the basement floor. Aaron dug into his pack and found his flashlight. Then they carried the cases together down the creaking steps in four trips.

"Hello?" Aaron announced after they had set down the last case at the base of the stairs.

Silence.

"Think anyone's down here?" Dr. Graves asked.

"Don't even ask that."

"Then why did you ask 'hello?'?"

"Just to confirm … just in case."

The basement was large, and the main room looked empty. Stud walls divided it into smaller rooms, but only a few had drywall. None looked weight-bearing. Steel poles spaced throughout the room appeared to provide the support. A dark lightbulb dangled from a cord in the middle of the room, subtly swinging in a small circle as if someone had just given it a gentle bump.

"You've exposed a lot of false paranormal activities over your career?" Aaron asked.

"Thousands," Dr. Graves replied.

"Care to explain to me why that lightbulb's swinging like that?"

The professor looked at it for a second. "It's barely moving. Hanging down here from a long cord like that, it's probably just caused by slight vibrations in the floorboard above, from our walking around in the house."

"All right," Aaron said. "I can buy that. Not bad, Professor."

Dr. Graves grinned. "Of course, it could be that paranormal entities are moving around the property and creating tiny electromagnetic disturbances that would push and pull a sensitive object hanging like that. Although I'm sure one of your scientific instruments can clear up that theory lickety-split."

"Oh, yeah. I've got just the thing for that." He opened one of the large cases and, with obvious pride, pulled out a black device that looked like a walkie-talkie. "Professor, allow me to introduce you to Mr. Mel Meter. This little baby can detect electromagnetic fields from both natural and man-made sources." He touched a short yellow fitting sticking out the top of the handheld device. It had an inch-long blue wire protruding from it. "And it even has an ATDD unit attached to it. Ambient Temperature Deviation Detection. It will sense if there are any sudden temperature changes nearby as we investigate the room. A high-pitched beep means the temperature has suddenly gone up; low-pitched means a drop. As you know, ghosts create pockets of energy that cause sudden chills in places they've been, and increases can indicate objects they're trying to move."

"Very impressive," Dr. Graves said. "What other magic tricks do you have?"

"Well, check this out," Aaron said, reaching into the case and pulling out a silver device about the same size as the Mel Meter. This looked more like a large cell phone from the age of the dinosaurs. "This," he said, "is an Olympus EVP recorder. It's top of the line."

"Electronic voice phenomena," Dr. Graves said, amused. "Sounds that many believe are ghosts' attempts at communicating with us from beyond our dimension. How the hell does that thing work?"

"It uses radio-frequency sweeps to generate white noise, which, theories suggest, give some entities the energy they need to be heard. When this occurs, you will sometimes hear voices or sounds coming through the static in their attempts to communicate."

"Theories suggest," Dr. Graves repeated. "Whose theories? I wonder. The scientific method is losing credible practitioners, I fear. Still, impressive. We can sense ghosts and hear their communications. Fantastic. What else do you have?"

"I have this bad boy," Aaron replied, holding up a black rectangular device the size of his palm, with four small white bulbs facing out from the front corners. Two yellow-striped strips of reflective tape stretched along the top and bottom of the face. A red switch stuck out from the side. "This is a wide-angle infrared floodlight. It will help the video recorder capture better evidence through its night-vision illuminator."

"What video recorder?"

Aaron grinned. "Keep your shirt on, Professor. We've got three full-spectrum-modified GoPro camcorders that sit on a three-sixty puck camera mount."

"I have no idea what that means," the professor said.

"It means I can place this device in the center of the room, and it will record a high-def, three-hundred-sixty-degree video in infrared light of everything around it—everything in the room. Its Bluetooth connection to our video monitor allows us to monitor it on our laptop anywhere within a hundred feet."

"Not bad, kid."

"That's not the half of it. We also have motion sensors, a laser grid scope, a—"

"Okay," Dr. Graves interrupted. "I get it. You're a ghost-gadget guy. So let's get this tech set up so we can get back to the others. We've been gone a long time."

He watched as Aaron stepped to the center of the room and put down the puck camera mount, which did indeed look like a hockey puck. He then attached three small silver cameras to it, each facing out to cover 120 degrees of arc. Aaron pressed a few buttons, flipped the red switch, then stood and stepped back as the device came alive like a miniature flashing, beeping android from a science fiction film. Then it went dark and silent.

"Is it broken?" Dr. Graves asked.

"Nah, it always gets a little testy when it's first turned on. But then it settles into stealth mode. It's recording us right now using infrared light. We can watch the live feed on my laptop when we're back upstairs. I also have another three-camera packet we can set up in the upstairs bedroom. We should just do a quick EMF and temperature sweep of the basement, then set up some sensors before heading back upstairs."

"Go for it," the professor said. "I'm following your lead."

Aaron held up the Mel Meter and made a slow sweeping motion across the room. It made a soft whisper of white noise with sporadic hisses cutting through the otherwise steady flow of static.

Dr. Graves listened carefully to the sounds, realizing just what a clever product this was. Designed for modern ghost hunters, it created indecipherable data that provided no information at all. But mix that data with an excited imagination, and any least anomaly became contact with a ghost, even when nothing at all was lurking in the dark.

"You hear that?" Aaron said when the sound rose slightly in pitch.

Dr. Graves smiled at the idea that this Mel Meter could somehow aid spirits in communicating with electromagnetic waves. While his belief in the afterlife had recently solidified, his knowledge of the real-life existence of scammers in the world of paranormal research was undeniable and extensive, and it included the purveyors of useless gimmicks to desperate ghost hunters with little academic-based experience in field investigations.

"What is it?" the professor asked, willing to play along with the kid's imagination.

"I don't know," Aaron said. "It's like there's a pocket of energy down here."

"Where?"

Aaron slowly moved the Mel Meter from left to right, then back again, sweeping the far side of the basement two more times. And each time, a sharp, excited burst of static hissed from the device at a particular point. "There," he said. "The center of the back wall. There's definitely some sort of energy field."

Dr. Graves was mildly intrigued. While he didn't think the Mel Meter did what Aaron believed it could do, he couldn't deny that the device had reacted three times to something in the direction of the far side of the basement. But *direction* was no indicator of *distance.*

"How do you know it's all the way at the back wall?" he asked. "Couldn't it be closer?"

Aaron didn't reply, but he seemed to realize what Dr. Graves was implying. He took slow, gingerly steps along the dusty floor, making a semicircle to change the angle between him and the center of the back wall. As he moved, he swept the Mel Meter between the center of the room and the back wall. The hissing static from the device rose each time it pointed at the wall, and went dead silent when directed elsewhere in the room.

And with each rise and fall of the electrical noise, Dr. Graves's nerves tensed. He found himself staring at the middle of the back wall as if trying to discern whether anything was standing there, hidden in the shadows. He tried to think of a scientific explanation for Aaron's readings: mineral deposits affecting nearby magnetic fields, geological changes from local shale-oil drilling activity, electronic feedback caused by all the other equipment they had lugged into the confined area belowground. But as the activity continued, he stopped trying to work through a logical explanation and found himself marveling at the effect he was witnessing.

"Have you ever seen activity like this before?" he asked.

"Never," Aaron whispered.

Aaron then took a step toward the wall. The Mel Meter got louder, and a blue LED flickered on at the top of the device. "Oh, man. The temperature just dropped three degrees." He took another step. "Now it's dropped another two."

"Colder near the edges—not unusual in a basement," Dr. Graves commented.

Aaron stepped back and turned the device to his right, near another concrete wall. The blue light blinked off. Then he returned it to the previous place, nearer the far wall. He grew animated when the blue LED blinked on again.

"Nope," he said. "Only this wall is colder."

"That doesn't make sense," Dr. Graves said as an icy chill ran up his spine.

"Here, hold this," Aaron said, reaching out to hand Dr. Graves the Mel Meter. "I want to see something."

Dr. Graves took the device and watched as the kid rushed back to the stairs and grabbed the EVP recorder. Realizing what he was going to do, Dr. Graves looked back down at the readings on the Mel Meter. He wanted to see if they changed when the kid tried to use the EVP recorder. The white needle was near zero, which meant he wasn't pointing it in the correct direction. Slightly right. He pulled it back left, and as the Mel Meter aligned toward the middle of the back wall, he saw the needle jump up to the halfway mark at the top of the gauge. Despite Aaron's claims these past few minutes, it had still surprised him when he first witnessed the needle jump. Turning the device left and right, he watched with fascination as the needle fell and rose, then fell and rose again, each time matching the fluctuations in the volume of static crackle.

And for the first time, he thought that something might actually be down here with them.

"Hold it steady," Aaron whispered with surprising authority. "And keep it pointed at the strongest spot."

Dr. Graves straightened up, sensing the urgency in the kid's voice. As he held the device steady, he saw the temperature drop by one point, to sixty-six degrees. Then to sixty-five. Then sixty-four.

"Wow ... Something's happening here," he said.

Sixty-three.

"What?"

Sixty-two.

"The temperature's dropping—fast."

Sixty-one. Sixty.

"What about the electromagnetic field readings?" Aaron asked.

"Yeah," Dr. Graves said, noticing the change in the needle. "It's moved up, maybe by ten percent."

"Keep holding it on that spot," Aaron said, rushing forward. "I'm gonna try to get an EVP recording."

Dr. Graves watched the temperature reading tick down. He kept glancing up at the wall, half expecting something to materialize at any moment. He also followed the rising needle gauge for the electromagnetic field. Meanwhile, Aaron stood beside him, pressing buttons on the handheld device. He held it out in front of him.

Immediately, the EVP recorder began to crackle with white noise. It sounded like listening to the ocean in a conch shell, magnified a hundred times. The delta waves washed through the basement, bouncing off the concrete walls and creating an ambient sound.

Dr. Graves strained his ears to hear within the noise any pattern that might be some form of communication. Only five minutes ago, he had been biting his tongue to keep from laughing at the ridiculous antics with the ghost-hunting equipment. Now he wasn't so sure.

The sounds coming from the EVP recorder could be mixed with something meaningful. They strained to hear it.

"S-s-s-s-h-h-h-h-l-l-l-l-a-a-a-a-n-n-n-n-y-y-y-y-s-s-s-s-h-h-h-h."

Aaron's eyes widened, but Dr. Graves wasn't sure why. It had sounded like there was something in the white noise, a doppler shift in the digital winds, but nothing more. There was no more meaningfulness in it than that of a car engine revving up and down as it sped around a race track. But because of Aaron's strange reaction, he listened even more closely to the scrambled noise spewing from the EVP recorder.

"W-w-w-w-r-r-r-r-s-s-s-s-h-h-h-h-a-a-a-a-n-n-n-n-y-y-y-y-s-s-s-s-h-h-h-h."

Aaron was about to burst with excitement. "You hear that, Professor?"

"I don't know," Graves said. "Maybe something, but my ears aren't as good as they used to be."

"I hear 'Annie,'" the kid said. "As in 'Annabel.' She's saying her name. She's right there, and she's trying to communicate with us."

"How do you hear that?"

"It's in the middle of the sound."

The EVP recorder crackled again. *"W-w-w-w-r-r-r-r-s-s-s-s-h-h-h-h-a-a-a-a-n-n-n-n-y-y-y-y-s-s-s-s-h-h-h-h."*

"Yes," Dr. Graves said. "I think—yes, maybe I hear it. I hear something … a repeated sequence …"

The sound turned to something deeper, almost like a growl from a wolf or other large carnivore.

"W-w-w-w-r-r-r-r … W-w-w-w-w-w-r-r-r-r-r-r."

Dr. Graves took a step back. Something was wrong. Something had changed. For the first time since setting foot in the basement, he worried that they may have ventured into some unknown danger. But why would Annabel be aggressive and violent to visitors here after showing no signs of malice at the hospital? What about this place could possibly be twisting her energy so negatively? What dark secret did she hold? Was it merely the memory of her murder? Had something else happened here? What was creating such a transformation in Annabel's spirit?

The growling from the EVP recorder intensified.

"I don't like this," Aaron said, all signs of eager enthusiasm gone. He seemed as unnerved as the professor. "Maybe we should leave."

Dr. Graves glanced down at the Mel Meter. "The temperature has gone back up," he said. "And the electromagnetic-wave readings have dropped. Is this right?"

The growling intensified.

"She's moving," Aaron said.

Moving? The professor hadn't thought of the spirit entity in those terms. But Aaron could be right. The EVP recorder clearly indicated that something was down here with them, but unlike the Mel Meter's sensors, it couldn't detect the direction of the source.

The professor began moving the device left and right, sweeping the basement while keeping his eyes on the Mel Meter's gauges. Then, as he had it pointed toward another corner of the basement, it became active again. "There," he said. "Temperature's down again, and EMF readings are above seventy-five percent."

The growling from the EVP recorder had become less loud. "She's leaving," Aaron said.

"I think you're right," Dr. Graves said. "The EMF is lower now, but she isn't moving around the room anymore."

"Vanishing into another dimension?"

"Maybe. Or maybe rising up through the ceiling into another room in the house. Where are the others?"

"In the bedroom, I think." Aaron paused, then added, "Two floors up from that corner. Professor ..."

"Yeah. Let's hurry."

Just as he spoke, the floorboards above them rattled for a few seconds before going still. A fine cloud of dust drifted down over them.

Leaving the rest of the equipment behind, he and Aaron rushed up the basement stairs. He didn't know what the others had been doing there, but something had drawn Annabel to them.

59

Rachel watched in silence as the others formed a small circle in the center of the bedroom. Madam Bovell had promised they wouldn't attempt another séance tonight. The circle would supposedly help them attract Annabel's ghost even if no medium was in a trance state to channel communications. Ghosts could influence physical objects and may even be able to conjure their appearance to the living. This, it seemed, was Madam Bovell's hope. And that was fine with Rachel, so long as she wasn't asked to reopen her mind to the spirit world. The experience had been both enlightening and exhilarating, but also exhausting and dangerous.

She was still trying to understand what happened to her only a moment ago. The stab in her abdomen was the most terrifying thing she had ever felt. And not just the physical pain—it had an emotional element, too. A layer of confusion and fear had embedded itself into her mind during the episode—fear that was not her own. It felt as if she was experiencing someone else's nightmare.

The obvious assumption was that she had picked up the phantom echo of Annabel's death. But this had felt too powerful to be some lingering cry from the past. It was as if she had sensed something occurring at this very moment.

Rapid pounding on the stairs startled everyone. The clatter grew until Aaron burst into the room, panting. Dr. Graves appeared a few seconds later, gasping as he leaned on the door frame. Both held up electronic devices, waving them around the room.

"What the devil?" Madam Bovell asked.

"Something's ... here," Dr. Graves wheezed.

"Annabel," Aaron added. "And she isn't happy."

"I told you," Jason said. "This isn't the same as the hospital. She's different here."

"You saw her?" Madam Bovell asked.

"We detected her," said Graves. "On these." He gestured to the device in his hand.

"Solid readings on the Mel Meter," Aaron said. "Twenty-degree temperature drop. Seventy-five percent of full electromagnetic field on spot location. And we're picking up massive EVPs, including jumbled pronunciations of 'Annie,' for 'Annabel.'"

"Holy crap," Tommy said. "We've never seen numbers like that—not even in the Badlands. And she actually tried to *speak* to you?"

"Yeah," Aaron said. "She was in the basement, then seemed to be moving up through the ceiling on this side of the house. We thought she was coming here."

Just then the EVP recorder came to life with a barrage of garbled noise.

"This is it," Aaron said. "She's here! This is happening!"

Rachel shot to her feet. She had also sensed the change in the room. She felt a heightened mental focus. New layers of light appeared. Things around her were now visible in minute detail she hadn't noticed a second ago. She could see the marks on the floor where the bedposts had once been. The wall across from the large back window showed the sun stains where a dresser and mirror had once been. A red sofa chair. How did she know it was red? But she did—somehow.

The entire room appeared before her eyes in a hollow, ghostly image of pale blue light. Was this a dream? A vision? A time slip from the past? A glimpse between dimensions?

"Do you guys see this?" she asked.

"See what?" Madam Bovell replied.

"She's trying to show me something," Rachel said.

"What?" Jason asked.

"No, don't tell us," Madam Bovell insisted. "Not now. Focus everything you have on her. Everyone else, be quiet. Don't distract her."

Rachel saw the former outlines of the room grow more distinct. The objects sometimes superimposed themselves translucently where others in the group happened to be sitting. But soon, she didn't even notice the others anymore. All her concentration centered on the objects of blue light.

More pronounced than anything else was the bed in the back center of the room. Stepping toward it, she saw the two dead bodies of the adulterous lovers lying naked on it. Even in the glowing blue light, she could see the details of their murdered bodies, twisted together like an erotic Greek sculpture. But if this was truly a glimpse of the past, then the woman, Annabel, must still be alive. For she had not died until she reached the hospital. Kneeling down to look closer, Rachel was confused to see not even the slightest trace of life from this woman.

Pulling back slowly, she saw movement in the corner of her eye. A tall man stood in the doorway. She recognized Annabel's husband from the newspaper articles. His face was twisted with rage and confusion. He had been staring at the bodies he had killed, but now he turned to Rachel. Stepping forward, he demanded, "Where's Annie?"

Startled, Rachel crawled backward a few feet until she bumped the wall.

He stepped closer and leaned into her. "WHERE'S ANNIE?"

Rachel screamed. Her shrill, bloodcurdling cry vibrated the blue rays of light.

"WHERE'S ANNIE?" the man yelled again as his outline faded and he vanished into the air.

All the other ghostly images of the past vanished with him. The room was once again empty except for the other ghost hunters, who stared at her in horror.

Then, suddenly, the stabbing pain in her abdomen returned. This time, however, it was worse than before. And the fear embedded with the pain had multiplied many times over. Fear that screamed for her to run from this place of horror and the evil things that still lurked within it. *Run. Hurry. He's coming back to kill you.*

"Are you okay?" Jason asked.

"What's wrong?" Madam Bovell said softly.

But Rachel couldn't think of answering them. The fear was crawling all over her skin like a thousand spiders. She struggled to her feet and barged out of the room, nearly losing her balance as she raced along the hallway and scrambled down the stairs. She could hear the others chasing after her and calling her name, but mad fright pushed her to escape the house.

She banged the stairway wall with her shoulder, shifting her descent enough that her left foot caught the banister's bottom post, sending her sprawling to the floor.

Escape. Hurry. Before he returns. Run!

Her mind swirled with thoughts of this house and its murders and the yelling husband, and the devil killing her mother and grandmother, and Annabel's spirit pleading for help in the hospital. But the source of this pain and fear was something altogether separate and unknown. This was happening right now, but not here and not to her.

Another poor soul was suffering at this moment.

Escape. Hurry, before he returns. Run!

She got to her feet as the others clambered down the stairs after her, trying to get her to stop.

He's coming. I hear him. Hurry, before it's too late. This is your only chance to live. Run!

She pushed off the wall and ran to the front door. Throwing it open, she dashed out onto the front porch and across the wooden planks. Rain drenched her hair before she had even jumped off the porch and raced across the dirt and grass of the side yard. She made for the trees, for something told her that darkness and cover were her only hope of survival.

She heard the others behind her as she ran through the dense boughs of the evergreen thicket. The needles scratched her skin. The trunks were barely visible, but somehow she kept moving fast for nearly a minute, finally breaking through the patch of woods, into a vast field.

She struggled to run through the rough field at night. The furrowed ground bore the remnants of the fall harvest, with broken stalks twisted along the dirt. Lightning flashed across the sky before her. She tripped and fell to the soft, wet earth. Her drenched hair had whipped around and wrapped over her face. She couldn't see or move or breathe. The pain in her stomach intensified.

He's here. He's found you. You ran, but you didn't escape. He's too strong. He has you.

"No!" she screamed. "Please, no!"

A sharp pain pierced her side, causing her to jerk to the left while still on her knees. Then another stab of pain.

"Stop! Stop. Please!"

Then another sharp pain. Then a strange feeling across her lower neck. Warm, slick liquid poured down her throat. Weakness followed. Then dizziness. She couldn't speak, and breathing became too difficult.

He's cut my throat. God, not yet, please. I had so much I still wanted to do ... Mom, Dad, I'm sorry ...

Rachel fell onto her side, curled up in a ball, and sobbed uncontrollably, shaking, twitching. The pain and fear were gone, but the echo of suffering wouldn't leave her. She heard the others, yelling her name in the distance. She needed them now more than ever. With what little strength she had, she raised an arm in the air. And as she did, the skies erupted in more lightning, and torrential rain descended on the field, drowning its echoes of death.

60

Jason was the first to see Rachel's arm sticking up from the dead field. It twisted awkwardly in the air while the rest of her body lay convulsing on its side. "There!" he yelled, jumping over a short mound of dirt and rushing through the corn stubble.

Lightning fired the sky as her arm dropped and her body fell still.

"Rachel!"

He slid into the fresh mud beside her. The others were not far behind him.

"Rachel!" He lifted her head. Her entire body was limp. "Rachel! Can you hear me? Open your eyes!"

He held her head on his lap and leaned over her as the rain pounded them.

"Rachel!"

"What's wrong?" Scott said, arriving and towering over him.

"Help me carry her back to the car!"

As Tommy and Jessica arrived, Jason and Scott lifted Rachel. They carried her back across the field, through the stand of trees, past the farmhouse, and into the back of the yellow Yukon that Dr. Graves and Madam Bovell had ready and running. They backed it up to the county road just to get her away from the house. Shelley and Jason stayed with Rachel while Tommy, Jessica, and Scott rushed back into the house to help Aaron gather the equipment from the basement. Once the truck and the Jeep were loaded with everything, they would leave.

Jason watched as Shelley tried to bring Rachel around. Rachel was breathing and didn't seem hurt. Both Dr. Graves and Madam Bovell felt she must have fallen into a trance and that the best thing to do was wait for her to come around naturally on her own. Watching her, he tried to imagine what horror could have made her rush from the farmhouse in such a mad fright. Madam Bovell had pressed a wrist to Rachel's forehead and announced that she was now safe and they just needed to wait.

Tommy and Jessica jumped into his truck. Aaron jumped in on the passenger side of Scott's Jeep, and Scott motioned that they were ready to go.

Dr. Graves threw the Yukon into drive and punched it. The wheels spun, kicking up gravel. Jason saw the pickup and the Jeep come roaring out of the driveway behind them. They couldn't get away fast enough from the farmhouse and its evils.

61

Rachel opened her eyes and found herself floating over a field of stars. Thin blue lights pulsated between the stars like billion-mile laser beams. There was no sound. Purple waves swirled above her as if she were underwater looking up at the ocean's surface in a silent storm. Everything else was shrouded in a black void, except for the movement that caught the corner of her eye.

Turning her head, she saw a girl floating beside her. The girl's eyes were open unnaturally wide, and her mouth moved as if to speak, but there was no sound.

Rachel tried to speak, but she couldn't even hear herself. This was not a place where sound waves could exist. She tried to use her mind to communicate. Gazing into the girl's terrified eyes, she tried to look past the fear and into her mind.

Who are you? Rachel projected the question with her mind.

The girl's behavior was unchanged. She was still pleading for help with her eyes, still moving her lips, struggling to speak.

Rachel focused harder. *Who are you?*

There, a change—a sparkle of light in the girl's eyes. And Rachel had felt an electric tingle in her own mind, as if she had made a connection.

Who are YOU*?*

The question echoed back at Rachel as if by sonar. But it wasn't in her mind's voice, so it wasn't really an echo. It was a reply.

I'm Rachel, she thought. *Who are you?*

Gin ...

Gin? Rachel had felt a hesitation from the girl.

Gin ... Jenny.

Rachel suddenly felt as if she knew this girl from somewhere. She couldn't recall her from anywhere, but she could almost swear that she had met her before somehow, somewhere in her past. It was there; she could feel it. She knew this girl but didn't know how.

Is he here? We need to hide!

The thought question reached Rachel's mind like an alarm bell.

Who?

The man.

She received the thought back, but the answer meant nothing to her.

Then suddenly, the girl's fear spiraled to panic. *They're here,* she thought, with more urgency than Rachel had sensed from her so far. Urgency, yes, but the panic was gone. The horror and fear had vanished, and only a concern for time remained. *They're here,* the thought repeated.

And then Rachel saw it, too. The blue lights.

Who are they?

I don't know. I'm scared.

Rachel focused on the lights. There was a warmth to them, and she could somehow sense that they were good: like a sunrise peeking over the horizon, or a lighthouse shining through the darkest night.

Don't be afraid, she thought-spoke to the girl. *The lights are good.*

They're here to take me, aren't they?

I don't know.

They are. I can hear them.

Who?

The voices in the lights. I recognize them.

Who are they?

My grandmothers. And others. Oh, my brother—he's here, too. So beautiful. I can't believe it's this beautiful. I never imagined. Not really, not like this. So beautiful.

The light was now surrounding her, creating a glow within her, and a safe orb of energy shielding her. She began to drift away from Rachel, looking back at her with tears.

You must find the man, she thought.

How? Rachel thought back. *Who is he?*

I don't know. Find me and you'll find him.

Find you?

Follow the trail. The bloodstain. It's still there. Find me and you'll find him. You must find him. You must ... But then her thoughts turned away. *It's so beautiful. Better. So much better. We're all together now. Everyone except my mom and dad. They would be so happy to know this. I can't believe it. So beautiful.*

The girl was drifting farther away, taking the light with her and leaving Rachel alone in the dark void. She heard the roll of distant thunder but somehow knew that the storm wasn't of this place. The ambient thunderclaps were intrusive in this parallel place. They rattled her as she watched the girl disappear in the distance. She was still marveling at the orbs of light encircling the girl ever more closely until she blurred into them. Then, in an eyeblink, she traveled farther and faster than Rachel could see.

The thunder grew louder. Her face now felt wet, and she heard voices calling her name. The void stretched away from her, warping and retreating in all directions. A pressure built in her forehead. And then she was attacked by a sudden vibration— a weight on her chest, a warmth on her lips.

The void was gone, and she opened her eyes to a giant lightning bolt that illuminated the jumbled dark clouds. Rain had drenched her face. She lay on her back on wet, hard ground. Her head rested on something soft, and Scott's mouth was pressed against hers. She flinched, causing Scott to jerk back. Then she saw a half-dozen heads silhouetted above her.

"Are you okay?" a woman's voice asked.

It took Rachel a few seconds to regain her focus and recognize the voice.

"Are you okay?" Madam Bovell asked again.

"We have to find her," Rachel said to everyone. She was squinting her eyes in the falling rain.

"Help her up before she drowns," the professor said.

"We have to find her," Rachel repeated.

"Find whom?" the professor asked.

"Something happened to her. Something bad. A man. We have to find him, and that happens only if we find her."

"Who is 'her'?" Jason asked. "What are you talking about?"

"Where were you?" Madam Bovell asked, concerned. "What did you see?"

"Jenny," Rachel said. "Her name's Jenny, and I think she's dead. I think I saw her taken to heaven."

"Heaven?"

"Or whatever you want to call it. It was someplace good. Someplace with loved ones who had passed. But she told me I had to find her, that it was important."

"Find her in heaven?" Scott asked, confused.

"No. Find her body. She said I had to find her to find 'him.'"

"Who's 'him'?"

"I have no idea. But whoever he is, he killed Jenny. And it just happened tonight. He's probably trying to get rid of her body right now. We might not have much time."

"Holy crap," Jessica said. "A murder … tonight?"

"I think that's what I was sensing at the farmhouse … when I panicked and ran. I think I was sensing her running at that very moment. And then I felt her being killed." She put a hand on her belly, remembering the excruciating pain.

"Somewhere around here?"

"I don't know. Not for sure. But I felt it so strongly that it couldn't have happened too far away from here."

Everyone else was silent. In the seconds that passed while she awaited some response, she finally took note of her position among them. She was sitting on the wet asphalt in the hotel parking lot as cold rain pounded down, splashing into the countless puddles scattered across the black surface.

"What are we doing out here, anyway?" she asked. "And why am I down here?"

"You were still unconscious when we got back to town," Jason said. "We discussed taking you to the hospital, but Madam Bovell didn't think that was a good idea."

"You appeared to be in a deep trance state," Madam Bovell said. "I've seen it before in mediums. I thought you would return naturally, as they had. And I was afraid that people at the hospital wouldn't understand anything about deep trances. They could try to stimulate or revive you in a way that is harmful to a mind drifting between dimensions."

"Plus, you seemed peaceful, like you were just sleeping," Scott added. "So we decided to bring you here to the hotel until your mind returned. You could rest in Madam Bovell's room. But once we had you out of the car and halfway across the parking lot, you began to spasm and—for a moment—even seemed to stop breathing."

"I see," Rachel said. "Well what do we do now?"

"I think we should all call it a night," the professor said. "If we want to try to contact Annabel again, then we have a big day tomorrow and a bigger night. We'll need to be rested."

"But there's a man out there somewhere probably burying a girl's body as we speak," she said.

"We don't know that," he replied. "And even if it were true, we have no idea where. We'd never find it."

"It might be too late to do any good tomorrow."

"It's late and it's dark and it's storming," the professor continued. "Our only smart choice is to get some sleep so that we're prepared to face everything tomorrow. We can't do any more tonight."

Everyone else agreed except for Rachel. She realized that the professor was probably right, but it was impossible to get this Jenny out of her head. It was already past two in the morning, and everyone in the group looked exhausted. So they split up. Madam Bovell and the professor and Jason walked to the hotel. And her friends all left for their homes.

But that night, as Rachel dreamed, her mind spun through one long, continuous nightmare of a faceless man digging a deep hole in a dark field in the rain, with a girl's body twisted unnaturally beside him.

SATURDAY

❋ ❋ ❋

HALLOWEEN

I can't describe to you all that passed on that horrible night.
  —J. S. Le Fanu, *Carmilla*

62

Rachel drifted in and out of sleep. Her muscles were relaxed, and her body felt as if floating into a dream. Someone called her name, but the voice came from the dreamscape. The real world had fallen away, ceding its authority to the infinite realm of the mind.

"Rachel," the voice said from the depths.

The accepted strangeness of dreams drew her further into the scene. The mind was at its most powerful when it dreamed, because it questioned nothing, and everything was possible.

"Rachel," the voice repeated.

She walked barefoot on snow that was not cold. A breeze washed gently over her as she trekked along a mountain path lining the edge of a wide, spiraling descent into a cavernous pit with no visible bottom. In the distance, she saw the other side of the pit and thought she could make out gateways and black rivers and a large waterfall on the lower levels. But then a dark fog crept in, limiting visibility to less than a hundred feet.

"Rachel."

She didn't answer, waiting for the voice to reveal its source.

A patch of fog drifted from the open air above the pit, down onto the rock path. On touching the path, it grew denser and darker until it formed an object the shape and size of a man. But just when she thought it would take some defined form, the edges became blurred like a cloud, and its core seemed to slosh like water in a bucket. It was completely black and devoid of all light.

As she looked into the darkness of this thing, she saw what it was.

"Have you come to take me?" she asked.

"I am not allowed," the voice answered. "You have free will."

"Then what do you want?"

"To persuade you."

"To tempt me," Rachel said. "To trick me."

"To show you the truth," the voice replied.

"They call you the Father of Lies," she challenged.

"I am called many things by those who do not understand me."

"I understand you. You're the devil," she said emphatically. "Lucifer. You killed my mother and my grandmother."

"I tried only to help them."

Rachel wondered why she wasn't terrified. This encounter had an unexpected civility, and a safety implicit in the strong possibility that this was all a dream.

"Why am I here?" she asked, stepping closer to the edge of the rocky path, as if daring this voice to take corporal shape and push her over the edge and into the pit.

"You are here because few true witches remain on Earth, and none are as strong as you."

"I'm not a witch," she replied in a calm, quiet voice.

"Call it what you will. You are more than you realize. I have been waiting so long for you. You do not yet comprehend your place in everything. The world has always feared those with abilities to reach beyond the barrier of death."

"I'm not a threat to anyone," she said. "No one needs to fear me."

"And yet, they do. They have always feared. Nearly fifty thousand were put to death through witch trials over the centuries." The voice paused for a deep, slow laugh before continuing. "And nearly all those killed were innocent. Their communities thought they were purging themselves of evil, but the reality was that through fear of me, *they* had become the evil. Oh, what terrible joy it was to watch mankind grow evil while believing they were good."

Rachel felt something brush against her ankles. Looking down, she was startled to find a large black snake sliding between her feet. Frozen, she stared at the faint reflection on its gleaming scales.

The voice, still coming from the cloudy shape in front of her, spoke as the serpent slithered on and vanished in the fog.

"I have played my role in dividing mankind over the centuries. Winnowing the faithless from the faithful. Even separating the faithful from each other. How many different theological philosophies are there? How many hawkers of religious fervor and false certainty? Oh, what joy I once took in shattering the harmony between souls."

Feeling a spark of anger, Rachel stepped closer to the edge of the pit.

"To think of the endless pain and suffering you've caused the world over the ages!"

"I served God," the voice said. "I did things that he wanted done but was not willing to do himself. He wants people to have free will, to make the choices in their lives that he hopes will lead them to his light. But he knows that if people are truly to have free will as he wishes, then his light cannot exist without my darkness. That's the *doctrine of providence*: everything happens in accordance to a divine plan for the benefit of those whom God chooses to save."

Rachel was so close to the dark cloud, she smelled the sulfurous smoke swirling around her. She looked with horrified awe into the void below her. Fires burned through the rocky surfaces on the far side of the pit. Screams echoed in the darkness, filling her eyes with tears for the forgotten souls of the damned.

"You truly blame God for the evil you oversee?" she managed to ask.

"You have free will to choose," said the voice in the smoke, "because God wants you to choose. And this means God condones innocent suffering, because he permits the existence of the evil that is wrought by free will. But free will doesn't mean one has to choose only between good and evil. Jung believed that everyone, no matter how good, had some evil buried within the psyche. He was not wrong."

"So we have free will," Rachel said. "Even if it limits us? Even if it *destroys* us? What's the point of that? Why plague humankind with countless choices between good and evil as we just take turns saving and destroying each other? How can God expect us to make the right choices when we can't even understand the purpose of our own lives?"

"I can change that," the voice said. "I can help you realize the full potential of your abilities. Your power will eclipse anything you could hope to achieve on your own."

"What is this gift?"

"Knowledge of things long forgotten by mankind. Ancient magical books and religious texts used by the branch of magic known as necromancy, last practiced in the Middle Ages before being lost to time. The greatest of these necromancers was a German student of theology I knew in the early sixteenth century, whom I helped become a professional fortune-teller. He later became the inspiration for the fictional character Faust, or

Dr. Faustus. But you, with careful study of these books of magic and religious text, could become the most powerful living spirit in nearly two thousand years."

"I don't believe you," she said. "I don't trust you."

"You already possess the gift. It's inside you. I am merely offering you what you need to complete your true self—to discover the person you were born to become."

"What could I do beyond what I'm already doing?"

"Much more," said the smoke. "It will allow you to bridge the separate prisons of the soul. The soul doesn't have to be trapped within flesh during what you call life, and it doesn't have to be an undefined form in what you call death. With my guidance and this lost knowledge, you can free all souls from their unnecessary limitations."

"And you have these lost books and texts?"

"It was I who took them from mankind. I was waiting for someone with the gifts to harness their power. I was waiting for you."

"I don't want them." She longed for a breeze to waft away the rotten-egg stench arising from the pit beside her.

"Yes, you do. You can bridge the divide between him and me. You can help heal the world of its greatest misfortune. You can be the one to unite forever the split powers of light and darkness."

"By learning from these scrolls?"

"Yes. And then spiritually bonding with me so that *he* will listen to us."

"And then you want me to reach out to him in prayer so he can forgive you and grant you salvation? So you may return to heaven?"

"Yes, yes. He will feel my change if it comes to him through you: a strong living spirit. If you accept my knowledge and power, you could reach him as if you were I, but with all the requisite innocence for an audience with his holy presence."

"But I still don't understand why you are so set on *me.* Just because I'm becoming a strong medium like my mother and grandmother? I can sense you're lying."

The dark, nebulous phantom expanded to twice its size. She saw what looked like little lightning strikes within its misty outlines, as if this shapeless being had become a window to a distant storm. Then the lightning strikes faded and the murky view vanished as the form returned to its roughly human size.

The voice returned.

"Before the 1500s, everyone believed that magic must be demonic. Then things changed as mankind made slow strides in exploring the mysteries of the natural world through science. For four hundred years, this knowledge was an innocent addition to religion. But eventually, as knowledge advanced, many felt their religions threatened by the unraveling of mysteries that had once fed faith. Darwin was the tipping point. By the early nineteenth century, science had mostly split from religion, and the desire to understand creation was the wedge between them. Alchemy, the morally questionable discipline involving angelic communications, enjoyed newfound popularity. Something I championed whenever possible—after all, once one learns how to summon angels, what is to prevent them from conjuring demons, too?"

The voice paused.

"What is so important about me?" Rachel demanded.

"More than you can fathom. It is your blood, your ancient ancestry. You are the last of a long line descending from the first satanic witch cult."

"Liar!"

"It was three thousand years ago, in the land now called Turkey, near the city of Istanbul—known as Constantinople in its glory days. Before that, it was called Byzantium, and before that, Lygos. Oh, the ages fall away so fast, but I remember them as if they were yesterday. Or perhaps I am remembering tomorrow. We are not linear beings as you think."

"Liar! My ancestors have no ties to you!"

A chilling laughter burst from the darkness. It faded, and the voice said, "You accuse me of deception, but *men* are the true deceivers of men. Even if I had never existed, men would have created me in their minds."

"Is that what you think?" she asked, looking around her as she spoke, searching for any avenue of escape. But the path was narrow, squeezed by the rocky cliff rising above on her right, and the pit on her left.

"I no longer need to exist the way I once did," the voice proclaimed. "I have served my purpose and wish only to return to God's side as I once was. Men can carry on in their conflicting ways without any assistance from me. In truth, I never did much to push them toward darkness. They did most of that on their own. I was just a convenient scapegoat for those unwilling to face the truth of their own nature: The bond that unites can just as easily become a wedge. And love and hate are two sides of the same coin."

Rachel spoke. "And you rejoice when that hate brings evil. You love that the world has become so violent, so used to evil, without people even giving lip service to your influence. When people today say 'evil,' they are thinking of evil *people,* not devils and demons. People still talk of God, but they no longer mention you like they did in the past."

"That is true. Andrew Delbanco observed this when he said, 'The work of the devil is everywhere, but no one knows where to find him. We live in the most brutal century in human history, but instead of stepping forward to take the credit, he has rendered himself invisible.' But that was twentieth century, in whose waning years I began to regret my actions. I realized I had taken things too far. I almost started World War Three with the Cuban Missile Crisis, but at the last minute I had a change of heart and relaxed my influence on certain people in power. Now my nature has changed completely. And I need your partnership to make that change apparent in God's eyes."

"But can Satan really change? Can you really become good?"

"Evil is the price of free will, as Saint Augustine liked to say. And I, too, have the free will to change, for I am not a *slave* to evil. I wish to be again as I once was with God, before the fall. A key belief in the doctrine of providence is that light comes out of darkness. And there has been no greater darkness than I, so through me can come one of the greatest lights of all time."

"But how can you undo all that you have done? Are you not truly evil incarnate?"

"Oh, sure, orthodox writers from the New Testament through today have insisted that I am eternally damned. But they are wrong. God loved me once. And yes, I did turn against him. I became the worst sinner, his greatest enemy. But if God can forgive humans who sin and then ask forgiveness, can he not forgive my infinite sins if I ask infinite forgiveness? Would not that be God's greatest forgiveness—his greatest act? Greater even than the sacrifice of his own son?"

A chill shot down Rachel's spin. The words were blasphemy. And yet, something in the voice tempted her to keep listening.

"Some would say it cannot happen," said the wraith of smoke. "Some would say the Bible insists it is forbidden. But forbidden by whom? God? Does he not have the power to overrule himself? Does humanity really suppose that it can comprehend the complexities of his thoughts and his will?"

"But what of those in hell?" Rachel asked.

"The Kingdom of Torment," the voice said. "All those billions of suffering souls in the charnel pits of damnation. What of them? you ask. God will know what to do about them."

"What, exactly, would you have me do?" She asked this cautiously, wondering for the first time whether there might be some hope for the devil's repentance, as God's masterstroke of divine providence.

"Pledge your loyalty to me, to my cause, so that through your free will I may talk directly to God. For he will not hear me as I am—not since I led the rebellion against him. But if you place your faith in me and give your free will to me, then I can speak to him through you, just as you can speak to all spirits. And I will ask him to grant me forgiveness."

Rachel was tempted by the opportunity to help heal the most grievous wound of all time. To help end the conflict living in all spirits and broker the greatest peace deal ever. Was this the answer to the violence and cruelty and injustice over the millennia of the modern human race? How much current and future suffering could she erase just by showing compassion for Satan? What if this one act of faith and healing was the destiny she was always meant to find? What if she could truly help the devil find salvation?

"Beware," her mother whispered in her mind. *"Remember the book."*

Gregory the Great. Rachel recalled the book on her shelf, Gregory's *Dialogues,* with her mother's insignia signed inside the cover, on the title page. For as long as she could recall, even back to the orphanage in Kansas City, she had kept the book in her possession. It was the only thing she owned that could be traced back to her mother. And within it, she would never forget the passage that her mother had underlined and marked with stars in the margin.

The process of demonic temptation. First, Satan implants "suggestion" into the mind; these produce a pleasurable response; and then the sinner acts to realize the imagined pleasures. Moreover, the enemy is a master psychologist who tailors his suggestions to his victims' sensibilities. Thus the "cunning deceiver" leads the pious to take pride in their spiritual accomplishments, while he baits simpler people with earthly pleasures.

It was the kind of realization that had been in her mind the entire time, but masked by the cloud of the dream. But now it was pushed to the front of her thoughts and could never be hidden from her again.

"Everything you've said was designed solely to tempt me," she said.

The devil's dark cloud tightened and withdrew a little from her.

"You have no desire for salvation," she said. "You only wish to trick me into pledging loyalty to you the way some witches have done in the past. You are a foul fallen angel with designs only for evil and the enslavement of souls. But I will never be deceived or tempted by you and your rank lies."

"Child, this is not true. I am only trying to show you the darkness in the light! It is God, not I, who is evil, for he allows evil to exist! But his weakness is his insistence on giving humans free will. His weakness is to forgive sins. We can use this against him to get me by his side once again, to give me access to all in heaven."

"Is this how you tried to deceive my ancestors?" Rachel snarled. "How many of them have you tried to tempt over the ages? But I know now that none of them has ever joined you. Never. Not in ancient times, not in the Middle Ages, and not in the centuries since. You couldn't corrupt my grandmother or my mother, and now you fail with me. I will refuse and resist you all the way to my final dying breath."

"Wretch!" the voice snarled. "You will burn and suffer by my hand in ways you cannot imagine!"

The air turned freezing.

"Death will find you!"

The fires from the pit grew brighter.

"As shall hell!"

The sulphur stench intensified.

"As shall I!"

The cloud darkened and swirled in tight circles with an aggressive, menacing speed.

"I will have every inch of skin peeled from your body. I will have your limbs eaten away by horrific creatures. Then I will have you buried to your neck in the rocky floor of hell, to suffer near me for all eternity."

Thick black ropes of smoke emerged from the cloud and unfurled toward her like tentacles. Rachel stepped back, but the ropes reached farther until they were almost touching her. Turning, she tried to run, but one of them grabbed her wrist and wrapped around it so tightly, she couldn't escape no matter how hard she tugged to get free. As more tentacles stretched out and were inches away from wrapping around her, she screamed.

In an instant, the hellscape vanished and she was back in her bed, staring up at the dark ceiling. Her heart raced. Sweating, she sat up in bed and turned on the lamp at the corner of her nightstand. It appeared that nothing else was in the room with her.

She panted for nearly a minute, staring intently at the closet door across the room as the dawn sunlight crawled down the wall. But as her mind steadied and slowed, her eyes turned down to her wrist. The black markings on it lingered for a second before fading away.

63

Jason stared at the blank piece of hotel stationery as the morning sun reached the edge of the paper. The sunlight had been a bright square on the wall when he sat down at the small desk in his hotel room. Now it had crawled the six inches down to the desk and had begun a stealthy slide along the wood. Soon, it would touch the paper, forcing him to acknowledge just how long he had been staring at the blank sheet, with pen in hand and no idea how to connect the intergalactic dots of the past few days.

The auditor in him insisted there must be some consolidated conclusion from all the pieces they had gathered. What was the bigger picture? What was he missing?

He felt his first clear idea forming as the light touched the page. He drew two circles just left and right of the page's center. Then he wrote "Annabel" in the top center and outlined the name in a rectangle. He drew an arrow from her name down to each circle, as if he were creating an organizational chart for a company. He wrote "Hospital" inside the left circle, and "Farmhouse" inside the right circle. Then he made a list under the hospital circle: •Rare sightings; •Roams halls; •Moves objects; •Difficulty speaking; •Peaceful; •Sad; •Wants help.

Below the farmhouse circle, he wrote: •Very active when provoked; •Aggressive; •Moves things violently with great energy; •Angry; •Threatening; •Resists visitors; •Dangerous.

When finishing the list, he kept looking back and forth at the two lists. Then he looked up at the word "Annabel" and shook his head. "Why are you so different?" he asked out loud.

He drew a timeline of key events: his arrival in North Dakota, the first night, when Annabel moved the chairs in the conference room, the chilling moment when he saw the reflection of her face, going out to the farmhouse alone and encountering the violent vibrations, tearing the screen and breaking the railing as he fled in fright. Below this timeline, he created a list of everything he remembered from the articles about the night Annabel was murdered by her husband.

He stared at the work he had done and all the information it contained. Then he closed his eyes and let his mind reshuffle the pieces of information with related data points and connections that he might not have realized.

A combination of interlinking thoughts began to grow and expand, strengthening until he realized that here was something no one else had considered. With his eyes still closed, he stepped back from the desk, as if the paper had become something dangerous. He stumbled against the edge of the bed and fell backward on the mattress, but still he wouldn't open his eyes. As in a dream, he felt himself on the verge of an idea that could explain much of the mystery surrounding Annabel—and he worried that if he opened his eyes, he might break the spell before the answer had fully revealed itself.

A knock came on his door, which pulled his attention away from his dreamlike thoughts for a half second. Startled, he slapped his palms over his ears.

There it was. He could see it now. All the pieces were fitting together. He almost had it. The last magic pieces were sliding into his thought puzzle.

The knocking intensified, and he thought he heard a muffled voice yelling through the door.

He rolled onto his side and pulled a pillow over his ears. He had almost grasped the final thought. Just a few more seconds. He must complete this developing epiphany before the unstable thought in his mind came tumbling down, broken and dead in the graveyard of lost thoughts.

The knocking amplified, filling the room. It seemed to be shaking the walls and vibrating the bed.

Ignoring the external din, he pulled himself deeper into his thoughts. He was almost there: the sadness versus the anger. The married couple and the pain they must have suffered for the husband to go insane and murder his wife. The stories of Annabel riding horseback through the fields and across the valley surrounding their farmhouse. But her husband never rode with her. He was not a horseman.

Then Jason saw the image Annabel had shown him of the distant farmhouse at night with the short flashes of light.

He opened his eyes. That was it! Sorrow and anger! Sadness and rage—two polar opposites! That was her secret!

He rolled off the bed and jumped to his feet, too excited even to put his shoes on. He had to talk to one of the others immediately. He made it to the door of his room before he noticed the persistent loud knocking.

Opening it, he saw Professor Graves standing in the doorway.

"There you are!" Dr. Graves gushed. "I was about to call management to open this door—thought maybe there was trouble. Your phone wasn't ..." He stopped as if startled by Jason's expression. "*Is* there trouble?"

"I've figured it out!" Jason said excitedly. "I know what Annabel's secret is."

"Her secret?"

"That's what Rachel calls it: Annabel's secret. I figured it out. I know why she's so violent at the farmhouse."

"I'm listening with both ears."

"Where's Madam Bovell?"

"In her room, I suppose."

"Let's go there. I want to tell you both at the same time."

He stepped around Dr. Graves and speed-walked down the hallway.

"You coming?"

64

Rachel woke up earlier than her adoptive parents and ate breakfast alone at their kitchen table. As she crunched her Grape-Nuts and milk, she stared out the window at the pasture of rippling tall grass. She left a note on the table saying she was going for a drive in the countryside, to take pictures for an art class. Her adoptive parents had always been gracious supporters of her photography and encouraged her to get involved with the high school newspaper.

Of course, the note was a lie.

She got in her rusty old VW Beetle and putted away from the house. She had just cleared the corner of the pasture when her phone chimed four bars from her favorite pop song. Braking at a stop sign, she looked at the new text.

You up?

It was from Scott. She smiled. *Yeah. Up and out.*

Where?

Just driving around.

You're searching for her, aren't you?

Guilty.

I'll help. Come get me.

She smiled again. She hadn't wanted to bother anyone else so early, but it would be good to have company. Especially if she actually found what she was looking for.

I'll be there in five, she replied. Then she set her phone back in the console, switched on her right signal, and made the turn toward Scott's house.

65

"What is it?" Madam Bovell asked the two visitors at her door.

"I think I know what's going on," Jason said. "I think I know what Annabel's trying to tell us."

She stepped aside and waved them inside. He walked past her, with Dr. Graves in tow. Stopping by the window, he looked out from the third floor and saw an old couple loading up a white sedan.

"All right, man," Dr. Graves said. "Out with it."

"We all agree that Annabel seems different at the farmhouse than at the hospital, right?" Jason asked.

"Yeah," the professor said. "She's angrier—maybe even violent."

"Much stronger negative energy," Madam Bovell added.

"She hasn't talked to us there," Jason continued. "I mean, she hasn't really even tried to communicate with us when we're there. Not like at the hospital. And she hasn't shown herself to us out there."

"She didn't really show herself at the hospital," Dr. Graves said.

"She did to me," Jason said. "And she was putting a lot of energy into trying to communicate with us at the hospital. But not at the farmhouse. She didn't even seem to *want* us there."

"Maybe she was trying to hide something," the professor said. "Or maybe she didn't recognize us. The dimensional fields could be different out there."

"Maybe she was reacting to the proximity of her murder scene," Madam Bovell suggested. "Not the location of her death, but the location of the violence against her."

"Maybe," Jason said. "Or maybe it wasn't really her at the farmhouse."

They both stared at him.

"Maybe it was another spirit," he added.

Silence hung in the air, and he let it. He wanted to wait for one of them to speak next. He needed to make sure they were thinking through his theory. Madam Bovell sat down in the desk chair and looked at the ground. Dr. Graves paced back and forth along the edge of the queen-size bed, his index finger pointing up as if he were working through a proposed calculation.

"Another spirit?" Dr. Graves finally said. "That's very unlikely."

"But not impossible," Madam Bovell offered. "And it would explain a lot."

"The difference in behavior?" the professor asked.

"Not just that," she said. "The overall energy felt different. Much darker. And it isn't usual for a spirit to drift from place to place if they're in a haunting mode. Ghosts are usually trapped in places—sometimes to objects, though we haven't been moving any talisman back and forth. Usually, a ghost would be trapped at the place of its death. And we know that Annabel died at the hospital."

"And her husband and her neighbor died at the house," the professor said. "So let's say it *is* a different spirit. We can assume it's one of them. But which one?"

"Probably the neighbor," Madam Bovell answered. "It's more likely to be a victim than the murderer."

"No, I think it's the husband," Jason said. "I think he's the ghost at the farmhouse."

"That would explain the violent reactions we've experienced there," the professor said. "That would explain why *it* doesn't want us to be there."

"And it explains the anger, too." Madam Bovell pondered. "Rage at finding his wife cheating on him. He must have held that same burning rage right up until the moment of his own death—which could have been enough to put his psyche in an unreconcilable state at the exact moment of death, which could have prevented him from passing on to the next dimension."

"You mean hell," the professor said.

"I don't know where he would have gone."

"You don't think a murderer would go to hell?"

"It's not my place to pass judgment. Besides, heaven and hell are just constructs that probably don't fully grasp the reality of whatever complex afterlife awaits us." She turned to Jason. "If you're right, then this changes everything."

"But what does it *mean*?" Jason asked. "What could Annabel possibly want from her husband's ghost after he murdered her? What could she possibly want from *us*?"

"Maybe she forgives him," Madam Bovell said. "Maybe she's sorry for what she did. Maybe she still loves him."

"Even after everything that's happened?" Dr. Graves asked.

"Yes," Madam Bovell answered. "You said the words, Jason. Sorrow and rage. Annabel and Rubin. Maybe she feels responsible for what happened. Maybe the only way for her sorrow to end is for Rubin's rage to end."

"And how the hell are we supposed to help that happen?" Dr. Graves asked.

The three stared at each other in silence, searching for an answer to this new question. And as the seconds crawled by and the silent moment stretched into a terrifying stalemate, Jason had the strange sensation that Rachel would provide the key to this riddle.

66

"Where are we heading?" Scott asked.

"Out of town," Rachel said as she turned right and drove toward the long bridge that arched over a half-dozen railroad tracks. "I figured we'd try some areas north first."

"Why out of town?"

"The field," she said. "It's the only thing I actually saw as I sensed what she was going through. The field and the rain and the brief glimpse of the man's silhouette chasing after her. It was too big to be a yard or park in town. Wherever she was trying to escape from, it was outside town."

"But you don't know how close," Scott said. "You don't even know if it happened in North Dakota."

"I don't think I would have felt it so strongly unless it happened very close to where we were last night. It had to be within a few counties of us—maybe the same county."

"That's still a big area. How are we going to find it?"

"The same way we learned about her in the first place." Rachel pulled the car to the shoulder after crossing the bridge. Leaving the engine running, she got out, walked around the hood, and opened Scott's door. "Time for you to drive."

"You tired?" he asked.

"I need to navigate."

"Whatever you say. I'm just here to help."

"You are helping. Thank you."

They switched. As he pulled the Beetle back onto the road, he asked, "Where to?"

"Straight ahead. Take us all the way out of town and keep going straight unless I say otherwise. Also, I probably won't be able to talk to you while I do this—other than give occasional directions. The fewer distractions, the better."

She reached forward and turned off the radio. Then she closed her eyes and began breathing deeply in a slow, steady rhythm. To help herself relax, she imagined the natural rhythms of the world: first, forest treetops swaying in a breeze, then ocean waves lapping against a shore, then the imagined heartbeat of every living creature as she looked down from a low Earth orbit. She breathed and breathed and breathed, sinking deeper into the recesses of her mind and absorbing the larger world of life and energy around her. She still felt the rhythm of the car moving over smooth pavement, but her senses now seemed to reach beyond the immediate surroundings. She felt the landscape, the way the low autumn sun warmed the plains, how the deep vibrations of the Earth's shifting plates above the core reached subtly up through the foundations of every structure in the town. Then, in a sudden moment of pure clarity and alertness, she sensed a pull slightly to the right of their forward path. The ever-so-slight pressure felt as if someone was gently pressing a finger to her forehead, just above her right eye. It was hardly noticeable, and she might not even have detected it if she weren't in such a state of deep, meditative concentration.

Then, without warning, the pressure point began to move, inching farther right along her forehead. It felt like a snail crawling across her skin. She understood the deep directional sense that lived inside the brains of migrating birds and sea turtles. Why not humans, too?

"Turn right as soon as you can," she said without opening her eyes.

"Next highway exit isn't for another mile," Scott said.

"*Sh-h-h.* I need to focus."

"Sorry."

She tried to evict his voice from her mind and concentrate on the pressure, which by now had migrated around to her temple. It moved farther right with every passing second. And it was strengthening, pressing deeper into her skin as they drove along.

She heard the turn signal clicking, sensed the car slowing, felt a right turn onto a gravel road. And as they made the turn, she felt the pressure swing around to the center of her forehead. She breathed more slowly, more deeply, trying to see their destination in her mind. Tall, dark grass drifted into her thoughts. But this time, she wasn't running, but floating. And below her was the girl's body, lying in a wet hole in the ground as mud was thrown over her in steady increments, burying her until she was covered by unmarked earth as if she had never existed. But in that moment, as if the soul resisted oblivion, Rachel felt a surge of energy rip through her mind. In a furious blast of images, she saw a sunny past: lizards scurrying along rocks encircling a flower bed, coco palms swaying in the backyard of a white stucco house, a trampoline, a small overturned fishing boat. Toys were scattered about: a tricycle, a plastic bucket and shovel, a pink ball. A mother calling to playing children. An open neighborhood street. Single-story houses lining the sidewalks. Now, somewhere else, a long pier reaching out into the ocean. A dolphin sticking its smooth gray head above the water along the wooden pilings. People fishing over both sides of the pier while others walked along its center. Happiness in childhood. Then came a troubled youth. Frustrations from poverty while ambitions grew. Rebellion. Arguments. Now a runaway on a

Greyhound bus rolling through the night toward North Dakota. The promise of a job that paid more money than she had ever imagined making at her age. Freedom and hope for a wonderful future. Then, suddenly, flashes of worry … fear … terror.

Rachel opened her eyes, gasping.

"You okay?" Scott asked, looking at her.

"I lost contact," she said, still rattled, trying to absorb her surroundings: the autumn sunlight, the cool car window, the empty fields on both sides—all of which felt like another world compared to the Florida of her fleeting vision. And again the continuing, incessant rumbling as the car sped over the gravel road.

"Contact with what?" he asked.

"The soul's echo."

He glanced at her.

"Every soul experiences a shock at the moment of the body's death," she explained. "The more prepared and accepting the soul is of approaching death, the less the shock. Violent deaths generally cause a great shock that sometimes causes an echo of the soul to linger as a faint energy source near the place of death—almost like how the scent of a living thing remains for a time after it has passed through a place."

"Is that what ghosts are?"

"No. Ghosts are souls that can't move beyond the shock. The experience of an unaccepting death can so twist the soul that it becomes trapped in the place where it was separated from the body. It is an energy force of the self, the person, and it is too traumatized to find its way naturally into the next dimension. A soul's *echo,* however, is the energy pocket of a copy of some thoughts from a soul that only barely succeeded in moving beyond this world."

"So the girl you say was killed—her soul has moved on?"

"Yes," Rachel said. "I saw it in my vision as it happened, and I felt it. But her soul's echo is still near her body, and it holds some memories of her death—also some from her life in Florida. These echoes will eventually dissipate, just as a lingering scent slowly dissipates. If we hope to learn anything, we must find it before it vanishes."

"Florida?"

"I think the girl was a teenage runaway who became a migrant worker up here."

"For the shale oil fields?"

"Either that or some job supporting the oil industry. What else is there?"

"Do you know how she died?"

"Only that she was running from someone in a field. A man, I think, judging by the large silhouette."

"And no clue yet where she is?"

"Somewhere in front of us," Rachel said. "Keep driving straight ahead. Follow this road as long as you can, unless I say otherwise. It was the last thing I felt. She's out there somewhere. I'm going to try to make contact again."

She leaned back, closed her eyes, and listened to the soothing rumble of tires moving fast over gravel as she searched the recesses of her mind for any signal from the girl's echo.

67

"How dangerous is he?" Jason asked. "Could he *kill*?"

"People have died during ghost encounters," Madam Bovell said. "Just as they have died from encounters with poltergeists and demons and the devil itself. They aren't stabbed or shot, but they have died. They died from sheer terror. Some have fallen down stairs or off a cliff or rooftop. Some were just so shocked by what they experienced, they had a heart attack. Some even killed themselves just to escape their torment."

"So Annabel's husband could kill again, even as a ghost?" Jason mused.

"But why is he here?" Dr. Graves wondered aloud.

"He's still enraged," Jason said. "Just as he must have been enraged when he caught Annabel in bed with their neighbor. Just as he must have been when he murdered them."

"And then he was killed by the police and carried that rage with him into death," Madam Bovell said in a low voice. "Twisting his soul into something that could not pass into the next dimension."

"So his soul is trapped," Jason said. "Like Annabel's."

"Yes, his soul is trapped, but not like Annabel's," Madam Bovell said. "She is trapped in sorrow, sadness, remorse. We know that from the séance with her spirit. Even now she seems to be trying to reach out from beyond death to communicate with us. But if her husband died in rage, then his soul is trapped in a place of anger and utter darkness. He would be blind to what has happened to him. He may not even understand that he's dead."

"That would explain why he's making the repairs," Jason said, nodding. He saw Dr. Graves look at him quizzically. "The first night I was there, the doorjamb upstairs got split, the front door screen got ripped, and the railing on the front porch broke away where I fell through it. But by the next night, all three were mostly repaired. The husband was said to have frequently made improvements to their farmhouse. He had a reputation as a real handyman. I thought it was strange that someone would have gone out there and repaired things in the twenty-four hours between my visits. Now I understand: the ghost is somehow making the repairs."

"Just as he would have done if he was still alive," Dr. Graves said.

"That's very unusual," Madam Bovell said. "It's really hard for ghosts to move things with any precision. They can shake things, spin things, move and throw things, slam doors. But to make repairs … Maybe he's somehow able to slowly regenerate the matter, the way some spirits do when creating ectoplasm during séances. I don't know. Very strange."

"So did he even understand we were there to contact him?" the professor asked.

"Probably not," she offered. "We probably seemed like intruders to him, although it's difficult to know how well he perceived us. He is still just outside our dimension."

Jason sat on the bed and rubbed his forehead. "So I'll ask again: Is he a threat to us? Can he kill?"

"He killed his wife and her lover when he was alive," Madam Bovell mused. "As a ghost with the rage still inside him, he is more dangerous now than ever."

"Then what do we do?" Jason asked.

"For one thing, we stick together. The more of us there are, the safer we'll be. Under no circumstances do we do anything to contact his ghost on our own—not until we determine just how strong his trapped spirit is … and just how much rage still burns in his murderous heart. Until we determine that, there is no way of telling just how dangerous he may be."

68

"Stop!"

The brakes locked, and the Volkswagen slid loudly on the gravel before jerking to a halt. Rachel held her eyes shut and raised a forefinger for silence. She had been following the trace signal of the soul's echo for the past five minutes.

"She's to our right," Rachel said, opening her eyes and looking out her window at the stubble field beside them. "Out there. Not far."

"I don't think any road takes us closer," Scott said.

"We walk." She opened her door. "Kill the engine and pop the trunk."

When he met her at the front of the Beetle, she had already opened the trunk and taken out what she wanted. He stared in surprise, and she realized that until now he hadn't fully considered what they were really doing out here.

"What are you planning to do with *that*?" he asked.

She held the shovel low to the ground. "I think you know."

"Shouldn't we call someone?"

"We can't until we know for sure. We at least have to dig up part of the body ourselves. Once we know we're right, we'll call the police."

"Isn't there a chance they'll suspect us?"

"For the girl's murder?"

"Maybe. Be hard to explain how we discovered her way out here. Telling them you have psychic powers or ESP might not fly."

"We can't think about the law right now. Her soul's echo is crying out. Something evil is hanging over this town. I've sensed it since I first started having visions of Annabel—something tied to the farmhouse. And whatever it is, it's tied to this girl's death and the dark silhouette she was running from."

She closed the trunk and stepped off the side of the road, down and across the ditch, and up to the barbed wire that lined the edge of the field. Scott followed and stopped beside her. She tossed the shovel over the fence and ducked through it as he stretched the two center strands apart. Then, once on the other side, she helped him through the same way.

"I can get this," he said, picking up the shovel. "You lead the way."

The field was clumpy with tall but thinning grass. No cattle were in sight.

They had moved across the field for five minutes when Rachel stopped. A sudden, nauseating pain in her gut dropped her to her knees. And as she pressed her hand against her abdomen and as tears of pain filled her eyes, she felt the pressure return to her forehead, stronger than ever.

"You okay?" Scott blurted as he rushed to her side.

"We're so close," she whispered through gritted teeth.

"This was a bad idea," Scott said. "We shouldn't have come out here alone."

"She's right here," Rachel groaned. "I need to get closer to her. I need to listen to her soul's echo."

"Where?" he asked, holding the shovel in front of them.

She raised a shaking arm and pointed at a spot in the mud three furrows away. She was too weak now to speak, and she concentrated her remaining strength on keeping her finger pointed toward the energy force as long as possible. She could almost see it now as a faint light overlaying her vision, an emerald glow breaking through from the wet soil below.

Scott took a few steps forward, stopped, and looked back at her. "Here?"

"Yes," she groaned. "That's it."

He looked down at the muddied soil. Hesitating, he seemed reluctant to act, as if the reality of what they were looking for had moved beyond the thrill of the search and now consisted only of the sad, gruesome tragedy that remained. As if realizing that their course was irreversible, his posture straightened, and his countenance hardened. He pushed the shovel into the earth.

*   *   *

Scott pushed his foot against the shovel's blade and levered up a big glop of soft soil. Dumping it to the side, he took another scoop. Then another. Soon, he had a little mound of earth beside a muddy hole. After a dozen more thrusts of the spade, he struck something tough. He felt suddenly queasy. Closing his eyes, he reminded himself that they were here to help the girl and that any indecencies they committed were unavoidable and for the purpose of good.

Kneeling with the shovel clutched in his hand, he wished they had thought of also bringing a smaller tool for more delicate work. Holding the shovel with both hands along its metal neck, he carefully scraped the edge across the last deep gash he had made in the soil. Soon he had raked away enough of the mud to expose a pale forearm and wrist and hand. Scott had just time enough to turn away and vomit onto the mound of dirt.

*   *   *

Rachel crawled forward until she could see into the hole Scott had dug.

"You can stop now," she said.

The pain in her gut had subsided. Getting to her feet, she stepped down into the mud and knelt by the body. With her hands, she gently cleared away enough mud to expose the girl's pale face. She looked older than she had in the vision. Death had removed the life force that was, perhaps, the very essence of youth.

"What could have done this?" Scott asked.

She turned her head and saw tears streaming down his cheeks.

"A monster," she said. "Something evil. A demon. Perhaps the devil himself."

"Was it Annabel?"

"I don't know. My mother's spirit warned me to be careful at the farmhouse, as if we might encounter some form of evil there."

"What do we do now?"

She looked up at him and said, "We call the police to report the body. But first, I need to try one last thing while we have the opportunity."

She reached down and took the girl's pale, clammy hand. Closing her eyes, she searched her mind for any trace of energy left in the decaying cells. Almost immediately, she felt something: a slight whisper from the beyond, like distant music across a still lake at night. Something was there, trying to tell her something, to show her something. She felt the girl alive again, felt her terrified. She saw the shadows before death, saw the phantom silhouette trying to kill her … saw the apparition following her as she ran through the field during the thunderstorm … saw the thing catch her and strike her abdomen with some sharp energy that caused great crippling pain … saw a force wrap around her neck and tighten harder and harder as her strength faded. And just before she slipped into death, a brilliant lightning strike skipped along the heavens above and gave her a fleeting glimpse of an immense black eagle's head.

And then everything went dark.

Rachel opened her eyes.

"You okay?" Scott asked.

"I think so."

"Did you feel anything?"

"Yeah. I felt her die. And I saw something that she saw just before her death. A huge eagle's head, I think. I don't know what it means."

"Did you see what killed her?"

"A shadow of some type. A figure, but it was hard to see at night. A phantom."

Scott leaned on the shovel. "What do we do now?"

She paused for a moment, hesitating from the lingering nightmare she had witnessed. "We call the police. And we tell them we've found a girl's body. I have my good Nikon in the car. We'll tell them we were driving around the countryside looking for good places to take pictures for my portfolio. From the road, we noticed some crows over here, and when we came over to check it out, we saw an exposed part of the arm. We say we cleared the mud around her arm and face because we thought it might be one of our friends from school. We were in shock. Then we realized we shouldn't be touching anything, so we stopped and called nine-one-one."

Scott pulled out his cell phone. "Do we wait here?"

"Back by the car," she said. "The police will need us to point out this spot. We can go over our story again while we wait, but the simpler we keep it, the better." She looked back at the body and teared up. "She was a good girl. She has family somewhere, maybe still in Florida. And she loves them very much. I could tell when I saw her."

Scott put his arms around her, and she buried her face in his shoulder and wept. She held him tight, then let go and wiped her eyes.

"I'll make the call," he said.

"And then we need to go find the others," Rachel decided. "I'm not exactly sure what happened to this girl last night, but this proves that whatever danger Annabel may present, whatever danger my mother's spirit was trying to warn me about, it's much more aggressive than we imagined."

As Scott made the call, she looked back down at the poor girl's face. She didn't look much older than Rachel. The mental images had given only a glimpse of the girl's life, but they showed a drive and courage that should have been rewarded, not destroyed. All that this girl could have done and become was now lost. Her future of limitless possibilities had been stolen from her. As a cold breeze swept across the field, Rachel knew that they faced a growing evil that would never stop on its own.

69

Dr. Graves walked among the tombstones, glancing at each with a passing curiosity. He considered the dates, historical period, and lifespan before imagining what they might have done with their limited years on Earth. He considered their family life based on loving epitaphs and nearby stones bearing the same surname. He felt happy when he found family groups resting together, bound in death as perhaps they were in life.

It had been a long time since he was in a cemetery during the day, although an endless reef of gray clouds cast everything in a charcoal gloom. A cool fall breeze passed through the thinning trees and whispered over the cold grass and wet leaves. He was surprised at how large this cemetery was. It made him consider just how many lives had passed through this North Dakota town over the past century and a half. He stopped before two of the more recent additions.

"Doesn't it seem strange they'd be buried next to each other?" he asked.

"Well, they *were* married," Madam Bovell answered.

"But he murdered her."

"It is strange," she conceded.

"Everyone talks about how in love they were," Jason said. "And both their parents are dead. They didn't have any other family in the area except each other. I guess somebody decided they should stay together."

"They may have already had an arrangement. Something that legally said they wanted to be buried here together."

"Obviously never having imagined how horrible their end would be," Dr. Graves concluded.

He saw a Volkswagen Beetle moving slowly toward them on the narrow gravel lane. It slowed and seemed to hesitate at a little shaded crossroads, then kept going. Then, as it crossed a stone bridge over a lazy creek, the car accelerated toward them.

"Is that her?" he asked, guessing the answer.

"Mmm," Jason mumbled. "And Scott."

"Where are the other kids?"

"At the high school."

"It's Saturday."

"The upperclassmen are doing a haunted house," Jason said. "Apparently, it's a tradition. Every year, the junior and senior classes turn the high school halls and grounds into a spook fest for the evening. The rest of the town brings their kids to the Fright Fair in the late afternoon, before the sun sets and the trick-or-treating starts."

The car stopped at the edge of the grass, and Rachel and Scott got out. They looked tired, and the professor wondered just how much of a toll it had taken on them to find the girl's body and then spend another hour waiting for the police and giving their statements.

"You guys okay?" Madam Bovell asked as they arrived.

Scott nodded. Rachel looked as if she had recently been crying.

"Do the police have any idea who did it?" Dr. Graves asked.

Rachel shook her head.

"Do *you*?" Madam Bovell asked.

Rachel closed her eyes, took a deep breath, and opened them. "I felt something dangerous when I touched the girl's body. Some life form was pursuing her last night, hunting her as if she had been marked by the devil."

"Do they know who she was?"

"No, but I got a glimpse of her life. She was a troubled teen, a runaway from somewhere in Florida. She came to North Dakota as a migrant worker looking for opportunities in the shale-oil business. Things were not going well, but she was working hard and hadn't yet given up hope. It was a struggle, but I sensed that given enough time, she would have found her way to a good life."

"And something was hunting her?"

"Yes."

"Something or some*one*?"

"Some*thing*," Rachel said. "I sensed an evil life force in her memories. And then I saw a dark image of an eagle's head. I think there's something very bad in this town—some darkness, an evil force. And I don't think it's Annabel's spirit."

"It's not," Jason said. "It's her *husband's* spirit."

"*What?*" Rachel said. She turned to Madam Bovell. "What's he talking about?"

"It's true," Madam Bovell said. "At least, we think it is."

"Jason came up with the theory," the professor chipped in. "And once we worked through the differences between the hospital and the farmhouse—along with other clues like the mysterious repairs occurring at the farmhouse—we concluded that somehow, both husband and wife became trapped spirits, unable to move out of the netherworld between this plane and the afterlife."

"*Both* are trapped?" Rachel asked. "Has anything like that ever happened before."

"There are many stories in ghost lore of entire groups of people dying together and becoming a haunting force," Dr.

Graves said. "Ghost ships of the dead. Recurring ghost battles at Gettysburg from the Civil War that are still heard on some nights. Large historic hotels often claim to have at least a few ghosts innocently haunting a room or floor."

"But in this case, you're talking two people at odds with each other," Scott said. "She betrayed him; he murdered her. And now you're telling me you think they're both still here—that *both* their spirits are haunting this town. One at the hospital. The other at the farmhouse."

"Is there anything we can do?" Rachel asked.

"There is long precedent for exorcisms by the Catholic Church," Madam Bovell said, "but that deals specifically with demon spirits possessing a living person. There is some precedent for cleansing haunted places like a house or ship, but it is unclear how many of those stories are legitimate. Maybe the Society for Psychical Research has dealt with something like this. Doctor Graves?"

The professor looked down. "If they were in the same place, we could, in theory, get them to at least communicate with each other. But the physical distance between the hospital and the farmhouse may be preventing them from reconciling their sins against each other."

"Can a ghost be moved from a place it's haunting?" Jason asked.

Madam Bovell grunted. "An object imprinted with a spirit's energy acts as a talisman, but it's rare. Spirits prefer stationary locations."

"Is there some way we can help them communicate across the distance?" Rachel asked.

"That's got to be at least ten miles," Madam Bovell said.

"Fifteen," Scott said.

"That's too far," said Bovell.

"What if it wasn't?" Rachel asked. "How would you do it?"

"Well, if we were close—like less than a mile—then we might be able to connect them telepathically."

"How?"

"Well, in theory, you would go to one location; I would go to the other. If we could somehow connect telepathically as we fell into our separate trances, then we could connect our separate séances into something like a shared dream. But this is just theory. I don't know of it ever being done before."

"Telepathy can't reach beyond a mile?"

"I don't know the limits," Madam Bovell said. "In 1745, Emanuel Swedenborg was at a garden party when he had a vision of a major fire that had just broken out in Stockholm three hundred miles away. He described it to sixteen guests in great detail as it was happening. Two days later, news reached them confirming the vision. Swedenborg was gifted with telepathy and traveling clairvoyance—when one's soul leaves the body and travels to distant places to obtain information. So fifteen miles between the hospital and farmhouse is *possible,* but the challenge is to achieve telepathy while falling into a trance. It's likely too complex for the mind to concentrate on both at the same time."

Dr. Graves caught a glint of sunlight off one of the many gemstones on Madam Bovell's necklaces. "What if something makes the connection for you?" he asked.

"Like what?" Rachel asked.

Dr. Graves met Madam Bovell's eyes. "What about crystals?"

"Crystals?"

"Yeah. Could it be done with crystals?"

She scratched her lower lip. "That's never been tried before, either, far as I know."

"But if you used the same type of crystal and it was properly charged and programmed, might that help?"

She frowned, then nodded. "It might."

"What are you guys talking about?" Jason asked.

"Crystals are efficient absorbers and transmitters of energy," Madam Bovell said. "We could use the psychic applications of crystals to strengthen a connection between Rachel and me while we're in separate séances."

"I still don't understand," Jason said.

"Neither do I," Rachel added.

Scott shook his head and said, "Well, that makes most of us."

"The superheated magma forming the Earth's mantle sometimes rises into the crust, where heat and pressure and supersaturated water can combine to form quartz crystals. Because of this, people have believed since ancient times that their structure allows crystals to absorb, conserve, focus, and emit energy, especially on the electromagnetic wave band."

A cool breeze blustered through, pushing and scattering dead leaves among the tombstones.

"All objects are made of individual vibrating molecules," Madam Bovell said. "And crystals are unique. Because of chemical impurities, radiation, solar emissions, and the means of their formation, every crystal has its own energetic frequency of vibration. Healing crystals have been used since ancient times. Crystal balls and bowls are used in seership rituals to seek images or symbols of the future. And some crystals have an extremely high vibration that raises consciousness and opens the higher chakras to communicate with other dimensions. Crystals can be programmed by imprinting one's life force onto them. And they can affect the energy all around them, including the human and spiritual energy fields."

Jason stared at her in disbelief. "Are you telling me your crystal ball from last night can do all this?"

"It was cut and shaped from one large natural quartz crystal," she answered. "It can be imprinted with energy and used for divination, seership, and necromancy. And its power to connect us to higher-frequency beings such as spirits will be at its very strongest tonight."

"Because it's Halloween?" Rachel guessed.

"No," she said. "Because tonight is a full moon. Crystals follow the lunar cycle, and they are most receptive to being charged with energy when the moon is full."

"So how do we use it?" Jason asked.

"First, we need to find a way to cut my crystal ball in half," she said. "If we split it in two, then Rachel and I would each have a piece during our separate séances. The two halves will be drawn to each other's energy. They're from the same source, with the same vibrational frequency, and have been together for thousands or millions of years. This will be our psychic energy bridge between the two simultaneous séances."

"Has anything like this ever been tried before?" Rachel asked.

"Never," Madam Bovell said. "These days, crystals are mostly used for healing purposes. Or for charms. Crystal balls are still used for crystal gazing—looking into the planes and occlusions within the ball to see the future reflected by your energy force. Few people use crystals to communicate with the dead anymore, and I'm not aware of anyone ever cutting a crystal ball in half to connect two simultaneous séances."

"And on Halloween," Rachel said.

"And during a full moon," Jason added.

"Oh, yeah, what could possibly go wrong?" Scott deadpanned.

"So we're doing it," Dr. Graves said. "It's a crazy plan, but this is a crazy situation. And it's going to take all of us for it to work."

"Crystals are unpredictable," Madam Bovell said, offering a final warning. "So are spirits."

"So is *everything*," Dr. Graves said. "If things don't go as planned and we have to pivot, then we'll pivot. But we have to try."

"So now what?" Jason asked.

The professor gazed out over the tombstones of the town's dead. Another strong gust whipped through the mostly bare trees. It reminded him of the ominous, mystical wind he had encountered at his son's grave in Chicago, at the beginning of this journey. He looked up at the branches above him, half expecting nuts to fall and magically form another message.

"You mentioned that Jessica restores classic cars with her dad," Graves said. "She must have access to drilling and cutting tools."

"Yeah," Rachel said. "She's got tools that should do the trick. Diamond drill bits and everything. But they'll be in her garage, which she's terrified to go into right now. She'll want all of us to be there with her when she drills and cuts the crystal ball."

"Of course we'll all be there," Madam Bovell said. "We're all in this together."

70

Dark thoughts assailed Rachel. It was her first time seeing a dead body in an undignified, raw setting. She had felt the girl's death as it was happening—experienced the horror of running wildly through a field in the rain at night, crying while desperately trying to escape a shadowy energy force of pure evil.

Rachel had bonded with the girl—first through her death, and then while helping guide her soul into the spirit realm. She was with the others in Jason's corner suite in the hotel. Sitting on the bed, she watched the orange blob of the sun sink into the horizon. And as she waited for the approaching darkness of All Hallows' Eve, her thoughts were consumed by a vague sense of the stirring souls of the dead.

Her growing gift now gave her a connection with the dead and dying in a way that others couldn't imagine. A calm confidence had taken root inside her. For what was death, really? She knew that it wasn't a void. It wasn't an empty nothingness. If anything, death was rich with energy. It was an infinite world, a cosmic jungle, an ocean of everything and everyone who had ever existed, of all things hidden beyond the boundary between life and death, between dimensions and planes of existence and whatever labels religion or science or philosophy or art wanted to give it.

But if she had learned anything from witnessing the girl move into the warm tunnel of light, it was that the dead should no more be trapped in this world than should a bird be caged or a person enslaved. And while she wasn't afraid of the dead, she was terrified of whatever truth must lie behind Annabel's and Rubin's imprisonment in their own little hell worlds. And she feared that the group was missing something important: that perhaps the souls of Annabel and Rubin were in a deeper, darker place than any of them realized.

She closed her eyes and tried to read the emotions of everyone else clustered in the hotel room. They had returned from successfully drilling through and splitting the crystal ball in Jessica's garage. Everyone was excited by how evenly it had split into two hemispheres and by the prospect of the coming séances. But beneath their excitement was a whole mix of emotions in anticipation of other, darker things that the night may hold in store. She could taste the pond water in Shelley's throat as it tried to drowned her. She could hear the wild gabbling of a possessed swarm of chickens scratching and pecking at Tommy. She could feel the hard weight of the Chevy as it bore relentlessly down on Jessica. And she felt the heat against Aaron's face as he struggled to drag his unconscious father across their deck. Rachel could sense the lingering fear in each of them. An evil presence inhabited the town, and she was quickly coming to realize that she must face it not only to help Annabel, but also to save her friends. And ultimately, she must face it to fulfill whatever fate had always held in store for her. For the crazier that things got, the more she believed that she had always been predestined to face some ancient evil on this Halloween night.

"You okay?" Scott asked, sitting down next to her on the bed. His weight sank the mattress and tipped her into him, which made her feel better.

"Yeah," she said. "Just a little anxious for the big event."

"This will work," he said, ever the optimist.

She pressed her thigh against his. "I can feel the crystal transmitting energy between its halves," she said, looking at the two hemispheres, sitting like a split cantaloupe on the table. But then her eyes found Madam Bovell's stare.

"You really sense the energy?" Bovell asked.

"A tingling on my fingertips," Rachel answered, extending her right hand with fingers splayed. "Warm, soft energy ... like sunlight on the skin."

Madam Bovell leaned forward at the table and held her fingers above the smooth surfaces. But Rachel could sense her wistfulness upon feeling none of the energy that Rachel could detect.

"You're remarkable," Madam Bovell said. "Such a gift." But then the woman became withdrawn, and Rachel could sense a great worry rising in the old medium—a deep concern that had been buried since they first met but that was now expanding fast.

"You don't think this will work," Rachel whispered.

"I never said that."

"You thought it."

"I didn't—not really."

"Then what are you worried about? You're afraid of something."

Madam Bovell stood up and stepped toward her, stopping so close to Rachel that their shoes almost touched. "Okay, stop it," she said under her breath. "I'll tell you, but for God's sake, stop probing." Then she leaned in and said, "It should be said in private. Follow me."

Rachel looked around the room. Jason and Dr. Graves had been telling Shelley and Aaron about the haunted rectory in central England. Tommy and Jessica were sitting close together on the short couch, talking about how the town had changed.

Rachel stood and followed Madam Bovell. The woman held the key to her room and was waving at her to catch up. Rachel met her in the hallway, and they walked in silence down to Madam Bovell's door.

Once inside the room, Rachel said, "Okay, what's going on?"

"It's the devil," Madam Bovell said.

Rachel froze. It was the instinctive type of fear, the kind one never imagined until their body tensed and goose bumps sprout across the skin, and the hairs rose on the back of the neck.

"You're certain?" she managed to ask. "No false warnings. No hyperbole. Not when we're speaking of the devil."

"I'm as certain as I can be," Madam Bovell vowed.

"Do I die?"

Rachel heard herself utter the question so calmly that she wondered whether she was suffering from shock. Then she mused, was it even possible for someone in shock to know they were in shock?

"I have a terrible fear that you will die tonight," Madam Bovell said, her expression melting. "I'm sorry."

"You saw my death?"

"I felt it."

"What the hell does that mean?" Rachel asked. "I thought your gift was weak, if not gone altogether. How could you feel something like that?"

"I don't know what else to say. I felt it."

"Well, what am I supposed to do with that? *The devil's out there, somewhere. And he's coming for you. You're going to die. Cheerio! Now, let's go communicate with the dead on Halloween using a murdered crystal ball!* No way. You've got to give me more than that."

"I'm sorry, I can't. I was afraid even to tell you this much, in case I'm wrong, but you sensed it in me and called me out. Forgive me."

"You have to tell me more than that. If you're right, if I'm to face whatever my mother and grandmother faced, whatever *killed* them, then you at least have to give me a chance."

"There's nothing I can do. When you're in a trance, you're alone."

"I'm surrounded by the dead."

"The dead can't help you."

"Why not?"

"Because the devil doesn't want them. Their paths have already been decided by their lives and the way they died, their state of mind—not at the moment of death, exactly, but at the moment *after* death, too. Everything a person was and is and will be seems to be part of where we go after we die. The devil can't change those already dead. That's not who the battle is over. It's the living who are at risk, along with those rare trapped souls like Annabel and Rubin."

"Is *that* what all this is really about? My soul? And theirs? Is this some kind of trade with the devil? My life and more to save their souls from eternal damnation?

"Maybe," Madam Bovell said.

"Annabel's husband should be in hell, but instead he's trapped here. And because he's trapped, Annabel has refused to move on to heaven, because maybe she believes there's still a chance for her husband and maybe she can't leave him because she still loves him."

"Maybe."

"Is that what this is? A love story? Between two ghosts being pulled apart by the devil?"

"And you are their savior."

"They've both done horrible things to each other. I'm not sure that I'm anyone's savior, but even if I were, do they even deserve one?"

"They do if they're still in love."

Rachel sat on the corner of the bed. The conversation seemed to have sucked the energy from her legs. Was there still love between Annabel and her husband? How could love survive in such darkness?

Her eyes fell to the thin carpet's swirling beige patterns. Everything had changed, and she was now more doubtful than ever about what to do. She felt Madam Bovell watching her.

"Annabel spoke of lies," Rachel said.

"Maybe she was referring to the continuing love between her and her husband beyond death. Naturally, people in town said bad things about them after the double murder-suicide."

"Naturally," said Rachel. "They still do. But how would any of that be considered *lies*? There must be something else here that we're missing."

"We'll know soon enough. Once we get a linked communication, I think that together we can coax the truth out of them. Remember to just focus on falling into the trance and connecting with any spirit guides or spirits that find you. Don't try to find me telepathically. If we're right about the crystals, then each half of the divided ball will form a psychic link stimulated by the spirit energy we attract in our separate séances. And again, if you don't think you can do this, it's not too late. But just remember that not doing the séance won't necessarily save you from the devil. That is a battle that you must face sooner or later."

Rachel stood up. "No, I'm okay. You've warned me of the dangers. But you've also convinced me that we must try to find the answers tonight—to find out why Annabel and her husband cannot move on, why their spirits are trapped. But before we go, you have to promise me one thing."

"Name it."

"Promise that if something happens to me tonight—if I die—promise that you'll try to contact me, to communicate with my spirit, just to make sure *I'm* not trapped in some dark netherworld for all eternity."

"I promise."

"You can do that? Even if your powers weaken again?"

"There's a place that I can go to magnify the power of communication with the spirit world."

"That cemetery in Kansas?"

Madam Bovell shook her head. "There's an ancient abbey on the island of Iona, in Scotland. It has a powerful tie to the spirit world. I would be able to contact your spirit from there."

"Iona?"

"Yes. I promise."

Rachel didn't know what the night had in store for them, but this gave her a tiny degree of comfort.

They left Madam Bovell's room and made their way back down the wide hallway, toward Jason's corner suite. Along the way, she heard ice cubes clattering from the machine into a bucket, a baby wailing, a television spewing noisy blather, a couple laughing. Then she sensed someone reading emails, another sipping a can of bitter beer while looking out the window, another sitting on the toilet, scrolling through newsfeeds on a cell phone. A couple having sex while others were alone and thinking of past lovers.

Energy flowed all around her. And so did the spirits of the dead. It was seven at night on Halloween, and the nearer it got to midnight, the closer they came to a gateway opening between worlds. The Vikings believed this was the most spiritual time, right before winter and the season of death—the long nights during the cold months when death most visited their people. All Hallows' Eve was both a last celebration of life and an honoring of those animal spirits of the dead who briefly rejoined the living.

Rachel took slow, steady breaths as she moved down the hallway, feeling the living and the dead circle in an ever-tightening orbit, sensing the approaching pinnacle of Halloween's power, and preparing herself for the possibility that she might pass from this world into another plane of existence before this night was over.

Everything was closing in on her.

Protect me, Mother, she thought. *If you can, please protect me. Please, give me the strength that you and your mother had. Please, help me face this evil.*

The elevator door dinged and opened as they walked past. Glancing inside, she saw that it was empty.

71

Dr. Graves gripped the Yukon's steering wheel as if he meant to strangle it. His thoughts drifted for the ten-thousandth time to another random memory of his son. He saw the squat three-year-old version of his son during a summer vacation in the Rocky Mountains of Colorado. He had taken little David on the historic tourist train from Silver Plume to Georgetown, though the boy, instead of observing the world outside, had spent most of the ride running a toy locomotive back and forth across his leg. Graves had bought the toy from the gift shop *before* the ride instead of after—in hindsight, not the best call. Soon realizing his mistake, he had spent the last half of the train ride disheartened and frustrated with himself. But now he held fast to that memory of his little boy rolling the little green choo-choo train across his legs and along the bench and up in magical circles into the air. Every year on his son's birthday, he would take a new toy train engine and place it at David's tombstone.

A voice burst from the darkness. "Professor, this is it! Slow down!"

A mailbox loomed out of the night and flew past on the left. Jolted from memory to the present, he slammed on the brakes in panic. The heavy Yukon slid a few dozen feet on the gravel and was still rocking as a brown cloud of dust overtook it.

"Sorry," he said, embarrassed.

He backed up until the white mailbox was in front of them again. Then, turning into the white rock driveway, he navigated around a dozen large potholes, past giant dark trees, to the front of the attached garage. Turning off the engine, he couldn't help scanning each of the unlit front-facing windows. Hidden eyes could be watching from any one of them.

A passenger door popped open behind him, triggering the dome light and wiping away the outside world, leaving only the reflection of his worn face. More doors popped open, and everyone but him and Madam Bovell slid out into the night.

"Kind of reminds me of that time in West Haven," she said.

"Oh, yeah," he confirmed quietly. "Those twin girls who heard strange, loud knocks from the closet door at night. Like the Fox sisters."

"The way those pine trees along the left side keep trying to touch the house. They did that at the twins' house, too."

"I remember that," he said. "People thought that was what made the knocking sound."

"But they were wrong, weren't they?"

"Yes, they were," he said sadly. "Is their mother still alive?"

"Far as I know," Madam Bovell answered.

"Still in the asylum?"

"I believe so."

"Evil comes in many horrible forms," he said somberly. "It makes you wonder sometimes how the good ever really have a chance."

"Yeah," she said. "Those poor little girls certainly didn't."

His mind returning from the past, he looked up just in time to see the full moon swallowed by clouds. "We haven't had a dry night since arriving in North Dakota. I thought we might actually get lunar light tonight. I guess the darker it is, the less our chances of anyone seeing us out here."

"This is a dark place," she said.

"Why is that, do you think?" he asked, realizing that she wasn't referring just to the weather, but to some other darkness hanging over the townspeople. "Because of Annabel's secret, her murder, or whatever evil thing her tormented spirit may have attracted to this town?"

"I think it's because this town is changing faster than the locals can accept. Lot of new people coming here. Lot of growth and change. The old town is vanishing and being replaced by something new. That creates a lot of anxiety and fear for those who have always called this place home."

She stopped suddenly, as if she'd had more to say before something silenced her. She seemed lost in thought, her eyes wide and focused on something near the house.

He followed her glare toward the trees. "What is it?"

"It's as if something is coming to destroy the whole town," she said. "And the people sense it. They don't understand it, but they can feel the change and they fear they won't survive it."

"Including them?" he asked, nodding toward Aaron and Tommy and Jessica. The three teenagers had grabbed the lighting equipment out of the Yukon and were walking with it through the headlights, toward the house.

"All of them," she said. "And it's spreading and growing across this town. Every day we've been here, it's gotten worse. And it's especially strong at this house. Come on. Follow me."

They got out, and she grabbed his wrist and marched toward the house. Under her other arm was the crystal hemisphere, wrapped in the brown potato sack. He let her pull him across the gravel and up the steps to the front porch. The long cedar planks creaked with each step. The screen door was ajar, drifting out a few inches before retreating, then out again, then back.

The house is breathing, Dr. Graves thought. *It knows why we've come, and is preparing for a fight. It doesn't want to give up its resident spirit. It doesn't want to reveal its darkest secrets.*

In this moment, he realized what a blind alley his own career had followed these past thirty years. He had been blind to the world of spirits that overlapped the natural world he lived in. Every medium he observed after his son's death had been guilty of fakery before he had even begun his investigations. He had prejudged and condemned the entire community of spiritualists and ghost hunters the moment his son's tombstone was erected. And whether it was anger, sorrow, or bitterness from the greatest loss imaginable, he had channeled it into a crusade to expose and discredit anyone claiming to connect the living with the dead. But the entire time, he had been on a self-serving quest to ease the pain of his loss, all the while ignoring all the signs that pointed to the possibility of life beyond life—because the idea of his son out there somewhere without him had terrified him beyond anything he ever knew.

"Here!" Madam Bovell said. She had led him past the front door, to the far side of the porch. She laid her hand on the wood railing near the outcropped edge. Closing her eyes, she took a few deep breaths. Her face tensed.

"What is it?" he asked.

"There's energy here."

"Rubin?"

She nodded and opened her eyes. Just then a metallic clanging came from the corner of the house. "That's it," she said, without looking toward the noise. Her gaze seemed lost in the evergreen branches swaying in the breeze.

Seeing that she wasn't going to investigate it, Graves moved toward the strange sound. Inching along the end of the porch, he saw a gray downspout at the corner of the house. He realized at once that it was the source of the tapping. And it grew louder and more pronounced as he drew near. He leaned his head out over the railing and stretched to get his ear as close as he could to the downspout. Along with the tapping, he now also heard a deep human moan and some inaudible words. The tapping came in six evenly spaced strikes, followed by a pause, then six more. Again and again the tapping reverberated along the downspout. It could be coming from any gutter or downspout connected to this one. The moaning seemed to be coming out from the puddle of muddy water at the bottom of the downspout.

He reached out his hand, hesitated, and tapped the downspout six times with his knuckles. The moaning and the tapping stopped. The abrupt silence froze him. He held his breath, waiting for the tapping to resume, but the dead silence continued.

"Donovan, look," Madam Bovell whispered.

He glanced back at her, then followed her outstretched arm pointing at the evergreens. The branches were no longer randomly swinging side to side. Impossibly, they were swaying in small perfect circles, making counterclockwise rotations, like hundreds of hands on watch faces trying to turn back time. And every branch moved in unison, perfectly in sync with the others. It was mesmerizing.

"What the hell is happening here?" he asked. "This thing you're worried about—has it found us?"

A sun-bright bolt of lightning flashed, and all the branches froze in a motionless rigidity every bit as unnerving in the buffeting wind as the perfect little circles had been. A bone-rattling thunder crack chased the lightning, and the branches returned to the natural swaying of a tree in gale.

He and Madam Bovell stared at each other with the unspoken awareness that there were many unnatural forces in the air tonight.

Tommy and Jessica rushed up under the porch roof with their lighting equipment cases. Aaron, caught closing up the Yukon when the rain hit, lumbered across the driveway with the last case.

"Why?" he complained to anyone interested as he joined the others on the porch.

"That everything?" Dr. Graves asked.

"Yes, thank God," Aaron answered.

"How long to get it all set up in the house?"

"Ten minutes."

The professor glanced at his watch, then said to Madam Bovell, "How much time do *you* need?"

"A few minutes of silence after everything's ready."

"Jessica, can you text Rachel to let her know we'll be ready to start in about fifteen minutes?"

She pulled her phone out. "I don't have a signal."

"Aaron? Tommy? Could one of you?" he asked.

"I've got nothing?" Tommy said, looking at his phone with bewilderment.

"Zip here, too," Aaron added, tapping his cell with a wet finger.

"Something's here," Madam Bovell warned, looking around as if she might see a minion of Satan lurking in the dark. "Something other than Rubin."

"What do you feel?" Dr. Graves asked.

"It's like a scent … a psychic scent. I don't know what it is, but it's different and it's here."

"We should leave," Aaron said, still looking at his cell phone. "We should have signals, but we don't. There's a cell tower only a mile that way. This is not a good idea. Something's really wrong here."

"We have to finish this," Tommy said. "No one else will."

"Whatever this thing is, we can't fight it. It's not just our cell phones. You didn't see what it can do."

"Oh, really?" Tommy said. "I saw thousands of chickens turn psycho and practically kill themselves for a chance to finish me off."

"Fine," said Aaron, "but you didn't see its face in the fire. It saw me. Looked right into my eyes. It felt like pure power and hatred. If it's here with us, then we need to leave now."

"And go where?" Jessica said. "Look, I'm scared, too. But this thing's already found each of us in our homes. We have to do something before it tries to kill us again."

"She's right," Dr. Graves said. "There's no where you can go to be safe. And tonight is likely our best chance to end this—maybe our *only* chance." He turned to Madam Bovell. "Can you still do this? Even if it is creating some sort of signal interference?"

"I don't know, but I don't think we'll get another chance to try."

"Okay," Dr. Graves said. "We said we'd start around ten—that's in just fifteen minutes. Rachel will plan to start then, too, even if we don't call. They'll probably try to call and will figure out that our phones aren't working, and they'll just continue as planned. It's all we can do, so let's keep moving."

Helping Madam Bovell into the house and up the stairs, he noticed the air getting colder with each step toward the second floor. The large house was dark and quiet except for the racket the others made lugging the gear through the shadows and on the creaking staircase. Already, his eyes were playing tricks on him—or so he hoped, for through the banister on the second floor, he thought he saw a long shadow sliding away from them as they ascended closer to that scene of death.

72

The north annex of the hospital was dark and silent—a limb severed from the newer, larger facilities humming in warm illumination just across the long grass yard. Scott had suggested parking in the main lot like last night because of beefed-up police presence on Halloween. Now Jason found himself in the half-lit no-man's-land between the old and the new, the dead and the living, as he followed Rachel and Scott and Shelley toward the haunted building he had first entered only five days ago.

He had no idea whether Rachel and Madam Bovell knew what they were talking about, saying they could communicate with multiple ghosts, from separate locations, at the same time. In his rushed study of medium and paranormal research, he hadn't come across anything like what they were trying tonight.

He saw Scott's arm stiffen toward them, with his fingers stretched out. He had stopped and knelt in the cold grass. Both girls stopped, too, and knelt on the hospital lawn.

Jason searched the shadows with his eyes, scanning across the dark field in front of him. Then he saw it: a group of dark shapes, barely visible, moving along the outside wall of the hospital annex. He looked hard, trying to determine the number of individuals. Three or four, at least—maybe as many as six. Then the hairs on the back of his neck stood up when the figures passed near a lamp. To his surprise, he saw the pack of werewolves, moving fast in a single line, slinking from the woods beyond the side parking lot, toward the more populated residence wing of the hospital. None of the ghost hunters was moving—they must all be as scared as he was. And he might have stayed locked in baffled fright if he hadn't heard the muffled laughter, instead of howls, that rose up toward the full moon.

They waited until the giggling werewolves had crept along the annex and disappeared under the second-story walkway to the main hospital building.

Scott stood up, and Rachel and Shelley joined him.

"High school friends of yours?" Jason whispered to Rachel.

She shrugged.

"Those fools are going to attract security," Scott said.

The soft night sounds stopped short as a haunting howl rose up from the other side of the hospital and toward the pale moon. A flight of birds darted over the treetops. Or bats? Jason felt a cold shudder run up his back, warning him of unnatural dangers. It was as if he suddenly felt the presence of an occult force, watching them from the darkness within the trees.

Scott was the first to jog toward the annex, still fifty yards away. Then Shelley and Rachel ran and caught up, then passed him. Jason took off behind them. As he drew abreast, they started running faster. It now felt like a race to be anywhere but at the back of the group, as if some horror were snapping at their heels. And running faster, they made more and more noise, which made them more panicked—which spurred them to even greater speed.

All four reached the annex door in a clatter of footfalls, heaving and huffing. Shouting came from the shadows on the other side of the yard. Shelley's hand shook, fumbling to get the key into the lock. The door opened, and they piled inside as one unit, closed the door, and peered through the small window at the unnerving stillness of the moonlit world outside.

Nothing moved. No sounds. No changing light.

"Did anyone see us?" Jason asked.

"No," Scott said, though he couldn't have known.

"Anything?" Jason asked Rachel in the darkness. She had been silent for too long.

"Someone just died," she answered.

"What? In the hospital?"

An exit sign lit their faces with a dim glow that made Rachel's eyes shine like emeralds right before she closed them.

"It was a man," she said. "He was very old. I felt him in his hospital bed, staring at the ceiling, on the verge of moving into the spirit world. Most of his life, he had been surrounded by many loved ones, but no one was with him now. He was a good man, and I didn't want him to be alone at the end, so I let him know I was present ... that I was with him, that he wasn't alone."

"Are you okay?" Scott asked, stepping around Jason and putting a hand on her shoulder.

"Yes," she said, now in a hushed voice. "But the night staff will need to take care of the body. And the werewolf pranksters will aggravate security with all their howling. There's too much activity. We're not prepared for this."

"We don't have much of a choice," Jason said.

"We should hurry," Scott said, consulting his sport watch in the dark. "We have less than ten minutes until they start."

"Go," Jason insisted. "Get set up. Get ready. I'll be right behind you."

As the group left him and ascended to the third floor, he rushed back to the side door. He pushed hard on the aluminum door to make sure it was latched and locked. Satisfied, he was about to turn away when a lightning bolt cast a brief splash of illumination across the field, revealing a solitary figure, with fur and what appeared to be a tail, staring at him from fifty yards away.

Jason continued to stare out the window, but with the next flash of lightning a few seconds later, the creature had vanished. Or was it still there, hidden in the night? Had it really seen him? He didn't know. Had it really even been there? He couldn't be sure. He prayed not. Stepping away from the door, he raced to the stairs and darted up them as fast as he could without tripping in the dark, then stopped at the half landing, ducked down, and looked one last time at the door and its little window right where a face could be. It was pitch black except for the rain streaming across it.

He felt he was being watched, and suddenly felt very uncomfortable being alone. He raced up the remaining stairs to find the others.

73

Madam Bovell sat on the wood floor on the spot where the murders had occurred. She had unwrapped the crystal hemisphere and folded a red velvet cloth corner-to-corner three times to make a thick triangle, which she laid flat on the plank, making sure to find a spot not too close to any flooring nails. Only then did she lift the crystal from her lap and, with two hands, place it on the cloth.

"How much time do we have?"

"Four minutes until ten."

"Everyone, sit in a circle. Donovan, please light the candles, and all turn off your flashlights."

Tommy, Jessica, and Aaron sat on the floor. Tommy looked tense, as if expecting a fight. Jessica, by contrast, looked supremely confident about placing her life in Madam Bovell's hands. Aaron was calm and studious as usual, his eyes tracking Dr. Graves's movements. The professor edged stiffly around the room, hunching down to ignite each of the dozen candles surrounding them. Then he returned to the center of the room and sat opposite Madam Bovell.

"Everyone, hold hands, please," she instructed.

The candles made tiny reflections of firelight in the crystal hemisphere. She felt at once mesmerized and alert in the dreamy commune of their small circle of souls in this quiet, dark place. A place of murder and death. And their brave group sat on the floor of this death chamber, hoping to discover the secrets of the damned and help right whatever wrong trapped them in their private hell.

Through all this, at the beginning of their final journey into the spirit world, she was ready to face Rubin. Her gaze drifted up from the dancing fires in the crystal. Her eyes closed, and she bowed her head.

At first, she could sense the flow of energy from their circle. She sensed Tommy visualizing himself on his farm, walking along the property line in silence, breathing the fresh morning air. She sensed Jessica visualizing herself cruising Main Street in a beautifully restored blue and white Chevy Bel Air with her dad. She sensed Aaron visualizing himself walking through the halls of MIT while dreaming up lab experiments with equally enthusiastic peers. And she sensed Dr. Graves visualizing a day, long past, when he was sledding with his son while his wife cheered them on from the top of the hill.

The energy flowed through them and glowed and did everything it was supposed to do at the start of a séance. She could feel the space around them begin to warp and open up to other places and the things within them. But then she sensed that something was off. They weren't making any connection with the séance at the hospital. She couldn't sense Rachel. Maybe something had gone wrong at the hospital, or something was blocking the connection between them. Then the positive energy Madam Bovell felt from her circle changed. The warmth turned cold; the glow turned dark. Something bad was happening, and she had to stop this before it was too late.

She tried to open her eyes, but they were stuck as if they had been sewn shut. She tried to speak but couldn't. Her mind was thick and heavy and drifting further and further away, until she could no longer stop herself from falling into a dark trance. And she couldn't even warn the others that something had gone horribly wrong.

74

Rachel had been sitting in near silence for five long minutes, holding hands in their little circle around the crystal hemisphere. While lightning flashed and thunder ripped outside, she tried to breathe deeply, sitting, waiting, willing herself to remain calm.

Then Jason raised an index finger while looking at his watch. His head bobbed subtly, as if miming the clicks of the final seconds. Then he dropped his hand.

Ten o'clock.

"Everyone, please remain quiet, stay calm, and focus on positive thoughts," Rachel said. "Positive energy is the way to reach Annabel. Just remember that she wants to communicate with us, that she needs our help, and that we *can* help her. There is nothing to be afraid of."

But inside, she was terrified.

She closed her eyes.

Her heart was racing. Was the devil out there somewhere, looking for her? Had it been a night like this when her mother died? And her grandmother? Had it been on nights like this that

God abandoned her family to Lucifer? What chance could she have against *that* ancient power? What hope?

Madam Bovell had told her that her concerns about such things weren't important. Whatever happened, she was exactly where she was supposed to be, doing exactly what destiny required of her. There were no coincidences in the cosmos. The adoption process could have sent her to any town in America, but as a child she had been sent *here,* to a small town in North Dakota, where she would eventually start to develop her very special gifts at the same time that this peaceful community was rocked by the most violent murders in its history.

She had to calm down. She knew she couldn't conduct the séance as an inexperienced, first-time medium if she were to have a panic attack. She had to stay focused and will herself to relax. To breathe. To trust in her natural gifts.

She inhaled slowly, held it, then exhaled in half the time it had taken to inhale: the way she was taught for deep meditation. And there, in the recesses of her mind, she felt a pull into another place—an alternate universe, a blue dreamscape of shadows and echoes of past lives wandering through a timeless spirit world.

It was not like her last vision. She was not floating in some intergalactic nebula. She was walking at night in a field of tall grass. The soft wet blades brushed her as she pushed through them. The rolling land sloped down, toward a valley along a meandering creek rimmed by a line of trees. A large farmhouse sat at the end of the field among some trees. Annabel's farmhouse. Lights were on inside. A red Jeep in the drive. A steady breeze splashed over her face, coming from the direction of the farmhouse. Rachel continued toward it, but time seemed to slip away and vanish as sharp cuts of darkness whisked in front of her. Before she knew it, she was standing in the backyard, with no memory of crossing the broad valley.

Annabel was standing near a small window inside. Her head was lowered, and her shoulders moved as if she was working on something. Then she turned and raised a cookie sheet into the light before slotting it into a cupboard space.

Rachel took slow steps across the yard. Now time seemed to freeze. She couldn't take her eyes off Annabel—the long red hair, pale skin, and full lips moving as she gently bobbed her head. She was singing softly while washing dishes. Perhaps, a radio was on inside. Perhaps, she just had a warm heart, the kind that sings in the silence just to make the world a happier, more beautiful place.

Rachel stopped twenty feet from the house when she saw a new light in the corner of her eye. She looked right. A car was coming down the driveway, its bright headlight beams throwing moving shadows through the trees clustering the side of the house. Looking back at the window, she saw Annabel was no longer there.

Rachel moved around the side of the house until she stood at the front corner near the driveway. The front door opened, and Annabel stepped out onto the porch. Her pale face showed concern when the vehicle stopped at the edge of the garage. A car door opened, and a man stepped out into a cloud of darkness that she couldn't penetrate no matter how hard she stared. And with every step he took, the shadows seemed to slide with him, to keep his face masked in darkness, as if this were the devil in the flesh, who had finally found Rachel in a trance state that she could not abandon.

She had sworn to discover Annabel's secret, even if it meant coming face-to-face with pure evil and all the lost spirits that *he* controlled. Everything about Annabel's spirit in the hospital had screamed of some injustice done, some secret buried with her murdered corpse, which must be revealed. But that was before this evil figure had appeared. The more Rachel watched it move through the shadows to the front porch, the more she realized that in some way, she truly was seeing the devil in the flesh.

But never once did he turn to look at her. His focus was on Annabel as if, in this moment, her warm soul was the most coveted object in all the world.

Suddenly, the house vanished and everything went dark. Then, in the black void, a voice whispered into her ear, "*Lies, lies, lies.*"

75

Madam Bovell found herself standing on loose gravel at night, behind a brown Ford pickup. Only a moment ago, she had been with Dr. Graves and the others, sitting in a circle. She had initiated the séance without even noticing the transition into a trance state, just as one can't register the moment of drifting off to sleep. So where was she now? Trance states, in those rare moments when she had achieved them over the past thirty years, were never as clear and vivid as what she now experienced. The Ford's bright red brake lights cast a flushed glow around her. Then they went out. A rusted door opened. She heard the driver get out and take a few short steps on the crunching gravel. Then the door was closed carefully, quietly.

The crunching moved away from her. Stepping around the truck, she noticed that she made no sound when moving over the gravel.

I'm not really here. I'm the spirit now, drifting in the echoing memory of someone else's thoughts. But where *am I?*

And then she saw not only where but also *when*. In front of her and the brown Ford, and in the direction the crunching footsteps were heading, was the dark outline of the farmhouse, in the pale glow of a full moon just emerged from a reef of clouds.

The crunching footsteps slowly formed into a figure that moved past three other vehicles parked near the farmhouse. And when the figure stepped up onto the front porch, the side of his face was briefly visible in the porch light. It was a hard, chiseled face. A tough face embodying the strength and resilience of an oil worker or farmer, both of which he was—or had been until this fateful night. And as she glimpsed the face, she recognized him from photos in a dozen old news articles she had seen over the past few days.

Rubin, Annabel's husband and killer, had brought Madam Bovell back in time, in his emotionally trapped soul, to witness murder, by his hand, of his wife and her secret lover.

76

Dr. Graves was witnessing the most remarkable séance of his career. Madam Bovell had been in a trance state for nearly five minutes, and right from the start, strange happenings had occurred. The four flashlights lying on the floor around the circle had all flickered on at the same time. Then they had flashed and gone out with the candles. The darkness had turned an already uneasy feeling inside him into real fright. And the others had felt it, too, and conveyed it by their tightened grip on his hands. Then came three loud bangs from the center of the room, in front of him, and, it seemed, from an elevated position floating somewhere between the floor and the ceiling. The sound hadn't come from anyone in the group.

The séance had begun with Madam Bovell repeatedly asking for the spirit of Rubin to communicate with them, but no one had spoken since she fell into a trance.

Dr. Graves determined that it was up to him to break the silence. He could sense Tommy, Jessica, and Aaron staring through the darkness in his direction, waiting for guidance.

"Rubin? Are you here?"

Nothing but darkness and the building storm outside. Soft, distant thunder and a bloom of lightning miles away.

"Are you here, Rubin? Are you with us in this house? Can you hear me?"

Nothing. But even though he couldn't see or hear it, he knew that something was happening, because Madam Bovell wasn't speaking. Either Rubin or her spirit guide or some other force in this room had taken control of her.

"Are there any spirits here?" he asked, going for a more oblique approach than a direct call to Rubin.

He hadn't expected Madam Bovell to go so silent so soon, and he wasn't prepared to take over for her. He had investigated over five hundred séances firsthand, in the room with mediums and participants, listening and observing for any number of a million tricks fraudsters could play: trapdoors, fishing line, magnets, and fluorescent-dyed string, to name a few. But in all his decades as a skeptical observer, he had never once had the role of leading a séance group into contact with the spirit world. Just a few days ago, he hadn't even believed it possible.

"Are there any spirits here that wish to communicate?" he asked again.

A long silence ensued, and after a short eternity he was considering another way to couch the same question.

But then a soft, higher-pitched voice came from Madam Bovell's spot in the dark. "Dad? It's me. Dad?"

A shock swept over him, chilling every nerve in his body, clenching his gut, and spinning his awareness out of reality and into a place where the tragedies of his past had never happened. Life, as he knew it, was explained as one long nightmare from which he had just now woken. And all his dreams were now a clear, convincing reality.

"David?"

"I'm here, Dad."

Dr. Graves felt his chest heaving. He forgot all about the teens sitting with him in the darkness. The possibility of being with his son dwarfed everything. He no longer wanted to challenge anything; he wanted only to believe.

"David, where are you?"

"Here."

Despite the passing of decades since his son's death, he could never forget the pitch and cadence of his voice. And although the voice was more mature, he could still sense the excitement.

He wanted to tell his son how sorry he was, how not a day passed when he wasn't tormented by his failure to protect his son from the disease, how his own life had essentially ended the day he lost David. How he had never felt joy or happiness since those best days of his life raising his son and watching him grow into the fearless, strong willed little boy who could have done anything when he grew up—if he had just been allowed to grow up.

But he couldn't say any of these things. He couldn't find the words or the strength.

So instead, he asked the only question that a still-grieving father could ask if given a second chance. "Are you okay, David? Do you *feel* okay?"

"I am fine, Dad. Death was not the end. I have grown in the final place."

"Grown how?" he asked, confused.

"Grown in thoughts, in understanding … in ability. You must not think of me as a child anymore."

Tears welled in his eyes, and he couldn't tell whether they were from happiness or loss.

"I have been in contact with our ancestors. They were waiting for me, aware and ready when I arrived. Everyone who arrives has ancestors waiting for them, some from so far back in the past, they would be strangers but for the shared bond of the chain of life—a bond even more powerful than love. And ancestors teach arrivals everything else one needs to know, including how to find other loved ones in the final place, and how to watch over and send signs to loved ones still living. But mostly, no one wants to leave. It is good here. No words can truly describe it."

Dr. Graves was unable to speak as his mind raced through everything David said. He tried to understand it, to imagine his son's soul growing to full maturity in whatever realm of the afterlife was out there—or the "final place," as his son called it. It wasn't a thought he had ever considered, but now that it was out there, he found it very satisfying.

"Is your mother in the final place with you? Did you find her?"

"*She* found *me* when I arrived."

"And my parents?"

"They have guided me from the beginning of my arrival. We are all in the final place—everyone except you."

The darkness around him felt heavier at the thought that he was the last one.

"Then what is the point of my life?" he asked David. "Why shouldn't I just die and join all of you?"

"Emotions do not exist here—not in the same way as in your realm. A part of your humanity will forever die with your physical death. Not every part of you moves on, so it is important that you live as long as possible, that you never wish for death and never stop fighting against it—that you never lose your will to live. It will make your eventual transition into the final place stronger. Time also does not exist here the way it does in your realm. Cherish every day of your life for as long as you can. Even the painful days are important. Everything that happens to you strengthens your soul. And everything that you do can make a difference in expanding the light."

"What light?"

"The light of the multiverse."

"I don't understand."

But at that moment, a faint tremble spread across the room. Although the group was still in near darkness, he could feel the subtle shaking along the floor and could hear the walls rattling. The change felt very wrong, like when water along a beach rapidly recedes from the coast in the moments before a tsunami. As much as he wanted to keep learning about his son's continued existence, the slight vibration warned of an unseen, immediate danger.

"He is here," David's voice said, loud enough to be heard over the growing commotion.

"Who? Rubin? Hasn't he been here the whole time?"

"Not Rubin. It is the bad one: Jeffrey. He has arrived."

"Who's Jeffrey?"

"You must get out," David said, louder to match the rising disturbances in the room. "Jeffrey is here. You must get out now."

"Who is shaking the room, David? Is it Jeffrey? Is it you?"

"Rubin is shaking the room because Jeffrey is coming. You must get out now."

A sharp cracking snapped from his right. Then a blue glow grew from the crystal hemisphere, casting soft but eerie illumination throughout the room. It was enough to reveal a dark crack zigzagging up the wall to his right. Then the nail heads began to move up and down like pistons as the floorboards rose and snapped back down. Then the window in the back of the house blew out, sending thousands of tiny shards glimmering into the night. A lightning bolt flashed somewhere above. A deafening thunderclap followed. Tommy's face was frozen, Jessica was shaking, and the whites of Aaron's eyes looked impossibly large in the pale light.

"Get out," growled a voice, no longer David's. "Run!" Then Madam Bovell collapsed to her side, and the bright blue light from inside the crystal went out, casting the still-rattling room in darkness.

And through everything, Dr. Graves thought he had seen new lights in the window, as if something was just outside the farmhouse.

77

Jason hadn't taken his eyes off Rachel since she fell into the trance. The group had spread three flashlights at the edges of the room, which cast an ominous glow of dim yellow light in select pockets around them. The illumination was just enough for Jason to make out the shifting shadows on Rachel's face as her expression changed due to her trance experience and whatever was happening inside her mind. She hadn't made a sound in over five minutes. He was starting to worry about her, but he knew enough to keep waiting without disturbing her.

And Scott and Shelley waited, too.

Lightning flashed outside the same window that had terrified him when he first arrived in this conference room five days ago.

Then all three flashlights went out simultaneously, like candles extinguished by a sudden gust of wind.

Then the crystal hemisphere began to glow, casting an ever-brightening blue warmth throughout the room.

A surge of excitement shot through his body. Their plan was working. Rachel was making contact with at least one spirit entity. He could tell by her slouched posture, the way her dark hair fell over the sides of her face while her lips moved as if she were whispering to someone. And the glowing blue half-orb meant—if Madam Bovell's theory was correct—that there was now a connection between the hospital séance and the farmhouse séance, fifteen miles away.

They were finally going to connect Annabel's spirit with the murderous spirit of her husband. They were finally going to learn what was preventing both spirits from moving on to whatever realms of the afterlife awaited them.

The blue glow intensified, and Rachel swayed a few inches left and right. He got the feeling that contact with the spirit world had been achieved. The group had decided in advance that he should lead any questioning since Annabel's spirit had shown more interest in him than in the others.

"Is there a spirit present?" he asked in a serious voice, doing his best to mimic the words and gravitas of the many séance stories he had read.

Rachel remained unchanged, and the group received no other signs of paranormal activity.

"We wish to communicate. Is a spirit present?"

Watching Rachel's face in the half-light, he noticed her lips tighten. He assumed that at this point she was in a deep trance, but he had no idea where, exactly, her mind had gone. But now it seemed that another spirit—probably Annabel's—was in this room and trying to communicate through her.

"Annabel? Are you here?"

Rachel groaned something inaudible.

"Annabel?"

"*No-o-o-o,*" whispered Rachel, still seemingly in a trance.

"Then identify yourself," Jason said, surprised to hear a hint of frustration in his own voice.

He tried to calm himself. He tried to focus on the importance of channeling positive energy to Rachel so she could build a psychic bridge between the living and the dead.

"Please identify yourself," he asked in a soft, pastoral tone.

Rachel's lips quivered. *"I am Elizabeth Black, daughter of Margaret Black, and mother of Rachel Black."*

Jason felt a shiver of excitement, but he willed himself to stay calm. "Does Rachel know you're here?"

"She does not know. She is with Annabel Heller. She is being shown the secrets."

"Is she safe?"

"She is in great danger."

"Should we bring her out of the trance?"

"That would place her in greater danger."

"Is there nothing we can do to help her?" he asked.

"Nothing you can do. But I am watching her. As is her grandmother."

"And you both can protect her?"

"We will try."

"Can you tell us Annabel's secrets?"

"Only Annabel can reveal her secrets. But she doesn't know how to tell them. Death has been difficult for her. Both her secrets and her experience since death have been complicated. She doesn't know how to explain her secrets in any other way than to show them."

"And she's showing them to Rachel now?"

"Yes, but she chose you first. She showed you first."

"I was never shown her secrets."

"You were—you just did not—realize it."

Jason was baffled. He was certain he hadn't seen anything and had no idea about Annabel's secrets. He tried to think of anything he had seen or heard since arriving in North Dakota that could have been Annabel giving him answers. Perhaps even in a now-forgotten dream.

"Help me understand," he said. "Was it in a dream? A pattern in the objects she moved around in the room the first night? Something with the way she arranged the chairs?"

"It was the vision she showed you."

"The farmhouse?" His mind raced back to the night he had gone into the small room on the upper floor of this hospital wing. He had been so freaked by the initial encounter—with Annabel's spirit right behind him, whispering in his ear—that he had fled the hospital. Soon after, he had been pulled over by the police and then had met Rachel. But what had Annabel shown him? The farmhouse in the valley, surrounded by hills on a misty night. How could that be her secrets? Wasn't she just telling him to go to the farmhouse? Or was there something else she had been trying to tell him, to show him.

He closed his eyes and tried to remember exactly what he had seen from her.

The farmhouse was in the distance, at least half a mile away. At that distance, it had been difficult to see if anyone was there. His view was of the back side, and a cluster of trees prevented him from getting even a partial look at anything along the front of the house. It was dark and overcast, so that, too, had limited what he could see of the area. Then suddenly, he remembered the one thing that had occurred at the end of the vision: the light that flashed inside the farmhouse.

"You remember," the spirit said.

Scott and Shelley had remained silent as he talked to the spirit of Rachel's mother, but now he noticed they had lifted their heads from a meditative pose and both were staring at him. But he was trying to stick with replaying the memory of the vision.

"I remember," he said. "The flashes of light."

"But you still don't understand," the spirit said.

"It was just light. A few flashes from a distance. I can't see anything else. I don't know what there could be to understand."

"Everything you need to understand, she showed you."

"How?"

"She chose you—for a reason," the spirit said. *"She thought you could understand."*

Jason shook his head, then closed his eyes. The more he tried to remember every detail of the vision, the more he saw only the brief flashes of light in the farmhouse's upper windows.

What was she trying to show him? *Flash-flash ... flash ... flash-flash.*

What was he supposed to see? What was her secret?

He couldn't understand why she had chosen him. Was it because he vaguely resembled her husband? Had she somehow decided that he was capable of complex, abstract problem solving? Did she see his skills as an investigative auditor and think they could be applied to discovering her own secrets? Or was it nothing more than her seeing him spend late nights in the hospital room where she had died?

His heart raced as his mind sped through space and time, searching for answers to her haunting.

In his mind's eye, he saw the repeated flashes.

As a financial investigator with a talent for remembering specifics from endless ledgers of accounting transactions, he remembered details that others might forget. And now he saw every detail of the farmhouse vision—every tree, every flash from the farmhouse. And the more he replayed the vision, the more he came back to the rhythm of the flashes.

Flash-flash ... flash ... flash-flash.

Two flashes. Then a pause. One flash. Another pause. Then two more flashes.

He had never noticed the rhythm until now, but this could be what Annabel had wanted him to see the whole time. Not the first two flashes. Not the last two. It was the flash in the middle, between the two pauses—yes, the *two* pauses. He focused on that last pause, that last *delay* before the final two flashes. That was where the secret lived: in that one little last delay.

He ran through the sequence of events, matching it with everything he had read about that horrible night in the old newspaper articles.

And then, with sudden terror as real as the raging storm outside, he realized the discrepancy, that there was no way the facts from the articles could be accurate if there had been a delay between the third flash and the last two. If the facts in the articles were true, then the last three flashes should have happened without any delays between them. He then understood just what kind of enemy they were up against and just how much danger they were all in.

Flash-flash ... flash ... flash-flash.

Lies, lies, lies.

"Oh, my God," he said.

"Now you understand," the spirit said.

He said to Scott and Shelley, "We have to get to the farmhouse immediately."

With no warning, Rachel fell sideways and collapsed to the floor. In that instant, her mother's spirit seemed to vanish from the room. The thunder outside sounded like Armageddon. And in that moment, Jason realized that while he had been searching with the spirit for Annabel's secrets, something horrible had happened to Rachel.

78

The darkness receded enough for Rachel to find her way onto the farmhouse porch. The dark clouds blocked any light from the sky, but a swirl of nebular wave energy still surrounded the area. Countless particle flakes floated around the house as if drawn by the life force inside. They glowed as she stepped through them, as if her presence was a welcome guest in the cold, forgotten memory lost to death.

But then something changed. A vacuum of icy, stale air surrounded her as she reached the front door and stepped onto the very place where the man had stood only moments ago. The glowing white particles moved away from her as if by magnetic repulsion. The danger felt real now, present and threatening.

But she had been called to this place by the spirit of a murdered woman, so she advanced with purpose.

Trying to calm her thoughts, Rachel stepped into the farmhouse. Ice crystals lined the walls and the staircase to her left. The air itself seemed to be shaking or swirling, as if this very plane of existence were teetering in an unbalanced state that could shatter and collapse upon itself like a crumbling sand castle. She couldn't tell whether these visions of past events were powered by her mind or if they were from Annabel, but she concentrated hard to hold the connection. She feared that if she relaxed her concentration, she might lose this moment, never to return to this place again.

She saw the man standing in the center of the living room. As he moved closer, Annabel stepped back and knocked into the coffee table. Then she pointed toward the door. But the man didn't care. He stepped forward again and tried to grab her arm. Twisting wildly away from him, she lost her balance and fell onto the couch behind the coffee table.

As Rachel watched, the man's figure grew less blurry. As he came into focus, she saw brown and blue and shiny black leather around the waist and hips, and a long stripe down the trouser leg.

Gradually, the image became clearer, the blurred lines sharper, until specific details emerged that were unrecognizable only moments ago. She didn't understand at first. The man was in a uniform, with a radio and gun on his belt. He was moving toward Annabel, who was scrambling across the couch to get away from him.

Rachel stepped farther into the room, but there was nothing she could do. This was the past, and she was merely a witness to what had already happened.

The man grabbed Annabel by the ankle, but she kicked his hand away with her other foot. Then she grabbed the television remote by the armrest and threw it at his face, hitting him in the nose. This bought her just enough time to roll off the couch and jump to her feet. Then Annabel raced toward the front door. Rachel stepped back and flinched, expecting Annabel to run into her. But at the last second, Annabel turned past the front door and ran up the staircase, pulled herself around the top banister, and raced across the open hallway into the bedroom.

The uniformed officer snapped his head up, and in that moment Rachel saw his face. It was Officer Jeffrey Connelly, who had grown up in Williston and even attended the same church as Rachel's family. The same officer that had pulled Jason over for speeding on Tuesday and had caught him trespassing at this house on Thursday. She couldn't believe what she was witnessing. But as she watched the events unfold, she found herself horrified by the certainty that all this had happened the night of Annabel's murder.

Officer Connelly ran up the staircase. He seemed to be yelling something, but this memory had no sound. The trance world created a partition, as if flexible panes of plastic separated Rachel from the past that she witnessed. No clattering. No yelling. And no cries for help.

She walked up the stairs as the officer raced across the hallway and forced his way into the locked bedroom. Rachel moved slowly, sensing that time didn't matter in this place and that she would see everything that Annabel's spirit wanted her to witness. Anxiety built with each step up. Reaching the top of the stairs, she could see shadows of frantic movement coming from inside the bedroom's open doorway. She inched along the hall toward the room, now afraid of what was happening inside. Finally, she reached the doorway and saw Annabel struggling with Officer Connelly, beside a nightstand. A drawer was open, and a large silver revolver lay on the floor along with a spilled yellow cardboard box of ammunition.

Watching events unfold, Rachel was no longer shocked or terrified. She felt only pain and sorrow for Annabel as she understood what really happened to her on the night of her death.

The officer grabbed the silver revolver she had just loaded, and tossed the gun away. It bounced once and flipped on its side, clattering on the wood floor and coming to a rest by the adjoining bathroom door. Then he lifted her and threw her onto the bed. He pulled his own black pistol from its holster and put it on the floor next to the nightstand. Next, he jumped onto the bed and crawled on top of Annabel, holding her arms and kissing her neck as she tried to jerk away from him and contorted in silent screams.

And all Rachel could do was stand in the doorway and watch. But it wasn't natural to do nothing. She didn't understand the more advanced theories of space and time and other dimensions. What if time wasn't really the straightforward continuum that people thought? What if the past also existed in the future, and vice versa? What if superstring theory was true and people lived in several dimensions? What if Rachel could somehow do something—could affect something?

She had to try.

Rachel screamed out for him to stop. She screamed at the top of her lungs. Sound existed for her now, and she heard her screams rise above Annabel's. But it did no good. They couldn't hear her, because this had already happened.

Then she saw a sliver of light grow across the ceiling and swipe from one side of the room to the other. Then it vanished.

Her eyes fell back to the bed. Officer Connelly had crawled further upon Annabel and now let go of her arms as he reached in and ripped her shirt open. She screamed louder and flailed her arms wildly, hitting him on the ribs and the back of his head. But he tolerated these blows as he yanked her bra down to her waist. She screamed even louder as he buried his face in her breasts.

Rachel felt dizzy. She didn't know how much more of this she could watch.

Then suddenly, she saw a holographic object of light walk out of her. When it materialized as another man, she realized that it was someone from the past, who had rushed down the hallway and passed through her when entering the room. And then, seeing the man, she remembered the neighbor who had also been killed at the farmhouse that night.

The neighbor rushed to the bed, grabbed the officer by both shoulders, and pulled him off Annabel. As Officer Connelly tried to rise to his feet during the attack, he stumbled sideways and crashed to the floor near the front wall. In a panic, the neighbor reached for the black police pistol on the floor by the nightstand. Connelly lunged forward and picked up the silver revolver in the bathroom doorway. This only hastened the neighbor's movements as he picked up the officer's pistol and pointed it at him. And the officer aimed the revolver back at the neighbor.

A single shot cracked.

The neighbor was hit in the forehead and thrown backward onto the bed. In a panic, Annabel picked up the policeman's gun—which had dropped from the neighbor's hands next to her—and aimed it at Officer Connelly. This time, there was a brief hesitation before the second shot exploded in the room. Annabel's head jerked back and twisted her body around like a rag doll as she fell on her stomach across the bed, with a large wound to her temple.

Rachel stepped towards the bed, almost unable to believe what she had just witnessed. She could see the entry wound on the side of Annabel's temple. And although the woman was motionless and looked dead, Rachel knew that she was still alive, with a faint heartbeat and some brain activity, because she hadn't been pronounced dead until she was at the hospital, where her ghost had become trapped.

So this is your secret, she thought with deep sorrow as she imagined the pain that Annabel's spirit had felt for the past year, with no one understanding her pleas for help. *This is what really happened that night. You weren't unfaithful. And your husband didn't murder you.*

"*Lies, lies, lies,*" whispered a disembodied voice near her ear.

Rachel nodded. "So many lies."

As she looked down on the bed, Officer Connelly scrambled to his feet and took slow, clumsy steps forward until he stood right next to Rachel. She turned and glared at him sharply, feeling a sudden anger build in her. Madam Bovell had warned her of the dangers of projecting negative energy while inside a world within a trance state, but a fury rose in her that she couldn't control. Everything about this man and what he had done was despicable—the pain and suffering and injustice caused by his selfish, violent acts. He hadn't just stolen the lives of Annabel and her neighbor. He had stolen the lives of any family that Annabel may have ever had: future children and grandchildren and untold generations that would have lived from her. All those many lives had been erased from space and time by this selfish, violent man who, in this moment, was the very essence of evil.

And then her fury intensified to a poisonous hatred as she saw what Officer Connelly did next. Pulling some plastic gloves from a small pouch on his belt, he put them on and proceeded to change the murder scene. He removed the rest of Annabel's clothes until she was completely naked. Then he did the same to the neighbor. Then he placed their bodies half on top of each other, as if they had tried to scramble at the moment the two fake lovers were discovered and murdered by her husband.

Lies, lies, lies.

Rachel screamed in rage and swung a fist at Officer Connelly, but her arm passed through him as if he were nothing more than a hologram.

Then—after wiping it off—he placed the silver revolver back by the nightstand. Then he took his own black pistol from beside Annabel's body and slid it back into his holster. He turned back to the bed and stared blankly down on his twisted tableau of the bloodied, naked bodies. His face sagged as if he was finally taking in the reality of what he had done. He pressed a palm to his forehead, then slid it down over his eyes and groaned. He slouched forward as if about to vomit. He held this bent posture for half a minute, breathing deeply, then stood up and walked out of the room.

Rachel followed him.

He opened the door at the other end of the hallway, pulled the chair out from the rolltop desk, and positioned it next to the wall, in the shadows. Then, leaving the door open, he turned out the lights and sat in the chair as darkness swallowed him.

Rachel stood in front of him. She couldn't believe what she had witnessed, and found it quite impossible to control her hatred. Again she heard Madam Bovell's warning on the dangers of having strong negative emotions during a trance, but still the anger grew inside her. She couldn't suppress it any longer.

She screamed at him. Her face was only inches from his, but he didn't even flinch. He couldn't see or hear her, which only infuriated her more. She screamed again and swung her arms at him, but she may as well try to punch her own shadow.

As she lashed out at him, she felt a change in the atmosphere. She stepped back. Something bad was happening to the trance itself. She had lost control and projected too many negative emotions in this halfway realm.

She heard a loud pop, and a large crack opened on the wall above the staircase. Then it raced up the wall and across the ceiling. A thunderous boom rattled the house. Pictures flipped upside down. Others were torn from the walls by an unseen force. The trance was collapsing.

The staircase crumbled as if it was made of sand. Then the entire house fell away and vanished in a billion particles of dirt and dust. She was now somewhere else. No more bodies, no more Officer Connelly waiting to complete his murderous night. No more anything except just herself, floating in cosmic space with distant stars above and below in ever-shifting, fluctuating waves of matter. She heard moans and saw faces and creatures appearing and then disappearing, one after another, like a thousand slow-motion strobe lights. The only constant thing was the dark crimson cloud circling around her, first at a great distance, but quickly drawing closer.

Then she realized with horror what had happened.

She had lost control during the trance. She had revealed the power of her darker side, and that had attracted the darkest, evilest of all things.

Floating helplessly in the deep, subconscious space of psychic dimensional shifts, she watched in horror as this nebulous hell closed on her.

She could feel evil, powerful eyes watching her with malicious satisfaction from within the giant cloud. Despite everything that so many had done to protect her, the devil had still found her. And now she could do nothing but face the same fate that had destroyed her mother and grandmother before her.

She felt her position changing, moving as if pulled by gravity. And all she could do was scream as she was pulled into the violent crimson cloud.

79

Madam Bovell followed Rubin Heller toward the farmhouse. The heavy footsteps of his work boots crunched along the gravel drive. And his large, bulky frame cast a giant shadow on the front of the farmhouse as he moved in front of the bright round headlights of his old Ford pickup. Then the man stopped, as if sensing something was wrong. He stared long and hard at the police car parked to one side of the drive. Then he studied the car directly behind the police cruiser.

Madam Bovell was as confused as Rubin seemed to be. She knew he had murdered his wife after catching her in bed with their neighbor, but it made no sense that the police were here before he even arrived home. And that made her question all the facts about this night.

Rubin turned from the cars and stared up at the house. A light was on in the upper right windows, which Madam Bovell knew to be the bedroom where all three bodies had been found. Lights were also on throughout the first floor. Only the upper left side of the house remained in darkness.

He stared in silence as the house stared silently back at him.

"They're already dead," Madam Bovell said in a flash of realization. She looked again at the police car, then jerked her head back toward Rubin as he started toward the front porch. "My God," she said, following him. "It wasn't you."

The best she could do was follow close behind him as he stepped onto the porch and moved in slow, careful steps over the dark planks. He seemed to know exactly where to place his feet to avoid making the wood creak. But no precaution could have eliminated the soft squeak of the screen door as he pulled it just wide enough to turn the brass knob of the front door, push it open, and slip inside.

Madam Bovell passed through the door after it had closed. She saw Rubin glancing around the room in bewilderment, staring a long time at the couch and coffee table. A few items appeared to be knocked over or out of place, but he seemed to be noticing a much stronger disturbance.

Then he looked up the staircase. He placed a hand on the banister and took a step up. Then another slow step. Then another. He continued his slow ascent into the silent void.

Madam Bovell followed him, her mind racing with fear of what was about to happen. Knowing the importance of always maintaining a positive, healthy emotional state to protect the mind when in a trance, she tried hard to imagine the love that had lived in this farmhouse before this terrible night. Despite what she feared she was about to witness, she focused on what must have been beautiful memories in this place the first year of Annabel and Rubin's marriage.

Rubin reached the top step and turned right toward the light coming from the bedroom's open doorway.

Madam Bovell looked left at the top of the stairs, but the hallway in that direction was dim, leading to a pitch-black room. Turning back to the right, she followed Rubin toward the bedroom. She couldn't tell whether she had sped up or he had slowed down, but she met him just as he reached the doorway.

The horror of the scene struck her eyes just as Rubin's deep cry of pain struck her ears. She stood motionless in the doorway as he rushed across the room to the bed.

Crawling onto the bed, he held his wife in his arms. "Annie! Annie!"

His screams echoed through the room.

Madam Bovell covered her mouth and felt sorrow swelling up as she realized just how much Rubin had loved Annabel. "Oh, you poor souls," she whispered as the crime against them became clear. "You poor, poor souls."

She shook her head in grief. Then her grief turned to an almost unbearable pain when she saw Rubin now looking at the naked body of his neighbor, in the bed next to his wife's naked body. Confusion washed over his face, then anger.

She could see all the negative emotions colliding within his mind, like a blunt-force trauma to the soul. And then, as she watched him fall into the bleak labyrinth of loss and anger and confusion, she felt something behind her. Turning, she saw the pale face of a killer emerging from the shadows of the hallway. The man slunk to the doorway, passing right through Madam Bovell into the bedroom before she could react. Spinning around, she saw that he was a policeman. He raised a gun from his side and pointed it toward the bed.

"Hey!" the policeman yelled.

Rubin jerked his head around and jumped to his feet. He had only just made eye contact with the officer when a shot flashed from the gun. Rubin's head whipped back, and a red mass splattered on the wall behind him. His body fell motionless on the bed, next to Annabel.

Madam Bovell was nearly in shock. Despite the horrors, she still needed to maintain a positive state of mind. She reminded herself that everything she was seeing had happened a year ago, that this was the past, and that she must somehow keep a positive mental state to hold the trance steady.

After a long pause, the police officer moved to the nightstand, put on some gloves, and picked up a shiny revolver that was there. He placed it in Rubin's dead hand, and aimed it right at Madam Bovell. She felt a sudden fear and even gave a little yelp when he fired two shots. The bullets passed right through her and splintered the wood paneling near the top of the stairs behind her. He dropped the revolver to the floor.

Then the officer lifted the phone off its receiver and dialed 911. He waited until he heard an emergency dispatcher on the other end before he smacked the phone a few times on the nightstand, then hung it up without a word.

Then he waited.

And Madam Bovell, horrified, waited with him.

The phone rang with a loud, sudden trill that screamed throughout the farmhouse. The answering machine picked up, but no message was left.

Another thirty seconds of deathly silence.

Then the policeman's radio on the man's hip crackled to life. He had turned it on after hanging up the phone. "Jeffrey, this is dispatch. We have a possible ten-sixty-seven on County Road Sixteen. House number Eight-fifty-one. That's the Heller farmhouse. Over."

"Copy that," the officer said into the radio. "I'm about ten minutes out. I'll head over there now. See if you can reach them in case it's a false alarm."

"We tried a call-back. No answer."

"Copy that. I'll check in on them. Over and out."

The officer slid the radio back into his belt. Then he bent over the bed, carefully reached inside Rubin's jeans pocket, and removed a set of keys on a ring. Then he headed for the door.

This time, Madam Bovell stepped aside as he rushed past her. He raced down the staircase and out the front door. Looking back at the three bodies, the realization hit her that this wasn't just the revelation of the awful secret that Annabel and Rubin had taken to their graves. This was also a warning of an existing threat—a triple murder in which the true killer had gotten away with the horrendous crime and was still free in the small, unsuspecting community.

The three bodies were twisted in death. The neighbor's spirit had not been encountered since the murders, so Madam Bovell felt that in his choice to fight, he had either consciously or subconsciously accepted the possibility of death, which would have aided his transition to the afterlife. But Annabel and Rubin were different. Tied together by a deep, true love, one had been unable to move on after realizing that the other had become trapped. But which had become trapped? And why?

It seemed that not all secrets had been revealed.

An engine roared to life outside. Stepping to the bedroom's front window, she saw the two round headlights of the pickup truck moving closer to the house and stopping next to Annabel's Jeep and the neighbor's van. Then the policeman killed the engine and the lights, got out, and walked with cautious steps to his patrol car. A second later, the car came to life. But minutes passed with it just idling, puffing warm exhaust out into the cold night.

Turning away from the window, she moved back to the bodies. This time, she noticed something in the heap of corpses … a slight movement … a sign of life. Leaning in closer, she saw the barest twitch beneath Annabel's eyelids.

Madam Bovell tried to hold her emotions in check. "You poor child," she whispered. "You're fighting so hard to stay alive. You're stronger than all these men combined. You don't want your life to end—and certainly not like this. Remembered in shame when, in truth, all three of you could not have lived and died with more courage and honor. And the killer lives on and moves with impunity throughout the town you loved."

The engine went silent. A car door closed. Footsteps crunched across the gravel.

Rubin and the neighbor were dead, while Annabel still fought to hold on to the faint life force within her. This told Madam Bovell that Annabel was the one who had kept her sanity at the moment of death later in the hospital, and that just as she had the extraordinary strength to fight death now, that same strength would enable her to resist the afterlife so she could struggle in hope of finding and saving Rubin's twisted, lost soul.

But how had Annabel known that Rubin needed her help?

Almost as soon as she had thought the question, the answer began to emerge in front of her. Stepping back, she marveled at the sudden added horror on this devilish night. Although she knew the truth of this tragedy, she had never expected to witness the part of this story that now revealed itself. In her career, she had imagined a moment like this ten thousand times but had never dreamed she would actually bear witness to the transition of a soul.

A light-blue glow had risen above Rubin's body. A life force of rare, brief beauty that floated like a heavenly masterpiece before it darkened and twisted on itself like a withering flower. Then the dark form seemed somehow to sense her, though Madam Bovell couldn't understand how that could be, since she was only *witnessing* the past and wasn't there when it happened. Yet somehow, this spirit sensed her presence in this place and manifested a humanoid shape long enough for her to make out the faint outline of Rubin, moaning in torment above his corpse. Then its motions turned sporadic, jerky, in bursts around the room, through the walls and floor, and returning again, seeming to want to flee like an animal escaping a cage without knowing exactly where to go. A confusion seemed to set in, which Madam Bovell understood to be some version of Rubin's soul still trapped in a spiritual insanity. The spirit then looked down on its own body and the bodies of Annabel and the neighbor.

She felt dizzy and astounded. Having devoted most of her life to communicating with spirits, she was actually seeing the first moments of a soul newly released from the body yet unable to move beyond the world of bodies. For a spiritualist or a medium, few things could be as exciting as bearing witness to this, even though what she was seeing came from the past.

And then she realized why Rubin had become trapped. For just as Annabel had loved him so much that she couldn't abandon his lost soul, he, too, had loved her so much that his soul could not abandon her while she was still alive and suffering.

Bovell heard footsteps on the stairs, then in the hallway. The policeman had returned to the room, hovering in the doorway as if he still possessed some shred of humanity within him that was horrified by what he had done. But his presence sparked a sudden rage from Rubin's spirit as it turned away from the bodies and advanced on the man.

Oblivious to the supernatural goings-on, the policeman pulled his radio off his belt and yelled, "Shots fired! Shots fired! This is Officer Connelly! I'm at the Heller farmhouse. I need ambulances now! Three people are down! Two victims of gunshot wounds! They may be dead! One assailant who fired on me in the house! I returned fire and hit him—I think he's dead! I think they're all dead!"

As the policeman shouted into the radio, the dark figure of Rubin's spirit flickered as if its very composition was unstable. She could even see distortions of rage in the fading image of Rubin's face. In a sudden, rapid movement, the spirit shot through the air across the room to the officer and raged against him like a chained dog.

But the policeman just kept right on relaying his lie into the radio. This confirmed to Madam Bovell what she had already suspected: the ghost of Rubin Heller, while visible to her in this time slip trance, had been no more apparent to the policeman than were the radio waves that transmitted his lies across the cold, dark fields.

And as she watched the ghost rage with poisonous fury at its inability to exact revenge on this breathing demon of a man, her heart wept. She now understood all the layers of torment that had twisted Rubin's spirit into a ghost trapped by endlessly echoing emotions.

Then suddenly, everything around her started to shake. The policeman continued to relay lie after lie after lie into the radio. Rubin's enraged ghost continued to scream and moan and pound the air. The neighbor's spirit was almost certainly away from here and in a better place. And Annabel was fighting for her life, deep within the subconscious strength of her dying mind.

The world was crumbling around Madam Bovell. The time slip was tearing apart, and the trance world was now unstable and seemed about to collapse into itself. At any moment, she would be ripped from this paranormal in-between, and if she couldn't get back into a positive state of mind, she may never be able to return to her own realm with her mind intact.

She knelt on the wood floor even as it rattled beneath her. There wasn't much time. Trying desperately to take her mind off the tragic horror of the murders, she envisioned the community of Lily Dale in New York. As a runaway, she had eventually found this community of people that accepted her for who she was. If anything could hold her in a positive state of mind, it was the memory of the bond she had felt with the other mediums at Lily Dale. But even as she clung to these thoughts, she felt the room shaking violently all around her.

With the murders completed, the killer escaped with his lies, and the souls of two lovers were trapped in their separate prisons.

The policeman was the source of everything bad that had happened and everything that was still happening.

The trance was collapsing.

And no matter how hard she now tried, she just couldn't suppress the horrors of these murders with any of her happy memories.

The room began to slip away while the negative emotions remained tragically locked in her mind. She was helpless to escape the danger of being pulled out of a trance while bearing such negative energy in her psyche. Losing her sense of balance, she fell sideways and landed hard on the wood floor of the bedroom, but in which realm or dimension, she had no idea. She couldn't tell which reality she was in.

The trance was over, but she hadn't woken up. She was lost in the cosmos.

80

Rachel screamed as she fell through the abyss. Blood-red clouds swirled violently around her, as if she were being pulled into some sort of cosmic maelstrom. Millions of burning faces would randomly emerge from the thick crimson clouds encircling her. The tormented beings reached out to her with arms of burnt flesh and screamed in anguish before unseen forces suddenly hauled them back into the nebula. And as she fell through the infinitely deep eye of the nebula, she heard louder waves of screams from some hidden horrors being inflicted within the thick red mist around her.

Pulling her arms in, she clasped her hands to her head, pressing on her temples in a desperate attempt to refocus her mind. She tried to think of her breath, imagined her heart pumping blood to her lungs, then sending it on, oxygenated, through smaller and smaller vessels to the rest of her body. Even though she knew that only her spirit had been taken to this place and that her physical body was back at the hospital, comatose,

Madam Bovell had told her that the emotions of the spirit can be tamed by imagining oneself as still in a physical form.

And as she imagined her body relaxing, her spirit calmed. Her own screaming stopped, and she sensed the slowing of her descent.

She eventually stopped falling and now floated suspended in space. The unnerving screams from the burning faces were as loud as before, but her horror at them had turned to pity. As she stared into the massive nebula, the thickness in one area briefly thinned enough to give her a foggy partial glimpse into it. Within the swirling gases, she thought she saw the faint image of naked bodies covered in blood, swimming through the crimson clouds. They were crawling over and past each other in the vain hope of escaping countless clawed hands that slithered after them like hunting serpents. Her eyes stung from the heat, and the screams repeatedly stabbed her ears. Vapors thickened and covered over the brief window, hiding again the torture and madness that this cursed, evil place seemed to feed on.

And below her, somewhere in the distant fires of the abyss, was the thing that fed more than anything else here. She could sense it. And she knew that it, too, could sense her.

Looking down, she saw a massive brimming, dancing fury of flames curving into each other like flares erupting from the solar surface. And within the fire were two large eyes.

She closed her eyes and focused only on escape. This was a battle that both her mother and her grandmother had lost. Concentrating on the energy surrounding her, she willed herself to rise gradually away from the thing's eyes, still a great distance below her.

Voices screamed all around her, and she sensed more eyes turning to her from within the surrounding crimson vapor.

She pushed her thoughts harder and felt an acceleration in her ascent. Looking above her, she saw a tiny speck of white light in the vast distance, like a star shining from an unfathomably faraway galaxy. Other than the burning nebula surrounding her, and the fire floating in the abyss below her, this tiny benevolent glint above her was the only other light visible in this dark netherworld.

But even as she rose, the swirling fires below her grew, racing toward her like a mine explosion. And as it grew, it further illuminated the wall of clouds surrounding her. She could now see that the wall extended far below her, all the way to the bottom flames, as if she were in a giant silo a hundred yards across and hundreds of miles deep—all while somehow drifting in the infinite space of the cosmos.

Then suddenly, her ascent stopped, and the vapor cloud encircling her began to shrink in toward her.

She hung in limbo, no longer drifting toward the speck of warm light above, but also not falling into the pit of fire. She may as well be falling, though, because the fiery pit's flames were still rapidly rising toward her.

A massive image began to form on the enormous wall of fire she faced in the nebula. Light shifted and swirled inside the massive flame until images slowly formed of the body of the girl who had been killed and buried in the shallow, muddy grave. But then the girl's eyes opened wide, screaming silently for help before countless worms wriggled onto her with impossible speed and completely covered her.

Then the light swirled and the image changed, revealing a terror-stricken Shelley running alone down a dirt road at night, frantically waving her arms like a deranged woman.

"Shelley!" Rachel screamed.

But Shelley couldn't hear her.

The light swirled again, and a new image formed. Scott lay in a bathtub, wearing dark jeans and the same red flannel shirt he had when she last saw him in the hospital. He was facing up at her, motionless, with a growing pool of blood forming behind his head and slowly creeping in a long stream past a broken hand and into the dark drain.

"Scott! No—no! SCOTT!"

Her screams prompted a chorus of wailing from the tormented, burning souls around her. Her hands were shaking, and she was slowly dragging her nails along her forehead. How long had she been trapped here? What had happened to her friends? Why was no one helping Scott?"

The image began to blur and swirl.

"No! Scott! Plee-ee-ease!"

A new image showed Tommy and Jessica sitting in the corner of a room, crying and holding each other as a massive floor-to-ceiling fire crawled toward them from every direction. And a body lay close to them, prostate and burning half inside the wall of enclosing fire. It was Aaron.

"God, no! What happened? Please! Why?"

The image changed again to reveal Madam Bovell, dead, her skull gruesomely bashed in.

Rachel felt weak, drained, broken. She couldn't even scream anymore. It was too much. She had been shown too much. She looked around helplessly and listened to the surrounding wails and screams of the countless damned souls being tortured in the blood-red nebula of fire. She was alone and could feel a darkness growing inside her. An anger turning to hatred because of everything that had been taken from her. Everything: her mother and grandmother, her friends—soon her own life and maybe even her very soul. Tears of rage welled in her burning eyes as she glared back at the image of Madam Bovell's corpse.

You did this to me, she thought. *You did this to all of us.*

Her nails dug deeper into the skin on her forehead.

You were sent here to help me, to protect me, but instead you pushed us toward this. We should never have opened this window. YOU *did this.*

Clinching her fists, she needed to hit something. But floating in this hellscape, she had nothing to hit except herself. So she pounded her fists against her thighs in wild, impotent rage.

You said this wouldn't happen. You said the devil couldn't win unless ... She paused, an idea fighting its way up from the ashes of her memory. *Unless we listened to him* ... She stared at Madam Bovell's lifeless body. *Unless we allowed him to manipulate us* ... Her heart slowed, and her mind raced as she stared at the image of the woman's lifeless body. *Unless we allowed him to tempt or trick us into evil.* The images were all fabrications. Everything she had seen in the fire was unreal. It was all ...

"Lies," she said softly.

The image swirled and changed to show Dr. Graves, dead, his skull also bashed in. He lay near Madam Bovell's body.

"Lies," she said more strongly.

The image swirled and changed again to show Jason, lying on his stomach in a bathroom with his arms wrapped around the base of a toilet, and his head turned sideways on the tiles, with his skull bashed in.

"Lies!" she yelled. "Lies! Lies! Lies!"

The image blurred, then dimmed, then burned away and vanished in the flames. She stared at the fire, waiting for the next image to appear. But nothing materialized. Then, from the bottomless depths beneath her, came a low, growling laughter. And overlaying the distant booming laughter was the loud *thump-thump, thump-thump* of a beating heart—*her* heart, for nothing else in this place was truly alive.

And as the laughter grew, she began to understand why the sound of her frantic, throbbing heart was coming from all around her. She had heard this laughter before—not in any recognized memory or dream or nightmare, but from deep in her past, almost in another life, in a forgotten memory that must have been suppressed until this moment, when this low, chilling laughter awoke the distant nightmare of her life. Slowly, in her mind's eye, the laughter pulled together the suppressed pieces of the memory from the final moments of her mother's life, which had been hidden from her until now. Rachel was four years old, back in the farmhouse in Kansas, hiding in the kitchen, peeking through the keyhole, watching the twelve grownups sitting around the dining table, holding hands while her mother helped them talk to dead people.

It was not the first time. The dead loved her mother. So did the grownups. But no one loved her mother as much as Rachel did. They had a powerful bond, a connection. Sometimes, they could even read each other's thoughts and talk to each other without moving their mouths. And that was why Rachel was the first that night to feel something going horribly wrong. She sensed something bad touching her mother's mind. She felt her mother's concern. She pressed hard against the keyhole just before her mother stiffened in the chair, and the table began to shake. Then Rachel began to hear an ambient laughter—that low, sinister laughter that came from a single source that was all around her. And as that chilling laughter echoed through her mind, Rachel saw that the grownups' faces around the table looked frozen in fright at some strange word her mother was repeating to them. The laughter grew louder, then growled in the dark, then broke once more into evil laughter. Her mother turned suddenly at the table, making eye contact with her through the keyhole. In that instant, Rachel saw her mother come briefly out of the trance, seeing her. Then her mother stuck her hand out in the air, toward Rachel, which somehow made the monster's laughter stop tormenting Rachel. Then, with sad love in her eyes, she spoke to Rachel's mind and told her she loved her and would always be watching over her. Then she buckled and collapsed to the floor, dead. And little four-year-old Rachel screamed and screamed and screamed.

Her little-girl screams now echoed across the hellscape and the blood-crimson clouds and the spindly creatures swimming through the nebula of burning souls. She had returned from the newly released nightmare memory of her mother's death to the present nightmare of the final minutes of her own life.

The memory must have been buried deep in her mind, because when the laughter below her flooded the memory back into her thoughts, it drained nearly all her energy. Had her mother done something to her to block the memory, to protect her from the pain? To hide her from the devil's awareness?

Now, as she tried to gather her remaining strength to face this sum and source of all evil, she could hear that same sinister laughter rising up, closer to her now. And as before, the laughter morphed into a growl—that same monster in the dark from the night her mother died. Thirteen years later, it had found her again.

And the two large eyes within those flames were locked on to her.

This was the pivotal moment she had feared since discovering the secrets of her ancestry. Unable to escape, she must fight the same battle that had killed both her mother and her grandmother.

She rotated to face this evil. The eyes glared with triumphant fury as they raced up this hellscape shaft toward her. The lying tongue of Lucifer had told the truth about one thing: He was going to destroy her. He was rushing toward her with terrifying speed. She had only seconds before his fires would enwrap her in death and damnation.

Rachel pressed her thumbs and fingers to her temples and tried to imagine everyone she had ever loved—even the lives of ancestors she had never known but who had given her life through their own struggles and love for each other. And she thought of how much she loved the world and the entire concept of the human race with all its cultures and triumphs and beauty.

Then she took that powerful cumulative feeling of love, imagined it as one ball of energy at the forefront of her mind, and gathered it into a bright white light. It glowed and expanded to form a sphere encompassing her in a clear cocoon of energy. She held her focus on the energy field as the rising flames hit her cocoon and swarmed around its surface without penetrating it. She felt the force trying to push in on the protective sphere, but she fought with all her power to keep it intact.

The translucent walls of the sphere allowed her to see a shift in the thing's fiery form. The molten mass condensed into a giant beast, which let out a deafening screech. Then the neck grew longer, then thickened as bones pushed out of it to form hundreds of little spikes. A deep, evil laugh bellowed from the scarred, bulky face. Gnarled hands clawed at the sphere, first with just a few swipes, then frantically, like a wild animal excited to tear into the flesh of trapped prey.

And as the beast clawed furiously, Rachel could feel the protective sphere weakening.

Though she didn't want to die, it was easy to accept that reality when face-to-face with this evil. But as the sphere continued to weaken, she knew she must do one last thing before she died. Her friends didn't know the truth about the killer. They had no idea how much danger they were in at the farmhouse. And despite the images she had been shown, she believed in her heart that her friends were still alive and that they could still be saved. If she diverted strength from her shield to sending them one last powerful communication through space and time before she died, she just might be able to warn them and save their lives.

She moved her hands away from her temples and extended them as far away from her core as she could, as if they had become antennas for transmitting the most important psychic message of her life.

Even as the beast bore down on the sphere, she searched past the flames and the infinite cylindrical wall of hidden horrors. She searched through the vacuum of space and ripped through the fabric to other dimensions, until she sensed a path, through some sort of psychic wormhole. It was as close to her physical body and friends in North Dakota as she was likely to find.

She gave all the energy she had left to send the message, praying the warning would reach her friends in time to save their lives. The message exploded from her mind with a powerful stream of radiance.

"No, no, no. We were wrong. Run. It's Officer Connelly. Officer Connelly killed them all. Get out of the farmhouse. Run!" But just as she sent it, she feared she had missed her target, that her message had reached her friends only after getting lost in another time dimension. For she realized she had already heard this message, from her future self, five days ago. It had come over the high school PA system as a garbled *"No, no, no ... Run Off Con ... Off Con ... Run!"*

At the time, none of them had realized just how important the garbled message had been. And now it was too late.

Too drained of energy to attempt another message, she felt the sphere collapsing without her power to maintain it. And the beast's laughter grew louder, more boisterous, more bellicose. The red eyes were growing larger. The claws now made a continuous deafening screech against her cracking energy shield, and from behind the large, jagged teeth poured a rancid, toxic breath, which started to seep into her weakening protective bubble.

Alone and exhausted, she had no screams left to give. She strained silently with what little strength she had left, turning her head away from the red eyes, trying to picture the faces of loved ones so that she might die in their presence instead of in this inferno of horror. But as hard as she tried, she could no longer visualize anything good in this demonic place.

As the sphere finally collapsed and the beast closed in, her weakened gaze saw a sudden brightening of the distant white star so far above her. It was as if a small pinprick in the black void had been ripped open and was blasting warm, blue rays into this pit of torment.

Rachel didn't fully understand what she was seeing, but it was so beautiful, it made her eyes tear up with joy.

The beast roared with acrid breath that burned away at the weakening white shield around her. Death was coming, and in this moment, she was prepared to embrace it. With teary eyes, her head fell back and she gazed at the light with wonder and marvel. Amid her surroundings of hate and chaos and suffering, her mind centered on the warm white light above. Much larger now, it looked less like a distant star and more like the beam of a lighthouse that had locked on to her in the darkness. And she must be turning delusional, because she thought she heard a harmonic tone in the air, then the voices of singing as if from a church choir, then harps. Then the light exploded with brilliance as trumpets and clarions blasted through the vacuum of space.

The beast reared back and screamed at the blast of light and sound from above. The things hidden inside the surrounding nebula shrieked and whimpered and went silent as if paralyzed by shock. The beast's claws released Rachel's sphere and swiped blindly at the dazzling stream of light. And as the beast raged against the light, Rachel felt two soft hands grab her wrists and pull her out of her protective sphere and up through the flood of white particles that swirled like snowflakes in a blizzard. Rising faster and faster through the cool, sparkling light, she still felt weak and wasn't completely sure what was happening, but as she turned her head sideways and glanced down, she saw the raging red pits of the nebula, now far below her. So much distance lay between them that the gigantic, monstrous beast now looked no bigger than her thumb. The beast was no longer focused on her but instead continued to rage against the all-powerful beam of light.

She tried to look up at the source of the majestic power, but her eyes could penetrate no more than a few feet above her. However, she could see the two hands pulling her by the wrists. And when she followed those hands upward, she saw what looked like two angelic beings pulling her in rapid flight up through the penetrating, protective light. She was weak, but her mind could still see and comprehend the miracle that was happening to her. Blinking the tears from her eyes, she looked closer at the angelic beings. They were the faces of her mother and grandmother.

She would have cried if she were not already breathless. This one pure moment of love in her darkest hour made up for an entire childhood of feeling alone in the world, wondering whether she truly belonged to anything, whether she was ever truly loved.

Their expressions were serious, and she could only imagine how they had discovered the peril she was in, and the struggle they must have endured to rally help from the great light and face the devil to save her.

They pulled her up into the seemingly endless light so fast that she could no longer see anything below her except the vibrant white beam of energy. A warmth spread through her as they rejuvenated her. After what seemed an eternity, they slowed their ascent and drifted outside the vibrant beam. Below her were millions of little white dots like distant stars, most of them clustered in swirling galaxies. And suddenly, everything made sense to her. The very nature of existence, and all the mysteries of its meaning, became clear in a realization that must happen to all souls when they transcended through death.

She looked above her and saw a massive light-blue nebula floating far above her, like a ceiling extending farther than she could see. Then its colors changed as waves of green washed through it. Then yellow and a warm orange. Then blue again. The lights and colors were washing and flowing and dancing in the slow, ecstatic motion, like a massive ocean reef full of life.

And she knew that this was the place where all souls wanted to go after transcending death. And she felt its warmth, its ecstasy, its joy and peace. And she was drawn to it, ready to enter this promised realm.

But then, to her surprise, the soft hands let her wrists go, and she drifted away from her mother and grandmother and the paradise waiting above them. She didn't understand. Their faces were warm, caring, nurturing. But they were letting her go. With their love, they were giving her the life they had been denied.

And she would live it with all the power and passion they had passed down to her. She would use it to love and do right and make a difference in people's lives. She would help the suffering understand the hope that pervaded the universe. She would help guide them out of the trappings of pain and suffering, help bridge the gaps between the souls of the living and the dead. She promised this to her mother and grandmother—not with words, but with the emotions softening her face, and the thoughts beaming between them. And along her journey, she would always know how to communicate with them if she needed to. And they would always be with her whenever she needed their help.

She kept drifting farther away, falling gently. She could barely make out their faces, as their figures receded in the expanding vastness of paradise.

Then she sensed something below her. Turning her head down, she saw yellow light coming from a rectangular opening in space. A doorway home. She was gravitating toward it, only seconds away from being pulled inside.

Looking back at her distant mother and grandmother, she reached out her hand toward them in a gesture of longing, wistful goodbye.

And they reached out their hands in return.

Then, with tears in her eyes, she fell into the blinding yellow light.

81

Madam Bovell was somehow aware that she had become lost within the deep recesses of her subconscious. It was something that, by its very definition, should have been impossible to know. Yet much of her life had been filled with experiences that many people believed impossible, so if her mind was telling her that she had become trapped within her own psyche, then she must try to find some way to escape.

Maybe this was something like being in a coma. If so, then she knew there was hope, for people sometimes mysteriously woke from comas.

She tried to remember what had happened to her before this moment. At first, there was nothing, and she was truly terrified. Then it all came back, blasting her like waves of sound: the group séance at the farmhouse, the trance, following Rubin Heller into the bedroom to discover his murdered wife, then witnessing his murder, the sorrow of Annabel, the fury of Rubin, and the evil of the killer. Then the destabilizing trance, her failed attempt to calm her psyche, then the collapsing of the trance before she could get out.

She drifted in a world of darkness and couldn't wake up. But with each new recollection, a layer of light grew from the void surrounding her. Eventually, she found herself standing on a firm, reflective surface, with walls of rainbows around her. It was a strange, otherworldly place of optical illusions amplified by long, spinning mirrors that floated like balloons. Bolts of electricity shot in mesmerizing slow motion from mirror to mirror, to mirror, with the violent randomness of lightning strikes in a massive storm.

Looking around her, she had the unsettling feeling of someone trapped for too long in a carnival fun house. She moved forward until she hit the strange barrier. Pressing against it, she felt the smooth, cold moisture give a little before resisting her force. She had the horrifying idea that she was physically trapped in a confined space.

She stepped back and tried another direction, only to meet a similar barrier. Again and again she tried, and again and again she failed to find a way out.

Then, just as she was losing hope, she heard a voice. She turned and spun and searched for the source of the unknown ambient voice. Mirrors reflected light from other mirrors in a visual complexity impossible to decipher.

Then, finally, she saw something. An opening in one of the mirrors looked like a ball of white light surrounded by a ring of fire. There was a slight distortion to the image, so she wasn't seeing it in perfect focus. But what struck her was that no other mirror was reflecting the image within this mirror.

As she stepped toward it, the voice became more decipherable. It sounded weak, almost in pain. Only some of the words were audible. She heard *"No ..."* followed by moaning. *"Officer ... Connelly ... Run!"*

It was a desperate message, as if weakly murmured in the seconds before death. Then it came again, softly, but with crystal clarity. *"We were wrong ... Officer Connelly killed them all ... Run!"*

Madam Bovell's heart leaped. It was Rachel's voice. After hearing that last reiteration of the message, she was certain. Somehow, Rachel had sent her this message telepathically and, in the process, was showing her how to escape—though Rachel couldn't have known that Bovell was in trouble.

She got as close to the mirror as possible. But there was no longer any trace of her reflection. It had changed. This mirror was no longer a mirror. It had turned into something else—a doorway, perhaps—but all she saw was the distant white light surrounded by fire, which seemed the source of Rachel's message.

She placed her hand into the gateway and watched it vanish as it crossed the plane. Then, without warning, something grabbed her wrist and pulled her into whatever awaited on the other side.

82

Dr. Graves rushed to Madam Bovell after she fell. The farmhouse shook so violently, he feared that it might collapse. He slid a hand between her head and the rattling planks. His other hand gently slapped her cheeks, then lifted an eyelid to find a dull, motionless stare.

"Come back to us," he said. "This instant!" He raised his hand in front of her face, like the stage magician he had once been. "Now!" he said, with a loud snap of his fingers. "Now!" *Snap.* "Now!" *Snap, snap.*

But her eyes didn't open.

"We really should get out of here," Tommy said over the noise.

"I agree," Jessica yelled.

"Is it okay to move her?" Aaron asked.

"I don't know," Dr. Graves replied. "It's better if we don't— not while she's still in a trance."

"It's getting pretty dicey in here," Tommy shouted just before a slapping floorboard knocked him off balance and sent him stumbling against the wall. A crack raced diagonally up the wall. "Holy bejeebers!"

"You all should go," the professor yelled.

He felt a sharp stab that made him wince. And surrounding the pain in his head, a shaking female voice said, *"Officer Connelly killed them all. Run!"*

Then both the pain and the voice stopped.

He clasped his forehead with his free hand and blinked. The room was still shaking. He looked around him. All the others were now on their hands and knees as if they, too, had felt the stab of pain.

"Oh, God," Jessica muttered.

"What the hell was that?" Tommy gasped.

"You felt it, too?" Aaron asked. "You *heard* that?"

"It was Rachel," Jessica said.

"Yeah," Aaron agreed. "Something about Officer Connelly killing ..."

"'Officer Connelly killed them all,'" Dr. Graves repeated. "'Run!' That's what she said."

"Yeah," Jessica said. "That's what I heard, too ... But I'm sure I just heard it in my head."

"Me, too," Tommy said.

"We all did," Dr. Graves said. "She spoke to each of us telepathically—all of us, separately but at once. What does it mean? Who is Officer Connelly?"

"A cop in town," Aaron said.

"It's actually someone from around here?" the professor said, aghast.

"Yeah," Jessica said. "We all know of him."

"Is he trouble?"

"No, he's just a cop."

The professor was trying to think, but the house seemed to be growing more violent. He wished they had received a longer message from Rachel. He could only assume that her message came from some revelation she had received while in her trance—perhaps the same trance connection that had trapped Madam Bovell.

He bent over Madam Bovell and yelled, "Wake up now!" *Snap.* "Now!" *Snap.*

Madam Bovell reached her arm up. He grabbed her hand, hoping the touch might bring her out of the trance. She gasped and sat upright with a jolt of energy as if she were possessed.

"Whoa!" Tommy breathed.

"You okay?" Dr. Graves asked her.

"We're in a lot of danger," she mumbled, still dazed. "We have to leave here now!"

"We are!"

"Now!" she urged. "Everyone was wrong! He killed all three of them right here. I saw him! Some policeman! We need to call the FBI or somebody. But first, we have to get out of here."

"All right," said Dr. Graves. "Just take a breath. We're getting out of here right now."

He grabbed her under both arms and helped her to her feet.

"Oh, no," Madam Bovell said, looking around the room. She seemed only now to notice the shaking walls and slapping floorboards, and cracks forming in the ceiling. "How long has this been happening?"

"Two or three minutes," Dr. Graves said.

"Rubin is doing this because he's *here.*"

"We know he's here."

"No," Madam Bovell said. "Rubin's doing this because *the policeman* is here."

"Where here?"

"I don't know. Somewhere on the property. Maybe even inside the house."

Dr. Graves felt a lump of fear in his gut. He rushed to the window and gasped at the dark shape of a police cruiser parked behind their vehicle in the driveway.

"We're in trouble," he said, jerking his head back toward the others. "He's here!"

83

Rachel's eyes opened. She had returned from the brink of hell and the threshold of heaven and was now back in the hospital, lying on the floor of the old emergency room, exactly where Annabel had died. At least, she thought it had been heaven and hell, but she wasn't sure. Had the trance really transported her? Or was it all just her own subconscious imagination? She may never know.

But that didn't matter right now. She was back in the hospital, with Jason and Scott and Shelley looking at her.

"Are you okay?" Jason asked. "You were gone a long time."

"How long?"

"The trance lasted maybe forty minutes, but then it broke and you collapsed for another forty minutes. Maybe longer. And it was really strange. A few times, you stopped breathing. But you told us earlier that no matter what happened, we weren't to disturb you or call for help during the séance, so we just waited."

"Have you heard from the others?"

Jason shook his head. "All our phones are still off and in the other room. We wanted as few signals as possible until you returned. Their phones were probably off, too."

"They're in danger if they're still at the farmhouse. We need to get there asap."

"Get the phones," he said to Shelley.

As she scurried out of the conference room and down the hallway, Jason and Scott helped Rachel to her feet.

"You sure you're all right?" Scott asked.

She wrapped her arms around him and clung to him. It was as if the question had pierced some invisible armor and broken down defenses she had built up around herself.

She held Scott and wept for what felt like a long time.

Shelley rushed back into the room with the cell phones and started passing them out. Rachel wiped her eyes and then carefully took the silk cloth from under the crystal hemisphere, unfolded it, and used it to wrap up the crystal. Then she carried it to her backpack in the corner of the room, put it inside, and slipped her arms through the straps.

"Let's go," she said.

Together, they all raced down the steps and out of the old hospital wing. Jogging across the dark lawn and parking lot, they piled into Scott's Jeep. They were a twenty-minute drive from the farmhouse.

84

"What did you say?" Madam Bovell asked, praying she had heard him wrong.

Dr. Graves stepped away from the window. "I said he's here!"

And as he spoke the words, she saw the long face of the policeman as he stepped out of the hallway shadows, just as he had done in her trance, before murdering Rubin. One hand was pressed against the doorjamb to brace against the farmhouse's tremors, while the other hand held a black pistol.

Madam Bovell was sick with horror to be facing the cop again. The house was now shaking so hard, she could barely keep her footing. Everyone else seemed to be holding on to something to keep balance. She was still light-headed from the trance, and the room seemed to be spinning. She felt Rubin's presence more than ever, and for the first time she understood his rage. For here was the man who had murdered his wife, standing in the same doorway from which he had killed Rubin, too, holding the same murder weapon.

"Stop!" Madam Bovell screamed at Officer Connelly. "Stop, you devil! Just stop!"

The man glared at her as if she, not he, were the devil. And in that moment, she read his gleaming dark eyes as if telepathically receiving information from his mind. And what she saw was pure hatred.

"Stop this!" she insisted.

"You did this, you evil witch!" Officer Connelly yelled, his face contorting with rage. "I've been watching! The past was dead! All of you should have stopped! Now you'll all burn!"

Madam Bovell tried to take a step back, but her heel caught on a loose floorboard and she banged into the wall. This drew Connelly's shaky aim to her alone, and Aaron seized the moment to rush the man. But Connelly turned and cracked him on the nose with the butt of the pistol. Aaron collapsed, moaning, with both hands cupped over his face.

The action had spurred something in Dr. Graves, too. He stepped toward Connelly from the opposite side of Aaron. But the cop spun around, smacked the professor across the face with the pistol, then brought the gun down hard on the back of his head. Dr. Graves dropped to the floor.

"Stop it!" Madam Bovell screamed.

New cracks ran up the wall.

Tommy started to move but stopped when Connelly pointed the gun at his chest.

"No more!" Connelly yelled. "No more!" And in his rage, he pointed the gun above Tommy's head and fired a shot.

At that instant, the vibrations throughout the farmhouse gave one last, terrifying jolt. In that moment, Madam Bovell caught a brief flash of blue light from the crystal, as if some force had just struck it. Then, just as suddenly, the room stopped shaking, the cracks in the wall stopped expanding, and the floorboards ceased their rattling. Then a blue crystal mist emanated from the walls and floorboards and began a slow whirling motion, like a miniature cyclone. Madam Bovell lost sight of everyone else in the room as she marveled at this metaphysical transformation, recognizing it as the manifestation of Rubin's tormented spirit. Something had happened to the spirit when the gun went off. It almost seemed as though the spirit had a traumatic reaction, as if the gunshot triggered the memory of being shot and killed right here last year.

She waited for the spirit to explode like an atomic bomb, but instead the circling blue mist just slowed and contracted inward. Then she realized that it was spinning directly above the gleaming hemisphere of quartz, still in the center of the room. There must be a lingering connection between the spirit and the energy of the crystal—something initiated by the séance and time-slip trance—which was now magnified by Officer Connelly's raging presence.

And perhaps it was all too much for Rubin's tortured spirit. Maybe the soul of this ghost had suffered as much as it could bear. Perhaps the officer's gunshot had so mirrored the moment of his own murder that it finally broke Rubin's traumatized, unstable soul.

Whatever was happening to Rubin's spirit, the gunshot had paralyzed its energy, and the crystal hemisphere was acting as some sort of mystical attractive force. The mist slowed and sank and slid onto the surface of the crystal. Then the crystal seemed to absorb it, and gave one last flash of blue light before going dark.

The flashlights turned on and blazed their beams throughout the room. Now that the farmhouse had stopped shaking, every minute sound could be heard: Jessica's crying, Tommy's heavy breathing, the soft moans from Aaron and Dr. Graves, and the heavy, clomping footsteps of Officer Connelly in the doorway. She watched silently as the man held the flashlight in one hand while handcuffing Dr. Graves to the old heater along the wall. Then he dragged Tommy and Aaron to separate steam pipes that ran from the heater, and quickly tied them up with a narrow rope he pulled from a duffel bag.

Jessica stood, rushed to pick up the crystal hemisphere, and charged at the officer with it raised high in both hands. Connelly turned just in time to parry her blow and knock her to the floor.

Madam Bovell knew that their only hope was for her to get outside to the Yukon, where they had left all their cell phones. Then, if she was fast, she could bang out a 911 call.

She sprang up and raced through the open door, into the hallway. In the corner of her eye, she saw the flashlight whip around and lock on to her. A hand grabbed at her from the darkness. Ducking and jerking sideways, she barely avoided it and pelted down the hallway.

She heard movement behind her and knew she was in trouble. Just as she neared the turn to go down the stairs, something hit her from behind, and she crashed to the floor. A heavy weight was on her. She tried to crawl forward, to wiggle free, but it was no use. He pushed himself up off her, then grabbed both her ankles and dragged her back toward the room while she screamed for help.

85

The Jeep bounced along the gravel road through the moonlit countryside.

"Turn up here," Rachel commanded, spotting a path half-hidden by tall grass.

"Where?" he asked, slowing.

"Here!"

Scott braked and slid twenty feet to a stop. Gravel dust washed over them and reflected in the headlights. He reversed through their dust and stopped beside the path's entrance.

"It's just a field road," Scott said.

"It heads in the direction of the land behind the farmhouse," Rachel said.

"You don't want to enter by the front?" Jason asked. "You think he's there!"

"I sense fear from Madam Bovell," Rachel replied. "It's weak. We're still far away, but I can sense something's wrong."

"You don't know it's the cop. It could be because of Rubin."

"She wouldn't be afraid of a spirit. Not like this."

"Then we should call the police," Shelley said.

"Officer Connelly *is* the police," Scott said.

"Not the only one in Williston. There are more than a dozen officers in the department."

"She's right," Jason said. "We have to call someone."

Shelley held down a button on her phone and then swiped the screen to make an emergency call without waiting for anyone else's approval. She put the cell to her ear and waited. After a few seconds, she lowered it and stared at the screen. "It didn't go through. I lost the signal."

"Me, too," Jason said, looking at his phone.

"Yeah, I've got nothing," Scott said.

"Our phones worked here the other night," Shelley said.

"He's blocking them," Rachel said quietly, her worst fears returning to her.

"How the hell could Officer Connelly do that?" Scott asked.

"Not him," Rachel said, unsure how to explain her intuition.

She glanced at the orange display on the Jeep's console. It was a quarter to midnight.

"We need to go down this path through the field, and we need to do it now. We don't have time to go for help. I think Connelly's going to kill them all when the clock strikes midnight."

Scott popped the Jeep into first gear, kicking up gravel as it lurched off the country road and onto the faint double track cutting into the field.

"How can he kill all of them?" Scott asked. "He could never cover that up."

"I think he feels he doesn't have a choice," Rachel said. "Not anymore. And he managed to cover up his triple murder a year ago, and he's gotten away with the other killings since then."

"He killed the girl?" Scott asked.

"Yes," Rachel said. "And many other people in the past year—migrant workers and homeless drifters. I sensed their deaths on him during the trance."

"The people that have been vanishing from this town," Jason said in a shaky voice.

"That's a monster," Scott said.

"Why midnight?" Jason asked.

"He's superstitious, maybe. I don't know. I just feel like something really bad is going to happen right at midnight."

The Jeep's console read 11:46. Rachel closed her eyes and looked out across the surrounding field. But nothing was out there. Only emptiness. She couldn't even find Madam Bovell anymore. Something was blocking her ability to receive nearby psychic energy.

The Jeep bounced on its stiff shocks as it rumbled over grates protecting part of an irrigation system. Corn stubble lined both sides of the path, giving only sporadic glimpses of the surrounding fields.

The path sloped up, and soon they were on a long rise that gave them their best view yet of the entire field. A quarter mile to their right, on the other side of the field, was the sparsely lit farmhouse.

"Turn off the headlights and stop here," Rachel said.

Scott killed the lights and hit the brakes.

They all got out and stood on the path, looking out over the field, at the back of the farmhouse. A light was coming from a few of the windows on the left side of the second floor, which was the master bedroom and where the group would have held their séance. The rest of the house was dark.

"I've seen this before," Jason said.

"What do you mean?" Rachel asked.

"From this angle, from this position, way out in this field, just like now. With those two windows lit and all the others dark. In the vision she gave me, Annabel showed me the farmhouse from this vantage point. I thought she was showing me the past—the murders—but she chose this unique vantage point, maybe knowing I would one day be standing right here. Maybe she was showing me the future at the same time she was showing me the past."

"Time dimensions don't exist for spirits the same way they do for us," Rachel said. "Did she show you anything about this moment that can help us?"

"When the vision faded, the last part that vanished was the top left portion of the house. There was even a tint of red before it vanished."

"So he's there," Rachel said, believing she understood the meaning.

"We have ten minutes until midnight," Scott warned.

"Do we have a plan?" Shelley asked.

"If Officer Connelly's got the others in that room, maybe we could just rush him," Scott said. "Strength in numbers."

"He'll be armed," Jason said. "We won't."

"We could distract him from outside," Shelley said. "Maybe get him to look out the front window so his back is to the door."

"That might work," Rachel said. "I could even try to hold him with my mind, maybe confuse him briefly—maybe giving you an extra few seconds to overcome him."

Scott nodded. "We can do this, right?" he asked Jason.

"Yeah. Because if we fail, he'll kill us all."

They ran out into the field, galumphing awkwardly over the mushy soil. A chilly breeze picked up strength as midnight approached. The four had spread out as they ran, like a hunting party stretching their front as they advanced through the field. The sounds of footfalls and snapping cornstalks created an unnerving dissonance that sharpened Rachel's anxiety. After a minute, they had covered a third of the distance to the farmhouse.

As Rachel ran, the images of her friends, dead, flashed back through her mind. Jason said he had been shown this future moment days ago. Maybe her vision had been the future, too. But before she had time to consider what that meant, a dry corn leaf gave her cheek a stinging cut. Then her eyes caught the one light in the farmhouse going out in the top left window. Whatever her future held, it was waiting for her in that room.

"Seven minutes till midnight," Scott wheezed, running beside her.

She turned to see him while they kept running through the dead stalks, but all she saw was his dead eyes staring up at her from a bathtub while blood ran from the back of his head down the length of the tub and into the drain.

They were nearing the end of the field. She didn't know what to believe about the visions, but there was no time left to ponder. If they didn't act now, their friends would die in that farmhouse at midnight. But she just couldn't get the images out of her head.

"Stay away from the bathrooms," she said between breaths.

"What?" Scott asked.

"I saw all of us dead in a vision. You were in a bathtub. I don't think it's real, but please just stay away from bathrooms when you're in that house."

"I'll try," he panted.

Finally leaving the field, they rushed through the backyard and darted right, around the corner of the farmhouse. Sprinting through a patch of a dozen tall trees, they reached the front porch.

"Go in now," Rachel told the guys. "Real quiet. We'll get his attention and hold it as long as we can."

Jason and Scott sneaked through the front door while the girls rushed off the porch and into the front drive.

"How do we do this?" Shelley asked.

Rachel looked around and stopped when her gaze landed on the police car. "You honk the horn, and I'll stand here and try to hold him when he looks out the window and sees me."

"*Hold* him?"

"If I can see inside his mind and push hard enough, I might be able to hold him paralyzed for a few seconds."

"Why can't you just do that now? You have to actually make eye contact with him?"

"Something's blocking me," Rachel said. "I can barely sense his conscience right now. Normally, it wouldn't be this hard, but something here is interfering with me. I think I can get through to him if we're looking at each other."

"If you're wrong, he might shoot you on the spot."

Lightning flashed across the sky, followed by a powerful thunderclap that shook the air around them. The full moon was still high in the sky, but black clouds would soon cover it.

"Honk the horn," Rachel said over the building wind. "It's almost midnight. Do it NOW!"

Shelley darted around the police car, opened the door, and got in. Her wide eyes made contact with Rachel as if needing one last reassurance before she drew the monster's attention.

Rachel nodded.

With her teeth clenched, Shelley pushed both hands down on the horn. It sounded impossibly loud.

Rachel looked up at the second-floor windows. Suddenly, the dim lighting in the room blinked out. Her chest tightened in panic. She had never faced evil in the flesh, and because those she loved were in danger, she found this moment every bit as terrifying as facing the devil itself. There was movement against the black windowpane. The outline of a large man had half-appeared from the shadows. And that man was looking directly at her.

She couldn't make out his face, but she recognized Officer Connelly's large head and imposing broad shoulders.

She touched her fingertips to her temples and unleashed the full force of her power to invade his mind. His head jerked back slightly, then froze. And in those few seconds, she saw the tragedy of his poisoned mind: his undeclared fondness for Annabel in high school, the heartbreak of a misplaced crush as he watched her fall in love with Rubin, the frustration over missing his chance, the bitter disappointments and loneliness of the years that followed. The brotherhood of the police force had given him a brief respite from his hidden emotional failures. He had found a satisfying drive in his life, and that had fixed everything—at least, for a while. But then, after years of lying dormant, his memories and feelings for Annabel had risen up inside him, confusing him, distracting him, growing like a cancer, gaining a strength that he couldn't ignore, darkening until it had metamorphosed into a burning lust that drove him insane and turned his heart toward selfishness and hatred. And surrounding that madness was the tormenting temptation offered by something that Rachel hadn't expected to discover in him— not something so much as some*one:* the prince of darkness and lies, the ultimate poisoner of souls. She couldn't see the devil, but she could sense the aftermath of his work. Within the poisonous rot of Officer Connelly's mind, she could trace the damage that Lucifer had done with his toxic, silver-tongued lies. He had poisoned this man's soul with layers of evil until he had become truly lost. And then she discovered within Officer Connelly the sudden, horrifying truth: all of it was because of *her.*

She fell to her knees in the driveway, still maintaining her lock on Connelly. She felt as if a semi were parked on her chest. She was at fault. All these deaths and twisted souls and tormented spirits—it was all because of her. She was the prize the devil had targeted since before she was born. He had tried with her grandmother and mother, but with their deaths she had been removed from the spiritualist community and ended up in North Dakota, far from Stull, Kansas—the place that would have pulled her toward her mediumistic ancestry. So Lucifer had contrived plans to awaken her natural abilities by tempting and poisoning and corrupting Officer Connelly into committing murders. And those killings would create tormented souls trapped and crying out for justice across the spiritual wavelengths that would have been magnified in Rachel's dreams as she came of age with her mediumistic powers.

Everything that had happened—all of it—had been an elaborate plot by Lucifer to bring her gifts out of the shadows so he could corrupt and co-opt her.

She screamed into the gathering storm. And as the horror of this complex realization struck her, she saw Officer Connelly's pale face lean forward into the faint outside light. And on the man's face was the bright, wide grin of Lucifer.

She fell back, terrified to witness traces of a demon inside the man. As a police officer, he had been a trusted authority in the community. But for many years, the devil had been tempting and turning and twisting this man's soul. And over the past twelve months, he had become a truly evil man poisoned by the devil.

And the devil had done all this just to bring her gifts out of the shadows. He had destroyed all those lives just to lure Rachel into his trap.

The sky opened up, and everything turned cold. The Lucifer grin widened for a second before shrinking into a closed, tight-lipped, hardened expression. Something had changed, and Rachel didn't realize what it was until she saw the quick blur of Jason and Scott tackling Connelly and vanishing from sight.

As Shelley got out of the patrol car, Rachel yelled to her over the rain, "Run toward town."

"What?"

"I'm going in to help them," Rachel said. "But we need to make sure at least one of us survives to warn others, in case we can't overpower him."

"We'll have a better chance if we stay together," Shelley pleaded.

"No, please. He's too dangerous to risk letting him get away undiscovered. I've seen what's inside him. We need a plan in case we can't stop him tonight. You have to do this. You have to be the guarantee that he won't get away with what he's done. Now, go!"

Convinced, Shelley turned and ran down the driveway, turned onto the country road, and disappeared into the rainy night.

Rachel turned and dashed onto the front porch and ran into the house. After seeing the strength of evil inside Officer Connelly, she didn't think Jason and Scott had much chance of overpowering him.

She feared it would be up to her to somehow stop the monster.

86

Jason and Scott slammed into Officer Connelly just as he turned from the window. All three fell through the next doorway and into the adjoining bathroom. Connelly became like a wild animal: grunting and snarling, twisting to fight back. And Jason realized they were in trouble. Despite how hard they had tackled him, the man seemed more angered than hurt. Jason had managed to climb across him on the floor and get him in a headlock, but Jason wasn't an experienced fighter and couldn't say how long the technique would hold. The guy was seriously strong. Connelly elbowed him so hard in the side that Jason nearly lost his hold. Scott, who was younger and more athletic than Jason, was trying to hit Connelly in the face, but the officer was blocking most of the blows with his left arm. One of Scott's frantic punches even missed and caught Jason with a glancing blow across his forehead.

The tide turned when Connelly managed to push Scott off him enough that he could cock his leg in and drive his boot heel into Scott's jaw. The young man fell back into the bathtub, whacking his head on the porcelain edge. His feet stuck out of the tub and he didn't move, and Jason didn't know whether he was still alive. With no one to help him fight the burly cop, he squeezed Connelly's neck harder, praying the man would just lose consciousness. But he soon took two more elbows to his ribs and then a backward head butt to the nose, which sent stars exploding in his vision. The man broke Jason's weakened stranglehold, turned, and pummeled him with repeated blows to his now bleeding face. He rolled backward and collapsed at the base of the toilet. With his mind clouded by blinding pain, he barely registered a soft clanking of metal. He tried to see what was happening, but his sight was blurry. Then he felt Connelly grab his wrists and pull his arms around both sides of the toilet base. Just as he was recovering his bearings, he felt the cuffs tighten around his wrists.

Then the chaos stopped. It was as if he was being mauled by a bear that suddenly lost interest. Silence had replaced the frantic sounds of the struggle. He tried to pull his hands back to his chest, but they were locked together on the opposite side of the toilet base, and the handcuffs cut into his wrist the harder he pulled.

He managed to blink away enough of the tears to see Officer Connelly getting up. And as this happened, Jason saw a large black tattoo of an eagle's head just below the man's throat, revealed by a popped button. It looked just like what Rachel had described from her vision of the girl who was murdered last night. He yanked harder on the handcuffs, but they weren't going to give. He watched as the man walked sluggishly out the door and back into the bedroom. A few of the team's flashlights were tucked into the corners—the sole source of illumination other than occasional blasts of lightning. He could see everyone from the farmhouse séance along the front wall, all with their backs to the heater pipe, hands tied or cuffed to the iron radiator fixture. He had barely had time to register them when he and Scott rushed into the bedroom at the sound of the horn. But now he studied each of them in the dim light. Madam Bovell was frazzled and sitting next to a stern-faced Dr. Graves. Tommy, Jessica, and Aaron were all tied to the extending pipe, beside Dr. Graves. Aaron's nose was bloodied and starting to swell near the eyes. They all appeared exhausted and weak. He then looked at Scott for any sign of life. Seeing none, he glared back at Connelly, who had returned to the front window and pressed his face to the pane. The man seemed to be searching for what Jason assumed were the girls. The horn was no longer honking, but the storm grew more violent. Heavy rain beat down on the roof, and thunderclaps rattled the walls.

Still struggling to see clearly, Jason managed to watch as Connelly rushed to a duffel bag near the doorway and moved it to the center of the room. He unzipped it and removed a handful of tall red candles that looked at first like sticks of dynamite. Circling the room, he leaned them against the corners. Then he pulled a shiny object from his pocket and turned it in the light.

"You've forced my hand," Connelly said to his captives. "Imagine my surprise when a group of ghost hunters decided to explore the one place in the world I didn't want anyone exploring. Imagine what went through my mind as I watched from a distance while you kept digging into a past that I thought was forever buried. Imagine when I realized that I would need to kill all of you just to keep my secret safe."

"You don't have to do this," Jessica said, crying.

Aaron was crying, too.

Dr. Graves just stared at the man's feet, as if his mind was elsewhere.

"This won't save you," Madam Bovell warned. "It will only further condemn you."

"Not if I don't get caught. Once you're all gone, my secret will be safe again."

"It was never safe," Madam Bovell said. "And it never will be safe. You cannot silence the spirits beyond this world. They know what you've done. There is no escaping it. One day, your spirit will answer for everything you've done—and everything that you do tonight."

"Fairy tales," he replied coldly. "Delusional fantasies embraced by the weak and the insane."

He flicked the shiny lighter in his hand, creating a tiny yellow dancing flame.

"Another tragic accident," he said. "A group of ghost hunters tried to contact a spirit in a haunted house, when a fire started from candles they were using in their ritual. The farmhouse caught fire and burned down, trapping and killing them." He shook his head sadly. "Some will naturally be suspicious. They'll wonder if your group wasn't really some cult that connected online and was performing a satanic ritual. After all, one of you is a modern-day witch." He nodded to Madam Bovell. "Some will wonder if the fire was really an accident. Some may even believe that the ghost itself started the fire to kill everyone in the group. A new gothic legend will be born. The site of this farmhouse will become a landmark for believers in the occult—hell, it may even get listed as one of the most haunted places in America. With so many horrific deaths on two Halloween nights in a row, you can all die at least knowing that your names will be remembered among fellow ghost hunters and that legends of your death will be told around campfires for decades to come."

He walked to the nearest candle and lit it. Immediately, the flame brushed against the wall and began to crawl up the wood paneling. He lit the other candles, then went back to the center of the room. Opening the duffel, he took out a black pistol and a thick police baton. He tucked the gun in the holster on his belt and slung the bag around his shoulder. Then, patting the club against his palm, he looked at Jason, then stared at Madam Bovell and Dr. Graves.

He said, "I'm gonna need all my handcuffs back now. Can't have those being found around your bones in the ashes.

Unfortunately, I think the only way the three of you will stay put is if I give you a good bashing on the head. Now, I know that skull fractures will look suspicious in some of the fire victims, but who's to say what, exactly, goes on during the ritual of a satanic suicide cult." He waved the baton around. "You know, the plates of the human skull are not all the same thickness. You want to try to hit someone on the frontal or temporal plates if possible, cause they're the thinnest and the trauma will make the deepest depressed fracture of skull bone into the brain, causing the worst hemorrhage and brain injury and—if hard enough—death." He pointed to his temple. "Right here is where I'll get you."

"Monster," Madam Bovell snarled.

The professor, who had been in an almost catatonic state, glanced up at Connelly. Then Jason saw his gaze turn from Connelly to something in the bedroom doorway. The fire was catching the wood paneling and seemed on the verge of blowing up fast. So Jason, too, followed the professor's glance at the door, as did Connelly. And there he saw Rachel, standing boldly in the brightening firelight.

Connelly stood still, as if cautioned by her strange confidence. Rachel fixed him with a steely gaze. Her black hair hung wet, and her clothes dripped rainwater. Without a word, she raised her hands up and out, like a TV preacher beseeching the Almighty. Then, in a sudden motion, she brought them down in a loud clap that filled the room. And at the moment of her forceful clap, the flames rising up the walls shrank back down and went out one by one with a soft pop.

Connelly hesitated a second longer, then raised the baton and charged with the fury of a savage beast.

Rachel's hands shot to her head, fingertips pressing her temples, eyes closed. And Jason couldn't fathom what he saw next: Connelly dropped to his knees only feet away from Rachel, and his baton went flying past her to clatter on the hallway floor.

The man was paralyzed by pain, with his hands clasping his head as he screamed in anguish. He had heard that Rachel could give someone a migraine if she concentrated hard enough on pressing deep into their mind, though he had no idea she could project it with such intensity. But from the intense effort on her face, he knew she couldn't hold Connelly for long.

Jason desperately yanked at the toilet, feeling it rock a little. Encouraged, he pulled and knocked and jerked the toilet desperately, but while it continued to rock, it showed no sign of breaking free from the floor and wall. Stopping for a second to think and marshal his strength, he noticed that Dr. Graves had pulled his feet in close to his body, in an unusual position that allowed him to arch his back away from the radiator. He then saw Madam Bovell trying to shuffle a few inches away from him, as if to give him a little more room.

Then Madam Bovell turned her head and glared at Dr. Graves. "Hurry up!"

"I'm almost there!" the professor said.

A bolt of excitement surged through Jason when he saw the professor fumbling with the handcuffs holding his back to the radiator. He tried to think of anything he could do to help. He whipped his head back to glance at the top of the toilet, then twisted his arms and rotated around so he was facing the wall. He could then slide to his back and kick a foot up to the top of the tank. His first strike knocked the porcelain lid up and off its place on the tank. The next kick jolted it halfway over the lip, and the next knocked it all the way off, to crash down on the tiles.

With his heel, he dragged the heavy lid away from the wall until he had it beside him. Then he ducked his head and rotated around so he was again facing the doorway to the bedroom. Dr. Graves was still struggling with the handcuffs, but more frightening was what was happening with Connelly and Rachel. While her strength seemed to be holding for now, Connelly had managed to put a hand on the ground for stability and was trying to grab the pistol from its holster. The man moved in slow motion as if every inch of his movement was in resistance to Rachel's paralyzing power over him. Still, he slowly pulled out the pistol and fought to raise it, inch by inch, pointing it at Rachel, while she fought to hold him motionless with her psychic pressure on his mind.

"Hold on!" Madam Bovell yelled at Rachel.

But Jason could tell that she was already doing everything she could. Her fists were clenched against her temples, and her lips were pulled back in a tight grimace.

She was about to lose whatever grip she had left on Connelly.

And the gun muzzle was rising ever closer to lining up on her torso.

Jason pivoted enough to grab the tank cover with the side of his foot and pull it in front of him. Looking up, he saw the professor finally lean forward as he whipped both hands in front of him with the handcuffs dangling from one wrist. As the professor stood, Jason yelled to him and kicked the tank cover as hard as he could with his heel, sending the heavy porcelain slab sliding to the professor's feet. Dr. Graves picked it up with both hands and took a few quick steps forward. Then, with a nice golf swing, he teed off on the side of Connelly's head. There was a grimly satisfying sound of cracking bone.

Connelly's body fell to the wood floor, blood spreading from his head and settling in the long cracks between the floorboards. Rachel slumped over, exhausted. And the professor stood over the killer's body with the blood-smeared white slab still dangling in his grip.

87

After five minutes, Rachel finally felt her strength returning. She was relieved that Officer Connelly was dead—not just because of the horrific crimes he had committed against the innocent, but also because she had sensed the devil's influence still on the man when she was holding him with her mind. Connelly was no longer a man who had the right to stand before a judge and jury with the legal protection of a defense attorney. She believed in the justice system, but she also understood the power of the devil. And this was one case where it was just better for all humanity that this corrupted, evil man had met the swift justice of a violent death.

As Rachel turned these dark thoughts around in her mind, she stared with cold determination at Connelly's body. She didn't like the body being in Annabel and Rubin's old bedroom, but they dare not move it, because this was now a crime scene once again, as it had been exactly a year ago. Madam Bovell had called 911, and first responders would arrive soon. Everyone else had gone downstairs to wait. Scott had hit his head hard on the bathtub, but he soon regained consciousness. No one else had been seriously hurt, but most had gotten banged up fighting the murderous policeman, and Madam Bovell was patching up some minor cuts with the first-aid kit in their Yukon.

But Rachel had chosen to stay up in the room by herself. She told the others she just needed some time alone, but that wasn't it. She had stuck around because she had to be sure that Officer Connelly was really gone. She needed to know that his spirit hadn't found a way to stay here in death.

She stared at the body, keeping her mind calm and open to receiving any hint of his spirit's presence. The room was quiet. The man's blood had stopped draining into the cracks between the floorboards and had begun to coagulate in dark, narrow rivulets. The storm outside had passed. The bloodied top of the toilet tank lay next to the body. The gun was beside it. The crystal hemisphere still gazed up like a monstrous eye from the floor along the room's back wall.

After a few more minutes, her concerns faded. She had felt such a mental lock with the man in the moments before his death that she didn't think his spirit could evade her detection if it were still here. The room felt devoid of paranormal energy.

She sighed and turned her eyes to the crystal hemisphere. She wondered how far Madam Bovell's group had gotten with their part of the dual séance before being interrupted. She hadn't even thought to ask them. She wondered if maybe they had finished; if maybe they had gotten as far with Rubin as her group at the hospital had gotten with Annabel. Then she wondered why she hadn't sensed Rubin's spirit since arriving here tonight. Staring hard at the crystal hemisphere, she wondered ... The crystal looked somehow different, darker, heavier. Then a new concern formed in her thoughts. Was it possible that ...?

Rachel suddenly felt an uneasy tingling in her stomach, as if she was about to be sick. At the same moment, her eyes caught a faint blue glow coming from the center of the crystal hemisphere. Fighting the discomfort in her belly, she went over to investigate the glimmer of light.

It was growing brighter and now had a more intense ball of blue light expanding within its center.

"Hey, guys!" she yelled. "Something's happening here!"

Dropping to her knees, she stared at the blue streaks growing from its center. The entire corner of the otherwise dark room was now bathed in a soft, tranquil blue glow.

Mesmerized, she reached out and touched it with both hands. The second her fingers connected with the crystal she felt a surge of energy. But it wasn't electrical energy; it was spiritual—the warm, contained power of a life force that reached out to other objects with a free will unfettered by the laws of physics. And instead of trying to flow through her body, the energy force stayed at her fingertips, as if some combination of the barriers between the crystal and her touch was holding it back.

"Madam Bovell!" Rachel yelled. "Madam Bovell! I need you! Now!"

A rumble of commotion came from the hallway and materialized when Tommy and Jason burst into the room.

She looked away from the glowing crystal just long enough to see who had responded to her cries for help. Turning her attention back to the growing energy force at her fingertips, she yelled, "Get Madam Bovell!"

"What's happening?" Jason asked.

"Get her now! It's Rubin! He's in the crystal. This could be our chance, but I can't hold him much longer by myself!"

Tommy shifted his weight and darted out the room.

A surge of pain erupted in her head. It lasted only a second, but that fleeting stab was worse than any migraine she ever had.

"What's wrong?" Jason said, rushing to her side.

"He's fighting to escape!"

Another sharp twinge fired through her nervous system. This time, it was so strong she could barely find the will to keep her fingertips on the crystal. As she sat forward with renewed concentration, she felt tears welling in her eyes.

"Rachel, stop! You'll hurt yourself!"

"We can't let him escape! He's become angrier than before! More confused! This might be our only chance to save him!"

"How?"

"Somehow, Rubin's spirit became trapped in the crystal during their séance. That means there's a chance Annabel's spirit is trapped inside the other half."

Another pain shot through her, and she let out a sharp cry. But still she managed to keep full contact with the crystal.

"Get the other half!" she yelled. "Hurry! There isn't much time!"

Jason scrambled to his feet and rushed out the door.

88

Madam Bovell was in the back seat of the rental car, carefully applying disinfectant to the cut on the back of Dr. Graves's head. They had called 911 and were told that the police and ambulances would be immediately dispatched to the farmhouse.

"What's that?" Dr. Graves asked.

She followed his gaze through the windshield to the front of the farmhouse. A blue glow was coming from the upstairs windows to the bedroom.

Just then Tommy bolted out the front door, darted across the porch, and raced down the gravel drive toward them. Dr. Graves tried to lean forward, but she gently pushed him back into the seat.

"Don't move until the ambulance gets here," she said. "Your head got gashed worse than you realize." She got out and walked around the front of the car. "What is it?" she said to Tommy.

"Rachel needs you! Now! Something's wrong! The crystal is doing something!"

Her eyes shot back up to the window. The blue light was even brighter now. The same blue glow that had flashed from the

crystal hemisphere when Rubin's soul vanished from the room.
"Oh, no," she said softly. She realized that because Officer
Connelly had disturbed the séance, Rubin's spirit had somehow
been left marooned inside the crystal. Under different
circumstances, this could have been a perfect opportunity to
guide him into the afterlife. But because they hadn't realized it in
time, the spirit was now trying frantically to escape the confines
of the crystal. And if that happened, the additional transference
of psychic energy would further dilute whatever elements of his
identity remained, diminishing his spirit to a hollow emotional
echo of himself, perhaps trapping him in this realm forever.

Bovell trundled toward the farmhouse as fast as she could
manage. "How long since it started?" she shouted.

"Maybe a minute."

Just then Jason burst out the front door and raced down to the
other end of the porch. To Madam Bovell's startled surprise, he
vaulted over the porch rail and hit the yard running hell-for-
leather toward the stubble field behind the farmhouse.

"What is it?" Tommy yelled at him.

The others stared after him from where they had been
waiting by the Yukon.

"Jason?" Madam Bovell shouted.

But he had vanished into the dark field without pausing to
explain.

"Hurry, please!" Tommy begged Madam Bovell.

"I am!" she insisted. She couldn't remember the last time she
had to run so hard. Even in Chicago, trying to escape Dr. Graves
earlier in the week, she hadn't moved this fast.

Tommy held the front door open, and she rushed in, using
the banister to help haul herself up the staircase.

Huffing and panting, she reached the upstairs hallway and
saw the blue glow emanating from the open bedroom door. Near
the room, she felt warm waves of energy pulsating through the
air. Each step forward was a slog, more difficult than the last. By

the time she reached the doorway, the resisting force had dropped her to her hands and knees as she fought her way forward. But despite the onslaught, she kept crawling. She had to save Rachel from being destroyed by a fatal collapse of Rubin's spirit energy.

She reached forward with both arms and grabbed the doorjamb. Taking a deep breath, she pulled herself the last few feet to get her head into the bedroom. And what she saw jolted her with a mixture of excitement and horror. Blue light oscillated throughout the room, like rolling ripples from a rock thrown into a still pond. And that someone was *them*—they themselves had disturbed this still pond of death by magnifying Rubin's ghost and disturbing the natural world. They had caused this by bringing his ghost out of a hidden dimension of death and into the mystical layer of the crystal without guiding him all the way to the next realm.

And in the center of the violently pulsing energy source was Rachel. Her hair was blowing up and back as if she were staring down a wind tunnel. The blue light splashed across her face—a tense, desperate expression of someone fighting with every ounce of their strength. The girl's arms were stretched out and down, and her hands had disappeared into the light.

"Rachel!" Bovell shouted.

But the girl gave no notice of her. It was as if her mind had been pulled into another realm.

"Rachel!" she yelled again, but this time she could barely hear herself. The source of the blue light was now generating a low, rhythmic pounding, combined with the near-blinding brightness and the physical force pushing everything away.

She dragged herself forward. She inched toward Rachel, toward the terrifying light. Somewhere within that bright, burning energy source were Rachel's hands, and Rubin's spirit trying to escape the dense layers of the crystal hemisphere.

This had been a mistake. All of it. And now Bovell was about to get the girl killed. She should have ignored the visions in her dreams, never gotten out her old Ouija board, never left Chicago for Kansas with Dr. Graves. They should never have sought out the spirits of Rachel's mother and grandmother in Stull Cemetery. Never followed the trail to North Dakota. Never tracked down Rachel and encouraged her to embrace and develop her gifts. Never encouraged the ghost-hunting club to take their efforts to the next level in an authentic séance. Never convinced them to provoke the dead by digging up the mysteries around their deaths—their *murders.* Never made themselves targets for a hidden killer. Never challenged the devil and his minions.

And now she feared the girl would die.

She continued to crawl forward. When she reached the center of the room, she tried again to get Rachel's attention. Calling out the girl's name, she still got no indication that she had been heard. With no choice, Madam Bovell continued on, crawling forward in slow, excruciating increments, until she found herself moving into the expanding orb of blue light. It was now so bright that she couldn't see anything else except for the cloud of tranquil blue pulsing around her.

As she moved farther into the light, she felt the jarring tingle of dancing between the realms of the living and the dead. This was not like being in a trance. Nor was it like mediumship table reading, when she would consciously ask questions and receive answers from other realms beyond this natural world. Nor was it like anything she had ever dreamed. This was physical. She was crawling into a space where the dead reached out to the living. A place where time did not exist and any attempt to understand mass and motion and energy was futile.

But soon all her focus fell to the glowing gaseous star growing within the crystal hemisphere. And holding desperately to this godlike energy were Rachel's quivering hands. Poor

Rachel, all alone, had been holding back a force more powerful than any that Madam Bovell had ever encountered. The girl was only beginning to discover her gifts, yet already she had been forced into a situation beyond anything that any living medium had ever encountered. Although Bovell didn't know what she could do to help, she had to try.

Learning of Rachel's existence was the most exciting thing that had happened to her, giving her life purpose after she had given up hope of doing anything else meaningful with her remaining years. And in the past few days, she had discovered that Rachel was the answer to all her fears. This girl was her hope for redemption for decades of fraud. For so long, she had just been going through the motions of life without really being alive. And until the vision from Rachel's mother, she hadn't even realized she had given up.

But hope had merely been lying dormant. And now it was wide awake.

The purpose of her entire life was to be right here to do everything she could to help Rachel.

Still crawling, Madam Bovell forced her right hand six inches forward. Then she dug deep and willed her left hand forward. Then her right knee. Then her left knee. Then her right hand again. And with each move, the pain increased.

Gale-force wind hit her in the face, blowing her hair back and making her cheeks ripple. Her baggy clothes felt as if they might be pulled right off her body.

Now well into the growing sphere of light, she saw Rachel's eyes open slightly and look up at her with desperation. And that plea for help drove Madam Bovell to strain herself beyond anything she had ever tried before—to push forward at the very moment her muscles were on fire and the pressure made her head feel as if it would implode.

Then she saw it: her crystal hemisphere, glowing from the spirit trapped inside it.

Rubin's spirit. Trapped and fighting to get out.

And there, holding back all this building energy, were Rachel's slender hands pressed against the sides of the glowing crystal.

Crawling the final few feet, Madam Bovell reached out to touch the crystal. Its texture had changed. It was no longer hard and smooth, but instead soft and scaly like snakeskin. And the energy within it—Rubin's spirit—was very much alive. She could feel its pulsing energy.

And then the pain intensified. She could feel the energy trying to seep through the side of the crystal the way that light changes and splits apart as it passes through a prism. She could *feel* Rubin trying to escape. She could feel his strength growing just as the crystal was weakening—just as Rachel was weakening. And although Madam Bovell could never hope to be as strong as the girl, she still felt a small measure of power within her old body. So she flattened her palms on the crystal to get as much surface area on it as possible. Then, as the pain and pressure built, she flashed one last glance at Rachel and closed her eyes to focus all her remaining energy on holding Rubin's spirit inside the crystal.

From the crystal hemisphere, a growing orb of brilliant blue stretched beyond the room into the hallway and out all the windows. But together, Madam Bovell and Rachel formed a bond of psychic power. And together they fought to contain the building energy that seemed on the verge of exploding.

89

Jason's lungs burned as he raced through the field. Dead corn stubble stuck out of the ground at odd angles. His feet sank into the soft earth as he raced over the furrowed ground. Scott's Jeep was fifty yards away.

His toe caught a dead root, nearly sending him pitching forward, but through some miracle of balance, he had waved his arms and pushed hard enough with his feet to keep himself upright and continue his sprint. Picking up his speed after regaining his balance, he clamored down a ditch at the end of the field and darted up the other side to reach the Jeep.

He yanked the back door open and grabbed the brown backpack tucked under the seat. Unzipping it, he felt inside to make sure the crystal hemisphere was still inside. Within a clump of the wrapped silk sheet, he felt the smooth, cold crystal.

Are you really in there, Annabel? he wondered. *Did we unknowingly trap you and remove you from the hospital after so long? Do you even realize that we've brought you back home?*

He zipped up the backpack, slung it over his shoulder, and slammed the door. Turning back toward the dead field, he was startled to see pale blue light coming from every window of the distant farmhouse. He stood frozen for a second or two —which was long enough to see that the blue light was growing brighter.

"Dear God," he murmured. The situation was escalating too fast.

He took off running over the dead cornfield. As he ran, he looped his other arm under the remaining strap. Moving faster now, he pumped his arms and took long, quick strides. His face was bruised from the fight with the officer, and his lungs hurt from the cold. A few rough, dry cornstalks reached out and scratched him on the arms and neck as he ran, but nothing slowed him. He kept his eyes mostly up and forward, watching the farmhouse grow closer and watching the ominous blue light grow brighter against the black night. Then a blue beam shot out of the bedroom window like a powerful spotlight.

He didn't know if the farmhouse was about to explode, catch fire, split in two, or sink into the earth. He had no idea what power Rubin's spirit was unleashing from within the crystal hemisphere. But the one thing he knew for certain was that Rachel would still be in the bedroom, desperately trying to stop it.

He pushed himself harder, exerting everything he had left in one frantic run, in what might be the most important moment of his young life.

More than halfway across the field now, he could make it to the farmhouse in just thirty more seconds. A second beam of blue light blasted from the right upstairs window, and he half expected the entire place to go supernova. He wasn't even sure their plan would work even if he did get there in time. In fact, he didn't even really know what the plan even *was*. But he trusted Rachel.

His back felt oddly warm. Cranking his head sideways, he looked back and saw a dim blue light behind him. Stretching his neck farther without breaking his stride, he glimpsed a stronger, brighter blue light coming from the backpack.

"Oh, God," he groaned, turning his head forward again.

He didn't have time to deal with whatever the hell was going on inside the backpack, but now he knew that Annabel was inside this half of the crystal ball. Rachel had been right, but she hadn't had time to tell him what the hell he was supposed to do about it. So all he could do was run as fast as his once-athletic accountant body could take him.

"I'm here!" he yelled into the night. His breath was short and he could barely get the words out, but he had to give them hope. "I'm here!"

In the far distance to his right, he saw a small line of flashing red lights crawling along the dark horizon. He was glad to see the first responders, but they were still minutes from arriving, and nothing in their training would help them with what was happening now.

He sprinted through the last rows of the stubble field, the farmhouse now in blazing blue before him. The dead corn was now cast in a hazy cerulean glow from the backpack. He wasn't sure which terrified him more at this point: the streaming beams of light making the house resemble a giant blue jack-o'-lantern, or the warm, glowing backpack pressed against him. Annabel's blazing blue light now made a huge orb that illuminated the entire field around him, except for the giant shadow gesticulating wildly in front of him as he sprinted toward the farmhouse.

"Hang on, Annabel!" he groaned through the pain as he neared the edge of the field. "We're almost there!"

He emerged from the field, rushed past the giant oak, and darted through the backyard. Yanking open the back door, he rushed inside into the blinding blue light.

90

Rachel's fingertips felt as if they were burning. And the crushing pressure against her right temple made her fear that she might pass out at any moment. She couldn't keep her eyes open for more than a few seconds at a time—the light was just too bright now. Air swirled around the bedroom as if a tornado were tearing through hell. The floor rattled so violently, she feared that the house might come apart.

But no matter how bad things got, she could not let go of the crystal. She could not allow Rubin's spirit to be released back into his tormented, haunted prison even more damaged than before.

She opened her eyes again just long enough to catch a glimpse of Madam Bovell on the other side of the crystal. The woman looked as if she was being electrocuted.

"I can't hold it," the woman yelled over the commotion.

"Just a little longer!" Rachel yelled back, though she could barely even hear herself.

Rachel believed that the other ghost hunters were in this room, too, somewhere outside the core of the energy. But there was nothing they could do to help. Not now. And if she had the ability to focus on anything other than Rubin, she would have warned them all to get away from the farmhouse in case this effort failed.

The violent shaking of the floorboards intensified. Her body itself vibrated so much, she feared it would knock her away from the crystal.

And then she felt it: the serene final moment that only the peace of coming death can give to a prepared soul. Time slowed for her just as it appeared to speed up for everyone else. Madam Bovell was thrown back from the light and was no longer in view. Only Rachel remained—Rachel and Rubin. For she felt him now—hurting and angry—furious enough to break out and roam the darkness for eternity. She felt him splitting from himself ... becoming something else ... something less than he had ever been: a split soul soon to be forever damned in a hidden dimension. His half-soul was starting to seep out of the crystal, like steam escaping boiling water. The vapor was dissolving into the light, vanishing forever.

Through her tears, she saw a figure appear in the light. At first, she thought it was Rubin, showing himself one last time. Then she thought it was God, finally showing himself to her. Then, as if looking up while drowning and finding an outstretched hand, she realized with sudden hope that it was Jason.

Crawling on his hands and knees, he battled his way closer to the light. She was amazed he had even made it this far. And she was even more amazed when he rolled onto his side and shucked off a backpack that was glowing the same bright blue as the crystal hemisphere she still held.

A prickle of excitement fired through her. Annabel's spirit *had* been trapped inside the other half of the crystal ball. And now here she was, returned to her house for the first time since her murder.

Rachel wondered what Annabel's spirit must be thinking at this moment. Would she be confused? Overwhelmed? Angry? Sad? Or would she be able to push all those disruptive emotions aside and focus only on the pain and suffering of her husband, and the difficulties he was having in processing the tragedy of their lives?

She felt a sudden burst of energy from the crystal. Rubin was becoming more violent, and she was terrified that he would escape at any moment. Tightening her concentration, she pushed him back with her mind. But the effort cost her: a surge of pain hit her like an excruciating migraine. She would not be able to hold it much longer.

Jason was closer now. She had been trying to look up and catch glimpses of him in the light as he inched forward on his side and worked to unzip the backpack, but she had her hands full with Rubin. Jason was now pulling the silk sheet out of the backpack and unwrapping the object inside it. Then, as his fingers removed the final layers of silk, she saw the bright blue glow of the other half of the crystal ball—Annabel's half. It absorbed and redirected energy from the sphere of light surrounding them, like a prism dividing blazing sunlight into its component colors. Suddenly, a scattering of little circular rainbows surrounded them, bobbing about like fireflies.

And in that moment, Rachel saw the way forward. She felt the hope of resolution. They just had to fight through the final overwhelming resistance. Just ten or fifteen more seconds—that was all they needed to save these two souls, and all the time they had before Annabel and Rubin were lost forever.

"NOW!" she yelled over the thunderous clamor around them. "Now, Jason! Do it now! DO IT NOW!"

The pain in her head intensified. She felt sick and dizzy and feared she might lose consciousness. From the clouded daze of her mind, she saw Jason holding the other half of the crystal ball in both hands. He was creeping forward on the floor as if fighting against a hurricane. And as he inched forward against the unnatural obstacles of pounding energy, Rachel saw, as if through drunken eyes, the slowly closing distance between the two halves of crystal. Another pain fired through her mind, and she heard herself growl.

Was the Devil still here?

Her thoughts spun and twisted.

Was there some other force at play here that she couldn't see? Was all this really coming from just Rubin—and now Annabel?

She felt another presence somewhere within this chaos—an evil energy.

Please, God, help me make this right. Help me honor my ancestors. Help me live up to my promise to Annabel. Help me achieve the promise that all my ancestors lived to pass on to me before they died. Help me give their sacrifices a purpose—let me help these lost lives, lost souls, lost lovers. Help me reunite those whom evil has ripped apart—those who loved so much that they refused to move on without each other ... those who are lost without each other.

Please, Lord, give me the strength. Just for ten seconds, give me the strength to right this great wrong.

Jason was yelling something to her. She couldn't hear his words, but she could read his thoughts. He was asking her what he should do now. And she told him—not with words, but with her thoughts. With her mind weakening, she sent him one simple message: *Reunite them.*

Then, with her fingers still on the crystal hemisphere, she pressed harder and tipped it up on its edge so that the split was facing Jason. The light intensified, and the vibrations increased, blaring white noise.

Jason pushed forward, trying to connect his crystal hemisphere with the other half, as Rachel tried to move her half closer. But a great force was resisting them, as if they were trying to push the same pole of two magnets together. A strong negative energy was here—something trying to prevent them from saving the two lost lovers. But Rachel was determined to end this now. With her last remaining strength, she formed her own energy field around both halves of the crystal ball and then tightened the field, shrinking it inward to pull both halves closer together. A cloud of red formed between the two halves once they were only six inches apart. The cloud moved fluidly like red ink being swirled in oil. She concentrated harder, tightening her energy field more until the red cloud suddenly dissipated and vanished. Then, with her last grain of power, she released her hands from the crystal, made two tight fists, gave one final push in her mind, and pulled the energy field inward until both halves of the crystal ball came together in perfect alignment.

The moment the two halves reunited, a warm shock wave rippled through the room. It pushed both Rachel and Jason onto their backs, but they were still inside the bright blue sphere. Rachel barely had the strength to remain conscious. But she managed to lean on one elbow and sit up enough to see a darker shade of blue radiating from directly above the crystal ball. This darker blue light rose and swirled, reshaping before her eyes, as if trying to coalesce into some kind of object. Through the light, she could see that Jason was also watching this. The light continued to swirl and blur together until two objects formed before her eyes. Mesmerized, she saw a translucent image of Annabel, looking at her with silent eyes. But the eyes weren't sad. Annabel was smiling, and her face held a warmth as if all the bad things and suffering that had occurred in the past year were finally over. Then the swirling blue light next to Annabel coalesced into Rubin. He looked at Annabel, dumbstruck. Then touching her hand, he leaned forward to place his forehead against her temple. Their arms wrapped around each other as they held each other tightly. Annabel's eyes closed, and her smile widened. Rachel thought she even saw tears on their faces.

Then a bright yellow light opened into a large square to Rachel's right. It was a gateway like the one she had passed through after waving goodbye to her mother and grandmother. Rachel was still dazed, but she understood what she was witnessing. Annabel and Rubin glided toward the square of light. They were holding hands. Once they reached the gateway, they both turned back to look at Rachel and Jason. Rubin nodded at them with joy in his eyes, and Annabel smiled blissfully and mouthed *thank you* to both of them. Then, turning, the reunited lovers entered the light and disappeared into its blinding glory.

The gateway closed. The yellow light vanished. An explosion of blue light shot out from the crystal ball, rapidly expanding the sphere. The light blasted to all corners of the room, through the entire farmhouse, and out the windows, into the night.

Then the light extinguished, and the crystal ball went dark and lifeless. Rachel and Jason were on the floor, leaning half upright on their elbows. She looked around and could see all the others in the room. Everyone else seemed to have been lying on the floor, too, and were slowly recovering.

"Did you see them?" she asked Jason. She felt weak, and her mind was foggy, so part of her couldn't even believe the memory of what she had just witnessed. Over the past week, her thoughts had been mixed with so many dreams and visions and trances that she needed confirmation.

"What was that?" Jason asked. "The light. Did they go into the wall?" He was shaken and rambling. "But it was right here in the middle of the room. What was it? A doorway? To another dimension? To heaven? Is that what it was? Did we just get a glimpse of heaven?"

"I don't know," Rachel said, overjoyed that he had seen it, too. "We got a glimpse of something ... special. Something ... beyond."

"They looked so happy," he said.

Rachel smiled, with tears welling up in her eyes. "Yes, they did." Her chest heaved as she took deep breaths and thought of the reunited lovers. "We did the right thing."

He looked at her strangely. "Of course we did."

"Thank you for believing in me," she said.

"Of course. Are you all right?"

She nodded. "It's just, I think I felt her pain the whole time. Ever since her murder. I didn't realize it until she left just now, because it's gone now. But the pain was always there, deep inside me, festering and crying and begging to be released." She could feel warm tears racing down her cheeks.

"It's okay," he said. "Everything's okay now. Rubin's free. Annabel's free. And they're together again, and they're ... I don't know where, but it's someplace good, someplace they were very happy to go to."

"I know," she said, wiping her eyes with her sleeve.

"And you believed me, too," Jason said. "Before anyone else did, you believed I had seen her in the hospital. If it wasn't for you, they probably would have locked me up in an institution for the insane."

She laughed slightly. "I think we're all lucky we didn't end up in straitjackets and padded rooms."

He laughed, too.

"What happened?" Madam Bovell asked groggily. She was the last of the group to sit up and look around the bedroom, at its cracked walls, blown-out windows, and loose floorboards.

"Did you see anything that happened after you were knocked back to the wall?" Rachel asked.

"No."

"Nothing?"

"I remember seeing a blinding ball of light that must have encompassed you and everything that was happening to you and Rubin. But I don't remember seeing much for very long. I think I lost consciousness."

"Nothing about Annabel or what happened when we rejoined the two halves of the crystal ball?"

"No, nothing." Madam Bovell paused, half lost in some new distant thought. Then it registered. "The crystal ball."

Rachel followed her gaze toward the place on the floor directly in front of her. The two halves of the crystal ball had reformed into a rough version of the original ball: smooth, with only a rough, melded indention circling it along the circumference line where it had been split and resealed.

"I didn't even feel anything," Madam Bovell said. "And I can't sense anything now, either. It's gone ... My gift—it's not there anymore."

"You exerted yourself," Rachel said. "I'm sure it will come back." But even as she said this, Rachel could sense the complete absence of Madam Bovell's abilities, and she knew that the woman's gift had finally been extinguished forever. And this wasn't all that she sensed. Looking around the room at everyone, Rachel had a strange inkling of their futures. It was more intuition than vision. Jason would return to Chicago and eventually find the woman of his dreams. Her friends would disband the Ghost Hunting Club and enjoy their senior year in less ghoulish ways. And as her powers continued to grow, she would help Madam Bovell and Dr. Graves contact his son's spirit again. Over time, she would help many others, too.

"What happened?" Madam Bovell repeated.

Rachel smiled with warm intoxication. "We succeeded," she said. "Annabel and Rubin are together again."

"Where?"

"Somewhere good," she answered, a tear welling in her eye. "Somewhere very, very good."

THE END

About The Author

Bryan Devore was born and raised in Manhattan, Kansas. He received his Bachelor's and Master's in Accountancy from Kansas State University. He also completed an exchange semester at the Leipzig Graduate School of Management in Leipzig, Germany. He is a CPA and lives in Denver, Colorado. He welcomes comments and feedback, and can be contacted at bryan.devore@gmail.com.

Novels by Bryan Devore:
The Aspen Account
The Price of Innocence
The Paris Protection
The Girl from Dark Dakota

www.bryandevore.com

Made in the USA
Columbia, SC
22 October 2021